Just Parker

A novel by K.C. O'Neill

Just Parker

Second Edition
First Printing, 2015

ISBN 1-943010-06-4

Cover design by Indie Solutions

This one is for you, Mom.

Because I wouldn't be here, either literally or figuratively, without you.

And because you're the best woman I know.

Chapter One

Parker

I WAS OFFICIALLY RUNNING LATE.

I couldn't say that I was surprised to be running late. I wouldn't even say that I was angry about being late. No, I was experiencing more of a deep, ugly, soul-wrenching frustration at being late. I hated being late – at all. I hated being late even more when it meant that I would be walking into the first class of my sophomore year of college ten minutes after said class started. That meant everyone would turn and stare as I made my way to my seat. That's what I hated the most.

I grabbed my bag as I put my car into park. My first class was Philosophy, which was required as an additional course for my major. I still haven't figured out what the heck I was thinking when I decided that I needed to take Philosophy at 8AM Mondays, Wednesdays and Fridays...

Well, that's not entirely true. It isn't like I've been lacking for distractions these days.

My problem was that I was *not* a morning person. At all. Not to mention, counting out all those pills for the day and grinding up medication while trying to make breakfast for two takes way longer than you'd expect.

I had already timed my commute to school the week before, so I had planned for the drive to take me about 15 minutes. But stupid me timed the drive in the middle of the day, and not in the morning - when I had to sit in tons of traffic. This meant my drive took twice as long as it should have. I should have gotten to campus fifteen minutes early, walked to my class, and I would have had about ten minutes to relax before it started.

Instead, class had started five minutes ago, and I still had to navigate across a campus that I hadn't set foot on in four months and find a classroom I'd never seen.

I hopped out of the car after putting it in park and then raced across the lot towards the beautiful white wood and red brick buildings that littered the campus. I had always loved the University of Virginia. I loved the history, I loved the architecture, and I loved the people. I did not like the five minute walk from my car to my class when I was already running late.

I had just made it to the other side of the parking lot when I froze mid-stride. *Shit. Where is my phone?* I reached into my brown canvas messenger bag, pushing my hand around the books, pens and papers – some of which were new, some leftovers from the year before. I frantically searched for the ancient, black flip-phone. I couldn't walk into class unless I had it with me.

Not finding it in the bag, I grabbed my keys and sprinted back to my car. Popping the locks, I pulled open the door and started searching the cup holders, console, and passenger seat. I could feel tears starting to well behind my eyes, and I leaned out of the car. I slammed my fist against the car's hard roof in frustration just before I noticed a girl walking past my trunk. She jumped at the sound and let out a short shriek. Her mouth dropped open a bit, then she squeaked and put her head down, scurrying away.

I let out a sigh and glanced down into the car again. *Wait a second, yes!* There, under the driver's seat, was my phone. I let out a small shout of victory and then slammed the door and ran the entire way to class.

By the time I arrived at the right building, I was out of breath, covered in sweat, and sure that my face was bright red. I tried to ease my heavy breathing as I wound through hallways and staircases and passed by offices and classrooms. The building was made up of mostly small rooms with a few mid-sized lecture halls, like the room I was headed towards. I counted the numbers affixed to the wall next to each door as they rose until I arrived at the right set of solid, wooden double doors. Already late, I wasn't about to procrastinate. I threw my weight into what definitely appeared to be a heavy door.

Except it wasn't a heavy door. I may not have a lot of extra weight, but I'm solid enough. The door flew open with the force of my body hitting it and it let out a huge BANG as, I'm assuming, it hit the wall. I couldn't react quickly enough and, before I knew it, the door had slammed right back into me, sending me straight onto my ass with a grunt.

"Oh my God," I whispered under my breath, clenching my fists until I felt my nails pressing into my skin. The pain would keep the tears from flowing down my face. *You have got to be freaking kidding me… Can't a girl just catch a single break?*

I heard a muttered, "Holy shit," in the silence that covered the room following the crash, and then a pair of legs appeared in front of me. They were nice legs, from what I could tell. A pair of really faded, slightly ripped jeans covered them. The jeans didn't look like the kind you bought from the store ripped and faded for a buttload of money. They looked like jeans that were lived in; they looked like pants with a memory.

"Are you okay?" is what I think the legs asked, but I didn't expect the legs to have such a deep, masculine, growly voice, not to mention, I was still a bit in shock from being taken down by a door.

"I like your pants," I croaked. *Wait, what? What the hell did I just say?*

I heard a deep chuckle as the legs bent. The denim stretched across knees and thighs (and I have to admit, I noticed that the legs looked even nicer as they bent - denim moving over tight, thick thigh muscles… *Um, yum*) and suddenly the legs attached themselves to a torso. My eyes moved up over strong shoulders and a wide chest to see a long, tan neck that supported the most beautifully masculine face I had ever seen. He had a strong jaw with just a hint of dark stubble, full lips, strong cheekbones and absolutely glorious eyes. I had never seen anything like them. They were a light shade of hazel, but right near his pupil there were so many gold flecks that they looked to be a glowing, solid gold.

"Oh my God," I moaned as I looked away quickly. I couldn't even look at him, he was that gorgeous. My mind offered a reasonable explanation: *Maybe you're dreaming...* *or maybe that door killed you. Maybe he's an angel!*

I thought about it. It made sense. He was too perfect to be real. Maybe I knocked my head harder than I thought. Maybe I *was* dead now.

I almost wished it was true as my gaze passed beyond his shoulder and I took in an entire classroom full of students staring at me. *Oh God oh God oh God.*

I sprang to my feet so fast I collided with the vision standing before me. I felt my face grow even more impossibly hot as he fell backwards onto his ass. A shocked expression was frozen on his face, and after a second he erupted into laughter.

"Oh my God, I'm so sorry," I told him as he sat on the floor, head thrown back as he made no attempt to hide how hilarious he found the situation. I looked past him and addressed the professor, a middle-aged man wearing slacks, a button down shirt with a sweater vest, and a surprised expression. "I'm so sorry," I repeated for his sake. I leaned down and extended my hand to the guy still sitting on the floor. He stifled his laughter and reached up to grab mine. The second his hand wrapped around my fingers I felt a jolt - like a spark of static electricity - shoot up my arm. I tensed and pulled as he lifted himself off the floor, still wearing a smile, and as soon as he was stable I let go.

"No worries. Really," he told me with a grin that was positively sinful. "I gotta say, that was one of the funniest things I've ever seen. It's not even eight thirty and you already made my day..."

His eyes looked lazy but I could see an alertness, a sort of tension underneath the calm exterior. But, before I could focus on that, I finally processed what he said about my grand entrance and my face began to burn yet again.

"Alright, alright!" I heard from the front of the room as the professor neurotically shuffled around stacks of papers on his desk. "Mr. Carter, please take your seat. Ms…" He looked to me, searching for a name.

"Uh, Parker." I offered with a scratchy voice. I cleared my throat and tried again, a bit louder. "Ms. Parker."

"Alright, well, Ms. Parker, please take one of these," he offered me what looked like a syllabus from the now disorganized mess on his desk, "and then find a seat. I was just telling the class a bit about what you can expect over the next semester."

I took the paper and walked back towards the rear of the room, up the risers and to an empty seat near the back. As I turned around to sink into my chair, I caught the guy who had helped me looking back from a seat near the front by the aisle. I gave him a small, apologetic smile that he didn't return. Instead, he shot me a hard stare, almost as if he was trying to figure out all my secrets with his eyes alone, and for some reason I couldn't pull mine away from his. Then, suddenly, he blinked. The look was gone, and before I could even try to figure it out, he turned back to face the front.

I let out a shaky breath as I tried to calm my still-racing heart. Once I was breathing normally again, I reached into my bag to grab a notebook and a pen. I also slid my phone out, turned it to vibrate, and then placed it in my lap so I could feel if it buzzed. Once I was situated, I tried to force myself to forget all about embarrassing entrances and beautiful man-boys and crushing responsibilities, and I focused on school.

Nothing but school. Nothing but classes and schedules and being a normal nineteen-year-old girl at college. My life may have been falling apart, but this was where I could pretend.

Chapter Two

Ash

I BARELY HEARD A WORD that Professor Ellis said during Philosophy. Not that it really mattered. I shouldn't have even had to be here. I already took this class. I sat through everything but the last three weeks and the final, but that didn't matter. I had to take it again if I wanted to get my life back on track.

I couldn't think about anything but the gorgeous blond with insanely green eyes that looked so full of pain it took my breath away. But it wasn't the pain that made me curious. I saw guilt too.

I knew guilt like that. I lived with it every day. It lived inside me in a way that I knew meant it'd never leave. And I couldn't figure out what a girl like that, a girl who looked like a cross between the shy, innocent, girl-next-door and Daisy Duke, could have possibly done to feel that way. I wanted to know why she looked like her life was over and she had lost all hope of redemption.

I sat through the whole class just staring at the desk in front of me. Before I even realized that it had been an hour, people were shuffling towards the door. I grabbed my book and pen and threw them into my bag before standing to search the back of the classroom. I wanted to find her, needed to at least know her name. I knew it was a little fucking irrational, but I needed to talk to her again. *Without an audience.*

I was 6′4″, so it was easy to see over the heads of most of the people who were left in the room, but I didn't see long blond hair and gorgeous green eyes. Didn't see the endless legs displayed in the sexiest pair of jean cut-off shorts ever conceived. Didn't see the tight, black tank-top that showed off flawless skin that was just olive-toned… but less tan than you'd expect with how hot summer in Virginia was. Everyone I knew from around here spent as much time outside – with as little clothing on - as they could.

Maybe she's not from Virginia, I thought as I rushed towards the door, wanting to see if she was still lingering outside the room. Pushing through the crowd, I made it into the hall but she was gone.

I really shouldn't have been disappointed. I mean, it's not like I wouldn't see her in class on Wednesday. But for some strange reason, I didn't think I could wait. It felt like every moment counted with her, and I didn't want to waste a single one.

What the fuck, Ash? You don't even know this girl's name. I headed out of the building and back across campus. I knew her last name was Parker, but that would hardly help me find her. This was a big school. Fuck it. I'd just have to wait to see her again.

I headed over to my favorite place to get coffee, and on my way my phone buzzed in my pocket. I pulled it out and turned it back off silent for the time being. I still had two hours before my next class, and if Rory called I wanted to be able to answer. I knew she was worried about me being back at school for the first time since everything had gone down. I felt bad that she was worrying, but I had told her not to... more than once. I was excited to be back at school. I was ready to move on. More than anything, I just wanted to get back to real life. School, work, all the other stuff I had missed out on for the past two years.

I checked my phone and saw a new text.

Lisa: **Had a great time last night. We should do it again soon ;)**

Fuck. Just thinking about last night made my stomach twist. I had no interest in going out, but Jimmy and Marco showed up at my door literally screaming about letting them in for our gay threesome. I didn't think my neighbors would appreciate my friends' unique sense of humor so I let them in, at which point they refused to leave until I got dressed to go out.

We had walked to a little dive bar a few blocks from my place, and then I remember a lot of alcohol. I hadn't drank much since I had been sprung, so to speak, so I probably should have paced myself a bit better. I vaguely remember playing pool, and then I remember Lisa practically attacking me with her mouth. I pushed her away, and then... The memories are really fuzzy now. More drinking. More pool. I remember leaving and, *fuck*. Lisa lives in the building two doors down from mine. It comes back to me slowly - heading home, Lisa following me out, following her back to her bed...

At least I wasn't so drunk that I crashed at her place – not that I remember getting home. I just know I woke up in my own bed alone this morning, which was the silver lining in this shitty situation. If nothing else, I needed a silver lining.

Me: **Last night was a mistake. I'm sorry.**

I felt like a dick when I pressed send, but it was the truth. Lisa was a bitch – I knew this firsthand. I also knew that if I gave even the slightest hint that last night meant more than it did, Lisa would be so far up my ass that I wouldn't be able to walk and that was a terrifying thought. I shoved my phone back into my bag and walked the rest of the way to get my coffee.

Steaming hot beverage in hand, I sat at one of the tables near the windows up front. I liked being able to see people walking past all the stores along the street. It reminded me that the world was still turning - that even though my life might be irredeemably fucked up, people were still working and loving and fighting and learning and living. I needed that reminder.

I pulled my notebook and a stack of papers out of my bag. I needed to figure out how to fix my life. I needed to figure out a way to get the train that was my future back on the right set of tracks.

Looking through the pages and pages of information that Dad printed for me, I could feel the anger and frustration growing inside. I knew it wasn't fair to him - I knew that I had singlehandedly caused every last one of my problems, and I knew that he was just trying to help. I just couldn't deal with the possibility that everything I'd ever worked for was gone before I even had it. I shoved the papers back into my bag as carefully as I could manage. I wanted to rip them, burn them until they were nothing but a pile of ashes - as if that would change the past. As if that would make my future any brighter.

I pulled my phone back out of my backpack, relieved to see that Lisa hadn't texted back, and sent a message to Marco.

Me: **You home?**

I set the phone on the table next to my half-drunk coffee. I was anxious, and the double shot cappuccino on top of my fraying emotional control left me feeling jittery. I turned the phone in my fingers, flipping it end over end on the table as I waited for a response. As usual, I didn't have to wait long.

Marco: **Yeah, dude. Come by.**

I flew out of my seat, remaining coffee in hand and headed out the door. I was pretty close to where I parked my truck so I walked the few blocks back and climbed in to the cab to drive to Marco's.

I was pulling up out front in less than ten minutes. Marco's dad worked for my dad, so his family was almost as filthy rich as mine and his dad paid for an awesome apartment close to campus. I parked out front and walked up to the door, buzzing the intercom when I reached the entrance.

"Let me up, asshole," I called through the speaker and heard the door buzz as the lock flipped open. I took the stairs two at a time up to the third floor. The apartments were massive, two large suites on each floor, and I turned to the door marked B as I knocked.

There were footsteps towards the door and then I was smacked in the face with the smell of burning weed as it swung in-wards. I saw Marco's bloodshot eyes for only a second before he turned and walked away from the door, leaving me to follow. I wasn't surprised by his outfit - a white t-shirt, boxers and an old blue robe hanging open over his lean frame. I watched him stumble into the living room and flop face-first onto the couch.

"You alright?" I asked as I made my way into the room behind him and settled into a wide leather armchair. The apartment had large rooms with tall ceilings and huge windows, so the space was flooded with natural light. Marco's dad hired a decorator to furnish the apartment, so it was stylish and classy, as opposed to what you would expect from a 22-year-old college senior who parties all the time.

"Yeah dude," Marco spoke into the couch. "But you interrupted the all-important wake-and-bake ceremony. My entire day is going to be chaos now."

I laughed. "Sorry about that, man. Recover from last night yet?"

"Absolutely not. I still have no fucking clue why you decided to schedule all of your classes for the morning. Seriously, if my first class was before 2PM there's no fucking way I'd be showing up."

"Some of us need to work, lead lives - stuff like that. We can't all sleep until noon and take classes whenever the fuck we want to." At that, Marco turned his head to glare at me.

"Is there a reason you're here at 9:30 in the morning, or do you just love to torture and guilt me with your impressive work ethic?"

"Mostly just the torture and guilt. Also, I wanted to personally deliver a giant fuck you for letting me go home with Lisa last night, asshole." Marco grinned.

"Dude, don't even tell me you didn't have fun."

"I barely even remember what happened, so I honestly couldn't tell you if she raped me. Seriously, what the fuck, man?" I realized I was yelling. I didn't mean to, but I was frustrated and annoyed and all I wanted to do was take that out on him. I might be a dick, but I was too pissed to care.

"What the fuck, what?" Marco shouted back at me. "You're not locked in that fucking house anymore, Ash. You're allowed to go out, have fun, spend time with your best friends, and get laid! You're twenty-fucking-two, not forty-two. Act it!"

"Yeah? Was I acting my age when I almost fucking..." I stopped, breathing heavy. This wasn't fair. This wasn't his fault, as much as I wanted it to be. As much as I wanted it to be *anyone* else's fault, I had done this all on my own.

"Sorry, dude," I told him quietly. "I'm just... My head's fucked up today."

He looked at me closely before I saw him let out a breath of air. "It's cool. And I'm sorry. I know you're dealing with a lot of shit right now, I just... I don't want you to forget how to live. You haven't really done that in a while."

I nodded, but inside I knew he was wrong. I wasn't forgetting, I had already forgotten. And that terrified me more than anything, because I had no idea how to remember. I had no fucking clue how to start living again.

Chapter Three

Parker

AFTER PHILOSOPHY, I HAD TWO more classes to sit through before I could run home to make sure that Diane had showed up as she was supposed to. I wanted to sneak away so I could call Mom and make sure she was alright, but I had planned all my classes so close together that I literally only had time to make it from one building to the next. I didn't have time to stay at school all day, as much as I wanted to.

Freshman year had been about as normal as anyone's freshman year of college could be. I lived in the dorms, made a few friends, and had a mostly good time. Nothing life shattering, no great adventures, just me starting my "college experience."

It was only the first day, but I knew that this year was going to be *nothing* like last year.

My second class was Statistics - something that, walking into it, I knew was going to be a problem. I sucked at math of any kind, and I had avoided taking this class (which I needed to graduate) last year, which was a *really* shitty decision. You know what they say about hindsight...

I tried to follow along in class, but my professor spoke so quietly I only heard about every fourth word, and of course there was the small fact that I didn't have my textbook yet. My last paycheck had gone to my Philosophy book, and I already knew my next check was going to bills and medical co-pays. For these reasons, as well as about a thousand more, I knew that this was going to be a *really* long semester.

After Stat was my Psych Research Methods class, which my advisor had recommended when I told her that I had no idea what I wanted to do after graduation. She was trying to help me cover all of my bases until I figured it out. The only problem was that I knew she wanted me to figure it out soon. But, with the way my life was going I had no idea where I was going to be next year, which kind of made planning for the next five incredibly difficult.

I tried to pay attention as the middle-aged man with a monotone voice dove into the material but my mind just wanted to wander. I found myself getting pulled away from the room and into my mind, backwards through time until I was once again a five-year-old girl with her toes in muck and the sunlight reflecting off her face.

It was the day after my fifth birthday. I woke up to a low voice whispering my name and my shoulder being lightly shaken.

"Daddy?" I asked groggily, trying to bring the hazy face fully into focus. I could only make out his small smile in the dark of my pre-dawn bedroom.

"Rise and shine, Lizzie girl. We're taking a drive. I have a surprise for you."

Instantly, I was out of bed and rushing to the dresser. I fumbled around trying to get dressed until Daddy helped me pull on a t-shirt, a pair of corduroys, and my running shoes. Then I was racing towards the bedroom door.

"Whoa there, sweetheart. I forgot to tell you the best part!" I froze, then turned to face him.

"What? What is it?" I asked when he didn't continue.

"Well, if we're gonna do this, we need to be super quiet. We're on a secret mission, and we can't let anyone see us."

"Like spies?!" I asked, my voice rising with astonishment. But, I mean, come on. Spies were the absolute coolest.

Daddy chuckled. "Yeah, Lizzie girl. Can you be like a spy for me?"

I nodded as I pretended to hold a key between my fingers, locking my lips with it to tell him I would be silent. Then, with extravagant sneaking motions, we both crept out the door and into his truck, only bursting into uncontrollable laughter once we were driving away into the darkness.

We drove for about half an hour before Daddy pulled onto a dirt road, finally parking near a dense forest. Daddy helped me climb out of the tall truck and we headed into the trees. The sun was just starting to come up over the horizon as we plunged further and further into the wood. I kept catching glimpses of the yellow light as it passed through the tree trunks, and it felt warm on my face. It was May, and the morning air was chilly, but I knew it would soon be sunny and hot.

We walked for what felt like forever until the trees finally showed signs of thinning. Out of nowhere, I was staring at the most beautiful thing I had ever seen in my five years on Earth.

A picture-perfect, glass-topped lake, complete with early morning sunlight and dark green trees reflected on the smooth, still surface.

"Wow, it's beautiful," I said in awe. I couldn't drag my eyes away.

"That's not even the best part, Lizzie girl. Come on, right over here." He led me to what looked like a pile of bright blue tarp. That is, until he pulled the tarp away and revealed everything we would need for a full day of fishing.

I jumped and squealed, breaking the serenity of the lake to shout, "Thank you, Daddy! This is the best birthday present ever!"

Daddy had lived in a place called Florida before he moved to where we live now and met Mommy. I knew this because he talked about it all the time. The stories were great, but the pictures were better, and in most of them he was holding a giant fish.

I knew that Daddy had loved fishing, and he told me all the time that "Fishing in Virginia... It's just not the same..." I didn't know what that meant, but Daddy was smart, so I knew that it was true.

I had been asking Daddy to take me fishing for as long as I could remember, but Mommy wouldn't let us go. She said it wasn't something that ladies did. I didn't know what that meant either, but Mommy wasn't smart like Daddy, so I didn't know if it was true or not. But I knew that I really didn't want to be a lady if it meant I couldn't go fishing with Daddy.

Mommy really didn't like it when I told her that.

But, in this moment, none of that mattered. I just wanted to fish with my daddy at the most beautiful place in the world.

We spent hours at that lake. Daddy had brought a cooler packed with sandwiches, snacks, and drinks and we ate lunch on the grass. We didn't catch much, just a few fish that Daddy put back into the water. He said that they were too small, and I was okay with that. I didn't want to eat the baby fish.

After lunch, it started to get hot so I took off my shoes and socks. I rolled up my pant legs and stepped into the mud that lined the water's edge, letting the muck work its way between my toes. It was cold and squishy, but felt good on my sweaty feet. I moved forward until the water was lapping at my ankles and my feet sunk deeper into the murky bottom. I kept still like a statue until I felt the minnows swimming around my toes. It ticked, so I let out a giggle which shook my body and scared them away.

Darn.

I was so focused on watching the fish as they darted around my feet that I hadn't noticed Daddy walking to stand behind me. He was a few feet back, feet firmly on dry land, but I heard his voice as if he was speaking into my ear.

"Lizzie girl, I want you to know that you were worth everything. You are the best thing I ever did, and I hope that you never forget that. You are beautiful, and special, and no one can ever take that away from you."

I didn't know what most of that meant, but I knew it sounded nice so I turned to look at him, a bright smile on my face.

It faded a bit when I saw the emotion clouding his eyes. It was something I was unfamiliar with. It worried me for a second. But Daddy just rubbed a hand across the bridge of his nose, swiped his eyes, and then shot me a happy smile. Just like that, everything was okay.

That day at the lake was the best I ever had. A few hours after Daddy had said those strange things, we packed up the gear and carted it back to his truck. Then, he drove us back to the house. Daddy pulled up out front and told me to head inside, that he had to head to work for a bit. I gave him a kiss on the cheek and *thanked him again for the amazing day. I hopped out of the truck and ran inside, grinning ear to ear.*

Daddy never came home that night. The next morning, Mom woke me to tell me that he was gone and never coming back. And that was the day that my life changed forever. For the first time, at least.

Chapter Four

Ash

BY THE TIME MY LAST class was over, I was exhausted. All I wanted to do was go back to my apartment and crash until tomorrow. But it was Monday and I had work.

I made my way towards the ice rink I worked at part-time with the radio in the truck turned all the way up. I didn't eat lunch and I was starving, but I knew I was cutting it close to being late for my shift, so I was prepared to wait until my dinner break and get a shitty hot dog and a bag of chips from the cafeteria. I pulled into the parking lot right when I was supposed to be clocking in, so I didn't waste any time getting inside.

It still hits me in the gut every time I walk into an ice rink. The smell and feel of the air brought back so many great memories. But even the best memories turn dark before the end. Everything was tainted.

I walked back to the locker room, threw my shit into the locker and pulled out the t-shirt that was really the only true element of our uniform. I changed as fast as I could and made my way back to the staff room to clock in. I saw Tim, the assistant manager, seated in the tiny office. I hastened my pace to get past him before he noticed me. No luck.

"You're five minutes late, Ash." I hated his voice. He talked through his nose. He was essentially that dorky guy from The Office, just wearing a windbreaker instead of a sport jacket.

I turned around to face him even as I kept moving towards the door to the floor. "Yeah, I'm sorry, first day of classes and all. Won't happen again," I told him with a smile before walking through the open door.

"It better not, or I won't be held responsible for what Chris has to say!" I heard his shout as I walked away but it didn't faze me at all. Chris loved me. He had been my coach for twelve years before he retired. Well, from coaching that is. He still ran the rink and treated me like I was his nephew, which was both a good and a bad thing, depending on the day.

I walked over to the skate rental booth and was surprised when I saw Jimmy.

"Hey, man. I didn't know that you were working tonight."

Jimmy grinned as he heard my voice. "I wasn't supposed to, but Mitch decided to be an asshole and get laid instead of showing up to work, so I got called in."

"Downside to being the boss's kid, huh?" We both laughed at that. Jimmy loved working at the rink, and had fully come to terms with the fact that he would one day inherit the family business. He had no problem with coming in to help his dad, especially since - more often than not, recently - I was here all the time too.

"Did you come in over the weekend?" he asked.

Jimmy was one of only two people in my life who knew I still skated. I wasn't ever going to play again - hockey was just an old memory for me, but I loved being on the ice too much to completely walk away. It was one of the only places I ever felt calm. Even in the middle of the most intense game of my life, the ice was where I belonged, and I had always just been a natural.

"Nah. Rory had a recital so Dad flew us up, and then I had to get books and shit. Just didn't have time."

"Gotcha."

"How are you feeling after last night?" I asked him.

"I felt like shit when I woke up, but my first class wasn't until 11, so I just stayed in bed drinking water until I had to get up. Marco called me, though."

I wasn't surprised. I had been a dick this morning, and I figured Marco would call Jimmy to make sure I was okay. That being said, I didn't really want to talk about it with anyone, even if Jimmy was my best friend. I was anxious. I hadn't been able to stop thinking about the girl from Philosophy that morning, and I just didn't have the energy. So I said nothing.

"So? Any particular reason you were freaking out this morning?" Apparently, Jimmy wasn't going to give up.

I let out a sigh. "Not really, just stressed I guess. It's weird being back here." He knew that I meant school.

Jimmy gazed out over the ice and nodded. "I can imagine that."

We fell into silence and I was glad he let the subject go.

Work was slow, and before I knew it the night was over. We cleaned up and shut down, and I headed out to my car to drive home. I still needed to look over the papers from

Dad, and as much as I was dreading it, I had to get it done. I couldn't avoid the issue forever.

I kept the radio off for the drive home, letting myself think about the girl from this morning once again. Her face had drifted through my head so many times at work that I was starting to worry that I was going crazy. I couldn't help but wonder about the look that I had seen in her eyes. What had she been through? What had she done?

You're losing your damn mind, Ash.

I probably was. Didn't that shit happen all the time? Normal people started going crazy little by little until one day they snapped and blew up a building – or walked into a shopping mall and started mowing down innocent bystanders?

Was I going to snap?

It seemed possible. I hadn't exactly felt sane in over a year.

By the time I got home, all I wanted to do was go to sleep. Instead, I forced myself to sit down at my shitty kitchen table and I grabbed the folder from my dad. I pulled the note off the top of the stack and reread what he had written.

Ashton,

I pulled all the information I could about places in the area that would let you volunteer. This will fulfill your community service requirement and look good for school. I know you think that the future you want is out of your reach, but I really think that you're underestimating yourself. Don't let your past keep you from living your life.

Dad.

A small part of me wished that he was right, that it was as simple as volunteer work and sending a check to the right people to keep the future that I had always envisioned for myself. But Dad couldn't understand that I didn't want his money to be the reason I got into the school I wanted to go to. I don't want to be reminded every time I walk into Carter Hall - or whatever - that my intelligence and my background meant nothing compared to my father's checkbook.

It might sound ridiculous - hell, that's what he said every time I brought it up. *You're being ridiculous, Ashton. You know it has nothing to do with that.* But that wasn't true at all, and we both knew it.

Looking through the rest of the papers, it was time to choose - a hospital or a nursing home? If I really needed to do this, I'd rather spend the time in a hospital, where I might actually learn something useful. Plus, I figured it'd look better on applications to grad schools. I wrote down a few phone numbers and decided I'd make a few calls tomorrow to see if any of them needed help.

After getting that out of the way, I walked to the bathroom to take a shower. I turned the heat up until the water was scalding and stood under the spray for what felt like hours. My skin started to prickle and burn, but I stayed under the downpour, trying to wash away the day. Trying to wash away my life.

The girl's face popped into my head again as I started to soap up, and I found my fingers moving down along my stomach before I even realized what I was doing. Once I wrapped my hand around my already hard length, I hesitated for a moment, really trying to think this through.

I knew I wanted to get to know this girl. I also knew that if she ever found out that I jacked off while thinking about her before I even knew her name she'd probably be pretty creeped out. However, with my hand on my junk and her face in my mind, her legs stretching out of those tiny cut-offs, I found that I just couldn't stop. All I could think about was the thick, honey blond hair that I wanted to wrap around my fist as I took her mouth with mine; the emerald green eyes that I wanted to stare into as I moved inside her and took her over the edge. With that image burning in my mind, my hands picked up speed until I groaned in the quiet of the bathroom and came into my hand.

After the shower I fell right into bed. I'd had a shit day, except for her, and I'm not just talking about the shower scene, although that really was pretty spectacular.

She felt like the only light in an existence that seemed so dark, so bleak that I wanted to scream. I tried to think about anything else, but despite my best efforts, I fell asleep to the image of her eyes burning into mine, begging me to save her, to heal her and make her whole.

But how the hell could I fix someone else if I couldn't even fix myself?

Chapter Five

Parker

TUESDAY'S CLASSES FLEW BY IN a flash, and (thankfully) everything went much more smoothly than it had on Monday. I had two psych classes and an English class - another prereq I hadn't gotten out of the way last year. Tuesdays were longer school days for me, and I had been worried the whole time I was at campus, but like Monday, there were no emergencies.

But now it was 7:30 Wednesday morning and I was walking towards Philosophy. Part of me wanted to drop the class, just to avoid Mr. Too-Beautiful-For-His-Own-Good, but I knew that was insane. Not only did I *need* the class, but it was kind of interesting, so I was determined to see it out.

I left my house even earlier than before this time. I wasn't going to be late again. When I made it to the room, I pushed open the door and found the place empty.

Thank God.

I went to the back and took the same seat I had sat in last time. I pulled out my textbook, notebook, and a pen. I checked my phone, silenced it, and set it on my lap. Then I started doodling.

I used to draw. As in actually draw, not just absentmindedly doodle. I used to do a lot of things, but drawing was one of my favorites. I loved working in pen and ink more than anything. The contrast of light and dark always felt significant, and to me, there was nothing more freeing than just creating something.

That was before. Now, doodles were all I had left in me. Trying to put a pen or pencil to a page to make something truly beautiful felt too risky... like I was going to cut myself open and bleed out onto the floor. I couldn't do it. Doodling was safe.

About fifteen minutes had passed before I felt heat spread across my right arm, right through the thin, long-sleeved shirt I was wearing. I kept my eyes down on the page, still circling, still looping. I heard a throat clear. I kept doodling. When I heard it again, I finally looked up.

"Hey."

Dear God, that smile. His hazel eyes were even more beautiful that I had remembered, and the scruff was a little bit longer than it had been the other day. I had no idea why he sat next to me, and I really had no clue why he was smiling at me like I was everything he ever wanted. My tongue turned to sandpaper as I tried to come up with something, anything to say.

"You're the legs."

Oh my fucking God, Parker. Really? Is that really the best you can do?

I watched as his smile grew even wider and his eyes began to crinkle, and I wanted to kill myself. "Uh, I mean, you. The pants. From yesterday."

I don't even know what to say. I'm an idiot.

"Well, I have different pants on today, but I'll keep the fact that you liked them in mind and wear 'em again for you sometime." He winked at me, and I think I had an orgasm.

"So," he continued, "how's your first week going?" As he spoke, his voice rumbled softly over my skin and I wanted to wrap myself up in it. It was like hot caramel over cool vanilla bean ice cream. *Nothing* better.

"Fine. I mean, as good as I could hope for, I guess." I was determined not to bring up my entrance to class on Monday again. I was going to prove that if you didn't talk about something out loud, it actually never happened.

"That's good. Are you a freshman?"

"No," I snorted. "Why, do I look like a freshman?"

"Not really, but you have this lost look about you. That's kind of a freshman thing."

I narrowed my eyes like he was crazy, even though I knew he was probably right. How he could tell that I was lost when I refused to even admit it to myself - that just didn't bear thinking about. Instead, I attempted a scowl.

"I'm not lost."

"I didn't say you were. I said you *looked* lost. But now, you're the one getting all defensive."

I knew he was just teasing, but I had no clue what to say. He was right, I was getting defensive. And no one had ever really teased me before, besides Jessie - but she didn't count because she'd been my best friend forever. Instead of answering, I looked back down at my notebook and started doodling again.

"Wow. That's a work of art, right there." He was looking at the notebook, at the swirls and circles and dark.

"No. That's just a doodle."

"Are you an artist?" *Was he actually interested?* I really wanted to be honest, to tell him how I used to love art more than anything in the world. But I couldn't.

"No. I just like to doodle."

"That's cool. So, what *do* you do?"

I stared at him. What did I *do*? I didn't do anything. I didn't have a life. I had no hobbies, no real friends within a hundred miles, nothing but the suckiness of my day to day existence.

"I, uh, I don't really do anything." I told him quietly, breaking eye contact again. Looking at him was too hard. It took too much energy to keep my shields up when I was staring into the most disarming eyes I had ever seen. And I knew that if I let those shields down around him, even for a second, I would be a goner.

"Huh." Then he fell silent.

I should have kept my mouth shut but, of course, I didn't. "Huh what?"

"I don't know. That's just weird. Why don't you do anything? You're young, in college, this should be the time of your life. Live a little. Go out. Join a club or something. People who do nothing all the time miss out on life. In case you weren't aware, it's happening, right outside, every day."

I bristled with anger. I knew it wouldn't be fair to take it out on him. He had no idea what my life was like. He didn't have a clue what I was up against, so I knew I shouldn't get pissed, but I did.

"That's kind of rude, don't you think? You don't know anything about me. I don't even know your name." As soon as I felt my voice rise, I stopped and took a deep breath. The room was about half full and these people already had more than enough reasons to think I was crazy.

"I'm Ash." He stuck out his hand as if I had been asking for his name rather than telling him to back the hell off.

"Cool."

"And you are...?"

"Does it matter?"

"It does to me. Come on, I tried to help you the other day. The rest of these assholes just sat around staring at the beautiful girl on the floor, but I was the Good Samaritan. Shouldn't I get some brownie points for that or something?"

Crap. I instantly reacted to three things. First and most importantly, he called me beautiful. That rocked through me like a tidal wave, drenching my insides with a warm, gooey feeling that made me uncomfortable as all hell. But, he also just called everyone in the room, which was definitely filling up, an asshole and he wasn't exactly quiet about it. And lastly, he kind of had a point about having been the only one to try and help me out. But I really didn't want to acknowledge that.

"I guess you're right. I'm sorry. I'm Parker." My words were short and I may have growled a bit as I spoke, but I hoped he didn't notice. I've never been very lucky.

"Damn." His face gave absolutely nothing away. "That was really hard for you to say, wasn't it?" I tried not to, but cracked a smile anyway. *Damn this hot boy to hell.* "And anyway," he continued, "I meant your first name. I already knew your last name."

"Oh, I, uh... It's just Parker."

He looked at me before shooting me a cocky grin. "Just Parker?"

I nodded slowly. "Yup, just Parker."

"So, are you a superhero or just really famous?"

"What are you talking about?"

"Well, Just Parker, the only people I know with only one name are superheroes and famous people. You know - like Madonna, Batman, Oprah, Catwoman... Which camp are you in?"

I let out a small laugh as I looked back down to my desk. "Neither. I'm just boring, average Parker."

"I don't believe that for a second." His voice was low and so serious that I had to look back up. He wasn't joking around anymore, and somehow I knew that whatever he was about to say was important.

"What do you mean?" I asked when I couldn't bear his silent gaze any more.

"There is not one thing about you that is boring or average."

He turned away as the professor walked into the room and dove right into his lecture. I stared at Ash for a few seconds before I realized what I was doing and looked back down to my notebook.

I wasn't sure why I was so affected by him. He was only good-looking. Well, maybe he was the most attractive guy I'd ever seen, but, still - that was just superficial. But it probably also had to do with the fact that he was funny and that he had a voice that warmed me from the inside out like hot chocolate. Maybe it was the way he so casually he called me beautiful, as if he believed it was really true, as if it was a fact - something accepted and known. It also could have been the way that he seemed to see inside me, as if everything I fought to hide was laid out on the floor at his feet for his approval.

I didn't know exactly why my body ached to get closer to his, what made my insides call out like he was vital for my continued survival, but I knew with every breath I took that Ash was bad news. I knew just looking at him that he was the type of person who would take everything I had and leave me with nothing but pain. The boy was a broken heart waiting to happen, and I wasn't going to let that heart be mine.

And it wasn't like I had time for a relationship, anyway. Maybe one day, years from now when my life was back under control. Maybe if I made it through everything that was going on around me, everything that was threatening to destroy me, and maybe if I had anything left by the time this was over, I could think about getting involved in a relationship.

But *definitely* not now.

Despite all that, even though I knew it was pointless, I couldn't help but wonder what it would be like to let myself fall for Ash. To live a different life, to be the girl who dated and kissed boys and fell in love, even if just for a little while. And I couldn't help but imagine Ash picking me up for dinner, taking me to the movies, kissing me at my door before whispering goodnight. It was a beautiful fantasy.

I knew it was impossible, but the fantasies made it a little easier to accept. After all, they were all I had.

Chapter Six

Ash

SITTING NEXT TO PARKER FOR an hour was pure torture of the absolute best variety. She smelled fresh, almost like a mixture of baby powder and wildflowers, and I wanted to bathe in that scent forever. I felt completely attuned to her natural frequency. Every time she moved, shifted, pulled that gorgeous blond hair over her shoulder, I felt it like a shock to my system. I wanted to put my hands on her, wanted to build her up and break her down and force her to admit all of the secrets I could see her hiding.

I kept sneaking glances throughout class. I couldn't help it. She surprised me. When I had called her beautiful she froze, as if no one had ever told her that before. As if she just had never happened to look in a mirror. I couldn't believe that she didn't know how stunning she was. Then again, people can hide a lot of things from themselves. I knew that firsthand.

After a half an hour, I couldn't take it anymore. I knew that I was being the world's biggest pussy, but I still wrote the note.

I knew she would probably laugh and take it back to her friends to mock later, but I didn't care. "Do you want to go out sometime?" I wrote "yes" and "no" and drew boxes beside each with the instructions at the bottom - "Check one." I folded the paper four times, back and forth and back and forth. Then, on the outside, I neatly wrote "Just Parker."

In a total loser move, I leaned back in my chair as I stretched my arms out like I needed to open up my body for the world's biggest yawn. I slid my arm behind her head and around her back as I dropped the note over her left shoulder. It hit her before bouncing down to land on the floor next to her bag. *Shit.*

Okay, okay, this might not be so bad. The note was a bad idea anyway. I saw her glance at me with narrowed eyes, I'm sure wondering what the creepy guy next to her was up to. I hid behind my best smile. Her face didn't move, and I was worried that she was literally the only person in the world who could resist the Ashton Carter Killer Smile, but she licked her lips just as her eyes darted down to my mouth and back up so fast I would have missed it if I blinked. Then, she rolled her eyes and turned back towards the front of the room. I let out a sigh of relief.

Maybe she won't notice the note at all, I found myself hoping. *Maybe I can just grow a set of balls, chill the fuck out for a second, and ask her out on a freaking date, like a normal person.*

Although I'd never really been normal, I figured that now was as good a time to start as any. This could be the New Ash, and he could be a good, normal guy. Someone who goes to school, volunteers at a hospital, gets into med school and dates a beautiful blonde with secrets and stunning green eyes. Someone who hasn't fucked up his entire life. I think that maybe I could be that guy, for her.

And then I remembered the blood and the breaking and the lights and everything else that was wrong with my life, and what I had done to get there, and I wasn't so sure...

But she made me want to try. And I don't think it's because she was beautiful beyond reason, or because her entire face lit up when she smiled, or because when I held her hand the other day it felt like my body was plugged back in - like I was alive and awake and real for the first time in a really long while.

I think it's because I knew that we could help each other. I knew that we could take the broken pieces of ourselves and make something out of them together.

Five minutes later, I was still breathing easy, sure that she still hadn't discovered the note. Then I saw her scribbling on her sheet. Then scribbling harder. *Shit*. All that doodling killed her pen. I knew she'd seen the note when she stopped reaching around in her bag (for, I'm sure, another pen) and froze for a few seconds, eye pointed at the floor. Then she grabbed the paper and dropped it quickly on the desk in front of her. I couldn't look away from it, but I managed to pull my eyes up to her face for a second. She wasn't smiling, but I could see the hint of a blush staining her cheeks. *She's always blushing.* It was the most adorable thing I'd ever seen.

I watched Parker slowly unfold the note. She still hadn't looked in my direction once. When she got to the last fold, I held my breath. When she flipped it open, I needed to look down. I stared at my textbook, waiting for something, anything.

And then... She snorted.

Seriously. Straight up snorted. Like a pig. I looked over and her whole face collapsed into silent giggles. They became vocal and she quickly tried to cover it up, pretending like she was coughing for the sake of the people turning around to see what was happening in the back of the room. I didn't know whether to laugh along with her or ask God to strike me down where I sat. I flashed a small smile but right away looked back down at my book as she gathered herself.

Once she quieted down and the room's attention was back off us, I saw her lean towards me. I could feel the energy pouring off her skin, and at the sensation of having her so close to me, I felt my heart start to race. I moved to meet her halfway and glanced at her out of the corner of my eye.

"Seriously?" she whispered. Her face looked so much lighter in that moment that all I could think was *I'll make her laugh every day if it makes her look exactly like that. Like everything everywhere is perfect.*

"Yes, seriously," I said, as straight-faced as I could manage. "And I don't appreciate your laughter. You really know how to make a guy feel good about himself, don't you?"

She rolled her eyes at me and muttered, "I hardly think you need any help with that."

"You have to check one of the boxes," I told her, choosing to ignore her last statement. "Don't leave me hanging here…" I pouted and gave her puppy dog eyes, which brightened her fading smile. I was struck with another burst of pride.

She really might have a point about the whole ego thing…

She leaned away and hid the note behind her arm like we were in elementary school and I wanted to cheat off her test. Although I guess I did kind of start it with my third-grade-style note passing. After making two quick scratches on the paper (with a new pen from her bag,) she folded it back up and instead of being an idiot like me, she just slid the note back onto my desk. I grabbed it and took a breath before I slowly opened its four folds. And then I exhaled.

She checked "no." And of course, at that moment, the professor dismissed the class.

Parker leapt out of her seat faster than I would have thought possible, but I was quicker and blocked her way to the aisle.

"Why don't you want to go out with me?" She had bent down to pick up her bag, and paused for just a second before she grabbed the handle.

"I have to go." She spoke with her eyes locked on my ear as she lunged to get around me, but she wasn't getting off that easy. I stepped right into her path, and she just barely avoided slamming into my chest. If I had moved forward three inches I would have be pressed against… *Fuck. Not now, little Ash.*

"Answer the question, Parker." I kept my voice quiet, but it was still an order. And she knew it because that's when her eyes narrowed on mine.

"Wow, Ash, since you asked *so* nicely…" She had a gift for sarcasm. Her voice was soft but there was the suggestion of steel behind it. She was pissed. And, the sucker that I was, I *liked* it. I tempered my smile so she didn't get even angrier. "I really do have to go. Like, *now*. I have to get to my next class." Her eyes moved towards the door and I could tell she was desperate to run.

"Well," I told her, looking at my watch, "the way I see it is, this class shouldn't have let out for another, oh... Five minutes. So, I say you have five minutes to tell me why you won't go out with me." I stood with my legs spread wide and crossed my arms on my chest to let her know that she wasn't getting away without answering the question. "Hurry up, you're the one who needs to leave in," I checked the time again, "four minutes now."

I heard a soft growl rumble in her throat and I had the insane impulse to kiss her. It was the second time she had growled at me, and both times she had been pissed. I wanted to see if I could make her growl for a different reason.

I thought I was up to the challenge.

"I don't have time to date." She was beyond cute. Her words were short, as if she was trying so hard to control her violent urges she was having trouble speaking.

"I doubt that. Everyone has time to date." This was true. I refused to believe that she didn't even have an hour to go eat a sandwich... or whatever people did on dates. I wouldn't know. I had never been on a date before.

Shit. I should probably talk to Jimmy about that. He'd know.

"Not me." She licked her lips. I wanted to lick her lips too.

"Well, what do you need to be doing when you should be going out with me?"

"Stuff." She looked uncertain of that.

"Really? *Stuff*?" I asked incredulously. "That's the best you could come up with? You could have literally said anything. I have to feed my cat. I have to feed my neighbor's cat. I have to mow the lawn. I have to get an oil change. I have to go to the store. I need to go get gas. I have to-"

"Okay, I get it!" she shouted. She was hiding a smile again, but poorly, and I knew I was winning. "Please, stop. Look, Ash, you seem like a nice guy, but I wasn't lying. I barely have enough hours in my day as it is. Now, I'm sorry, but I have to get to Stat. I swear, it's the second day and I already know I'm going to fail and..." She trailed off, looking up at me expectantly. I knew she wanted me to let her by, but now I had my way in.

"Did you say Stat? As in, Statistics?" I grinned.

"Yes," she replied and I could tell she was getting really annoyed. "Can I go now?"

"Do you need a tutor?"

She didn't expect that. She straightened her posture and stared at me with a strange expression. I could only assume it was a look of shock that a guy as classically handsome as myself might actually have a brain inside his head. It annoyed me a little, but I was used to it. I'd been getting that look for most of my life.

"I don't really think that's a good idea," she told me quietly.

"Why?" I asked. "Are you assuming that I'm a shit tutor because of whatever stereotypes you're imagining right now, or are you assuming that I have less than honorable intentions when it comes to helping a fellow classmate pass a class that I aced four years ago and could take in my sleep?"

She leaned back and her eyes widened a bit at my slightly hostile outburst. "Fuck, I'm sorry Parker. I didn't mean to totally sound like a dick. But, I mean it. I'd like to help. And seriously, I'm awesome at math." I gave her a cocky grin and watched as she stared into my eyes, probably trying to figure out if I was completely insane or not.

"Okay," she finally gave in. "I'd actually really, really appreciate that." She gifted me with a small, genuine smile and I gave myself a mental high-five.

"Great! When do you want to start?"

"Uh, well, actually probably not for another week or so. I still don't have my book, and I can't..." She trailed off. I waited for her to continue but when it became clear she wasn't going to, I broke the silence.

"If we don't start for a few weeks, then by the time we start you'll be a few weeks behind. There are only sixteen weeks in a semester, Parker. Not as many as it sounds. Why won't you have a book for a few more weeks?"

She looked down at the ground and then back up and stared right at my shoulder. *Damn, this girl couldn't lie for shit.* "I, uh, ordered my book online, but it was backordered. I'm waiting for it to come in now, but I'm not sure when I'm going to get it."

"Oh-kay," I said slowly. "Well, that's fine. I have a book you can borrow in the meantime. What's your number?"

"What?" She looked like a deer caught in the headlights, and I couldn't stop the small chuckle that slipped out of my chest. Thankfully, she didn't notice it.

"Your phone number, Parker," I told her, pulling my phone out of my pocket and flashing it in her direction. "I'll text you so you have my number."

"Why do I need your number?" she asked quietly, looking completely bewildered and I found myself frozen at the expression on her gorgeous face.

Fuck.

This was so going to happen. I was going to make sure of it. I would be as patient as I had to, but I wanted Parker more than I had ever wanted anyone. And not just physically - I wanted to know her. I wanted to help her. I wanted to be a part of her life.

"I'm assuming," I told her quietly, "that if you don't have time to date, you don't have a lot of extra time to spend with a tutor. Am I right?"

She thought about that for a second. "Yes."

"Okay. You text me, any time, if you have a spare hour or two. I'll work around your schedule as much as I can. I do have a job, but truthfully, if you don't mind coming to me, you could come there, hang out while I work, and we could do our thing."

"Your boss would let you do that?" She looked like she couldn't believe that was true.

"You'd be amazed the shit my boss would let me do. Number, beautiful?"

That earned me another smile and a few seconds where she stared at me like I was both the cure for cancer and the object of all of her hottest fantasies. *Holy. Shit.*

She realized I was waiting and rattled off her phone number so I could save it in my contacts. As I pushed the menu button I noticed the time.

"And now you need to run, or you're going to be late."

I watched the smile fade from her face as she processed what I said.

"Shit," she whispered, and took off at top speed right into my side. I laughed and jumped out of her way as she ran down the steps like she was on fire.

"Talk to you later, Parker!" I shouted as she ran out the door. She waved an arm without looking back and I watched her fly out of sight.

As I walked out the door to go get coffee, I could already tell that today was going to be a much better day than usual. It took a while for the smile to fade from my face, but even once it did, all it took was a quick thought of her and I was grinning like a fool.

I was seriously in trouble when it came to Just Parker.

Chapter Seven

Parker

THROUGHOUT THE REST OF MY classes, I waited for my phone to vibrate. Ash didn't seem like a very patient guy, and for some reason he seemed really – weirdly - determined to do the whole tutoring thing, for whatever reason.

I already knew that I couldn't trust myself around him. I'd kissed a couple of guys in high school, experienced occasional heavy petting, but that was it. And not only was I sure he had way more experience than I did (*hell, any experience would make him more experienced than me,*) Ash had a weird sort of hold over me. I was in awe of the way I reacted to him almost as much as I was terrified by it.

When I walked out of my last class, I was nearly convinced that I had imagined the entire conversation from this morning. The stress of my life was finally getting to me and I was starting to hallucinate. *Yeah, that's definitely it.*

I spent the drive home pushing Ash and tutoring and gorgeous golden eyes to the back of my mind, where I would force them to stay. By the time I got home I was just Parker again, not the girl who worried about if the cute boy would text her or not. That wasn't me, and I couldn't forget.

I grabbed my bag and crashed through the front door. I heaved myself up four flights of stairs after a quick brood over the "Out Of Order" sign still hanging on the elevator. I had sent letter after letter after letter to the manager of the building about that broken elevator. It'd been two months and I had yet to see a single worker in the building. I was ready to search for a YouTube video on elevator repair and fix the damn thing myself, and I was considering the probability of my doing that successfully as I lurched down the hall and unlocked the door.

I hated this apartment. I hated this building. I hated why we lived here.

The tiny living room was empty except for the old brown couch. That was strange. Mom spent most of every afternoon on that couch. I went down the hallway towards Mom's room but I ran into Diane as she quietly closed the door behind her.

"Hey, Diane. How is she today?"

"Good, sweetie. She woke up with extra energy, so we went for a walk this morning. But it tired her out pretty good, so we ate an early lunch. I just finished helping her get ready for a nap."

Diane was a godsend. One of the doctors had told me about some volunteer organizations that would arrange to have people come to your house if you didn't have money or insurance that covered in-home nurses. I'd left Mom home alone twice before I realized I couldn't do it anymore. Both times she forgot to take her medicine at the right time and I came home to her crying on the bathroom floor because she was sick, and she hurt, and she hadn't known where I was.

Mom normally was not the most stable person in the world. Actually, that's being too generous. Mom, "normally," was a wreck. But Mom, on cocktails of pain killers, antibiotics and cancer meds, was downright volatile.

So, before school started, I made some calls and found a company in Charlottesville who could send someone out when I had school and work. Diane was scheduled to come on Mondays, Wednesdays and Fridays while I was at classes. We had met twice before the school year started, both days that I had to go to school for registration stuff. I guessed that she was in her seventies, but I couldn't be sure. Some days it seemed like she felt younger than I did. She was also the sweetest woman I'd ever met. The type of woman you wished was your grandma.

"Did she take all the right pills?"

"Yeah, sweetheart, I got them out of the box you filled."

I nodded, trying to think of any other questions I need to ask.

"Everything's alright, Eileen. I promise. Now, I'm going to head out of here. My grandson is coming over for dinner tonight and I need to make a chocolate cream pie. It's his favorite."

I smiled as the jealousy sliced through me. I wanted a grandma who made me chocolate cream pie. Or key lime - that was my favorite. Or any pie, really. Hell, I'd just take a grandma.

"Well, get out of here, then. Thanks, Diane."

She gave me a sweet smile as she headed out the door with a wave. I locked the door behind her and headed back to my mom's room. I quietly opened the door and stepped a few feet into the room. I could hear her breathing - it was little more than a sick rattle that never stopped when she laid in bed on her back. She was losing weight, and I couldn't help but think that she was starting to develop the whole bag-of-bones look. I tiptoed a few steps closer, quietly, even though I really didn't have to be. Since she took a walk, she'd probably sleep for a couple hours if I left her alone, especially if she just took her meds. I checked the port that entered the skin of her right shoulder, made sure she wasn't laying on any tubes, and pulled the blanket up to her chin. Once I was sure she was sleeping okay, I made my way back out of the room and closed the door softly behind me.

Back in the living room, I picked up my bag from where I'd dropped it by the door. Then I walked to my bedroom and sat at my desk. I had to study. I pulled a few books out of my bag and set them on my desk, along with my reusable water bottle and my phone.

I was halfway through the first chapter of my philosophy book when my phone beeped.

Unknown: **Hey there, Just Parker**

I couldn't help but smile, which seriously annoyed me. I put my phone back down. He waited all day to text me, he could wait another five minutes for me to text back.

I shifted my attention back to my textbook and tried to read the same paragraph five times before I gave up and grabbed my phone again. I saved his number before I responded.

Me: **Do I know you?**

I smiled at my little joke before I realized that sarcasm didn't really translate through text very well. *What if he thought I gave my number out to every guy I meet? What if...*
My phone dinged again.

Ash: **I'm insulted. Do you give your phone number out to every passably handsome stranger you meet on the street?**

I snorted. *I worry too much.* I typed out my response and then considered it for a minute before hitting send.

Me: **Not the passably handsome ones. Just the ones that take my breath away.**

Shit. Why did I say that? That's like crazy talk. I shouldn't have-
My stomach dropped as the phone began to ring in my hand. *Stupid text messages. Why oh why did I do this stuff to myself?* I counted to five as my ringtone grew louder and louder before I finally flipped the phone open to answer.
"Hello?"
"So I take your breath away?"
I tried to come up with some sort of response that would sound cool without sounding flirty. I knew that I shouldn't be leading Ash on about the possibility of a future between

us, but it was so fun to play with him and imagine that this was my life.

"I think it's probably just the pants…"

Wow, Park. You couldn't be cooler if you tried.

"You seem awfully fixated on those pants, sweetheart. You got something you want to tell me?"

I decided that, before I managed to get my foot from where it currently resided in my mouth to where it was headed, which was halfway down my esophagus, I was going to try and salvage my pride, as well as the conversation.

"Is there a reason you're calling me, or do you just need someone to make you feel good about yourself?"

"I wouldn't have called you for that. You are like ego-kryptonite."

"Well, some girls need more than a pretty boy batting his eyes at them to give it up. I happen to be one of them." Not that I had ever, you know, given it up.

"See? Exactly that. You managed to insult me twice in a sentence that, on the outside, seemed to be completely about you. That's sheer talent."

I laughed and waited, but all I heard was the sound of his breathing. "What are you doing?" I finally asked, both to break the silence and hear his voice again.

"I'm on my way to class. What are you doing?"

"Oh, I'm just sitting at home. I was studying, but this really annoying guy called and interrupted."

"And the hits just keep on coming…" He muttered. "Well, I wanted you to have my number, and now you do. And I also wanted to tell you that, I really meant what I said to you earlier. I want to help you out. With Stat, I mean. And I can. Just give me a shot."

Crap. That was nice. *Why was he so nice?*

"I will. And, I know I was kind of a bitch and I'm sorry. I just… I'm not really used to having friends, I guess. We're friends, right?" I'm sure he probably thought it was a stupid girl question, but I realized I wanted to be his friend, at least as much as I could. He made things feel… easier. Or at least made me feel like the weight of everything wasn't crushing me as much. I felt like Ash would be a good friend to have.

"Yeah, Just Parker. We're friends." His quiet voice was rumbly and warm, and for some reason, even as it drove me crazy, the nickname made me smile.

And of course, at that moment I heard a thud from the other end of the apartment.

"Shit," I blurted, "I gotta go." I didn't wait for a response before I flipped the phone shut and dashed out of the room. "Mom?" I shouted, running towards and then through her door.

She was pushing herself up in bed on her tiny arms, a confused look on her face. I could see her shaking as she tried to sit up. I rushed to her side and lightly pushed her shoulder back to help her get seated. Once she was stable, I saw the tube from the port stretched across her chest and down towards the mattress. I glanced down and noticed the device that held the chemo meds and delivered them around the clock sitting on the floor, and I let out a relieved sigh. The pack was heavy, and the walls were so thin. I was sure that was the sound that I heard.

"Wha… What happened?" Mom asked in a dry, scratchy voice. She sounded exhausted. She always sounded exhausted.

"It's okay, your pack fell off the bed and hit the floor. Lay back down." I reached down to grab the pack and I placed it on her nightstand.

"Why were you yelling, Eileen? I was sleeping, I'm so tired and you shouldn't be yelling!" She tried to shout but her voice came out weaker and thinner the longer she spoke. "It hurts, it always hurts. Except when I sleep. Just let me sleep." I watched the tears work their way out of the corners of her eyes and clenched my fist until I felt the bite of my nails against the soft skin of my palm.

"I know, Ma, I'm sorry. Please, just lay back down."

I managed to get her settled after helping her drink some water and then I left her to (hopefully) fall back asleep. I went to the kitchen and laid my head against the cool metal door of the fridge.

The doctors had talked to me after we got the official diagnosis. They had explained that between emotions, hormones, and the drugs that they would be pumping into my mother's body, she wouldn't be her normal self. I mean, obviously - could you really expect a person to not change after you told them they were dying? But they had explained to me that I needed to be patient with her, that she was going to be emotionally unstable, and I should just try to "roll with the punches." They had given me a handout with a list of support groups for caregivers and family members of terminally ill people. I still had it, but I knew that I couldn't handle that. Sitting in a room with people who were already mourning the loved ones in their lives that they couldn't imagine living without. I didn't belong there.

I couldn't explain that I hated my mom. I couldn't tell them that, if it wasn't for her cancer, I would have nothing to do with her. I didn't deserve support, I didn't deserve to feel better about the fact that I was literally watching her die. Not after I had wished so many times for her to disappear from my life.

I pushed myself off the fridge and opened the door to grab a string cheese. I made it back to my room and settled in to finish the chapter that I had walked away from. I made it through two paragraphs and the entire log of cheese when my phone beeped from the desk. I grabbed it and flipped it open.

Well, shit. Two missed calls and four text messages.

Ash: **Parker, are you okay?**
Ash: **Why aren't you answering your phone?**
Ash: **Please call me back, I'm freaking out.**
Ash: **I'm about to call 911 and have them trace your cell.**

I sighed and sent him a quick text.

Me: **I'm fine.**

I set the phone down and tried to read but two seconds later my phone was ringing. I growled in my throat before hitting the ignore button. Then, because we were "friends," I texted him.

Me: **Seriously, everything's fine. I need to study. I'll text you about the tutoring thing.**

This time, I flipped the phone shut and threw it at my bed. It bounced once and flopped to the floor, where I left it. I heard it beep once, but I ignored it and all things Ash. I was too raw, too angry to talk to him.

I was going to study. I needed to finish school. I needed to do well and not lose sight of the future. A future where, for better or worse, this would all be over and done. I needed to remember that because, at this point, it was the only thing keeping me alive.

Chapter Eight

Ash

SO, I WAS KIND OF still freaked the fuck out about the way Parker hung up, even after Bio Lab two hours later. Everything had been fine, great even, and then she just panicked about something and hung up. In hindsight, I probably shouldn't have called her twice and texted her four times, but I was worried! I mean, all I could think was that someone had broken into her house to rob and rape her or something. Or, possibly worse, that she had a crazy jealous boyfriend who had showed up and she didn't want to be seen on the phone with another guy.

I didn't believe that she had a boyfriend, or maybe I just didn't *want* to believe. But Parker just didn't seem like that type of girl, and I felt like she would have mentioned if there was another guy. Then again, maybe not because, as she said, we were just "friends."

Shit, when her quiet voice asked me if we were friends, I wanted to burst out laughing, but I knew she wouldn't like that. So I held it in and just told her that, yes, we were friends. I was about tell her that we were going to be a fuck of a lot more but I figured I'd keep that to myself for now.

But then, she was gone and I freaked out, and… *I'll text you about that tutoring thing?* I mean, what the fuck was that?

I needed to calm down before I did something stupid. I didn't know what that something stupid would be, but I had discovered that when I was angry I didn't always display the best judgment, and I was working on controlling that. So I called Marco. Jimmy would want to talk, and I wasn't in the mood to talk.

"Yo, man," was his answer. I could already tell he was high, but then again, Marco was always high.

"What are you doing?"

"Sitting at home playing Madden with Jimmy."

Shit. "Oh."

"Wanna come by?"

I hesitated, but I figured if they were playing Madden there would be a good chance that Jimmy was high too, so I told him "yeah" and hung up. I made the drive to his house and he buzzed me up when I arrived, leaving the front door open so that I could let myself in when I got up the stairs. By the time I reach his door, the entire stairwell smelled like weed.

"Dude, you might want to be a little bit more careful about leaving your door open like that," I said as I entered the living room. I was right, they were both staring at the TV screen with tired, red eyes and stupid smiles on their faces.

"Dick, I sell shit to almost every person in this building."

I kept my mouth quiet because he knew how I felt about his selling. Marco was smart, way too smart for his own good, actually, and I had known him since third grade. Back then, he was this quiet, tiny kid who didn't talk to anyone. Jimmy and I befriended him for one of those weird, elementary school reasons and he had just stuck. He was third in our graduating class, and could have gone to school anywhere, but picked UVA to stay close to home. He was in the process of getting his business degree, and he had been selling pot for the past three years, despite both mine and Jimmy's thoughts on the matter.

Jimmy changed the subject. "So why do you look so pissed?" I clenched my jaw.

"I'm fine."

Marco laughed and Jimmy just stared at me harder. "Ash..."

I sighed. "I'm fine, really. I just - I met this girl, and she's driving me crazy."

Marco, who had still been chuckling about my attempt to claim that I wasn't angry, chuckled so hard that he rolled off of the couch and onto the floor, knocking into the coffee table on the floor as he convulsed with laughter. Jimmy, on the other hand, just stared at me with his mouth open.

"What?" I asked him, impatient with their show.

"You know *what*!" he shouted at me, and I did. "I never, not once, thought that I'd hear you say those words in my lifetime! Holy fuck. Oh my God, my dad's gonna shit himself. Oh my God, your dad's *really* gonna shit himself. Did you tell your mom? Don't tell your mom, man, she'll be planning your wedding and-"

"Just shut the fuck up!" I yelled at both him and Marco, who was still laughing on the ground.

"Dude," he said, staring at me as a goofy grin spread across his face. "Chill out, I'm just happy for you. So, who is she, what's she look like, and what's she like in bed?"

I sighed before I answered. "Her name is Parker, I met her in my philosophy class. She's fucking beautiful, and for your information, I haven't slept with her but I promise that when I do, I won't tell you shit about it."

"Oh my God," he shouted again. "You haven't even slept with this girl yet and you're freaking out over her? Is the great Ashton Carter actually..." he paused for dramatic effect, "in *love*?" Marco's laughter burst through the room again, and I really wanted to punch him.

"Fuck you, man." I told him, even as I cracked a small smile. "She's just, I don't know. There's just something about her that's... different..."

"Does she have big hands? Because if she does, maybe she's not actually a woman..."

I glared at him. "You're a dick, dude."

He just laughed off the insult. "Come on, Ash. Do you remember the raft of shit you gave me when I met Maddie? This is only the beginning."

He had a point. Maddie was great, and I knew Jimmy loved the shit out of her, but when they met senior year of high school, I made it a point to let him know that he was completely whipped. And he still was - Maddie went to the College of William and Mary and even long-distance, Jimmy and Maddie were solid. They'd been together for four years, the last three only seeing each other at most every few weeks.

"Point taken."

"So," Jimmy asked, "are you actually going to take this girl out?"

"Yeah. Well, I hope so. I tried to ask her today but she said no."

"She said no? That can happen to you?"

I laughed. "I know, right? But, I still got her number."

"How did she turn you down and then give you her number? You didn't get your dad to do weird spy shit, did you?"

"No, asshole. She mentioned being worried about her Stat class, and I offered to tutor her. When she tried to say no, I made her feel bad about stereotyping me as an idiot just because I'm beautiful. She couldn't say no after that."

Jimmy grinned. "Wow, you sure are boyfriend-material, aren't you?"

I sighed at that. I knew he was just messing with me, but it hit a little too close for comfort. "I don't even know what the fuck that is... I have no idea what I'm doing around this girl."

"Yeah, I remember that." He smiled but left it at that. His eyes glazed a bit. Guess I wasn't getting any help there.

Jimmy, Marco, and I played a few games before I calmed down enough that I didn't want to track Parker down and force whatever the hell had happened earlier out of her. About two hours later, I told them both I'd see them later and drove home to take a shower and get ready for dinner.

House arrest had sucked for a lot of reasons. One of the biggest ones for me was not seeing my Grandma. She's as close to sacred to me as anything in my life gets. I'll put up with a lot, but you don't mess with Grandma.

My dad and I never got along well. Things got worse as Aurora got older. I knew he loved me, but we were just way too alike. So Grandma would invite me to dinner, just me. It was our special thing. Every Wednesday night I would go to her house, we would eat dinner, and then we'd spend a few hours playing Scrabble or cards or something.

The weekly dinners didn't stop until I went on lock down. I knew I disappointed her, so I wasn't really surprised. I remember the first time she came to the house after everything happened - she looked down at the tracker around my ankle and a single tear rolled down her face. I turned away and blocked it all out. We didn't talk at all until she was getting ready to leave. She came up to me, wrapped her arms around my chest, and whispered that she loved me, no matter what. I waited until she left and then went to my room and screamed into my pillow until the screams became sobs and I passed out.

So, needless to say, when my Grandma had called me last week and asked me to come to dinner tonight, I was ecstatic.

When I pulled up in front of the little bungalow that she had lived in all my life, it hit me (not for the first time) that this place felt more like home to me than my parent's house ever had. I parked the truck and headed up the sidewalk, waiting for almost a minute after I knocked before the door swung open. I felt the smile stretch itself across my face, and I knew it matched in every way the wide one that greeted me, cracking her face near in half.

"Ashton," she said quietly. "Well, come on, give me a hug."

I laughed and pulled her into my arms. Grandma was sturdy but much shorter than I was and, as I grabbed her, I picked her up off the floor in a bear hug. She laughed before she shouted, "Put me down," whacking me on the back of the head. I set her gently back on her feet and followed her into the house and to the kitchen. I sat down at the counter as she busied herself getting me a glass of iced tea, like she did every time I walked in the door.

"So, how's school going?"

"Great. All my classes seem good, and I like the professors. I'm retaking a few classes, but they're all pretty easy so it should be fine." I sat up as I noticed the pie sitting on the countertop. I knew it was for me. Chocolate cream, of course. While she was facing the other direction, I stuck out a finger and dragged it through the cream. I lifted the finger to my mouth to lick it clean when she whacked me on the ear.

"Ashton Daniel Carter. I know your Momma taught you better than that. And if she didn't, I sure as heck did." She glared and I grinned as I ate the cream. *Delicious.*

"Sorry, Grandma. But you know how I feel about your pie."

"Yeah, yeah... So, what else is new?" she asked as she gave me the tea before shuffling across the kitchen to finish preparing dinner. I helped her set the table as we caught up, ignoring the fact that this was the first time we had had dinner in the four months since I was set free. We both ignored that giant elephant in the room.

When dinner was ready, we sat to eat. I smiled to see her homemade chicken and dumplings. It was my favorite meal, and another attempt to ignore the elephant. This time, I think she hoped feeding it would make it go away. After we cleared away the plates, we broke out the Scrabble board and set up the game.

I had tons of memories of playing Scrabble with my grandma when I was younger. I'm convinced she's the reason I'm as smart as I am today - while other kids were playing at the park, I was spelling out mischief on a triple word score at age seven.

"I've been thinking about something, and I wanted to talk to you about it..." Her eyes shifted to mine, and she seemed to be assessing my mood as she continued. "I met this girl, and I think that you really need to meet her. You'd just love her, Ashton. I swear-"

I interrupted her before she could continue. There was nothing new to this. Grandma was convinced I needed a woman in my life to "set me on the straight and narrow." It was about three years late for that.

"I told you this before. I don't need you to set me up Grandma. And anyway, where do you even meet all these young girls? Or is this one from community center? Trying to find me a cougar?" I winked at her. She rolled her eyes.

"I met her at work. Her mom is sick, cancer, and she's going to school, working, and doing everything on her own. Incredibly strong girl. And young. She goes to UVA, maybe you've even seen her around..."

"I appreciate the help, Grandma, but really, it's okay. I promise I'll settle down one day..."

"Yeah, yeah, so you say, but you've never even had a girlfriend! That's not normal, Ashton." Her eyes widened. "Are you gay?"

I choked on the breath I was taking. "Wait, what?!"

"I said are you gay? It's fine if you are. A friend of mine has a gay grandson. He's quite handsome. Maybe you could meet him?"

"No! Grandma, I am not gay!"

"Okay, calm down. I just figured I'd ask... No one's judging, sweetheart. You can love whomever you want to love."

"Please, *please* just let me be in charge of my own love life," I said. I could tell she wasn't happy, but she was giving up, at least for now.

"Oh, all right. I just want to see some great-grandbabies before I die, and it's not like your sister…" I clenched my jaw as she trailed off. "I just want to see both of my grandkids happy." She smiled at me, but it was so much weaker than the one she gave me at the door.

"I am happy," I told her, "and I'll be happier after I kick your butt at Scrabble."

"Oh please, I'll see you married before you beat me at scrabble."

I laughed. And later that night, as I made my way home, I realized we were both right. She had won, but I was *definitely* happier.

Chapter Nine

Parker

I WAS STANDING BACKSTAGE AT the community center next to my elementary school. I was excited, but a little bit worried that I was going to throw up. I had to keep it down because I didn't want to ruin my costume. It was finally my big night.

Jessie's parents had bought me a VHS copy of Annie, the musical, for my seventh birthday. They knew that it was my all-time favorite movie because I begged to watch it at every single sleepover Jessie and I had. We used to dress up in sheets (we thought we could make them look like rags) and sing "It's a Hard Knock Life" and "Tomorrow" at the top of our lungs. Jessie had no idea that I used to imagine that I was Annie, and my mom was going to disappear (I never thought about where, she just was always gone in my fantasies.) I'd pretend that my own Daddy Warbucks was going to show up and take me away and make me his princess.

So, in fifth grade, when I found out that the spring play at school was going to be Annie, I decided to try out. Surprising even myself, I got the lead role. I wasn't a bad singer and I knew the part like it was my life (probably because I wanted it to be so bad.)

I loved everything about being in that play. I loved practicing for the show, and dress rehearsals, and wearing the curly red wig. For the first time, I was really proud of myself.

I told my mom, over and over and over, what night the play was. I even posted a flier on the fridge with magnets. And I had left a note on the counter when I left for school that morning, reminding her that she needed to be at the community center by 6:00. I told her that her ticket was at the door, and that I couldn't wait for her to see the show.

Backstage, I peeked out at the auditorium, looking for her dirty blond hair and dark brown eyes, but I couldn't find her. There were more people than I had expected, but I wasn't nervous. I just wanted my mom to be there. I wanted to make her proud, for the first time in my life. I wanted her to be happy instead of disappointed and mean.

I headed backstage to get ready. I don't remember the play... just bits and pieces. I remember the lights, I remember the sound of the applause. I remember feeling like I could do anything I wanted.

I remember changing back into my clothes after the show and heading towards where I knew she would be waiting. I had a smile on my face, ready to see her, ready for her to tell me that I did a good job, that I didn't make a single mistake. I needed that.

I remember waiting. And waiting. And waiting. Thinking maybe she ran to the bathroom or maybe she's still in the auditorium. It wasn't until my teacher saw me standing outside the auditorium doors and asked me if I needed a ride home that I realized that she wasn't there. She hadn't come. I tried to say I was fine, that I was just going to walk home, but it was already almost nine and the sun had gone down, so she told me to get in *her car. When we got to the dark house she tried to walk me in, but I made up a lie about my mom being at work. I assured her I would be fine, and thanked her for the ride before running into the house, using my key to open the locked door.*

As soon as I walked in, I noticed the smell. The house smelled horrible, like old throw up. I walked into the living room then back through the dining room and into the kitchen. I saw the shadow on the floor when I got into the room and I turned the light on, almost wishing I hadn't.

She was lying on the floor, face down. There was a pool of vomit surrounding her face, soaking into her hair. There was a bunch of broken glass and what looked like the top of a clear bottle lying on the floor next to her. I noticed a few small cuts bleeding on her hands, but nothing looked too bad. Still, she wasn't moving.

I had seen Mom passed out before, but usually she was on a chair, or a couch, or a bed. Face down in a pile of throw-up on the floor? That was new.

I remember being angry. I wasn't scared, I was angry. I was angry that she hadn't come to the play. I was angry that she might be dead on the floor. And I was angry at myself because part of me hoped that she was.

I inched closer, shoving my ked-covered toe into her shoulder. Nothing. I nudged her again, this time adding a loud, "Mom!" Then she groaned and jerked her shoulder away from my foot. I wanted to scream and cry and break something. I wanted to leave, and I wanted her to leave, and I didn't know what to do.

I was ten, and I had no one else in the world. At least no one that wanted me. My own Dad had left me behind, and I had no grandparents, no aunts, and no uncles. I was completely alone, and I had no clue what to do or where to go.

I left her on the floor. I left her, surrounded by glass, lying in vomit, on the kitchen floor. And then I went to my room, closed and locked the door, and cried until I fell asleep.

When I woke up, I was covered in sweat and my sheet was tangled around my legs. I looked at the clock. 5:45. I wanted to roll over and go back to sleep, but I forced myself out of bed and into the shower after I checked in on my mom. She was still asleep in bed, which was good. After the shower, I threw on a pair of jeans and a Brand New t-shirt. It was already feeling like an angry music day, and when it came to angry music, Brand New was one my favorites. I left my hair to dry down my back after running a brush through it. It was a bit pathetic, but the one really great thing about my life was my hair. I did absolutely nothing to it besides let it air dry, and it always just magically looked amazing. I *loved* my hair.

Once I was ready, I threw the books that I had left on the desk the day before into my bag and then took my stuff out to the kitchen. I grabbed the pill sorter from the cabinet that was filled with prescription bottles and medical supplies. I pulled out the 6 pills that Mom had to swallow by mouth. Then I took out the three painkillers and tossed them into the mortar that was now a fixture on the counter. I ground them up, added a bit of water and poured the white mixture into a measuring cup.

I set everything on the counter with a glass of water and then headed back to her room. When I reached the side of the bed, I leaned down to squeeze her bony shoulder.

"Ma, I need you to get up to take your meds." I shook her gently, and she groaned. "Mom, come on. We need to get up to eat and take some medicine, okay?"

"Go away," she muttered.

"Mom, please, I just need you to get up for a little bit. Then you can lay back down. I promise."

"Damn it, Eileen. I need to sleep."

"I know, and you can, As soon as we eat some food and take some medicine."

I managed to get her to sit up. Before I pulled her out of the room, I pressed a thermometer to her forehead. With her immune system as compromised as it was, I always needed to be checking for a fever. Once I knew she wasn't getting sick, we slowly made our way out the door and through the hall.

She moaned the entire way, both in pain and annoyance. I got her into a chair at the dining room table and handed her the water and the pills. I set the cup of crushed pills and water in front of her, and then headed to make her some toast. While I waited for that to pop, I grabbed a bowl and some cereal, and set them by the seat across from her. I poured a glass of apple juice for Mom and set that at her place, grabbed the toast and threw it on a plate. Then I grabbed the milk and a spoon and sat down at the table with her to eat.

For the longest time, the only sound was the crunching of her toast and my cereal. I stared at the nicked wooden table I bought at a secondhand store and traced the lines in the wood with my eyes.

"Eileen," Mom rasped, "when do I go back to the doctors?"

"Monday," I said around a mouth of cereal. Her eyes narrowed.

"That's disgusting. Swallow before you talk. Show a little class for once."

I squeezed the crappy metal spoon so hard it started to bend and held her eyes as I chewed and swallowed. "Monday," I annunciated once I had finished.

She rolled her eyes and fell silent for a few minutes.

Quietly, she asked, "What is today?"

I took a deep breath, hearing the confusion in her voice. "It's Friday, Mom," I answered, just as quietly. She nodded quickly as I took the last few bites of cereal. I took my bowl to the sink. Then I went back to the table and cleaned up the rest my breakfast stuff as well as the plate from her toast.

"Do you want to drink your juice?" I asked her as she rose unsteadily from the table.

"No. It burns my stomach. I told you that."

"This is apple juice. You said the orange juice-"

"No, I didn't Eileen! You heard what you wanted to hear, as usual."

As she walked back to her room, I grabbed the glass and poured it down the drain. I wanted to slam the glass into the sink until it shattered, but I settled for rinsing it out and leaving it for later. I walked back to her room where she was already settled in bed with the TV remote clutched in her hand.

"I'm heading out, okay, Ma? I need to get to class, but Diane will be here soon." She ignored me and turned on the TV, flipping through channels before finally settling on the Home Shopping Network. "Mom, did you hear me?" I called from the doorway, louder that time and she waved a hand in my direction.

I was dismissed.

I walked back to the kitchen, grabbed my bag, resisted screaming some really nasty words, and then headed out the door to drive to class.

By the time I had arrived at campus, I still hadn't calmed down. I pulled into a parking space and turned the car off.

I didn't want to be here. I didn't want to be at home. I didn't want to see anyone. Especially not a dark-haired boy with hazel eyes whom I had been a total bitch to.

I had finally checked my phone yesterday morning to see his text from the night before.

Ash: **I'm sorry I freaked. I was worried. I really am here if you need anything at all.**

Since I was the world's biggest coward, I had completely ignored him. He hadn't texted or called at all yesterday, so I assumed he was pissed that I basically blew him off. That was fine with me. However, as stupid as it may have been, I didn't want to see him and know that I screwed things up - even if there wasn't anything to screw up in the first place. But it wasn't like I was just going to walk into class and he would sit next to me again and everything would be like it was the other day. I knew that much, at least.

I was already falling apart at the seams. I knew that one more tug would break me completely. So I sat in my car for a couple more minutes before finally climbing out the door.

Even though it was the first week of classes and I knew it was a terrible, completely irresponsible idea, I decided to play hooky.

Chapter Ten

Ash

SHE DIDN'T SHOW UP TO class.

All day yesterday, I left her alone. I figured I'd give her space and she'd text me back. I didn't want to freak her out, so I just went to class, went to work, and went home. When I woke up that morning, I figured I'd at least see her in class, but she wasn't there. Part of me wanted to walk out twenty minutes after it started, which was when I realized that she wasn't coming, but I forced myself to stay until we were done. This turned out to be an especially good thing, since the professor assigned a five page paper that was due Monday. I was sure Parker would like to hear about that.

I left the room and walked straight to my car, pulling my phone out as I went. I hit call, but after one ring, I heard her voicemail. I was beginning to really hate the way she used the ignore button.

Once I settled into the driver's seat, I texted her.

Me: **Where are you?**

I tapped my fingers on the steering wheel, trying to release some of the energy flowing through my body, energy that wanted me to put the truck in gear and drive around until I found her so that she could tell me exactly what was going on. I waited a full five minutes and was debating whether or not I should call her again when she finally answered.

Parker: **I'm fine. Don't worry. I just needed to do something.**

I had no reason not to, but I didn't believe a word she said. I knew something was wrong - I knew that she was hiding something. Whatever it was, I knew it was dark.

Me: **Can you please just tell me where you are?**

I only had to wait three minutes this time.

Parker: **I told you, I'm fine.**

Me: **Okay, I just figured you might want to know about the five page paper due Monday in Philosophy.**

This time, she responded within seconds.

Parker: **Hey Ash, can you pretty please tell me about the paper due Monday for Philosophy?**

Me: **Tell me where you are.**

Five minutes later, nothing, so I texted her again.

Me: **I'll tell you in person.**

Parker: **Isn't this, like, extortion or something?**

Me: **Or something. Where are you?**

Parker: **Library.**

I sighed and climbed back out of the truck. Once I got to the library, I texted again to ask where she was - the library was huge and I didn't feel like exploring every room to find her (although I probably would have.) She answered with "**McGregor Room**," so I headed to the second floor.

The McGregor room was arguably the best spot in the library. I didn't spend a lot of time in the building, but the dimly-lit space filled with antique-looking bookshelves and big leather armchairs was a cool place to just hang out and work. I saw her sitting back in the corner - chair pulled up to the window, just staring through the glass. She had that lost look in her eyes again and I hated it. I wanted her to smile. I wanted her life to be happy and easy, but I was starting to really get the impression that that wasn't the case.

"Hey," I said quietly when I reached her chair. She didn't answer, and I understood why when I noticed the white cords attached to the iPod in her hand. I gently reached out to pull one of the earbuds from her ear, and she jumped five inches in the air as she twisted back to finally see my face.

"Holy crap, you scared me," she whispered, placing her hand on her heart. "Don't be all quiet like that next time."

"I could have walked up screaming and you wouldn't have heard," I told her, gesturing to the earbuds, which were still emitting muted - but audible - noise. "Geez, you're gonna blow out your eardrums."

"I am not," she huffed as she turned off the music and wound the cord around the small device. I stared at her hands as they moved - transfixed by her long, graceful fingers and beautiful, soft-looking skin. I finally broke out of the trance when she tossed the iPod into the bag at her feet. I looked back up to her face in time to see her eyes dart back to the window. She let out a deep breath as she stood. "I should probably do something instead of just sitting here like a loser."

"Wanna go get some coffee?"

She gave me a long look before nodding. "Sure. I've already missed the first twenty minutes of Stat. Why not?"

We walked out of the library and headed towards the closest coffee place. When we got inside, I asked her what she wanted (a small hot chocolate, I swear to God.) I walked up to the counter, and ordered while she found us a table. With my coffee and her child's beverage in hand, I went back to her and sat down.

"So, what's up with the hot chocolate?" I asked as I slid it across the table. She furrowed her eyebrows.

"What do you mean?"

"I mean, I don't think I've met anyone over the age of ten who drinks hot chocolate. Do you like coffee?"

"I don't hate it, but I'm not really a fan. Besides, caffeine makes me bounce off the walls."

I laughed at that. "But a cup of liquid sugar keeps you nice and mellow?"

She allowed herself to smile. It was weak, but it was a smile. I watched until she looked away, and then I stared down at the table for a minute before I broke the silence.

"So…" I began. "Want to tell me why when I got to the library you were staring out the window like you thought the world was beautiful and you wished you could be a part of it?"

Her eyes widened in what appeared to be confusion and shock. Then she slid both her gaze and her hands to the coffee sleeve and started picking at the cardboard.

"Is that even a thing? Because, I don't know how you could even 'see' something like that. You say it as if it's… a *thing*. Like, someone, somewhere, has felt that exact way and now it's just… a thing."

"Okay, let's get a couple things straight. First, you have no idea what I see when I look at you. I see you, Parker. Not the person you want me to see, not the person you show to the outside world. I. See. You." Her eyes darted from her cup to me and back again as she pulled her bottom lip between her teeth. I knew she was uncomfortable, but she needed to hear this. "I see your anger, your guilt, your strength, your beauty, and I see the shields you keep throwing up to keep me out. But I gotta tell you, it's not going to work.

"Secondly, I know what I'm talking about. I felt that exact way for over a year. I know you don't really know me yet, but I promise… you can trust me. Friends tell each other things. Please, just tell me what's going on."

Her indecision was obvious. She couldn't decide if it was worth it. If it was worth giving up a piece of herself. And I realized when I saw her sigh that she was even more stubborn than I had thought.

"It's really... nothing. Just fighting with my mom - stupid stuff like that. I just didn't think I could handle being in class."

She was still lying. Or, at least withholding part of the truth. But, I figured I'd give her that for now.

"Do you get along with your mom?" I asked.

"That's complicated."

"I'm pretty sure that all parent-child relationships are complicated in some way."

She glared at me for an instant before dropping her eyes to the table again. "I know, it's just..." She paused to take a sip from her cup, and I couldn't help but watch her long, delicate throat work as she drank. God, the sight was absolutely intoxicating, and I fell into a stupor that I had to fight to shake off when she resumed her thought. "We fight. A lot. Always have. She's just, my mom's something else..."

"I can understand that," I told her, leaning back in my chair. "Me and my dad are like that. We're way too much alike, and we both have a pretty nasty temper. It's not that we don't love each other, because we do. We just..." I paused. "See, complicated?" I told her with a shrug and a short laugh. "We mostly deal with it for my mom's sake, but it boils over occasionally."

I kind of hoped that she would be inspired by my candor to tell me her life story, but no luck.

"So, what about your dad?" I asked.

"He left two days after I turned five," she said, matter-of-factly.

"Damn, that sucks. Do you ever see him?"

"Nope. I haven't seen or heard from him since. I barely remember him." She took another sip.

Fuck. Doesn't get along with her mom and no dad. That's shitty.

"Do you have any brothers or sisters?" I continued my game of twenty questions.

"No."

I nodded, sagely. "'Only Child Syndrome.' I see it all over you."

Her eyes cut up to me, "I don't have-" she snapped before she saw the grin spread across my face. That earned me another small smile.

"Ha ha," she deadpanned. "How about you, any siblings at home that you tortured growing up? It seems like you've had lots of practice."

"I do. A little sister. And you are absolutely right, I tortured her so bad she had to move to Massachusetts to get away from it." She gave me a quizzical look.

"School," I explained. "She's a freshman at some swanky music school in Boston. She sings and plays piano."

"That's awesome." Another smile.

"You have no idea. She's amazing. She's been through…" I paused, trying to find the best way to say this, and then I totally copped-out. "Well, some serious shit, but she worked her ass off and now she's making all of her dreams come true." Her small smile grew wider as I spoke. I let the silence linger for a moment before I asked, "So, what are your dreams, Parker?"

She tensed at the change of subject. "Survive this year. Once I do that, finish school. And then I have no idea."

"What's your major?"

"Psych, but I'm not sure what I want to do with it. What about you?"

"Bio."

"You're a Biology major?"

I nodded. "Why do you seem to find that hard to believe?"

"I just…" she blushed and swallowed. "I don't know." Her smile became apologetic. "What are you planning on doing after school?"

"I'm pre-med, actually. Hoping to get into the med program here, but I'm not totally sure about all that yet."

"Why not?"

I paused. "Just a lot of things to consider…"

She nodded like she could relate to that, and then let it go. I changed the subject again and described the paper for Monday and then we talked about our classes for a few more minutes.

"I should probably go," she said suddenly, standing up from the table. "It'd be a good idea to make it to at least one of my classes today."

I nodded, and stood as well. "Probably." I followed her out the door where she turned around to face me.

"Thanks for the hot chocolate," she said, lifting her cup in my direction as we stood by the door.

I wanted to keep her here, I wanted to talk some more and really start to get to know her, but I knew I needed to let her go to class.

"Anytime," I responded with a smile. "And you're going to text me about Stat, right?"

"Sir, yes sir," she answered. "I'll see you later, Ash."

"See ya, Just Parker."

I watched her walk away, and it was as if I could feel the cold start to sink back into my body. Being around her made me feel something I hadn't felt in a long time. And now that she had started filling in the blanks about her life, all I wanted to do was learn more.

I decided that I'd give her until Monday. I'd let her have the weekend, and then I was going to start making her mine.

Chapter Eleven

Parker

I MADE IT TO CLASS early, which was a relief. The hour flew by as my professor talked and talked, but I didn't hear a word he said. I was thinking about Ash.

I was a little shocked when he showed up at the library. I figured he'd lose interest when I wasn't in class, if he hadn't already when I blew off his text. I really never expected him to force me into giving up my location so he could make sure I was okay. Add in him buying me a hot chocolate and just sitting and talking to me like he had absolutely nothing better to be doing and it was officially one of the strangest experiences of my life.

Still, it had felt good. Too good. I didn't want to get used to Ash being sweet and caring, or else I wouldn't be able to keep myself away from him. That - well, I couldn't even think about that.

After class let out, I headed straight home. Mom was watching a movie on the couch with Diane. When I walked in, both sets of eyes came right to me. Mom's attention just shifted back to the TV, but Diane smiled.

"Hey there, sweetheart. How's your day been so far?"

I smiled, just a little bit. "Fine, thanks. How's everything here?" I looked towards Mom in time to see her let out a huff of air as she rolled her eyes to the ceiling.

"Everything's fine, Eileen. I'm still alive, right? Or were you hoping that I died while you were gone? Is that why you're never here anymore? Are you hoping you'll leave and come back to find me rotting on the floor?"

I flinched. It felt like she had punched me right in the stomach. Diane was shocked. She looked at my mom out of the corner of her eye. Mom had never done this in front of Diane, or anyone really. Katherine Rose Parker always made sure to put the best foot forward when she had an audience. It wouldn't do for people to know what things were like when no one else was around. Ladies didn't act like that in public.

"Diane, thanks. I have some homework," I said, ignoring Mom's comment completely, and starting back towards the hall. I could feel the tears gathering behind my eyes, and I didn't want to be standing here when they started to fall. "I'll see you next week, alright?"

She nodded as I turned and trudged straight to my room. Shutting the door, I leaned my head against the wood and focused on the air rushing in and out of my mouth. I heard Mom and Diane exchange a few muffled words before the quiet thumps of the front door opening and closing. I'd managed to breathe away the impending tears, so I pushed myself off the door and walked to my desk. I set the alarm on my phone for five, so I'd have time to make dinner and then I laid on the bed and tried to sleep.

It took a while. First, all I could hear was my mom's voice. *Is that why you're never here anymore? Hoping you'll leave and come back to find me rotting on the floor?* Over and over again it repeated. Once I had pushed that from my mind, the emptiness was filled with memories of my morning with Ash. It was an even worse form of torture. *I see you, Parker. Your anger, your guilt, your strength, your beauty…*

I wasn't sure, but I thought he might have been telling the truth, which absolutely terrified me. I'd worked all my life to keep people out, to avoid letting anyone see the real me. The only person I'd ever let in was Jessie.

I'd met Jessie in first grade. It was lunchtime and I had been sitting by myself, like I did every day. I'd just started eating my sandwich when a tiny redhead with a smattering of freckles across her nose dropped into the seat next to me. Without saying a word, she reached out and grabbed my container of pudding. She grabbed the lid and started to pull it off, and then I was unfrozen. I shouted "Hey!" and flung out my hand to smack the cup away. As I did, somehow pudding flew into the air, completely covering both me and the attempted pudding thief to my right. We both stared at each other for a minute. A giant glob of chocolate, sugary goodness dripped from her ear and her shoulder.

It broke the spell. We both erupted in giggles, practically falling off our seats. That was that. We had been best friends ever since.

Or at least until she moved away five months ago to live with her dad and go to school in New York City.

We still talked a lot, but it was different not having her around. Since my mom got sick, we'd been talking even less. It wasn't that I was trying to avoid her, I just didn't want her to worry about me - which I knew she would. Jessie was like a momma bear when it came to protecting me. I had never actually told her how bad things were with my mom - still, I knew she had her suspicions. She'd never brought them up, thankfully. She knew that was what I wanted.

I thought about calling her, but decided against it. In order to tell her what was going on, I'd have to tell her my mom was sick. I know I probably seem like the world's worst best friend for keeping so many secrets, but Jess left just before Mom got diagnosed. I knew that if I had told her she would have seen it as an act of God and come back, and I didn't want that. I knew how much she wanted to go to New York and, even if it left me lonelier than I had been before, I wasn't going to be the reason she didn't get to live her dream.

So I just I covered my head with a pillow and practiced my deep breathing until I finally fell asleep.

My phone started blaring Blink-182 two hours after I finally passed out. I sat up and rubbed my eyes blearily before shutting off the music. After rolling out of bed, I headed to the kitchen. I could see that the living room was empty, which I figured meant that Mom was lying down in bed. I started pulling objects out of the cabinets to make pasta bake for dinner. I didn't have the energy for anything more complicated than that. Even after taking my nap, I still felt mentally exhausted. I moved around the kitchen in a fog, almost blindly getting dinner ready and into the oven.

Once that was done, I set two places at the table and then prepared Mom's dinnertime meds. I lined them up at her spot, and fortified myself with a deep breath before heading back to get her up.

Thankfully, when I knocked and cracked the door to her room, she was sitting up, eyes trained on the TV against the wall.

"Hey, dinner will be ready in about five minutes," I said from the doorway. She nodded without looking away from the show and I shut the door and walked back out.

Five minutes later, she walked out of her room and sat at the table just as I was setting the dish on the hotplate. I used a spoon to fill her plate before doing the same to mine while she swallowed the collection of pills. We ate in silence. Except for the scratching of our forks against the plates, there was no noise but the constant, slow drip of the crappy kitchen sink. I was used to this. It wasn't unusual for us to go days without speaking, and truthfully, I really preferred the quiet.

After we finished, she disappeared to her room. I cleaned up and put away the leftovers before settling down on the couch. Grabbing the remote, I flipped through channels until I finally decided on a documentary about whales. When that was over I watched the next program (about sharks) and the next (about penguins) before I finally unstuck myself from the couch to head to the kitchen.

I got Mom's bedtime meds ready and walked back to her room with a glass of water. I watched her swallow everything down and, once I checked her temperature, I headed back to my room to go to bed.

It was only 9:30, which was pretty early for me, but I still laid down and tried to fall asleep. However, I was finally feeling the energy from my nap and I was restless just lying in bed. I tried listening to music, reading, and studying, but I wasn't able to keep myself focused. I couldn't help but wonder what Ash was doing. It was the first weekend of the school year, so I figured he'd probably be out, at a bar or maybe a party. Drinking, smiling, maybe dancing with a girl…

I slid out of bed and paced the floor. Why did I care that he might be out putting the moves on some strange girl? I decided that it was best to ignore that and I focused on all the ways she was probably prettier than me and more fun to be around.

I hated her.

And then, I realized that I was hating a completely imaginary person because of a guy who I had absolutely no claim to whatsoever.

I seriously needed professional help.

Before I could even think about the repercussions of my actions, I had my phone in hand.

I typed out a message and stared at it for ten minutes before finally hitting send.

Me: **Hey**

God, I am such *a loser.*

I wanted to throw my phone at the wall, hopefully breaking it into tiny pieces so I'd never have to look at it again. I was still trying to decide if this was a good idea when it chirped in my hand.

Ash: **Well, hey there, Just Parker**

I stared at the message, reading his nickname for me over and over, and feeling strangely warm inside. *How's that for scary?*

I was still staring at the message when my phone beeped again.

Ash: **You there?**

I quickly typed back.

Me: **Yeah. Sorry, I hope I'm not interrupting your night...**

The response was almost instant.

Ash: **Not at all. I always have time for you. What's up?**

Crap. What *was* up? I couldn't exactly tell him that I'd been thinking about him all day, and that I wasn't really sure why I had texted him in the first place. I thought about asking him when we could get together to study, but I still wasn't sure that that was even a good idea. I mean, obviously he was smart - he *was* pre-med. But it wasn't just that - I could tell when I talked to him that he was intelligent - just in the way he spoke and the things he said.

I just didn't trust myself around him.

You didn't really think about that when you texted him, did you?! my brain shouted at me. I didn't answer, because at that second my phone started ringing in my hand.

"Oh my god," I whispered as his name appeared on the screen. I flipped the phone open and pressed it to my ear with a shaky hand.

"Hel-" my voice broke and I cleared it, "Hello?" *Crap*. I still sounded all breathy and waspish.

"Parker?" I heard him ask. "Are you okay?" He sounded hesitant.

"Yeah," I told him, this time in an extremely high, way-too-perky voice. "Totally. One hundred percent fine."

It was quiet for a few seconds and I heard muted music in the background.

"Are you busy? I'm sorry, I'll let you go..."

"No," he said quickly, "not at all. I'm at my friend's house, he's having some people over, but it's not really my scene... What were you doing when I called?"

I hesitated before speaking. "Nothing really... I couldn't sleep..."

"Ah," he told me, and I could clearly hear the smile in his voice. "So, you were lying in bed and thinking about me... Go on."

I smiled. "In your dreams. I, uh, honestly, I don't even know why I texted you. I just... you're really the only friend I have." My voice was quiet, and I think I was half hoping that he wouldn't hear the confession.

"Do you want to study?"

"What?" The sudden change of pace confused me.

"Do you want to study? I can come over, I'll bring my Stat book and we can start working on it."

He wanted to come over? *Now*?

"But, it's Friday... You're at a party and..."

"Seriously, Parker. Not my thing. And even if it was, I'd much rather be helping you with Stat than doing anything else right now."

I couldn't breathe. The sincerity in his words was overwhelming and suddenly I wanted nothing more than to see him. To look into his hazel eyes and feel just a little bit less alone.

"Hold on a sec," I said. I placed my phone on the bed and quietly walked out of my room. I moved lightly over the floor to my mom's room where I knocked softly on the door once. When I didn't get an answer I pushed the door open an inch and peeked inside. The TV was off and Mom was sleeping in bed. I listened to the rhythmic, raspy breathing for a moment before shutting the door and running back to my room. I grabbed the phone, smiling like an idiot.

"Hey, you there?"

"Yeah," he said in his deep baritone. "You okay?"

"Yeah. Great. If you still want to, I'd really appreciate you coming over. I could definitely use the help."

"Say no more. I'm on my way. Where do you live?"

I rattled off my address and told him to text when he got close. He said he was about ten minutes away. I heard his "I'll see you soon," and then the line went dead.

Okay, so apparently Ash is on his way. Here. To see me, or study me - I mean help me study, Or whatever.

Oh my God.

Ash was on his way here.

I glanced down at my clothes (an old t-shirt and a pair of ratty shorts, I wasn't really into the whole cute pj's thing) and then raced to my dresser. I changed into a pair of cutoffs and a cute t-shirt. Then I realized that I had told him that I was trying to sleep, and no one sleeps in cutoffs. I whipped them off and threw on a comfy pair of yoga pants. They made my butt look great and it wouldn't look like I was trying too hard. I exchanged the t-shirt for a tank-top and then tossed a cute, lightweight hoodie over top, zipping it halfway. Once I was dressed, I threw my hair into a ponytail, quickly straightened up my room, and then sat on my bed, trying not to panic.

It didn't work. I *definitely* panicked.

Chapter Twelve

Ash

I WAS ON MY WAY to Parker's house and completely failing at controlling the giant grin that was breaking my face in half. To think that this night had started off as a train wreck...

When Marco had said to come over, I told him I didn't want to. He promised me that it wasn't going to be anything crazy. He said that he had just invited a few of the guys. A chill night.

I shouldn't have even walked in the door. As soon as I got into the staircase I knew he had lied. I could hear the music from three floors down. But I forced myself to go up and at least tell Marco to fuck himself face to face. As soon as I got inside, I was ready to leave. The apartment (which was by no means small) was absolutely filled with people. I could smell weed and beer, and within five minutes I saw two people leave the bathroom wiping powder off their noses. But Marco and Jimmy cornered me and told me that I needed to live a little. They wouldn't give up, so I finally caved.

But as soon as Parker texted me, I knew exactly where I wanted to be.

I hadn't really expected her to invite me over. More so, I hadn't expected to *ask* her to invite me over. She had just sounded so strange on the phone that I started to worry. When she said that I was her only friend, the loneliness in her voice told me that was probably true. I needed to make it go away. I figured I'd distract her from whatever was bothering her with Statistics and that Ashton Carter Killer Smile.

I texted her when I got close, as she had asked me to. I pulled up a minute later and found a place to park outside the apartment building. There were no lights outside the door, and the whole place looked tired - almost like it could fall over any minute. I didn't know what Parker's situation was like, but I knew it must have been worse than I'd imagined if she was living in a place like this.

As I climbed from the truck, Stat book in hand (I had kept it with me for when I saw her again) and headed up to the front door, I noticed a shadow topped by a head of honey-blond hair. I smiled as she pushed the door open and let me inside.

"Hey," I told her, with a grin too strong to suppress. I begged myself to act cool, but I was completely out of control right now. If Parker told me to jump, I'd ask how high - and do it with this stupid smile on my face.

She looked up at me and stared at my mouth for a minute before smiling herself. "Hey…"

She waved for me to follow her, and we began up the stairs, passing by an elevator with an out of order sign across its doors.

"What floor are you?" I asked as we started to climb.

"Fourth," she told me with a small, sideways glance. She led the way, and I'm only a little bit ashamed to admit that, as we climbed all four flights of stairs, I let myself fall behind and stared at her ass – which was in the sexiest pair of pants I had ever seen. I mean, come on. I'm a man, and she's, well, she's Parker.

We arrived at the right floor and she led me down a hall to what I assumed was her front door before we stopped.

"Listen, I uh… We have to be quiet." She seemed uncomfortable, but I wasn't sure why. Then again, it could have just been that she was bringing a relative stranger into her home.

"You have a roommate?" I asked, assuming that's why we were being quiet.

"Uh, yeah, and she's asleep. And a total bitch, so, we just need to make sure she stays asleep."

"No problem." I saw the tension drain from her shoulders, and I couldn't help but think that her roommate must be a pretty huge bitch for her to be that worried about waking her up. And then I wondered why Parker chose to live with someone she didn't like. I mean, it wasn't a dorm. She didn't have to stay, and if it was her place, she could kick the girl out.

Parker unlocked and opened the door, leading me through and locking it behind us. She grabbed my hand and pulled me across the room. I ignored the electricity shooting into my body from where her skin touched mine, and I looked around quickly, trying to take the space in. We had entered into the living room. There was a comfy-looking but visibly worn couch facing a TV placed along the wall next to the door. Behind the couch was a dining room table, and then eventually a counter that separated the kitchen from the rest of the space. I saw a hallway leading off each side of the kitchen but Parker led me towards the single door down the hallway to the right. She opened the door and led me through.

I sucked in a breath as I stepped inside her bedroom - it was nothing like I'd expected. I'm not saying that I'd given much thought to what the inside of Parker's bedroom would look like, but if I'd had to guess, I would have been dead wrong.

The walls, at least what I could see, were green - a bright, almost grassy green. The bedspread was orange, there was a big purple bean bag chair in the corner, and the lamp on the desk had a bright pink lampshade. She had color everywhere. Bright, bold color. The walls were mostly covered in posters for a bunch of different bands, some I recognized, some I didn't. The space that wasn't covered in posters was taken up by a collection of artwork, some charcoal pieces, a few watercolors, but mostly pen and ink designs. I immediately thought of her doodles.

But she said she wasn't an artist...

I walked closer to take a better look at one particularly beautiful drawing. It was a multitude of circles, large and small, separate and intersecting. The way they grew and shrank gave the picture life, but what made it truly beautiful were the vivid blue accents she'd added. They popped up in the places where the black ink was thickest, providing just a flash of color in the darkness.

"Did you do this?" I asked, not able to tear my eyes from the drawing. She was silent, so finally I glanced at her. I met her eyes and she nodded slowly. "Parker, this is great. Really great. Did you do all of these?" I asked, gesturing at the rest of the drawings hanging on the walls. Another hesitant nod. "So, why'd you tell me you weren't an artist?"

"I'm not." I gave her a look, which she answered with a roll of her eyes. "Anymore, at least. I just don't really have the time. I was into it in high school, and last year a bit, but..." She trailed off.

"What happened to change that?" I asked quietly.

She looked to the drawing that had captured my attention and stared at it for a moment, lost in thought. "I just... It took too much energy. I guess life happened, and I had more important things to focus on."

I nodded at her slowly, trying to make sense of that somewhat odd answer, and finished my perusal of her room. The desk was cluttered with papers, books, and schoolwork. There was a laptop, closed and sitting on the foot of the bed. A dresser in the corner covered in a bunch of girl crap and a door that I assumed led to a closet. Besides that, there was just us.

"So..." she started.

"So..." I repeated with a smile, which got a smile out of her. "Why do you seem so terrified of me right now?" She was across the room, arms crossed over her chest, staring at me like I was going to eat her.

She snorted and her shoulders relaxed a little bit more. "I'm not terrified. Sorry, this is just, weirder than I thought it'd be."

I stiffened at that, but decided to play it off as a joke. "Are you saying that hanging out with me is weird, or are you saying that I'm weird?"

"Neither, I swear. I just mean, it's kind of... Surreal." She smiled at me and I swear, I stopped breathing. "In a good way," she added before moving to sit on the bed. "So, Statistics?"

I watched her get settled and I swallowed before I moved to sit next to her, book in hand. "Statistics," I replied with grin.

An hour later, I was convinced she had to be fucking with me. It was like we were speaking two different languages. She really had no idea what I was talking about.

"So you're saying that the correlation coefficient is the measure of variation for a set of data, right?"

I let out a quiet sigh. "No. That's the standard deviation. The correlation coefficient is kind of like, how much a line matches the data. You need to use this equation," I told her pointing to the book on her lap.

She growled (I fucking loved that growl) and then flopped herself backwards, her head landing on her pillow. We were sitting side by side - she was facing the foot of the bed, I was facing the headboard. From where I was, the view with her lying down wasn't too far from what I would have gotten if I was between her legs, and I felt myself start to get hard. *Fuck.*

"This is stupid," she told me. "I mean, I am never going to use this. I just want to drop the class. There is no way I'm going to pass."

I swung around so I was facing the same direction as Parker and I leaned back onto an elbow, resting on my side next to her. Her eyes were closed, and there was one lock of hair that had fallen onto her forehead. I wanted to push it back and then wind my fingers into her hair. I resisted… but barely.

"Hey," I said softly, leaning down to look at her. "You are not going to fail. I promise, I won't let that happen. I don't care if I have to work with you every day, I'm not going to let you fail."

She opened her eyes to take me in. She looked wary, as if she couldn't figure out what to expect from me. "Why are you doing this?" she asked quietly. "Not... not just the tutoring thing, but all of it. Why are you being so nice to me?"

She sounded completely broken, and it scored my insides. I wanted to pull her into my arms, I wanted to press my lips to hers. I wanted to fix her.

"I told you, I see you, Parker. I see all of you. And I may not understand everything that I see, but I know that I want to. I know that I want *you*."

Her eyes widened as I spoke, and then she shuddered with emotion. "You don't."

"I do."

"Okay, well, then, you won't. I know what I am. You don't, so trust me on this one, Ash." Her eyes burned as she looked at me and her voice was laced with anger. I knew that she believed every word she had said. She thought she was tainted, or unlovable. And she was so wrong. I didn't know what she'd been through, but I knew that whatever it was, it wouldn't change the way I felt. I couldn't even begin to explain it, but she was starting to feel... essential.

"Park, I know that you think that shit you just gave me is true, but I swear, I'm gonna prove you wrong." Her gorgeous green eyes just stared into mine, lost and confused, and I couldn't resist any longer. I moved slowly, broadcasting my intentions so she knew exactly what I was doing. I expected her hands to press into my chest, for her to push me away or tell me no, but she stayed silent and still. I leaned down until I could feel her breath against my lips. It was quick and choppy, her chest falling and rising way too fast.

"Just breathe, gorgeous," I whispered, letting my lips brush against hers as I spoke. Then, I closed the distance. I didn't move at first, just kept a light pressure, before slowly stroking her mouth with mine in a light caress. She didn't move at all. I moved my mouth to the corner of hers and pressed a soft kiss there. Then, I did the same on the other side of her lips. Moving back to the center of her mouth, I kissed her again. This time though, I didn't pull back. I added just a bit more pressure, and slowly slid my tongue out to lightly taste the seam of her closed mouth. I heard the groan burst from my throat and finally moved to pull back. She tasted way too fucking good, and I needed to stop now if she wasn't ready.

My lips were an inch from hers when I heard a soft growl and her fingers slid up my neck and into my hair. Then, with a sharp tug, she pulled me back down and pressed her mouth to mine.

There was nothing soft about this kiss. I pushed my body closer to hers and placed my free hand on her jaw, angling her face towards mine as I kissed her deeper. She let a soft moan escape into my mouth and my pelvis, which was lined up with her hip, bucked uncontrollably, grinding against her. God, everything about her was incredible - the way her hands felt as they moved around my back and pulled on my shirt, the way her lips felt as they worked against mine, desperate and searching, the way I felt her shake underneath me as if she was about to burst out of her skin from just the feeling of my mouth against hers. And I knew just what she was feeling, because I felt it too.

It was as if someone had plugged us in - electricity was coursing through our bodies and sparks flew everywhere our skin touched. It was unlike anything I'd ever felt in my life, and it branded me, deep in my soul.

I knew that Parker was smart, and beautiful, and funny, and sexy. I knew she was hurting, and I knew I wanted to help her heal the wounds that scarred her heart. I also knew that she could be the person to help soothe the aches in mine. But, if I'd had any doubts before about how much I wanted - no - how much I needed Parker, our kiss would have demolished them all.

She was mine.

Chapter Thirteen

Parker

MY BRAIN HAD COMPLETELY LEFT the building. We're talking full and total desertion.

That motherfucker was A.W.O.L.

It had begun its escape when Ash went on about how he wasn't going to let me fail Stat. It started full out running from the room when he told me in that soft but impassioned voice that I was wrong when I said he eventually wouldn't want me.

By the time he pressed his lips to mine, my brain had hit the state line. I had been completely unable to move - too wrapped up in feeling his mouth against mine. But when I heard his groan (a.k.a. the sexiest sound in the entire freaking world) I kind of lost it. I grabbed his hair and pushed myself into him. If I'd had any sense left, I probably would have been mortified at the way that I threw myself at him. It was as if I wanted to climb inside his body and live there forever.

I'd let my hands travel over him, feeling the tight muscles moving in his back as he leaned over me. I pulled on his white t-shirt, and then pushed my fingers under the soft fabric. My hands worked up to his stomach where I felt the definition of his - 2, 4, 6, 8 pack? *Dear God, this boy is way too sexy for his own good.* After feeling each bump and valley, I moved my hands up to his chest. The entire time, his mouth continued to work at mine, tasting and teasing. It seemed like he was trying to memorize the way I felt, and the way he kissed me was almost reverent. I say almost because I could tell it was taking everything in his power to keep control and not let things go too far. I felt the tension in his body, tension I knew was running through me too. It was like we were being pulled together by an invisible force and it wouldn't be satisfied until we were as close as we could possibly be.

All of the sensations and emotions rampaging through my body should have absolutely terrified me, but, by this point, my brain was overseas.

My hands left his chest and moved around to his back again, this time traveling down until I could feel the waistband of his jeans. I played with the edge of the fabric before pushing one finger below the denim.

Suddenly, Ash's face pulled away from mine and his hand moved to grab my fingers from behind his back. He pulled my hand to his mouth and pressed a gentle kiss to my palm before twining his fingers with mine and laying our hands on my chest. His eyes stared into mine and they were positively glowing as he fought to catch his breath from our kiss. I was having trouble breathing at all in the face of the look of pure desire he was giving me.

"Parker, I want this more than you could possibly know, but not like this."

I felt my face fall. "Why not?"

He smiled and it took some of the sting away from the rejection. "Because, baby, when this happens for the first time, it's going to be special. And I'm fine with waiting for special."

I was having a hard time keeping up. "What do you mean, *special*?"

He chuckled quietly. "I know this is probably going way too fast for you to follow, but focus for a second, yeah? This," he pointed to both him and I, "is going to happen. You might not realize it yet, but you've been mine from the minute you slammed yourself into the door in Philosophy 101. So, when we finally have sex, it's going to be like nothing you've ever experienced. I promise you that."

My mouth dropped open. And, because my brain had taken my filter with it, I actually said what I said next.

"But I've never experienced anything."

Ash stared at me for a minute before narrowing his eyes. He spoke slowly when he finally said, "Are you saying that you're a virgin?"

A slight flush rose up my cheeks and I looked away before I nodded.

I felt his hand under my jaw and I let him pull my eyes back to his. When I looked at him, he was smiling warmly and his eyes, impossibly, were even brighter.

"Don't be embarrassed. Not with me. Do you have any idea how happy you just made me?"

Now, I was really freaking confused. My expression must have shown it because he let out a soft chuckle.

"Never mind. If you don't know, I'm not telling." He pressed a light kiss to my temple as he finished speaking and I felt it throb through my entire body. He sighed against my skin before pulling away. "I guess I should probably get going, huh? I'm actually a little surprised you didn't kick me out earlier." I could tell by his voice he didn't want to leave, and since I still didn't have a brain, I came up with, quite possibly, the worst idea ever.

"Do you think you could stay a little longer? I just... It feels good here, with you next to me. I just want to lay like this for a little while... Would that be okay?"

He gazed at me with an unreadable expression before pressing a kiss to my forehead as he sucked in a breath through his nose. "Absolutely, baby. I'd love that." As I felt his lips press against my skin, my whole body shivered.

We both lay back down and got comfortable. Ash wrapped both of his arms around me, turned to face where I lay on my back. My cheek rested on his arm and I kept my eyes locked onto his as we laid in my bed. We didn't talk much, and what we said didn't mean anything, but it was still one of the most profound experiences of my life. I felt peaceful. It was as if Ash had wiped away all of my worry and I could just relax and be.

Before I knew it, I was asleep in his arms.

I knew the moment I woke up that I was alone. And that, apparently, my brain had decided to return sometime during the night. The room was dark and quiet, and I laid in bed as my mind replayed the night before.

So, yeah. I totally let him kiss me, and then I completely kissed him back like a sex addict who hadn't touched a man in years. I then basically tried to offer him my virginity, (*do you see now, Brain, why I'd really rather you stick around?*) and I topped it all off by asking him to cuddle with me.

And that's just the shit that *I* did.

I wasn't even prepared to freak about everything that Ash had done - like kissing me, telling me that I was apparently his (whatever the frig *that* meant), and saying something about "this" happening. I wasn't really sure what "this" was, but I was starting to form a general idea, and I really didn't like the conclusions that I was drawing.

I decided denial was my best option. I took a shower, then hung out in my room listening to music and reading, trying to overwhelm my brain so it had no option but to participate in the denial plan. Once it was late enough, I got Mom up and medicated, and fed us both. After that, I left her to hang out in the living room while I sat at the kitchen counter and worked on my Stat homework. That, unfortunately reminded me of Ash, so in less than a half an hour I threw the book aside and turned to my computer. I checked Facebook (which was about a once a month activity for me, I hated Facebook but was never able to give it up entirely.) That led to stalking Ash, so I quickly switched to reddit. I was clicking through the front page when I realized that every single post I saw somehow reminded me of Ash. *Oh, look at that adorable bunny wearing a suit - I wonder what Ash looks like wearing a suit... Oh, drama in the Middle East - I wonder what Ash would have to say about that. Oh, Florida Man drove a tractor into a convenience store - I wonder what it'd be like to visit Florida with Ash, maybe years from now, when we take our kids to Disney World for the first time...*

And that was the point where I slammed the computer shut with an annoyed growl. Luckily, five minutes later, Charles walked in the door. Charles was from the same company that sent Diane, and he came on the weekends when I had to work.

I worked Saturdays and Sundays at a crappy diner near school. I liked the owners, and they understood when I told them I needed to switch from working five days a week to only working weekends. They were good people.

Charles was a forty-something, attractive, gay man. I knew he used to be a nurse, but had quit to get out of hospitals. He was super sweet, but didn't take any shit. I loved him - just not quite as much as Diane.

I ran to my room and got ready for work and then said goodbye to Mom and Charles before running out the door. I was ready to mindlessly serve customers for a few hours. Anything to get my mind off of a beautiful boy who kissed me senseless and held me until I fell asleep.

God, I was *so* screwed.

Chapter Fourteen

Ash

WHEN MY PHONE RANG SUNDAY afternoon, I didn't want to answer. But I'd been avoiding my dad for a week, and I knew I couldn't do it any longer.

"Hey, Dad," I said as I picked up.

"Hey, Ash. What are you up to?"

"Not much. Just hanging out at home…" I fell quiet and waited for him to tell me why he called. I didn't have to wait for long.

"I want you to come to dinner tonight."

I let out a tired sigh. "Dad…"

"No, Ash. You're never here anymore. Your mom misses you. But this wasn't even our idea. Grandma is coming too, and she wants us all together."

I rubbed a hand over my face as I considered how much shit I'd catch if I told him I couldn't make it. The answer was way more than I was willing to accept.

"Fine. What time?"

"Come over whenever. We're just hanging at home."

Fuck that. I was going to show up when dinner was being placed on the table and leave when it was done.

"Dad, what time?"

I heard his sigh. "Be here at six."

"See you then." I didn't wait for the response before I hung up the phone.

At 6:15 I was walking up the sidewalk to my parent's front door, and completely dreading having to walk inside.

I hadn't always hated this house. Still, after fifteen months inside these walls, a large part of me wanted to refuse to spend another second in there. But this was the house where Rory and I grew up, and, knowing that my parents will live here for the rest of their lives, I had resigned myself to trying to get used to the drowning sensation I experienced every time I walked through the door.

I pushed through the unlocked door and headed into the house, taking a large breath as I moved. Walking through the foyer, I made it to the huge, modern kitchen but still didn't see anyone. I could smell food cooking though, and it smelled amazing.

"Hello?" I shouted to the quiet house.

"In the den," I heard Dad call. I made my way towards the sunken family room that my parents liked to refer to as a den. Once I got to the steps that lead down into the room, I finally saw Mom, Dad, and Grandma all sitting around the heavy wooden coffee table.

I walked up to Mom first. Leaning down, I gave her a kiss on the cheek and a small smile. I looked a lot like my mom, especially when I smiled.

"Hey, Ma."

She shot me a huge grin as she blinked up at me. "Hi, Ashton. I've missed you."

That clenched my gut. She missed me because she was used to living with me. I was locked inside this house for over a year. I forced my smile to widen as I said, "Me too."

"Alright, alright, want to say hello to anyone else?" I heard Grandma's voice and my forced smile became a little more natural. I gave her a kiss and nodded to my dad before settling into the one available armchair. It was wide backed and leather, but wicked comfortable.

"Really? Photo albums?" I asked the group at large, gesturing to the pile of books spread across the table in front of them. I tried to mask the bitterness in my voice, but I didn't really succeed. Mom smiled, Dad stared and Grandma let out a small laugh.

"Do you hate the memories that much?" Grandma asked in a playful voice. I swallowed uncomfortably because I didn't want to tell her the truth. I didn't want to break her heart and say yes. Instead, I rolled my eyes and sat back in my chair.

Mom could tell I was uncomfortable; I felt her eyes keep coming to me, and I wanted to leave. I couldn't handle just sitting still. I felt trapped again. When the tension started visibly pouring out of my body, she hopped up and headed to the kitchen. Five minutes later, she called out that dinner was ready.

I practically raced to the table, ready to eat so I could get out. I felt like I couldn't breathe, like the walls were closing in around me and the air was growing thin.

Dinner was quiet and a bit awkward, but there were no major disasters. Dad asked about the volunteer work, and I told him that I had set up a meeting with someone at the UVA hospital for later that week. I was pretty sure they would take me on. Grandma brought up the girl that she had mentioned Wednesday again. Apparently, her name was Eileen and Grandma wanted to adopt her. I thought that was a bit extreme, but Grandma wouldn't explain. She just said that Eileen was fantastic and that she really wanted to arrange a meeting between us. I politely, but forcefully, declined again. I wanted to tell Grandma about Parker, but I didn't want to say anything in front of my parents. I could tell by her expression that Mom was already jumping on board with Grandma's attempts to fix me up with Eileen. I didn't need to tell them I actually had a girlfriend. Well, a kind-of girlfriend. Or... something like that.

By the time we were done eating I had relaxed a bit. I was just about to let them know that I was heading home when I saw Dad turn to face me.

"Ash, I wanted to tell you, I sent a letter to Robert, my friend from college. He's on the admissions board at UVA Med., and I let him know that you were interested. He called me the other day, and we talked for a while but he wants to talk to you. He told me to give you his number."

I was livid, and the guilt I felt over it wasn't enough to stop me from reacting. I knew he was trying to help, but I was pissed at him for doing the one thing that I had explicitly asked him not to do - which was to get involved with my application to Med School. And yet, like always, he just couldn't help but intervene.

"Yeah? Did you tell him about the nice donation that you'll make if they let the reformed criminal into their hallowed halls?" My voice was low and vibrating with anger, but I was hanging onto my control, even if just barely.

"Ash, stop," Dad began in his most patronizing voice. "You know that-"

"Yeah, that has nothing to do with it. Look, I know you don't get it, but it's my future. It's my decision to make, and I don't need your help."

"Yeah, well, that wasn't true when you tried to tell me the same thing a year and a half ago, and it's sure as fuck not true now."

I heard Mom gasp just as Grandma muttered, "Paul..."

I decided to ignore the comment. I wasn't about to do this again. "Mom, Grandma, it's always a pleasure." Then I turned, walked back to the door, and let myself out.

When I climbed into my truck, I had no idea where to go. All I knew was that I didn't want to go home. I sat in the cab trying to figure it out when I realized exactly where I wanted to be. Where I *needed* to be.

I sent the text, waited for the response, and then put the truck in drive.

Chapter Fifteen

Parker

WHEN ASH TEXTED ME TO tell me he was on his way, I thought about arguing. But, for some reason, I had a bad feeling in the pit of my stomach. It felt like something was wrong, so I just said, "Okay." Anyway, Mom was asleep, and if I was going to be honest, I wanted to see him.

My phone rang twenty minutes later. I had already freaked out and changed my clothes twice (ending up in the sweatpants and tank top I had been wearing in the first place) and pulled my hair up three times before pulling the tie back out. When the room filled with the music of Regina Spektor (my ringtone of the week) I jumped off the bed before opening the phone with shaky hands.

"Hey," I told him.

"Hey, I'm here." His voice was quiet, and I knew right away that my gut feeling had been correct. Something was wrong.

"The downstairs door doesn't lock. Do you remember how to get to my door?"

"Yeah. I'll be right there."

I left my room and headed to the door. Two minutes later I heard the knock and I quickly let him in. He walked past me and headed straight for my room. I locked the door and hurried after him, walking in to find him sitting on my bed, staring at a picture across the room. It was a watercolor I'd painted - a picture of cherry trees in bloom. I'd painted it after a high school field trip to Washington D.C. I had thought that those trees were the most beautiful thing on the planet when I saw them. I knew now that that was just because I hadn't met Ash yet. His eyes would beat out the cherry blossoms every single time.

I walked to the bed and sat down next to him, leaving a good foot of space between us. I wasn't sure what was going on and I didn't want to crowd him.

"Are you okay?" I asked quietly. He was still staring at the picture. His hands were curled into fists and as I spoke I saw them tighten for a second before relaxing again.

"No."

I stayed silent for a minute, completely terrified and totally unsure of what to do next. Thankfully, Ash clued me in a bit more.

"Why are you so far away?" His voice was quiet, almost afraid. The sound scared me so much that I moved instantly. I wasn't scared *of* him, I was scared *for* him. He didn't look at me when I plastered myself to his side and dropped my head against his shoulder. I pulled up my feet and set them on the edge of the bed and then let my knees fall to the side until my legs were resting against his thigh. Next, I slid my hand along his arm slowly. I didn't want to go too far and freak him out. Once I got to his fist, I moved my thumb softly along his knuckles twice before his hand relaxed and opened. He slid his hand to the side until my fingers fell into the spaces between his and then he gripped tight, curling them together.

I felt his chest move as he took in a deep breath. Finally he looked away from the picture and pressed his lips softly into the top of my head. Looking up from where our hands were linked together resting on his thigh, I caught him staring at me. I held his eyes and watched as the anger started to fade from his face. Breathing in deeply, I relaxed a bit. I had no clue what had happened, but I wanted to try and make him smile.

"Hey," I whispered, pulling my lips into a small smile.

He stared at me for a few long seconds before his lips tipped up and he whispered, "Hey."

I let my smile fall a bit and then chewed my bottom lip for a second, letting my eyes drop to the slight layer of stubble that decorated his jaw.

"Do you want to talk about it?" I finally asked him, moving my eyes back to his.

His looked away before quickly shaking his head. I nodded when he looked back to me.

"Do you want to work on Stat with me?"

This time his gaze dropped to my mouth before his lips slowly formed a small grin and he gave me a much slower head shake.

Crap. I was out of ideas.

"So, what do you want to do?"

The question hung in the room, and the only sound I heard was Ash's slow, steady breathing. My lungs had stopped working entirely.

His hand came to my mouth where I was biting my lip and he rubbed his thumb under the tender spot, causing my teeth to release it. "Hey, Parker?" he called. His soft voice seriously affected me. It was better than caramel on ice cream. Way better.

"Yeah?" I asked in a breathy squeak. I couldn't get enough air.

Oh my God, I am going to die. I am going to suffocate and die. Cause of death? Hormone-Induced Asphyxiation.

He smiled his lazy smile as his face moved towards mine. He stopped less than an inch away. I felt every smooth breath that flowed from his mouth as his air brushed against my lips. The sensation made my head feel light, and I had to close my eyes. It was too much. The things he made me feel were all too much.

"Breathe."

Then, his lips were on mine. I'm almost ashamed to admit it, but I didn't hesitate at all. The second our lips touched, I attacked him. My hands worked up into his hair and I pushed my chest against his. I tasted him and let my tongue explore his mouth as he did the same. His lips were warm, wet and urgent as they moved against mine and before I could stop it from coming out, I heard a moan escape from my mouth into his.

From there, things went wild. Ash pushed me back to the bed until he was lying on top of me, and one of his hard, warm thighs worked its way between my legs. His arms kept most of his weight off me, but his mouth never left my skin. When he wasn't kissing my lips, his mouth moved along my jaw and neck, planting small, wet kisses that drove me absolutely insane with need for him, especially when he started adding small bites and tiny tongue touches as he lightly tasted my skin. I pushed my hips up into his, searching for pressure. I felt an ache building, low in my belly. It grew and moved until the area between my legs was throbbing. When I felt his hand land at my hip, it sent a bolt of heat through my body and I couldn't take it anymore.

"Ash," I heard myself growl, almost incoherently. "I need... more."

That quick, he was gone. I blinked as a wave of cold air washed over me and I opened my eyes to see nothing but the ceiling above. I took a second to collect myself before pushing up onto my elbows. By the time I looked up he was sitting on the edge of the bed, elbows against his knees and head hung low.

"I..." I started before falling quiet. I sat up slowly and then, in a voice so low it was almost inaudible, asked, "Did I do something wrong?"

His eyes snapped to me, and they were narrowed. "*Fuck*," he hissed before softening his voice. "No, not at all. I'm so sorry, Parker. This really isn't why I came here..."

I cleared my throat and tried to gather my thoughts. "So, why did you come here?"

He stared at the floor for so long that I was afraid he wasn't going to answer. "You make me feel alive. And you make me feel whole." His voice was quiet but strong, and it was underlined with pure sincerity. It made me feel warm inside, to know that I did that for him. Especially when he did the exact same thing for me.

"I'm sorry. I didn't mean to let things get so... out of control," he told me with a small smile. "Although, I'm quickly learning that have I have very little of that when you're involved." That made me smile.

"I'm sorry for..." I felt my cheeks burn as I gestured to the bed behind me.

"No, don't ever apologize for that. I love the way you react to me. Every time I kiss you, you go crazy. It's the sexiest thing I have ever seen. So, don't apologize."

I didn't know what to do with that so I kept silent as he stood.

"I should head home." I could tell by his voice he didn't want to go but I needed space to get my head together, so instead of arguing I let him lead me to the front door. Ash froze with his hand on the doorknob before turning around to face me.

"Thank you. I was pissed, earlier. Thank you for letting me show up, and thank you for making it better." He leaned forward to give me a soft and sweet kiss that was over way too soon but still curled my toes.

Then, he was gone. And I spent a restless night thinking about nothing but him and the array of terrifying feelings that were already growing in my heart for him.

I couldn't do this. I couldn't get attached to him. I may not have known much about Ash, but I knew that he was pure good. I knew I could never give him everything that he deserved, and when he realized that and walked away, it would destroy me. I needed to shut it down, to keep dealing with life on my own. Because if I allowed myself to pretend... If I let myself get used to Ash making me feel alive and whole, I would never recover when it fell apart, just like I knew it eventually would.

With the way that I already felt about Ash, letting him in any further would be a mistake I would never allow myself to make.

Chapter Sixteen

Ash

WALKING INTO PHILOSOPHY THE DAY after I showed up at Parker's house, I was somewhere between nervous and excited. Excited because I was going to see Parker. Nervous because I didn't know how she was going to feel after last night. But I needed to talk to her. After everything that happened over the weekend, I wanted to make sure she knew where we stood. I wanted everyone to know that she was mine, but I needed to make sure that she knew it first.

So when I took the seat next to her and she gave me a small smile that suggested we were casual acquaintances instead of two people who came way closer to having sex than I was comfortable with the night before, I *probably* didn't react in the best possible way.

"Fuck," I said, rolling my eyes. "Are we back to this? Really?"

She turned to me and glared. *"Excuse* me?"

"You, trying to pretend like nothing is happening here? Let me guess - we can make out all you want in your bed, but once we're out in public you're going to try to act like you don't know me?"

Her mouth fell open and I knew I had screwed up. I also knew that I wasn't mad, but hurt. It was fucked up to treat her like crap because of it, but I was seriously falling hard and fast for this girl. And I had lost too much time already, I wasn't going to screw around when I knew what I wanted. Not to mention I knew she wanted it too. She was just too afraid and too stubborn to show any vulnerability.

I knew she was about to say something but at that exact moment Professor Ellis walked in. *Saved by the bell, so to speak.*

Class was torture. Not the good kind, like last week. This was serious, painful torture. I could feel the hostility rolling off Parker, and every time she moved, her actions were jerky with repressed rage. Feeling it probably should have calmed me down - or at least made me consider my actions (and reactions) a little more carefully - but the hour-long class and feeling Parker's excessive anger just worked me up. She couldn't throw herself at me on Sunday night and then pretend like she didn't know me on Monday morning. I wasn't going to accept it.

By the time class was drawing to a close, I could tell that she was preparing to make a quick getaway. At ten minutes left, she started putting all her stuff in her bag. She grabbed the strap with a white-knuckled death grip and then pushed her body to the absolute edge of her chair. Her feet bounced on the floor with nervous energy, and she trained her eyes on the door. When the professor dismissed the class two minutes later, she burst from her seat, ready to make a run for it.

Unfortunately for her, I was still faster.

I rocketed to my feet and put my arms out as she crashed directly into my chest. I rocked back a step but wrapped my arms around her to keep us both from falling to the ground. The second after she was sure we weren't going to hit the floor, she glared up at me and her body grew tense.

"Get. Off of me. *Now*." I was amazed fire wasn't shooting out of her eyes she was so pissed, and despite the anger I'd been nursing through class, I had to work to fight off a grin that I knew would make her lose her mind. She was insanely sexy all riled up, and the same part of me that wanted to make her smile every day now wanted to piss her off every day just to watch her react. Her eyes were bright and her cheeks were flushed, although that also could have been due to the fact that her body was pressed tight against mine. I felt the current flowing between us, and I knew she felt it too.

"Parker, stop. Just listen," I told her quietly, trying to reason with her. Her eyes bored into my shoulder and she was still pushing against my arms behind her back, but I decided to trust that she was listening. "I'm sorry. It was a dick thing to say. And I know that we haven't really had this discussion yet, but you need to understand that I want this, and I know you want this, and when you try to avoid me or act like you don't know me, it really makes me feel like shit." I knew I scored a point with that when I felt her body lose a tiny bit of the tension that was still holding her immobile. "I know I said we're moving slow, but that being said, we're still moving forward, together. And that applies to when we're here, too. Or anywhere, for that matter - not just in your bedroom."

"Can you please let go of me now?" she asked quietly, still staring at my shoulder. I considered her for a moment and tried to decide if I thought she was going to attempt a quick escape. Then I let my arms drop. The second they fell, Parker took a step back and looked up, finally meeting my eyes. I *really* didn't like what I saw.

"I apologize if my behavior this weekend gave you the wrong impression about us. I'm sorry, Ash, but *this*," she gestured between us with a hand, *"we're* not moving forward with anything. I told you I don't have time for a relationship and I meant it. I'm sorry. If you think you can handle helping me study without any repeats of what happened this weekend, then I'll accept that, but if not, I'll understand. I can find someone else."

I felt my eyes narrow at her, but she just stared at me with mild indifference. A million thoughts raced through my head, but I knew that anything I said would be wrong and would make the situation way worse than it already was. Instead, I decided I needed to give her time. Time to work out her shit and realize that she needed me as much as I was starting to need her. So, I gave her nothing more than a short nod before turning around and walking away.

A half hour later, I was sitting next to Marco, watching as he packed a bowl and wishing I wouldn't completely hate myself for getting high. Right now, I wanted nothing more than to block out the bad shit and just feel good. But I knew after the good there would be a whole lot of self-loathing so I watched him self-medicate alone in silence. Fifteen minutes after I got there, he finally addressed it.

"So, I'm assuming it's your girl that's got your head all fucked up."

I didn't acknowledge his words, just stared at the black TV screen. I heard an impatient sigh once he realized that I wasn't going to talk

"Look, man, I know that this is new shit for you to deal with, but sitting there looking like you wanna tear someone's head off isn't going to make it better. What's going on?"

"I don't even fucking know..." I told him. "We spent time together this weekend, at her place. It was great, fucking fantastic, and I thought we were finally on the same page. But today she acted like she didn't know me, and then told me that nothing was happening, and nothing was going to happen. I just, I honestly don't get it. I don't know what's going on that's making her so miserable and afraid, but she won't open up to me at all, and I have no fucking clue what to do." I leaned forward to rest my arms on my knees, then rubbed my hands down my face. The situation made me feel helpless and completely out of control, and I couldn't handle it. I'd lived long enough feeling like my life was out of my control and I wasn't sure that I was ready to do it again.

"Are you sure she wants you? I mean, could you just be totally reading the situation wrong?"

I glared at him. "No, I mean... Yes, I'm sure. We have... I don't know man, I can't describe it. It's just a... connection."

I knew that probably didn't make any sense, but to my slight surprise Marco nodded as if he totally understood.

"So, what's your plan?"

I sighed. "I don't know. Part of me wants to push, but I don't want to push her away. I kind of feel like I should give her time, but I'm worried she'll just use it to shut me out completely. I have no fucking clue."

We were both quiet for a few minutes before Marco spoke again. "Did Jimmy ever tell you about Emily?"

Looking at Marco, I shook my head. "Who's Emily?"

This time it was Marco's turn to focus his eyes on the TV. I watched him take a deep breath before he answered. "Emily was… She, I don't even know how to describe her, man. She was everything."

He was quiet then, and I had no clue what to say. I'd known Marco practically forever. I mean, sure, I'd always been closer to Jimmy, but still, I had no idea that Marco had ever even been in a relationship, let alone an apparently serious one.

"Do I know her?" I asked.

He shook his head. "Nah, man. She didn't go to school with us. We met in Fredricksburg the summer before senior year. She went to school around there, and we hung out all the time. As soon as I met her, I knew I wanted her. She refused to let me in. We were 'friends,' her word choice, not mine, all through senior year. After graduation… Well, let's just say that a lot of shit went down, some really good, some bad. I laid it out for her. Finally pulled my head out of my ass and told her that I loved her. She pulled away. So, I decided I'd give her time and I backed off. Two days later, she ran. Completely fucking disappeared. I spent weeks trying to track her down. I talked to her friends that I knew, but no one knew where she was. I went to her house, her dad completely refused to speak to me. To this day, I have no idea where she went. I fucking Googled her name, for Christ's sake. She was just gone."

This made absolutely no sense to me. So, I asked what seemed like the most important question. "How is it possible that I didn't know about this?" He shrugged in response. "And Jimmy knows?"

"Only because he found me at home wasted one night right before we started school. I was real messed up; it was about six weeks after she left and I was worried sick. I got shit-faced and he showed up at my house. We ended up getting into it and then I told him about her.

"We were all busy senior year. You guys were playing hockey, and I didn't bring her around, mostly because she wouldn't let me. Look, I'm not telling you this shit now because I want to... clear the air or whatever. I'm telling you, if you know it's real, don't let go. I know you haven't known her long, but I also know that I've never seen you give a shit about someone like this. She's clearly under your skin. If that feels right to you, trust it, be honest about it, and don't let her go."

I nodded slowly, but my head was spinning. I felt like an asshole for not realizing that one of my best friends went through shit that I knew nothing about. I looked up to apologize for being a shitty friend, but he cut me off with a look.

"Stop. I know that look. I didn't want anyone to know. Emily was mine, but she wasn't at the same time, and the whole thing... I hid it, for a long time. And once I was ready to be done hiding, she was gone. Don't feel like an asshole because I purposely kept something from you."

I gave him a reluctant nod and let the conversation go.

I knew I needed to sort out my head. Then, once I was back on even ground, I needed to talk to Parker. I needed to be honest and I needed to get her to let me in.

I just had no idea how to do any of that.

Chapter Seventeen

Parker

AFTER CLASSES MONDAY, I WENT home and, after checking in with Diane and sending her home, I headed straight to my room. Mom was resting before we had to head to her doctor's appointment, and all I wanted to do was put on music and block out the world.

I felt like crap. I knew I had hurt Ash this morning, and even worse, it had hurt me to talk to him like that. But I hadn't lied. Well, not completely. The truth was, I really didn't have time to "move forward" as he wanted to do. And I knew, even if things had seemed great the few times he had come over, eventually he would want more. He'd want dates and family meetings, and I couldn't do any of those things. I couldn't leave Mom alone, and I would never let him anywhere near her.

Ash was all good. The way he made me feel, the way he seemed to care - really care - it was all pure and beautiful. And my mom ruined everything that she touched. I wasn't willing to let those worlds collide.

I grabbed my iPod from my desk and scrolled right to Bright Eyes. I left the volume low enough that I could hear Mom if she needed me, and then I let the music of Conor Oberst work its way into my soul.

Multiple hours and two albums later, I was knocked out of my deep trance when I heard my ringtone start playing. Grabbing my phone, I checked the display, saw Ash's name, and hit ignore. Twenty-five seconds later the phone rang again. I hit ignore again. A minute later, the text came through.

Ash: **I'll keep calling until you answer.**

I ignored that, but my phone was ringing in my hand almost immediately. My finger hovered over the ignore button, but I really believed that he wouldn't stop calling until I answered. Pulling out my headphones and hitting pause on the music, I flipped the phone open and pressed it to my ear.

"Has anyone ever told you that you should seek professional help?" I snapped.

"Hi to you too, darling," he drawled. "For your information, I have had professional help. Has anyone ever told you that it's rude to ignore people's phone calls? What if I'm calling because of an emergency?"

"Is it an emergency?"

"Not this time, but my point is that you never know. What are you doing?"

His rapid change of subject threw me for a second, and I had to recover before I could speak again.

"I *was* lying in bed listening to music until some crazy person started blowing up my phone. Why are you calling, Ash?"

"I'm on my way to work, but I wanted to know if I could come over when I get off."

"What...?" I spluttered. "No!"

"Why not?"

I took a deep breath to keep myself from screaming at him. "Did you miss the conversation that we had earlier today? Whatever happened this weekend was a mistake on my part, and it will *not* be happening again."

"Seriously, Just Parker? A mistake? We both know that the only mistake either of us made was me being a dick this morning. The weekend was perfect."

I sucked in a breath at that. His voice was quiet and honest.

"Ash..."

"Don't. Don't say it again, I hate hearing it. We need to talk. We should have done it this weekend but, as previously stated, I have no control around you. But we really need to. There are some things that you need to know, and there are quite a few things that you need to tell me."

"No, we don't need to talk. We don't need to do anything. This is not happening."

Ash laughed softly. "Parker, it already happened. You might not want to accept it yet, but you're already mine."

I was quiet for a minute trying to figure out how to get myself out of this situation.

"I don't get it. Why does this, why do I, matter to you so much?" I finally asked.

His answer was immediate. "Because you make me feel like I can do anything, and you make me look forward to a future, but only so long as that future includes you. You have no idea… For so long, I've felt completely hopeless, Park. And the only time that goes away is when you're around."

Well shit.

I had nothing to counter that with.

Ash knew it, so he continued.

"I'm going to let you go, but I'll text you. Please, please think about letting me come over."

"Ash…"

"No, Park, just think about it. I'll talk to you later."

"Okay," I whispered into the phone just before the line disconnected.

I sat staring at the ceiling for ten minutes trying to find some way, some possible future that could contain Ash and I together. I wanted it so bad that I could taste it, but no matter how I tried to consider it, I knew it was impossible.

I let out a sigh and pushed myself up in bed. A five minute phone call had effectively ruined the relaxed mood I had been trying to create and my mind was officially racing again but, glancing at the clock, I knew I needed to start getting Mom ready for the doctor's. Which was awesome, because taking Mom to the doctors was something that I wanted to do slightly less than having my fingernails ripped off slowly while I watched Ash with another girl - a gorgeous, perfect girl who was doing all of the things that I would never get to do - smiling at me as I died on the inside.

Mom's oncologist was named Dr. Bradley. His office was a thirty minute drive from our apartment, which really sucked because Mom hated riding in my car. But he was a good doctor and I liked him. He was fairly attractive - I'd guess in his early- to mid-thirties - with tanned skin and a reassuring face. He was fantastic at making you feel comfortable while he told you that you or your loved ones were dying, and I'd guessed that was why he was as successful as he seemed to be. His office was always full and he dressed really well.

After the nurses checked Mom's weight and vitals, they took us back to a small exam room with a tall padded bench, a stool on wheels in front of a small counter, and a single chair. I tried to help Mom onto the bench, but she smacked my hand as I reached for her elbow.

"I can handle it, Eileen," she snapped. I bit my lip and moved to sit in the chair as I felt my phone vibrate in my back pocket. I pulled it out and flipped it open as I lowered myself into the seat.

Ash: **I'm at work. It's dead, and I'm bored. What are you doing?**

I rolled my eyes and flipped the phone shut, shoving it back into my pocket. I glanced at the walls, reading the different posters. Typical doctor's office stuff - drug advertisements and diagrams of the human body - and it all seemed so innocent that I could almost pretend.

When I was younger, I had loved going to the doctor's. As stupid as it sounds, I liked knowing that I was growing right and healthy, especially considering I was the one that was making that happen. Mom would rather get drunk and rant about my dad than make dinner and help me take a bath, so I learned how to take care of myself pretty early on. For some reason, I felt proud every time I walked into a doctor's office for a check-up because I knew that I was keeping myself alive.

As soon as Mom got sick, my entire concept of healthcare changed and doctor's visits became one degree short of terrifying for me. I had gotten better at handling things for my mom's sake, but I hated dealing with doctors, hospitals, medicine, and cancer in general. Like, really, I was over it.

Ten minutes of uncomfortable silence later, Mom and I were still waiting for the doctor when my phone buzzed again.

Ash: **I really hope that you're busy and not just ignoring me.**

I ignored that message as well.

Dr. Bradley showed up five minutes later.

"Hey there, Katherine," he said to Mom with a smile. She smiled wide and lifted a hand to run her fingers through her thinning hair as she told him hello.

"Hey, Parker. How's school going?" he asked me warmly. I heard Mom sigh at the nickname, but I ignored it.

"Really good, thanks."

"Alright, ladies. Let's do this so we can get you out of here. I'm sure you both have plenty of things you'd rather be doing than sitting here with me."

Dr. Bradley asked Mom how she was feeling dealing with the latest Chemo schedule. Where some people went to sit in a room and get Chemotherapy drugs pumped into their veins every so often, Mom was too sick for that. She carried her pack around for three days straight and then took three days off. This had been going on for four weeks and, today, a nurse had come to the house to disconnect the pump while I was at school. After about ten minutes of discussion about Mom's energy, nausea, and pain levels and a short exam that left Mom groaning in pain from the doctor's gentle poking and prodding, a nurse came in to draw blood. Five uncomfortably large vials later, she was finally done.

"I'm going to send those to the lab and I should have the results in a few days. I want to check all of your levels before we decide exactly what we're going to do from here. I'll have the girls give you a call once we get the results and we'll have you come in then, okay?"

Mom and I both nodded and then said goodbye to the doctor as he headed out the door with a wave and a smile. I made it to the door and held it open for Mom, who rolled her eyes at me yet again as we walked through.

We moved back out through the lobby and I took a look around at the people who were still sitting in the waiting room. My eyes fell onto one woman in particular. She was tiny, nothing but skin and bones, and she looked half dead already. I couldn't help but picture my mom like that, wasting away to practically nothing, and the image burned itself into my brain. I wasn't ready for that, to be faced with that image in real life. Honestly, Mom was holding up better than I expected. She had always had thick hair, so when she started Chemo she didn't lose it all - it just thinned. She looked tired and definitely too thin, but after years of drinking, that was still pretty normal for her.

The drive home was silent and, as soon as we got inside, I made dinner and got her meds together. After cleaning the dishes and putting away the leftovers, I headed into my room. I had felt my phone vibrate a few times after leaving the doctor's, but I hadn't checked it yet. As I expected, the three texts were all from Ash.

Ash: **If I asked if you were ignoring me, would you give me an honest answer?**
Ash: **You're gonna let me come over after work, right?**
Ash: **Good idea. We'll just wait to talk until I get there.**

I continued ignoring him and pulled out my books to get some homework done. Two hours later I gave Mom more meds and put her to bed. I had just finished getting changed when my phone vibrated from the bed with an incoming call from Ash. I let it go to voicemail. He tried once more, and again I just let it ring until voicemail picked up the call. I hoped he'd assume that I was sleeping since I didn't use the "FU" button.. When the phone didn't ring again, I found myself disturbingly disappointed. I chastised myself and then tried to fall asleep.

It took hours. And when I finally did, I dreamt of Ash.

Chapter Eighteen

Ash

BY WEDNESDAY AFTERNOON, I WAS seriously pissed. Parker had ignored all four texts and three calls I made on Tuesday. I thought about just showing up at her house, but she was always so cagey about her place that I didn't want to cross a line, or possibly run into the dreaded evil roommate.

I figured that I'd at least talk to her this morning in Philosophy, but the girl showed up three minutes late and avoided my eyes as she took a seat two rows from the front, instead of with me where we always sat together. She didn't even look at me once, and I know this for a fact because I stared at nothing but the back of her head for the entire hour that we spent in the room. After class, I took off to chase her out the door, but by the time I reached the hallway she had completely disappeared. She was like a fucking jungle cat the way that she moved, her sole intention evasion. I found it to be both a serious turn-on and seriously fucking annoying.

I spent the hours until my next class staring out the window of the coffee shop and drinking way too much caffeine. I was jittery and on edge through my next two classes. Once all that was finally done, I practically raced to my truck and climbed into the driver's seat. Then I texted her.

Me: **What the fuck, Parker?**

I gave her five minutes to answer. When she didn't, I texted again.

Me: **Seriously, if you don't answer I'm coming to your apartment.**

That got me a response.

Parker: **What do you want, Ash?**

Me: **Why are you avoiding me?**

Parker: **I'm not avoiding you.**

I really wanted to shake some sense into this girl. I started to text back and then changed my mind. Instead, I listened to the phone ring, swearing that if she didn't answer I was driving to see her.

"Oh my God, Ash. Do you know how to take a hint?"

"What the fuck?" I asked, ignoring her (lack of a) greeting. "What happened this morning?"

"I was late! I didn't want to make a scene walking to the back of the room!"

"Bullshit. You're avoiding me, just like you've been doing since Monday."

She laughed, but it wasn't a happy sound. "Because everything I do revolves around you, right?"

Now I was done fucking around. "What the hell are you so afraid of, Parker?"

I heard her suck in air over the phone before she could recover. "I'm not afraid," she replied with more attitude than was really necessary.

"That's bullshit, too," I told her quietly. "You're so afraid you can't breathe. I see it, I feel it, I know it. I just want you to tell me what you're scared of."

There was silence for a minute, and I knew she was processing what I said. When she finally spoke, there was a disturbing blank tone to her voice.

"You're wrong, Ash. I just have too much going on for this. I have to go."

Before I could respond, the line went dead and she was gone.

For the first time ever, I was dreading going to Grandma's. I was in a shit mood from my phone call with Parker, and I was starting to realize that sorting things out with her was going to be really fucking difficult. She had more walls built up than any other person I'd ever met (myself included,) and every time I started to break through one, it was like she put up three more to keep me out.

Grandma, being Grandma, knew something was up the second I walked in. Despite that, she took me to the kitchen, sat me on a stool, and asked me about school like nothing was wrong. I drank iced tea and told her about my classes and she talked a bit about her work. I relaxed as we got dinner on the table, and we talked comfortably as we ate. It wasn't until afterwards, once we had cleared the table, refilled our glasses, and pulled out the Scrabble board that she decided to address it.

"What's going on, Ash?" she asked quietly. "Something's not right, I can tell."

I took a long sip of tea, really wanting to ignore the question. I knew there was no way she'd let me get away with that.

"I, uh, I met a girl."

Grandma let out a relieved sigh. "Oh. Well, isn't that supposed to be exciting? Why do you look like someone ran over your dog?"

"It's complicated," I told her. "I think there's something wrong, with her or her situation maybe. I don't know, but she's really guarded. We have an amazing connection, and when we're together, it's just... perfect. She's perfect. But I think she's scared, and she won't let me in."

"What do you mean she won't let you in?"

"She won't tell me what's going on, or why she supposedly has no time for a relationship. I can see it when I look at her... There's something off. She looks like I looked last year, lost and alone and afraid. I've told her that I want to help her, but she just won't accept it."

Grandma nodded slowly before speaking again. "It sounds like you're right - she probably has something going on. But if she doesn't want to let you in, you can't force it, honey."

I knew that was true, even if I hated it.

"I know... I just want to make her happy."

Grandma gave me a sweet smile. "So be there for her. You don't have to know everything about her life to be a good friend and make her smile. And who knows, maybe once she sees that you just want to see her happy, she'll trust you more and start opening up. Just show her that you're going to be there for her."

I nodded. "That makes sense."

Grandma laughed. "I have my moments every now and again. Now tell me about this girl while I kick your butt at this game. It might make you feel better about losing every week."

Seriously. I loved my grandma.

That night, after I got home from Grandma's I thought about calling Parker. Instead, I settled for a text.

Me: **You might not have time, but I'm not going anywhere. I'm here for you, anytime you need me.**

She didn't respond, and I didn't expect her to. I just set my phone on the nightstand and thought about her until I passed out. And then, just like I had for the past few nights, I let her come to me in my dreams.

I'm not gonna lie, the dreams were fucking amazing. Still, I wasn't a fan of waking up every morning craving more.

Chapter Nineteen

Parker

BY DINNERTIME FRIDAY I WAS ready to lose my mind. All week I'd been avoiding Ash, and it was making me absolutely miserable. I hated how much I missed him, but I didn't trust myself around him - at all. Case in point, this morning in Philosophy. I thought about showing up late to avoid sitting with him again (despite the fact that he had seemed really pissed about that maneuver when I talked to him on the phone Wednesday,) but I got to campus early and decided that I could handle it.

I was frighteningly wrong.

Just ten minutes into class - dealing with the sensation of his heat next to me and trying to calm the electric tingles racing along my skin and smelling him every time he moved - and I was ready to both profess my undying love for him and beg him to just take me somewhere to do delicious things to me with his body. Seriously, I had no idea what was going on with my body, but this relative stranger physically affected me more than anyone else I'd ever met. Okay, so he wasn't really a stranger, but still, we barely knew each other. I didn't count the incredibly freaky physical reaction that we seemed to both experience when we were together as actually knowing each other.

I'm not entirely sure how I made it through the class without fully acknowledging him. I said "Hi" when he came in and nodded a few times, but I refused to make eye contact. I heard his sigh when (I'm assuming) he realized this, but I stayed strong.

I was woman, and I was in control.

And then he moved, and I watched out of the corner of my eye as he leaned down to grab something out of his bag on the floor. I stared at his t-shirt, stretching across all those rippling muscles, and I felt my legs turn to something slightly less resilient than Jell-O as my breathing turned shallow. From there, I had to force myself into some weird sort of zen, meditative state to block him out. It worked for the rest of class, but just barely.

Thankfully, class let out three minutes over and he didn't fight me when I told him I had to run or I'd be late. I focused on my lectures the rest of the day to avoid thinking about Ash (which *almost* worked) and then headed home for what was sure to be an incredibly long weekend.

Diane warned me before she left that Mom was in a mood. I kept my distance while she lounged in her room. I got her medicated and we were eating dinner when she finally broke the tense silence.

"We need to get rid of Diane."

I coughed on the meatloaf I was chewing. Taking a sip of water, I washed it down before asking, "Why?"

"We just do."

I took a deep breath to prepare myself before I responded, "Okay. And I'm asking if there's any reason or logic behind that idea."

"Because she just makes things worse. And we shouldn't need her anyway. You should be here, not some strange woman I don't know."

"Mom, you know I would, but I have class-"

"Really, Eileen? You do realize I'm dying, right? Are you really telling me that going to school is more important than taking care of your soon-to-be-dead mother?"

I felt that blast of cold freeze my insides as she spoke, and for a minute I didn't know what to say.

"I'm not saying that, but we're talking about my future," I told her quietly.

"Yeah? And I'll be dead in that future, right?"

"Can you please stop-"

"Stop what?" she interrupted. "Stop telling the truth? I can't believe that you are so selfish that, while I'm at home dying, you're out doing God knows what with God knows who-"

"Seriously?" I asked, my voice rising. "I don't do anything but go to school, go to work, and take care of you. Diane has been nothing but helpful, and-"

"Diane isn't my daughter. After everything I've done for you, I deserve that much."

Her words rocked me. I wanted to tell her exactly what she deserved for letting me raise myself, for drinking all the time and telling me that I was worthless and stupid. I wanted to tell her the only thing she ever did for me was somehow keep me alive long enough to bring me into the world (because I wasn't sure how she managed even that,) but I bit my tongue. I didn't stop until the metallic taste of blood filled my mouth.

I left the food on the table and walked to my room without another word. I heard her get up a few minutes later and shuffle back to her bed. When it was time for her PM meds, I walked out and got them ready. I took them to her room and handed them over in silence. After that, I cleared the table, cleaned the kitchen, and went back to my room.

I paced for a half an hour, trying to calm myself down. It didn't work. So I changed into a pair of jeans and threw on a sweatshirt. I walked to Mom's room and made sure that she was sleeping before I grabbed my keys and my phone and headed out the door.

I was still driving around aimlessly a half an hour later. I had no idea where to go or what to do, but I couldn't be at home. When I passed a playground a few minutes later, I pulled over and parked. I sat on a swing and tried to calm my brain. No success. Then, almost before I even realized what I was doing, I texted Ash.

Me: **Where are you?**

He answered almost immediately.

Ash: **My friend Marco's. He's having a party.**
Ash: **Are you okay?**

Me: **Yeah. Can I come?**

Ash: **Do you want me to come to you?**

Me: **No, I want to come there.**

Ash said sure and texted the address and I immediately headed over. I was only about fifteen minutes away, which was good because it meant I didn't have time to consider all the reasons why this was in no way a good idea.

I pulled up out front of a large, impressive-looking apartment building. Appreciating the brightly lit path (something that my place lacked, which I really hated,) I made my way to the door, which was propped open with a brick and walked inside. I headed upstairs for the third floor and walked in the open door.

The apartment was huge, at least three times as big as mine, from what I could see, and it was absolutely filled with people. I had been to a few parties in high school, but never anything like this. Music blared through the space and people were dancing and grinding together all over the place. I walked through a few clouds of pot smoke and passed a few people snorting lines of what looked like cocaine. I finally made it into the kitchen where the counters were covered in bottles of liquor and various beer cans. I still didn't see Ash, so I kept moving.

I was back in the living room when I felt heat hit my back. I turned quickly, assuming it was Ash, but a tall, lanky blond kid stood leaning over me.

"Hey, gorgeous," he slurred. "What's your name?"

I felt his hand squeeze my hip and I tried to take a step back. At that moment, my foot caught on the carpet and suddenly I was falling backwards.

I landed with a groan against something hard and warm. I felt two very familiar arms wrap around me before his growly voice spoke near my ear.

"She's here for me, Petey," Ash said to the guy. "Leave her alone."

Petey held his hands up and backed away but I focused on the body behind me. Now that he was here, I had no clue what I was doing.

So I used that moment to take stock of the situation. My mom wanted me to drop out of college to take care of her until she died. I was trying to avoid facing my feelings for the guy standing directly behind me, but that was really hard to do without a large amount of physical distance, and right now that distance was completely nonexistent. I was at my first college party, and from what I knew about college parties, it seemed to be a pretty epic one.

So, I decided to do something I hadn't done in years.

I decided to forget about it all.

Chapter Twenty

Ash

WHEN PARKER TEXTED ME AND asked if she could come to Marco's, I really didn't want to say yes. But I wanted to see her and if she wouldn't let me go to her, I was just glad that I would still get to spend some time with her, however we spent it.

If I hadn't already realized how gone I was for this girl, I would have known it the instant I saw Petey put his hand on her hip. I wanted to hit him. No, actually it was worse than that; I wanted to tear his head off for touching her. But when Parker fell trying to get away and literally landed right in my arms, I considered that an act of divine intervention.

I pulled Parker behind me as I headed towards Marco and Jimmy, who were playing flip cup in one of the rooms in the back. There were less people back here, and I wanted her to myself, at least as much as possible while we were surrounded by this insanity.

"Where are we going?" she asked breathlessly as I dragged her.

"Come on," I kind-of answered, pulling her into the room. Jimmy and Marco both looked up when we walked in the room and I watched as they both slowly realized who she was. Marco smiled but Jimmy just looked her up and down before looking back to the game. *Hm, that was weird.*

"Parker," I told her, gesturing to the guys, "this is Jimmy and Marco. Guys, this is Parker."

"Hey, Parker," Marco said, and she smiled at him. "I see Ash didn't get you a drink. Can I grab you something?"

Parker's smile widened before she said, "Yeah, that'd be great. No beer, liquor. Rum and coke if you got it."

"I can handle that," he replied, then winked before walking out.

I grabbed her hand and pulled her towards the wall, waiting for her to focus back on me before I spoke.

"I'm glad you're here," I told her quietly.

"Me too," she told me, even as she looked everywhere but at me.

"Is everything okay?" I asked tentatively.

"Yeah, of course," she replied. "I just needed to get out."

I nodded and Marco came back with her drink. He handed it over before leaning against the wall next to her instead of jumping back into the game. They started talking about school as she took frequent, long sips from her cup. In minutes it was gone and I volunteered to go get her refill before Marco could. I knew he was heavy-handed with the liquor, and I didn't want Parker to drink too much.

Unfortunately, she seemed to disagree with that idea, because the next drink - actually, the next three - she made herself. I was getting ready to ask her if she really needed any more when a body filled the door and caught my eye. I went still as I watched the tall, scrawny figure walk towards me with a cocky grin on his face.

"Hey, Ash. Long time, no see…"

Marco looked over at him, and I saw annoyance masking a layer of anger when he spoke. "What the fuck, Ty? You can't be here."

Ty ignored Marco, instead turning to look at Parker. I watched his eyes move up and down her body and I had to clench my hands into fists to keep from hitting the fucker. Ty was about two inches taller than me, but stupid, clearly because not only had he seen, firsthand, what I was capable of, but he also couldn't miss the fact that I had thirty five pounds on him and it was pure muscle.

Looking back to me, Ty spoke again. "Damn, she's a nice little piece. I didn't think you could get pussy like that."

I took a step forward but Marco was there with his hand in my chest. "Stop, Ash. Fucking stop," he said quietly to me. "Get the fuck out, Ty. Now." That wasn't quiet.

He didn't get out. He smirked at me and asked, "How's Rory?"

I moved again, not even acknowledging that Marco was already swinging at him. He nailed Ty across the jaw and then grabbed onto me again before I made it to the asshole.

"I swear to God, motherfucker, you ever say her name to me again and what happened to Will'll seem like nothing after I'm done with you!" I snapped. Jimmy was on my other side now, trying to calm me down, but I was already done. "I'm fine," I told the guys, shaking them off. Jimmy walked back to the table, ignoring us again as I watched Marco push Ty out the door, only relaxing once he was out of the room. Taking three steps back, I leaned against the wall. I felt Parker staring at me, but I had no idea what to tell her.

"Well, that was interesting," she finally said. "Care to explain?" Her voice was just starting to slur, and I didn't like hearing it. It didn't sound like her, like my Parker.

"Not right now."

She was quiet for a minute before nodding. "Great. Okay. Well, I'm going to get another drink." Then she was gone.

Marco returned as she left the room and came straight to me. "You alright?"

"Yeah, fine."

He nodded before jerking his head towards Jimmy across the room. "What's up with him?"

I shrugged. "I have no fucking clue." Marco nodded again before walking to the bong he'd set on the table earlier. He was halfway through packing it when Parker came back.

I saw her eying Marco as he finished packing the piece and took his first hit. He began to pass it around and I watched her eyes follow it around the room. When it finally got back to Marco, I realized that he had noticed it too. He looked up and offered it to Parker. I saw a flash of uncertainty in her eyes that she quickly covered before walking across the room to him.

I jumped behind her and grabbed her arm. "Are you sure you want to do that?" I asked carefully. I didn't know Parker that well, and maybe she partied like this all the time. Still, I got the feeling that wasn't the case, and I was starting to get worried. I didn't want her doing all this if it was just a way to escape.

Her eyes narrowed on my arm. "Let go. I know what I'm doing."

"Parker, calm down, I just want to make sure that you're okay."

"I'm fine, Ash. Now, can you please stop babysitting me?" My back went straight at the tone of her voice, but I nodded and let her go. Then, I watched as she got high with my friend and pretended like everything was fine. The problem with that was, as she got more fucked up, I saw the panic in her eyes get more and more pronounced.

When she went to get her next drink, I was out of patience. I knew something was up, and I was going to find out what. I followed her as she left the room, and when she moved to turn right, I grabbed her arm and pulled her to the left, into Marco's dark and, thankfully empty, bedroom. She let out a small shriek until I turned on the light, at which point her expression morphed from afraid to pissed.

"What the fuck, Ash?"

"Seriously, Park? That's what you want to start with?" Her eyebrows drew together and I knew that she was confused so I continued. "Let me help you out here. You could decide to tell me what the fuck you're doing here tonight. You could decide to tell me why you're hell bent on getting blitzed. You could decide to tell me why you've avoided me for the last week. But, I'd really appreciate you not starting this conversation pissed at me because I'm worried. Since you haven't seemed to figure this out yet, I give a shit about you. I don't want to see you hurting, and I really don't want to watch you do whatever the fuck it is that you're doing here tonight."

"You can't give a shit about me, Ash," she shot back. "You don't know me. For all you know, I do this shit every God damned weekend. And it's not your job to take care of me!"

"I know that!" I shouted. "Because you won't let me. But I want to, Parker! You need someone taking care of you, and I don't understand why you won't let that be me!"

"I don't need anyone!" She was loud and angry, but even as she shouted I saw her eyes start to shine with tears. "I've been taking care of myself my entire life. I don't need you."

"That's bullshit and you know it."

"No, it's not. I don't need you and I definitely don't want you."

"That's bullshit, too, Parker. Wanna know how I know?"

"Sure, since you apparently know everything about everyone. Tell me how you know."

I moved. One second there was five feet between us and the next, my mouth was on hers. And, just like I knew she would, she reacted. Her hands went into my hair and she opened up and gave me everything. The second our mouths touched the feeling came back - the electricity, the perfection. I wanted to live in that moment.

Then, I heard a choked sound as Parker shoved against my chest. I wasn't prepared and I had to take two steps back to stay standing. Tears were streaming down her face and she looked completely broken.

Faster than I thought she could move, she was out the door.

Leaving me behind.

Again.

Chapter Twenty-One

Parker

I MADE IT OUTSIDE IN under a minute and a half. The air helped calm me down a bit and I ran towards my car as quickly as I could. But, Goddammit, he was just so fast.

"Parker!" Ash screamed from behind me. "Fucking stop, Parker!"

At that, the little bit of calm I had achieved evaporated and my hands shook while I tried to get the key in to unlock the car door. Before I could manage that, he had pulled my keys from my hand and pressed his body against the back of mine, pushing me into the car.

"Calm down, Park. Just breathe."

"Give me my keys."

"I know you think I'm doing this to be a dick, but you are completely insane if you think I'm letting you drive home. You had like, six drinks. No way."

"I just want to go home..." I whispered, suddenly exhausted.

Ash was quiet for a few seconds, and then, "Okay. I'll take you home."

"Didn't you…" I started to ask before trailing off, but he must have known what I meant.

"No. I don't really drink much in general, but I don't ever drink at Marco's."

Ash stepped back and grabbed my arm. His touch was gentle, and he pulled me away from my car and down the street, slipping my keys into his pocket and then stopping in front of a dark pick-up truck. It was old, and pretty small compared to some of the monstrous trucks I'd seen around town, the ones that I was sure were driven by guys with shockingly small hardware. Ash helped me into the passenger seat and made sure I was buckled before walking around the hood and climbing in behind the wheel.

From the moment he started the truck, I kept my mouth shut. I had way too much going on in my head, and silence was the safest option available to me. I tried to use the drive home to get my shit together, but the alcohol and pot in my system weren't really letting that happen.

When Ash parked in front of my apartment, I let him lead me up to the front door. I tried to take my keys and tell him goodnight before entering the building, but he just shook his head and started pushing me inside. He followed me all the way to my door and used my keys to let me through before coming in and locking the door behind him.

"What are you doing?" I whispered.

"We're going to talk."

"What?!" I shout-whispered.

He shushed me and pushed me through the apartment towards my bedroom. Once we were inside he moved to sit on the bed and patted the spot next to him.

"Come here, Park," he told me, as I stood just inside the door. "We need to talk, and if you're loosened up right now, I'm sorry, but I'm going to take advantage of it to try and get some answers."

I slowly made my way across the room, but instead of sitting next to him I sat down in the desk chair. I needed distance.

"Why did you come to the party?"

Shit. Did we need to start with that? I couldn't talk about Mom.

I shook my head and he sighed, but also nodded.

"Okay, why have you avoided me the past week?"

I decided I was going to stick with the lie I had already told.

"I wasn't avoiding you."

That earned me a glare. "You know, this really won't work if you won't be honest with me..."

And that was when I snapped.

"Seriously?" I asked him. "I never said I wanted 'this' to work, whatever that means. And can we try to remember that, while you ask all these freaking questions, I know almost nothing about you, either! It's not like you're Mr. Forthcoming."

"What do you want to know?" he shot back, no hesitation.

"Who was that guy at the party?"

Ash sighed. "It's a long story, but basically he's a dick who's friends with an even bigger dick."

I nodded. "Wow. That cleared everything right up. Thanks." He didn't miss the sarcasm, but honestly, he couldn't have if he tried. I paused before continuing with a question that I knew would reveal way too much, but I had to know. "Who's Rory? Is that a long story too?"

Ash looked at me with a mask of pure confusion that I didn't buy for a second, but then his face cracked into a giant grin. "Are you jealous right now?"

Yep. Definitely gave too much away.

"No!" I shouted. "I just think it's ridiculous for you to get pissed at me when you and your friends are getting in fights in front of me over your freaking exes!"

"Baby," Ash said in a low voice, "Rory is Aurora. My sister."

Shit.

I was a complete idiot.

"You were totally jealous," Ash said with a smug smile.

"Was not," I responded like a child.

"Okay," he said, still grinning and completely not buying it.

We fell quiet for a minute, which I couldn't deal with. Unfortunately, I also couldn't really speak, so I suffered in the silence until he broke it.

"Why'd you come find me at the party?" The grin was gone and replaced with a look of concern. It almost broke me, and I couldn't help but give him as much truth as I was able.

"I got in a fight with my mom. It was ugly. I just needed... I needed to escape."

He nodded. "I can understand that. I've ended up at Marco's more times than I can count after fights with my dad." His eyes drifted to my mouth for a moment before they moved back up. "Well, I'm sorry about the fight, but I'm glad I got to see you. That said, you're probably gonna feel like crap tomorrow. Why don't you let me get you some water and a couple Advil and then I can help you get into bed? Then we can talk a bit more, at least until you pass out on me."

That sounded really nice, but I couldn't let him get me medicine... for so many reasons.

"Nah, it's alright. I'll grab it. Just stay here and I'll be right back."

I thought he was going to argue for a second, but he just gave me a short nod as I moved from the chair towards the door. I headed to the kitchen and grabbed two glasses, filling them both with water before setting them on the counter so I could sort through Mom's nine hundred medicine bottles to find the Advil. I swallowed two and then carried the glasses back to my room.

Ash smiled when I handed him a glass and took a sip before thanking me. I set mine on the nightstand and then walked to my dresser.

"I, um..." Shit, why was this so uncomfortable? "I'm gonna get changed real quick."

"Oh!" Ash said, hopping off the bed. "Do you want me to..." He pointed to the door, and I smiled as I shook my head.

"I appreciate the offer, but you're good. I have a bathroom," I gestured over my shoulder to the door behind me. Unable to stand still anymore, I grabbed a pair of yoga pants and a t-shirt from the drawers and then rushed into the tiny room, locking the door behind me. I ran cool water and then splashed some on my face before I caught myself procrastinating. Then I changed my clothes, leaving my jeans, bra, shirt and sweatshirt in a pile on the floor of the tiny bathroom.

I took a deep breath with my hand on the doorknob, and then immediately decided that I needed another.

Finally, I flipped the lock and walked back out.

Ash was across the room, standing in front of another of my drawings. It was one of my stranger pieces, an homage to one of my favorite songs by The Decemberists.

I was standing a few feet behind him when he asked, "Is this... Jonah?"

I laughed softly. "No, it's a scene from a song. The song's called The Mariner's Revenge Song. It's kind of a sea shanty about getting payback. It's great."

Ash shook his head as he turned to give me a look before focusing on the drawing again. "Whatever the inspiration, this is absolutely fantastic, Park. The way you drew the whale, and the wreckage in the background. God, and the expressions on their faces. It's incredible..."

I smiled broadly. "Thanks, but really, not my creation. That guy," I pointed to the man with the smirk, "is about to torture the shit out of the guy who looks like he's about to pee himself. I've just always loved the song, so I decided to draw it one day."

Ash turned around and grabbed my hand, using it to pull me against him. I sucked in a nervous breath, but my still fairly drunken body betrayed me and relaxed against him.

God, he felt good.

It was like I had finally found the place that I had always belonged.

As I realized this, I waited for the terror to strike. I waited for the panic and the need to pull away... but it didn't come. And as much as it freaked me out, I decided to roll with it.

"You're incredible, and you don't even know it," he whispered against the top of my head in his low rumbling voice, and I had to bring my free hand up to his chest, gripping his shirt tightly to keep from falling over as my legs tried to give out.

I felt him let out a sigh and he took a slow step backward, taking the time to make sure I was standing on my own.

"Come on, let's get you into bed." I let him lead me across the room, and he held my hand as he pulled back the covers, gently tucking them around me before sitting down next to me on the edge of the mattress.

"You okay?" he asked quietly.

"No." I saw the concern flash through his eyes, so I quickly added, "Why are you so far away?"

He settled and then gave me a small smile before lying down next to me. I put my head on his shoulder and we laid together in the most comfortable silence I'd ever been a part of. I loved every second.

But, after a while I realized that after everything he'd done for me, I really owed him something. So I decided to give him the thing he seemed to want most. A little bit of honesty.

"I'm terrified, Ash," I whispered. I felt him still, but I kept talking before I lost my nerve. "Of you, and the way you make me feel. I already feel myself falling for you, and... You don't understand-"

"I know I don't, but I want to," he interrupted.

"I know that, and I think I want you to, too, but... I've never had anyone who cared about me. Never had anyone who loved me or tried to take care of me. Maybe before my dad left, but I don't even really remember what that was like. I'm terrified to let you in because, I'm telling you now,

I already know that if I ever lost you it would destroy me. I'm used to having absolutely nothing. I don't want to try to get used to having everything if it's just going to be taken away again."

I didn't realize that I had started crying until I felt Ash's thumbs gently wipe away the wetness from under my eyes.

"Look at me, Parker. What you just gave me - that honest admission - that was the first taste I got of something that I want more than I've ever wanted anything. I want to know you, inside and out. And I can't make promises about what the future is gonna be like, but I can tell you... The way I feel about you? I've never felt anything like that before in my life. I'm already falling for you too, Parker, and I have been since you knocked me on my ass the first day of classes. Honestly, at this point I don't have too much further to go before I'll hit rock bottom."

I couldn't breathe. I really couldn't draw in air. Thankfully, he didn't notice and just kept talking like I wasn't dying next to him.

"I'm not going anywhere." His voice was rough and firm, and maybe I'm an idiot, but I believed him. Which is why I shifted my body until I was able to push up and press my lips against his.

Ash kissed me like he wanted to send a message, and I have to say, even dealing with a slowly fading buzz and the inability to take a steady breath, I received that message loud and clear.

I was his. Completely.

Chapter Twenty-Two

Ash

AS I WALKED TO PHILOSOPHY at 7:45, I was reminded why I hated Mondays. Honestly, if it wasn't for the fact that I was dying to see Parker, I probably wouldn't have forced myself out of bed this morning. But waking up to the alarm clock blaring and the fading memory of a dream that ended at the exact moment that she had just wrapped her mouth and tongue around me both pissed me off and motivated me to fly out of bed and into the shower to deal with my... situation.

I missed her - that was my problem. And I knew that I probably shouldn't be missing her, or at least not as much as I was, but I couldn't help it. I wanted to spend every minute of every day with Parker and it felt like she was still avoiding me. I mean, things were definitely better than they had been. We texted back and forth all the time and she stopped ignoring my phone calls... for the most part. But it still felt like it wasn't enough. I needed her - her presence was a tether that kept me anchored to the ground, and I was quickly becoming addicted to the way that I felt when she was nearby.

Friday night, after a kiss that left me painfully hard and regretting my decision to "make it special" for her first time, I left Parker in bed with a kiss on the forehead and the promise that I would text her. Which I did. Once as soon as I got into my truck. Once when I got home from her house. Once when I climbed into bed. And then once again, just for the fuck of it. I was trying to make her smile, and while I'm not sure if I succeeded, I convinced myself that I did, and it made me feel a bit better.

Saturday was pretty good, actually. Well, for me at least. Parker woke me up with a phone call at 10:30, freaking out and begging me for a ride to work since her car was parked at Marco's and I still had her keys. I thanked any God that felt like listening for that fortunate set of circumstances and promised to be there in a half an hour to pick her up. That meant I barely had time to get out of bed, throw on a pair of jeans and a tee, and eat two slices of toast before I was out the door, both sets of keys in hand.

I made it to her house with five minutes to spare and texted her to let her know that I was out front. Two minutes later she was running out the door towards the truck, wearing a tight white t-shirt and a pair of tiny shorts that really showed off her legs. Legs that I seriously wanted wrapped around my back. And legs that I really didn't want anyone else looking at.

I wonder if I could convince her to wear only baggy sweatpants when she's out in public?

I stopped that thought dead as she climbed into the truck.

"Hey! Oh my God, thank you so much for showing up, I can't even believe I didn't think about this last night. I'm so sorry-"

"Hey, stop," I interrupted, further discouraging any attempt to speak on her part by sliding across the bench seat and pressing my mouth to hers. I opened her up and tasted her fully before pulling back, smiling at the dazed look in her eyes. I kissed her once on the forehead before sliding back to the wheel and pulling out onto the road, heading towards the diner she had told me she worked at.

"You don't have to thank me. Ever. I'm glad I got to do this for you, even if it was kind of my fault that you didn't have your car."

Her eyes were a little unfocused and I could tell that she was still recovering from the kiss, which made me smile. She answered with a breathy "Okay."

"So, here's the plan. Wait, what time are you done work?" I asked.

"Five."

"Right, so here's the plan. I'm going to drive you to work. And then, I'll show up there at five and pick you up, and we'll go get dinner. Wherever you want, my treat. After that, I'll drive you to Marco's to get your car. Perfect plan, right?" I asked her with a smile. It wasn't as bright as the Ashton Carter Killer Smile, but I was trying to work her up to that. I didn't want to overwhelm my girl.

I looked away from the road to see her answer with a small smile of her own, but it didn't reach her eyes as she turned back. "It sounds absolutely perfect, but I can't. I need to get home right after work."

I shrugged. "That's fine. I'll take you to Marco's to get your car and you can head home. I'll swing by the store and grab shit to cook you dinner, and we can just hang at your place."

She looked at me with a mixture of amusement and slight shock when she asked, "Please tell me you're joking and you don't really cook?"

I let my smile fade as I lifted a shoulder. "Well, I could, but I don't like to lie to beautiful girls. I cook, and I cook damn well. You don't even know what you're in for, baby." I gave her a playful grin, hoping to get one in return, but her face fell a bit.

"You just keep getting better and better... As amazing as that really does sound though, I, uh, I can't."

"Why? And if you tell me that it has to do with your crazy roommate, I'll just let you know now, it takes a whole fucking lot of crazy to scare me."

"Well, obviously," Parker fired back. "I mean, you seem to have a thing for me, so..."

I burst out laughing and watched out of the corner of my eye as she turned to face me. Once I had calmed myself down, I reached out and grabbed her hand, winding her fingers through mine before placing them on my thigh.

"This is true, so you see, I'm not easily cowed."

"Wow, nice vocab word. Okay, well, I believe you, but, it's just complicated and... Ash, I promise you that I'm trying here, but you just need to... Just give me time."

I let out a quiet sigh, but nodded. "Okay. I'll try, but I can't promise to be very patient. I want to spend time with you, Park. And as much as I enjoy it, I don't just mean when we're alone in your bedroom. I want to take you out, and I want everyone to know that you're mine. And that includes bitchy roommates for as long as they're living with my Parker."

I saw her shaky smile and gave her hand a tight squeeze as she breathed, "Okay. I'll figure it out quick. I just... I can't tonight."

"That's fine. For now, I'll take whatever you're willing to give me." I grinned but kept my eyes focused on the road. The last five minutes we spent in silence, and I was beginning to love the way that we could just sit and... be. Like nothing mattered in the world, and all we needed to feel okay was to sit and hold onto each other's hands.

I picked her up after she finished at work, which led to another fantastic forty-five minutes that I spent driving her to her car, and then convincing her to make out with me. She did, and things quickly got hot and heavy, too hot and way too heavy, until I finally had to force her out of the truck in order to quickly drive home. Once there, I took a long shower and made myself come, once again, to the image of Parker's face in my mind.

Still, besides those few minutes in my truck, I hadn't spent any time with her. Saturday night she told me she was just going to crash early, and after work on Sunday she told me she had homework and that she would just see me tomorrow.

I knew that we talked, and things were supposed to be good now, but I'm wasn't gonna lie - pulling open the door to walk into class, knowing that I was about to see her, I felt a tiny flash of fear. I'd started to crave this girl's presence like a drug, but every time we spent a few days apart, she threw up more walls - barriers designed to keep me out.

I was terrified to see her still pushing me away.

So, to say the least, it was a huge fucking relief when I pointed my eyes to the back of the room and they immediately found hers. Not a second later, her face broke into a wide smile.

My heart literally stopped for a second. She looked so happy that I had no control over the grin that surfaced. She watched me as I got closer, and her eyes moved down over my body. By the look on her face, I knew she liked what she saw. When her eyes came back to mine, they had a mischievous glint, but she stayed silent as I dropped into the seat next to her.

"Well, someone seems happy this morning," I said, taking the time to pull my shit out of my bag before turning to take her in. She looked absolutely beautiful, but then, she always did. Today her hair was pulled to the side in a messy braid, and she was wearing jeans and a long-sleeved green shirt that made her eyes look brighter than normal. Parker had the most natural beauty I've ever seen before – it was completely effortless - like she couldn't care less what you thought of her - but she still managed to take my breath away every time I saw her.

"Eh," she responded with a shrug, "I had a pretty great weekend. Nice jeans, by the way."

I couldn't help it - I laughed. I knew she had noticed, but I was so glad she pointed it out.

"Do you want the truth?" I asked her, leaning close to her ear. I watched a slight shiver race down her spine, but she played along, stretching towards me to hear. "I was scared. I thought you were going to try to blow me off again, so I wore these as a back-up plan."

I watched as her smile faded a bit, but she turned to meet my eyes. We were suddenly way too close, and I had to fight the urge to press my mouth against hers. Probably not a great idea, considering our current surroundings.

"Well, they would have worked, if I was going to keep running. But, for now, I'm trying out a new way of dealing with things. I think it might be time for me to start letting people in."

"People?" I asked quietly.

She shrugged, her eyes dropping to my mouth for a moment before moving back up. "You."

I wanted to kiss her.

I really, *really* wanted to kiss her.

So, it's probably a good thing that at that precise moment the professor walked in, and we both leaned back.

Yeah, it's probably a really good thing because in that moment, knowing that she wanted to be with me and she was going to try to let me in, I wanted to kiss her in a way that meant I wouldn't be able to stop.

Chapter Twenty-Three

Parker

BY THE END OF THE week, I was expecting to wake up from what was quickly becoming the best dream that I'd ever had.

Ash was incredible. He texted me every day to say good morning. He texted me throughout the day to tell me he was thinking of me, or just to tell me what he was doing, and we talked on the phone almost every night. He told me about growing up with his parents and his sister, which, I will admit, made me a little bit jealous, but mostly just made me happy that he grew up in a loving household. I knew he and his dad butted heads a lot, but I also knew that they all loved each other and I was so glad that he knew he had people who loved him in his life.

I told him how much I had always wanted a sibling and about growing up with Jessie. He asked about my mom, and while I didn't lie, I did skirt around the truth. I knew that he knew I wasn't really being honest, and I knew it bothered him, but I think he understood that I wasn't ready. At least, I *hoped* that he understood.

It wasn't just Ash that had me waiting for the other foot to drop. Things at the apartment had been better than usual. When I got home from class Friday, I spent a few minutes talking to Diane. She really was the sweetest woman and she made me laugh. She had told me last week that she had been looking to fix me up with her grandson, but she'd just found out that he had a girlfriend. I had laughed but politely told her, even if he was single, I wasn't interested. Still, it had become a bit of a joke between us, as odd as that might seem.

Once I sent Diane home and checked in on Mom, who was napping in bed, I went to my room and turned on some music. I had a paper to write for Monday, and I decided to get a jump on it.

The next thing I knew it was four o'clock. I heard Mom moving around in the kitchen, so I left my papers on my bed and walked out of my room, where I saw her grabbing a bottle of water from the fridge.

"Hey, Ma," I called, walking over to her. She glanced up at me and gave a disinterested nod in my direction. I ignored it and went to the fridge, trying to plan out what I felt like making for dinner. I found some defrosted chicken in the fridge, along with everything else I needed for Chicken Alfredo, so I set about getting things together in the kitchen as Mom settled onto the couch and turned on the TV.

I was getting ready to start making the sauce when I heard my phone ringing from my room. I ran to grab it, knowing it had to be Ash.

"Hey," I answered somewhat breathlessly as I flipped the phone open.

"Hey, beautiful. Everything okay?" God, I loved it when he called me beautiful.

"Yeah, all good here. I was in the other room getting dinner together when I heard the phone ringing."

"Gotcha. I called to see if I could get you to come out to dinner with me, but if you're cooking, I'm hoping that you're about to invite me over to have dinner there..."

I winced, suddenly wanting nothing more than Ash sitting down to eat a meal that I had made. I found myself wishing, not for the first time, that I lived a different life.

"I can't tonight."

"Why?" His voice was guarded, and I hated it.

I tried to come up with something that wouldn't sound totally bitchy, and when I couldn't bring myself to outright lie, I decided to tell him a backwards form of the truth.

"I'm having dinner with my mom."

"Okay..." he replied in a voice that made it sound like it really wasn't. "Am I the only one who's actually a part of this relationship?"

I sucked in a breath that hurt my chest and my ass landed on my bed. "N- No. Why..." I couldn't finish the thought.

Ash softened his voice when he spoke again. "Baby, I've figured out by now that your home life wasn't great growing up. I get it if things are weird with your mom, but I'm assuming, if you're having dinner with her that she's going to be a part of your life for the foreseeable future, and right now, I'm hoping like fuck that that future involves me. So it stands to reason that I'm going to have to meet your mom at some point. Now I can understand if you're nervous to introduce me to her so soon, I get that. I just thought... Christ, I've barely seen you in six days."

I could hear the frustration in his voice, and I knew exactly how he felt because I felt it, too. It had been almost painful to sit next to him in class this week - I hated being so close without being able to touch him.

"I know…" I told him. "And I'm sorry. I just, I haven't really told my mom about you yet, so I just, I can't tonight. I want to… more than you know. But I can't." I tried to convey through my words how sorry I was, I just hoped that he heard it.

He didn't give me a clue when he let out a tired sigh. "You need to let me in, Park."

"Trust me, Ash, you're more 'in' than anyone else I've ever known."

"I know, baby, but honestly, that just worries me more. I know you're afraid, but whatever it is, you can tell me. Your secrets are safe with me, Parker."

I dragged in a shaky breath at that. I wanted to believe him, more than anything. I wanted to give him everything, I wanted to let him take it, even if it was just for a little while.

But I had no fucking clue how.

"I want you to come to dinner at my parent's house on Sunday," he announced suddenly.

"I, uh…"

"Seriously, Park," he spoke up, and his voice was low and serious, "this is important to me. My grandma will be there, and my parents. And, I need to see you this weekend."

Crap. I couldn't say no, but I had no idea what to do about Mom.

"I have work on Sunday…" I told him slowly.

"We can wait until you get off. Aren't you done at five, usually? We never eat until six anyway."

I figured he'd say that.

"I, uh, can I let you know tomorrow? I want to, I really do, I just need to check a few things first."

Ash was quiet for a minute before he let out a slow breath. "Sure, Parker. Tell me tomorrow."

I tried to say thank you but he had already hung up.

Well, shit.

I absolutely hated hurting Ash, and I knew that I had just done exactly that. So, I decided that there was no way I was going to miss dinner. At this point, I was running the risk of losing him altogether and that thought absolutely terrified me. I wasn't ready to give him up, and I wasn't going to throw him away by bailing on family dinner.

So, I was just going to have to find a way to figure my shit out.

Chapter Twenty-Four

Ash

I WAS STILL FRUSTRATED WHEN I woke up Saturday morning. I knew I was kind of being an ass, but it hurt when Parker told me that she wasn't ready to introduce me to her mom yet. Our relationship may still have been new, but we talked almost all day, every day, and spent hours on the phone each night. I was learning loads of little things about her, but almost every time I brought up her childhood, or her family, she avoided my questions. It both annoyed and terrified the shit out of me.

The problem was that I was quickly moving towards being completely in love with her. And the fact that she was still trying to keep me out made me worry that she didn't feel the same. I just didn't understand what she was so afraid to tell me. I knew she was keeping something huge a secret, and I grew more and more unnerved by it every day.

After texting her **Good Morning,** I hopped into the shower. Once I was done, I threw on a pair of khaki pants and a white tee before grabbing my keys and heading out the door.

I drove to the university hospital and found a place to park a few blocks from the main entrance. The day was bright and sunny, but it did nothing to lighten the unease and frustration I felt every time I thought of Parker. I forced the depressing thoughts from my head in order to focus of what I needed to do as I walked into the spacious and brightly-lit lobby.

I found my way pretty easily, navigating towards an office area separated from the main entrance by a long hallway. I finally found the office I was looking for and knocked on the closed door. After I heard a familiar voice yell for me to walk in, I opened the door.

At the desk was a heavyset woman who looked to be in her early fifties. She was wearing a bright purple dress and she smiled at me as I entered.

"You must be Ashton," she said as she stood from the desk and walked towards me with her hand outstretched. I took it and gave it a quick shake.

"Yeah, I'm Ash. Nice to meet you, Mrs. Paulson."

"Call me Nancy," she said, smiling. "Take a seat and give me just a sec, and then I'll give you a tour, okay?"

I nodded and looked around the office. I had spoken to Nancy twice before: once when she called to return my initial call and discuss the requirements of my community service, and a second time when she called to ask me to start today. Both times we had chatted a bit, so I had been prepared for her friendly demeanor. She knew a little about my plans for the future - namely that I was headed towards med school - and she had seemed excited to bring me on, even knowing that I was fulfilling a court order. It surprised me, but I wasn't about to complain.

Nancy sat at her desk shuffling through some paperwork before she finally found whatever she was looking for and then grabbed a pen. After making a few notes on the paper, she looked up and smiled.

"Right, so before we take a walk, I just want to talk for a minute and explain my thoughts for your time with us."

"Sounds good," I told her with a nod.

"I know that you're interested in a career in medicine, and I gather that you're a bit confused about the specifics of that future. The hospital, of course, has groups of volunteers who come in to help with patient morale and other odd jobs, but I had another idea in mind for you.

"I've spoken to the heads of just about every department, and everyone has agreed that they could use a hand with certain... odd jobs here and there. This way, you'll be meeting your requirements but also getting to see a bit of what goes on in each different area of the hospital."

I had no idea what to say. This was the last thing I had expected when I got out of bed this morning.

"Can I ask why? I'm not saying that I don't really appreciate that, but I'm just curious." I kept my voice quiet. I was almost nervous to even voice the question, but a part of me was dying to know why Nancy would be doing this for me.

"I have a few reasons," she told me, looking down to the papers on her desk again. "Mostly, I just want to make this as worthwhile as I can for all involved parties. From what I've heard, you're a smart, determined kid. I figure it'd be a waste to not put you to good use."

I wasn't entirely sure what that meant, but I found myself nodding all the same. Nancy smiled, and then pushed herself out of her chair.

"Alright, well, let's show you around then!"

After Nancy gave me a tour of pretty much the entire hospital, making tons of introductions that I knew meant nothing and would fly from my mind as soon as I left each room, she sent me straight to the radiology department. Apparently, they had "claimed" me first. When I got there, I met two techs, a guy who looked to be around my age named Chris, and a woman named Silvie. I guessed that she was about ten years older than me, although she wasted no time in sending the message that that didn't bother her a bit when it came to sex. She did this by gluing herself to my side, finding every opportunity she could to put her hands on me, and suggesting multiple times that we should get together for drinks sometime. I made a point to avoid her hands and discouraged her as much as possible without straight up telling her to back off, even speaking loudly to Chris while she was in earshot about my beautiful, amazing girlfriend who was meeting my parents tomorrow in the hopes that she would get the message. She didn't.

Talking about dinner made me worry about Parker again, and then worry about what I would do if she decided to blow off meeting my family. I didn't think it would be pretty. I pushed those thoughts to the back of my head and spent four hours doing random shit to help get the office space in radiology into better shape. It was currently a mess of paperwork and various equipment. By the time shift changes came around, I had made a good dent in my task.

Nancy called down and told me to head home, and I left the hospital feeling good about what I had gotten done, as well as about the time I would spend there in the future.

I shot Parker a quick text as I walked to my truck and told her to call me when she left work. I needed to know what the plan for tomorrow was... Preferably before I went crazy thinking about it.

When I got home, I spent time trying to get some work done for school, but I couldn't stay focused. I checked my phone every five minutes, hoping to see a text message, but it stayed menacingly silent. Finally, I left my school shit on the table and grabbed my guitar, a vintage Gibson Hummingbird, from the stand in my bedroom and took it out to the couch. I tuned the strings, and then I was ready to lose myself.

When Rory and I were younger, Mom had forced us both to learn an instrument on top of participating in some sort of athletic activity. Rory started playing piano and took dance lessons, while I took up the guitar and joined the hockey team. Rory eventually lost interest in dance, even though she was great at that too. She just absolutely loved making music and she knew that that was what she wanted to do with her life.

I loved music too, but I wanted nothing to do with that life. I didn't want to write music, I just loved it, either listening to a recording or playing my guitar. It was something that had always grounded me. Where hockey amped me up, playing guitar centered me, and right now I could use a bit of that.

I started by moving my fingers around the frets, just mindlessly picking at the strings. Then a few chords started to string themselves together and before I knew it I was playing one of my favorite Ray Lamontagne songs. I sang the words quietly, and I knew in the back of my head that the lyrics, which were a soft plea from the singer to the woman he loved, asking her to let him be the one she leaned on, were my quiet prayer to Parker, one that she would never hear.

I played until my fingertips ached, only putting the guitar down when I heard my phone start to ring where I had left it on the table. I picked it up and I saw her name on the screen. The nerves that I had been trying to play out all came rushing back with full force. I hit the screen to answer and reminded myself to play it cool as I held the phone to my ear.

"Hey." *Good, that was cool.*

"Hey," was her quiet response, and I knew she was nervous about where things stood between us after last night. Maybe cool wasn't the way to play this.

"Please tell me that you're coming to dinner tomorrow?" I asked quickly, rushing over the words to force them out.

It was quiet for a moment and I heard her draw in breath. "Ash, I would love to come to dinner and meet your family tomorrow night."

The air rushed out of my lungs on a silent wheeze and I had to sit down at the wave of relief I felt blast through me.

"Thank God," I whispered, and I heard her quiet laughter through the phone. I decided to change the subject immediately, I didn't want to jinx it. "How was work, baby?"

"It was okay. I was distracted, thinking about my super-hot boyfriend."

"Oh yeah?" I asked with a smile. "Does he distract you a lot?"

"Well, yeah, I mean, I pretty much think about him all the time, but today was worse. I was worried all day. I kinda thought that he was mad at me…"

"Not mad. Just afraid," I told her honestly. "Parker, I'm crazy about you. And I know that this has all moved kinda fast, but honest to God, it feels so right to me that I don't want to fight it. I was just worried, when you *did* want to fight it, that you might feel differently."

She was quiet for a moment before she whispered, "I'm kind of crazy about you too, Ash."

I smiled, and all my fear from the day was an ancient memory. It was insane to think about the amount of power that this girl had over me, but like I had just told Parker, I wasn't about to fight it.

"You driving home?" I asked.

"Yeah, almost there now."

"Alright, well, text me when you get there safe."

"I will. Talk to you soon."

I heard her disconnect and dropped my phone back on the table, still wearing my goofy grin. For the rest of the night, all I had to do was replay her words in my ear and the smile came back. *I'm kind of crazy about you too, Ash.*

I didn't let myself worry about dinner the next night, or school, or any of the thousand other things that usually stressed me out on a daily basis. Through the rest of the night the only thing I let myself focus on was the fact that I was taking a girl home for what was the first - and hopefully, last - time. And, even knowing I was headed back inside those walls, that night, I slept deep. And, of course, I dreamt of Parker.

Chapter Twenty-Five

Parker

So, NEEDLESS TO SAY, I pretty much started freaking out the moment I got off the phone with Ash on Saturday. I had talked to Charles and asked him to stay late Sunday night, totally lying and telling him that they had asked me to work extra hours and I couldn't turn down the money. I felt really shitty about lying so that I could go to dinner at my boyfriend's parents' house, but I had needed a solution, and it had seemed like the easiest one at the time. Part of me was almost hoping that he'd tell me he was busy as part of my karmic punishment, but he seemed more than happy to lend an extra helping hand when I asked, and it really just made me feel like crap.

I packed clothes into a backpack that I took with me to work, and got changed in the bathroom at the diner after I clocked out. At home, I had decided on a knee length, kind of flowy black skirt. I topped it with a green shirt that was both cute and presentable without making me look like I was trying too hard. I wore a pair of black flats and braided my hair to one side, which helped cover up the fact that I had just worked eight hours in a diner.

Ash had texted me his address and told me to head there after work so that he could take us to dinner and I panicked for the entire drive, for a few reasons. One, I wasn't convinced that my outfit was right. If I'd have been able to go home after work, I probably would have ended up changing my mind about four times, and since I hadn't been able to do that, I was worried. Two, I hadn't been to Ash's apartment yet. I mean, I know it wasn't like he was asking me to move in, but I still felt weird about the fact that I was going to see the place where he lived for the first time. I know, I know, I'm totally weird, but these were the types of things that made me panic. Reason three, which was last but *definitely* not least, I had completely convinced myself that his family was going to totally hate me.

I had never really known any real *adults*, at least on a personal level. I knew that Jessie's parents cared about me, but they didn't really know me, and it wasn't like I was there to spend time with them. Jessie and I had always spent our time either out of the house or in her bedroom. The only adults I had ever really interacted with, besides my mom, were teachers, so I wasn't really sure how I was supposed to act around Ash's parents.

Ash put all of my fears to rest pretty quickly once I got to his place. I parked my car and headed towards the building, but I was still making my way along the main path when he walked out the front door with a wide smile on his face. My lips turned up automatically as he moved straight for me, wrapping his arms around my waist when he got close and then plastering our bodies together in the tightest hug I had ever received. I took a moment to focus on how absolutely *incredible* he felt pressed to me, and then I was distracted by his mouth at my temple, where he pressed a soft kiss into my skin before tilting his head to whisper into my ear.

"I missed you."

I took a deep breath with my face against his chest and my hands gripping his t-shirt-covered sides and I just soaked him in, feeling a large chunk of my panic melt away as his warmth worked its way inside my body.

"I missed you, too," I told him quietly, leaning back to look in his eyes as he loosened his arms. He pressed a quick kiss into my lips before stepping back and trailing his eyes down to my shoes before slowly moving them back up again.

"You look fucking gorgeous, as usual," he told me with a grin that lit me up in places I didn't want to even think about while I sat with his parents in his childhood home. "Now, come on. I'm ready to go show you off, even if it's only to Grandma."

There you go. Fears one and two, swiftly taken care of. I smiled, in a total daze as he grabbed my hand and pulled me to his truck, pausing when we got to the door for another quick kiss before helping me get situated on the passenger seat. Once he'd buckled me in, he quickly walked around to the driver's side and then we were on our way.

The ride was way too short, but Ash held my hand the entire time, rubbing his thumb lightly along my knuckles in a way that slowly relaxed me. On the drive, he assured me that his family would love me, and he told me over and over again not to worry. I still worried, but I appreciated the fact that he knew I was stressing and tried to make it better.

When we pulled up out front of a white colonial-style house that looked a bit like where Jessie had grown up, I found myself relaxing a bit more. Just seeing the place where Ash grew up, looking so much like a normal, family home, I again caught myself feeling weirdly grateful that he had had this as a child – a safe place filled with people who loved him.

Ash held my hand as we walked to the door, and I was only a little surprised when he didn't knock. He just pushed the unlocked door open and pulled me inside behind him.

"Hey, guys!" he shouted. He led me into the foyer and down a hallway towards what I could tell was a kitchen. I heard a few quiet voices and then, "We're in the den," shouted by a female voice. As we got into and through the kitchen, Ash led me further into the house and towards a small flight of stairs.

"Hey, everybody, this is Parker," Ash began as he pulled me behind him down the stairs, blocking my view of the room as he introduced me. "Parker, this is my mom, dad, and Grandma." Ash finally stepped aside and I got a chance to take in his parents. The older Mr. Carter was attractive, and I could see a lot of him in Ash. They had the same dark, thick hair and strong, angled jaw. Sitting next to him was a gorgeous woman who was smiling warmly at me, and even if I hadn't known who she was, the smile would have been a dead giveaway. I started to tell them hello but was interrupted by a voice that I knew. I just couldn't figure out why I was hearing it.

"Eileen?" I heard Diane ask, and my eyes quickly moved around the room, right to an easy chair that sat caddy-corner from the sofa. She was wearing a small smile as she looked from me to Ash and then back again, and then she let out a laugh. "Oh my goodness, this is just way too good. What does he call you?" she asked me, and I couldn't find my voice.

"What..." Ash began, staring at his grandmother before turning to face me. "Eileen?" he asked me quietly, almost as if he was asking me to contradict her. I took a quick breath to steel myself, and then let it out slowly as I nodded.

"Yeah, Eileen Parker. Eileen *Elizabeth* Parker."

His face was completely blank, and I hadn't the slightest clue as to what he was thinking, but I also knew that his entire family was watching us with blatant curiosity, so instead of trying to deal with him, I looked to Diane.

"Please, call me Parker. My mom is literally the only person, well, besides you, that is, who calls me Eileen." I took in Ash's parents as I spoke, and they both wore identical confused expressions, but Diane's expression soured a bit as my words sunk in and she gave me a small nod before her smile faded.

"All right, Parker," Ash's dad finally spoke after a short but very awkward silence, "Well, it's nice to meet you. We've heard a lot about you."

"Thanks, Mr. Carter," I told him with a genuine smile. "It's nice to meet you too."

"Please, call me Paul. And this is Eliza," he told me, gesturing to his wife.

I smiled and Ash led me to the unoccupied love seat that was sitting across from the armchair. He sat and, still holding my hand, pulled me down to sit next to him. It was a tight fit, and my side was pressed against his in a way that made my heart race and my skin feel tight. But he was way too still, and if he hadn't been holding my hand, I would have been positive that he was angry. Which made me wonder if Diane had mentioned me to him before, and if so, what he possibly knew.

I knew the answer to that, and it absolutely, one hundred percent, scared the shit out of me.

Thankfully, Diane kept mostly quiet as Eliza started to ask me about school, and what I was working towards. I felt a little embarrassed to admit that I didn't really know what I wanted to do, but they seemed to think that was fine. We continued to talk, and I found myself slipping into the easy conversation quickly. I asked them what they did, and Paul told me that he worked for a tech development company. When I asked what they developed, he gave me a strange smile and told me, "If I told you, I'd have to kill you." I decided to let the topic go.

Thankfully, Eliza jumped into the conversation and told me about her work with a non-profit company she had founded with a few friends back in college, which was now apparently one of the largest companies in the US providing assistance to all kinds of people with mental and behavioral health issues. I was pretty blown away, and we talked for a bit about the reasons that she had gotten involved in the work in the first place.

"Growing up, I saw a lot of people in my life end up self-medicating because they couldn't fix the problems in their head, and even with programs like NA or AA, most of the time, if you don't fix the problem that caused the destructive behavior, you're never going to stop that behavior. I wanted to find a way to help, and I'm just glad that I can say that I've made a difference."

Her words made my chest grow tight and before I knew it, I was squeezing Ash's hand so hard that *my* fingers hurt. His hand gave a small jerk and I dropped it quickly, trying to calm my racing heartbeat. I knew that they didn't know, that they *couldn't* know what my mom was like but I still felt the heat of embarrassment flood my face. I dropped my eyes to my lap and took a deep breath, clearing my throat before I said, "That sounds really fantastic. I'm glad that you've made a difference, too."

My voice sounded high and strained and I could feel Ash's eyes burning a hole in the side of my head but I refused to look at him. Instead, I focused on Diane as I asked, "Could you please show me where the bathroom is?"

She glanced at Ash and frowned a bit before looking back to me. "Sure, sweetheart. Come on." She rose out of her chair and I moved to follow, but as I stood, Ash wrapped his fingers around my wrist, not enough to hurt, just enough to stop me and get my attention. When I finally risked bringing my eyes to his, I saw the questions shining there. I quickly focused on his mouth as I whispered, "I'll be right back." I pulled against his hand and, despite his obvious hesitancy, he let me go without a word. I shot his parents a weak smile before racing towards the stairs to follow Diane. She led me to a small powder room down the hall, and I smiled at her as she flipped on the light.

"Thank you," I told her.

She stared at me for a moment, then nodded towards the door. "Go ahead, sweetie. Rein it in. But later, you need to talk to my boy. He doesn't know anything, does he?"

I hiccuped as a sob tried to force its way from my throat. I looked to the floor before I shook my head, and I felt her hand come to my cheek, gently pulling my gaze back to hers.

"Sweetheart, I've been praying a long time for God to send someone to take care of you, and I told you myself that I wanted it to be Ashton. That boy is absolutely crazy about you, and, you give him this… If you let him take that pain from you, I promise he will not make you regret it."

I couldn't take anymore, so I nodded quickly and rushed through the door, closing and locking it behind me. Thankfully, when I had my breakdown, the sobs were silent.

Chapter Twenty-Six

Ash

I COULD NOT FUCKING BELIEVE it.

I couldn't believe that Parker was the girl that Grandma had told me about. Which meant Parker's mom was sick. Like, really sick. Suddenly, things started making sense - the mysterious roommate and the fact that she never left her house. But, I had no fucking clue why she would try to hide something like this from me.

Then, when she practically broke my hand in half in the den while my mom talked about her work - I mean, what the actual fuck was that?

I was confused and angry and hurt, and when she asked Grandma to take her to the bathroom, I didn't want to let her out of my sight. I was terrified that if I let her go now, I would lose her forever. I was about to chase after her when Mom looked at me with an expression that broke my heart and asked, "What did I say?"

It killed me to say it, but I had to tell her the truth. "Honestly, I have no idea…"

Dad gave me an odd look and I got up from my seat as Grandma walked back down the steps.

"I think we need to go get dinner on the table. Come on, guys. Lets relocate this party to the kitchen." I started to walk past her, but she grabbed my arm and whispered, "Give her a minute, darlin'. She's not going anywhere."

My jaw grew tight but I nodded and headed towards the kitchen to help set the table.

Parker emerged from the bathroom ten excruciating minutes later. My eyes snapped to her as she walked into the kitchen and headed straight to me. I took in the sight of her slightly puffy eyes and the red rings that hadn't been there before and I pulled her into a tight hug. I almost expected her to resist, but she didn't. She completely melted against me and I tried to let her feel the emotion swamping me through the embrace. I needed her to know what she was to me, and that I wasn't going anywhere.

I finally felt her let out a sigh and she pulled back against my arms. I reluctantly let her go and she looked up and gave me a weak smile before looking behind me to where Mom and Grandma were piling food onto the table.

"Sorry about that, everyone, I, uh..." She clearly had no idea how to explain whatever had just happened, but my mom decided to let her off the hook.

"Don't worry about it, sweetie," she said, shooting Parker a smile. "Dinner's ready, guys, why don't you take a seat?"

Parker nodded and I grabbed her hand and led her to a chair at the table. Once she was seated, I gave her shoulders a light squeeze and then sat down next to her.

With everyone around the table, we all dug in pretty quickly. Mom had made pot roast, which was delicious, and the conversation, thankfully, flowed easily. Grandma was quieter than usual, and I could tell that she was watching both Parker and I closely, but we both managed to relax after the evening's rocky start, and I actually found myself enjoying the night.

After dinner, Mom pulled out an apple cake and we all ate dessert. Parker raved about the cake, which made Mom smile brightly. I thought it was cute, and I couldn't stop myself from leaning over and planting a quick kiss on her cheek, which made her blush and smile at me.

I was so wrapped up in her, I didn't see my dad reach for his water, taking a sip before clearing his throat.

"Parker, I just have to say," he began, and my eyes shot to him, but he was totally focused on the girl next to me, "thank you. After the past two years, I was worried Ashton would never get over what happened. And I really never thought I'd see him smile in this house again."

I was frozen completely still with my eyes locked on my father. He didn't notice, and I began desperately hoping he would shut his mouth before I had to do something about it. And then, he continued speaking.

"You know, the day he was released from house arrest-"

"Dad!" I said forcefully, and he finally shut his mouth and looked at me. His face paled a bit and I saw the apology that he was afraid to voice in his eyes.

Parker had gone totally solid next to me, but as the room fell silent she looked up and met my father's eyes.

"Please don't thank me. Ash is a pretty incredible guy, and there's not much that I think he couldn't do, if he put his mind to it. Don't give me the credit."

Her eyes dropped to her plate as I watched her shoulders slump, and I decided that it was definitely time that we got out of there. I needed to deal with this situation, and I needed to do it now.

"Park, you ready to go?" I asked her quietly, and she nodded without meeting my eyes. I stood and everyone else rose with me.

"Thank you so much for having me tonight," I heard her quietly say to my mom. Mom pulled her into a hug before leaning back and squeezing her arms gently.

"Thank you for coming. You're welcome anytime, Parker."

"It was great meeting you guys," she told the room at large, shooting everyone a weak smile.

Grandma walked from where she was standing by her chair and wrapped her arms around Parker. I could tell that she was surprised at first, but she quickly returned the embrace. I saw Grandma whisper something that I couldn't hear, and when they pulled away and I saw the tears shining in Parker's eyes, I wanted to know what had been said. Instead of asking, I leaned down to kiss Mom and then Grandma before grabbing Parker's hand tightly in mine. I shouted a quick goodbye and then we were moving out the door.

She was silent as I led her to the truck and helped her climb up. I walked around and climbed into the cab, starting the engine before leaning back in the seat to take her in. I watched her stare at the dashboard for a few seconds before she finally spoke.

"Ash, I need to get home."

My chest hurt at the sound of her voice. It was flat and lifeless, and I realized I had no idea what had happened in there, but I was sure as fuck going to find out.

"We need to talk first."

"Please just take me to my car."

"No, Park. You need to decide right now. We can sit here for the next hour and you can tell me what happened in there, and then you can tell me all the other shit you've been keeping from me, or we can drive to my place and talk there. I'm giving you the choice now, but I promise you, if you say you want to talk at my place, and when we get there you try to take off and shut me out, I'm really not gonna be happy."

She let out a sigh and looked out the window. I followed her gaze and saw the curtain in the front room moving.

"Fuck it, I'm not doing this sitting here. We're going to my place."

That said, I shut my mouth and put the truck in drive.

Chapter Twenty-Seven

Parker

FOR THE FIRST TIME IN my life, a life that had included being carted around in an automobile by my drunk and high mother, I was seriously considering jumping from a moving vehicle.

The problem with my plan was that my car was still parked out front of his house, so I knew he'd just be waiting for me when I finally showed up to collect it.

I didn't want to talk. I didn't want to deal with the fact that dinner really, probably couldn't have gone worse. I didn't want Ash to ask about my mother. Mostly, I didn't want to try to explain that I was quite possibly the worst daughter in the world, and that I couldn't get over the past in order to take care of a terminally ill parent, who happened to be the only one I had.

On top of my anxiety about the "Mom conversation," I was constantly reminding myself that I couldn't even get mad that I had to hear from his dad that he had apparently been on house arrest. I wanted to scream at him that he was pressuring me to give him all of me when he was still holding back, but I knew that wasn't fair. That wasn't the way relationships worked, and as much as I hated it, I kept my mouth shut.

The drive was agonizing, and I was almost glad when we pulled up to his building. I froze when he turned off the truck and climbed out. When he opened my door, I took his hand and let him lead me towards the spot where I had met him just a little while before. He tugged me to the front door and then led me to a stairwell. We walked up one floor and then down a long, dimly lit hallway before he used his keys to let us into his apartment.

Despite my earlier fear about seeing this space, I didn't even let myself look around to take in his domain. I heard Ash's keys hit a table that was just inside the door and then he pulled me across the floor before settling us both down onto a soft blue couch. I was a little startled when he pulled me into his lap, and I stiffened as he wrapped his arms around me, but within seconds I relaxed into him. He made me feel safe, and while I still didn't really know what to do with that sensation, I absolutely loved it.

Ash pushed his face into my neck and I felt his lips press a soft kiss into my skin. Then I felt him blow out a burst of air as he shook his head against my shoulder.

"I gotta say it, baby: I'm kind of upset that I didn't even know your first name."

I was really glad that we were starting there. That was definitely the easiest thing to talk about.

"I meant what I said," I told him quietly. "No one calls me that but my mom. I hate the name. My dad did too, from what I remember. He refused to use it. He called me Lizzie Girl."

"Why do you hate it?"

"It was my mom's mom's name, and my mom picked it hoping that her parents would let us back into the family fold, I guess, but it didn't work. That being said, I just hate the name, always have, and I started telling people that my name was Parker in kindergarten, right after my dad left, actually. I don't use it, like, at all."

I felt him nod and then his arms unwrapped me. I thought he was going to let me move, but his hands landed on my hips and he turned me so that I was seated half on him and half on the couch, with my legs draped over his. One of his hands moved up to my neck and he wove his fingers softly into my braid right at the nape of my neck. This forced my eyes up to his face, and as much as I wanted to break away, I held his gaze.

"Why didn't you tell me about your mom?" His voice was low but steady, and I had to force myself to keep breathing.

"It's not..." I started and then stopped, trying to come up with some explanation that would make sense to him, but nothing was making sense to me at the moment, so I couldn't figure out how to pull that off. "It's hard to explain..."

"I can see that, baby. I'm just asking you to try."

"My mom... I told you, we have a weird relationship. It can get a little tense between us sometimes, and I really just don't like talking about it."

"But, Parker, you're nineteen years old and trying to take care of your dying mother, completely on your own while you also go to school and work part time. That is your life, and considering that she takes up a big part of that life, and seeing as I'm hoping to also become a big part of that life, I cannot, for the life of me, figure out why you wouldn't just tell me what was going on. I can't even imagine how hard this all must be for you. I mean, I think I'd understand. I get pissed at my dad, but if he was dying I'd be fucking devastated. I know you've been doing this alone, but you don't have to anymore."

I wanted to scream and cry and tell him that that was exactly it, he didn't understand. I had wished for years for this to happen, and both my mother and I deserved everything that we were going through. But how could I possibly ever tell him that? He would know that I am the worst kind of person, and if he was smart, and I knew that he was, he'd want absolutely nothing to do with me.

I felt my heart begin to crack as he guided my head to rest on his shoulder, and I felt his hand start to move up and down my leg, gently and reassuringly. For the first time though, his touch didn't soothe me. I was angry, and I hated it, but I wanted to take a little bit of that anger out on him.

"Can we talk about something else for a second?" I asked suddenly, pushing up with a hand on his chest to meet his eyes.

"Okay," he answered in a way that, paired with his guarded expression, I knew meant he was bracing.

"How about we talk about house arrest?" I suggested in a way that it wasn't really a suggestion.

"Right," he replied, "I was waiting for this. I know you probably feel a little pissed because I'm sure you think that I tried to hide this from you, even though that's not remotely the case. You know, if you had actually asked sometime in the past few weeks why I was 22 and still two years shy of graduation, I would have told you in a heartbeat. You deserve to know, and I want you to know exactly why and how I fucked up my life. But right now, fuck that. I'm sorry, Parker, but the fact that you're still sitting here holding back from me means that you don't trust me, which means the chances of us making this work in the long run are growing slimmer by the day. I'll gladly give you all my secrets the day you give me yours. Until then, I can't do it."

The crack that had formed in my heart grew a little wider, but I only nodded. He was right, completely right and I knew I had to let it go. We were quiet for a few minutes and I frantically tried to figure out a way to make this better, but the only thing I could think of that would help was the one thing that I just couldn't do. I couldn't force my mouth to say the things that he wanted to hear.

"Parker," he finally said quietly, "I'm going to keep pushing this. I'm not ready to give up on you yet. But you need to find a way to work this shit in your brain out. I want to help you, but if you're not willing to accept that help, then that's on you. Regardless, you still need to figure it out."

I nodded and then, before he could stretch that crack in my heart any further, I untangled myself from his arms. I needed to get out, and I needed to do it now.

I knew it wasn't the right thing to do, but without another word I walked away from Ash, through the door and out of the building. Without looking back, I climbed into my car and headed for home.

Chapter Twenty-Eight

Ash

I SLEPT LIKE SHIT, BUT still dragged my ass out of bed Monday morning to get to Philosophy on time, just on the off chance that she showed up. I really wasn't all that surprised when she didn't.

I didn't pay attention to a word that was said in any of my classes. All I could think about was the way that Parker had walked out of my place without even a word the night before. All night I had wanted to text her, but I refused, stubbornly deciding that she needed to be the one to reach out to me this time. I thought about going to Marco's between classes, but decided against it. I felt too shitty to even deal with him. Instead, I sat on a bench outside the Bio building and got lost in watching the people passing me by. For three hours.

By the time I was done at school, I was seriously considering calling out of work, but I decided that at the very least I could use the distraction. I blared Chiodos as I drove, the volume up as loud as it would go, in an attempt to block out the shit swirling around in my head. It didn't help.

When I pulled into work ten minutes early, I seriously tried to convince myself that calling Parker would be a good idea. Even I couldn't pull that off, and I ended up leaving my phone in the center console, just in case my resolve weakened while I was sitting in the rink.

After I got changed, I clocked in and waved to Chris, who was sitting in the office.

"Hey, kid," he said, but I avoided his eyes and just headed to the deployment on the wall. I was in the rental booth, so I walked straight there.

I relieved Evan, a thirty-something guy who worked days, and he thanked me before shuffling off to head home. Half an hour later, Jimmy walked into the booth and sat down on the stool next to mine.

"Hey," he said quietly. "How you been, man?"

I hadn't talked to Jimmy since Marco's party, and sitting there, I realized that I was still kind of pissed about the way he had acted towards Parker.

"Fine. You?" I asked.

He shrugged. "How are things with your girl?"

"Why are you even asking? It didn't seem like you gave a shit the other night."

"Sorry, man, I've just been dealing with some shit, and…"

"Honestly, I'm sorry, but I don't really give a fuck." At my outburst, Jimmy turned his surprised face my way before narrowing his eyes at me.

"What the hell crawled up your ass?"

I tried to rein it in but I was angry and hurt and I needed to lash out.

"You, motherfucker!" I exploded off the stool and turned to face him. "I'm sick of dealing with your bullshit, and I'm pretty over the fact that we only seem to be friends when it's fucking convenient for you!"

"My bullshit?" He forced out an angry laugh. "That's really fucking rich, coming from you. Look, I'm sorry that you're having problems with your amazing girlfriend because she doesn't want to tell you how many guys she's fucked, or whatever bullshit you're dealing with, but I actually have a real fucking problem, and where the fuck have you been? Getting your dick wet with your princess?"

I couldn't help it - he was my best friend but no one talked about Parker like that to me. I swung.

Jimmy saw it coming but didn't move fast enough to avoid it. Instead, he dropped with the hit and then immediately plowed into my middle. I felt his fist slam into my ribs and I grunted through the pain, bringing my knee up to hit his stomach.

The next thing I heard was a thundered "What the fuck is going on here?!" I stopped trying to bash Jimmy's face in as I looked up to see Chris towering over the two of us, a serious amount of rage coloring his face.

"Someone needs to fucking explain to me why you two are going at it in the rental booth, right the fuck now!"

We both kept silent, like little fucking kids who got caught with their hands in the cookie jar.

He gave us a minute and then nodded slowly. "Right. Jimmy, I get it, you're miserable. That doesn't mean you take that shit out on your best friend. And you, Ash, I don't get this at all from you. I want you out of here. Don't come back to work until you sort out your shit and pull your head out of your ass."

"Chris, I'm sorry, but I swear-" I started, but he cut me off.

"I don't give a shit. Just fucking sort your shit, yeah?" His eyes stared into mine, and I realized just how big of an asshole I had been.

I nodded. "Yes, sir."

"Good," he grunted. "Now, get the fuck out of here."

Without even a glance at Jimmy, I clocked out and headed back outside.

I spent an hour in my truck, trying to talk myself out of going. But, the second Chris had told me to leave, I knew I was going to end up at her place. I almost decided to just call her, but I knew, no matter what, I wouldn't feel okay until was close enough to touch her. So, with nothing but the thought of seeing her in my head, I headed to Parker.

Chapter Twenty-Nine

Parker

I HAD JUST GOTTEN MOM settled in her room after dinner, and was looking forward to relaxing in bed with my headphones in when I heard the knock at the door.

It had been an absolutely horrible day. I woke up feeling exhausted, like I didn't sleep at all because, well, I hadn't. Mom woke up crying because the pain was so bad, and I ended up sending Diane home as soon as she showed up. I knew she was concerned - that was written plain on her face - but I convinced her that we were both fine and she finally left.

Mom did nothing but bitch all day, mostly about me and how worthless I am. I didn't even have the energy to fight with her. And when nine o'clock came and went with no text from Ash to see why I wasn't in class, I ended up face down in bed, crying my eyes out, absolutely positive that I had ruined the best thing that ever happened to me.

I spent the rest of the afternoon in an exhaustion-fueled daze, but dinner had been mostly silent, allowing time for the thoughts I had been managing to avoid to begin creeping back in. Now I wanted nothing more than to put on music and block out the world.

What I really didn't want to do was answer the door. Especially since somehow, standing with my hand on the knob, I knew it was him. I never thought that I was actually one of "those girls," but when I opened the door and he was standing on the other side, looking more beautiful than ever, my knees went weak and I had to grab the door frame to remain standing.

His eyes scanned the empty living room behind me before they came back to mine.

"Hey," he whispered.

"Hi," I managed to croak out over the emotion that was clogging my throat.

"I needed to see you. Can I come in?"

I wanted to say no. I wanted to tell him that he couldn't be here, that she was awake and I didn't want him to ever have to meet her, but in that moment, the need to have him nearby outweighed all of my fears.

"Sure..." I replied, leaning back to let him in. I shut the door and then caught him once again looking around the space, I'm sure trying to see the other occupant. I was just praying at this point that we could sort ourselves out and I could get him out of here before she came out to see what was going on.

"I missed you in class today," he told me, taking a seat on the couch. I followed his lead and sat beside him, keeping a few inches that felt like miles between us.

"Oh," I told him. "I, uh, Mom wasn't feeling great, so I just decided to stay home."

He nodded, but kept his eyes trained on his shoes, arms crossed across his chest.

"I got into a fight with my best friend tonight," he suddenly said. "It was so fucking stupid, but I was at work and he made some comment about you, and I didn't even think, I just hit him."

That both surprised me, and made me feel really guilty. "Ash, I don't want you to fight someone over me, especially not someone that you care about that much."

"See, that's the thing," he said suddenly, "I do care about Jimmy. He's been my best friend for years. But he said some shit about you, and I had no problem hitting him. What does that say about how I feel about you?"

His voice dripped with defeat, and his shoulders were hunched over like the weight of his own body was too much to bear.

"Ash," I told him, "I'm really sorry about last night, about everything... I shouldn't have left you like that, I just... I was falling apart and I didn't know what else to do. I've never done this before, and you're... I don't know how to rely on someone else."

He was quiet for a few, long seconds before finally looking up to meet my eyes for the first time since we sat down. "Let me teach you, Parker. Let me be the one who takes care of you, and, I swear, I'll make it easy for you." His eyes were glowing with sincerity, and I couldn't fight it - I gave in. I slid over until our legs were pressed together and I wrapped my hands around his strong neck, resting my forehead against his before gently nodding.

"Okay," I whispered, and before I could even finish speaking his mouth was on mine. The kiss started soft, sweet, and tender as his lips danced around mine lightly, almost teasingly. Then, I let out a quiet moan and everything changed. Ash's hand dove into my hair and he slanted his head, holding me in place as he opened me up and ravished my mouth. I felt my hands moving up and down his chest but I had no control over my body: I was running on autopilot, all of my energy and attention focused on the way that his mouth and hands were making me feel.

I was about to pull him into my bedroom when I heard the voice clearing. He must have heard it too because he jumped and shot away from me, quickly standing and taking a deep breath before turning around to greet whoever was there.

I already knew who it was, and based on the look on her face, this was going to be really ugly.

"Hi, Mrs. Parker," Ash said brightly, "I'm Ashton Carter, I'm a friend of Parker's."

She took him in in a long glance that started at his head and worked downwards, all the way to his shoes before working back up again. Her face said that she was not impressed, and she didn't even bother to respond to his words.

Completely ignoring Ash's presence, Mom looked straight at me. "This is the reason that you're out, whoring around all the time, isn't it?"

I saw the confusion flash across Ash's face before his jaw grew tight.

"Mom," I started, "please, don't. Ash is-"

"Don't say his name to me!" she snapped. "I don't want to hear you talk about the reason that you refuse to stay home to take care of me while I sit here dying! You know, Eileen, I really expected more from you."

"Mom! You have no idea what you're talking about!" I shouted angrily, refusing to even look in Ash's direction at this point. I felt my face burning, and I had never been more embarrassed, or angrier with my mother.

"Don't tell me I don't know what I'm talking about! I know exactly what I'm talking about." She let out a low, mocking laugh before she continued. "Keep it up, Eileen. Keep spreading your legs and see what happens when you get knocked up. You want to experience exactly how you ruined my life, keep doing *exactly what you're doing*. Just remember, I won't be around when this one gets tired of your shit and leaves, just like everyone else in your life."

With that incredibly successful parting shot, she turned around and walked back to bed.

I stood, frozen in shock, processing her words and not much else until I heard his voice.

"Parker," he said as he started to move towards me, and that snapped me out of it. I dodged him and ran around the couch, avoiding his eyes as I backed towards my bedroom and spoke so quietly I wasn't sure if he could hear.

"I'm so sorry, but you need to go. I just, I need you to leave, now, please," and then I was moving towards my room. I grabbed the door to slam it shut but Ash was already there, blocking me from locking him out.

"Fuck that, Park, let me in."

"No, Ash, really-"

"I'm not fucking leaving!" he snapped, loudly, and I automatically stepped back away from him. Suddenly, I heard my mom's voice in my head again, saying all of those absolutely horrible things about him and me and I felt the tears start to fall as I finally looked up into his eyes.

"I'm sorry. I'm so, so sorry. I didn't want you to have to meet her. I didn't want her to do that to you. I'm so sorry, Ash." He cut off my rambling apologies by wrapping his arms around me so tightly I could barely breathe, but I couldn't have cared less. I let go. I sobbed so hard that my knees gave out, and I would have collapsed if Ash hadn't kept me standing. Then, I barely noticed as he picked me up into his arms, carrying me to the bed where he sat, gently arranging me in his lap where I continued to cry. His one hand rubbed soft, soothing circles on my back while the other played with my hair, and it still took me ten minutes to calm myself down. I was trying to get control of my breathing when I felt Ash pull in a deep breath.

"You know, I think you have to be the quietest crier that I've ever met. Or even seen. I could feel your entire body shaking, but you were almost silent." His voice was playful and I knew he was trying to make a joke to cheer me up, but he had no idea that he'd said the wrong thing for that.

"I know," I told him flatly, "I trained myself to do it."

He was quiet for a moment while I felt his eyes probe me. "What are you talking about?"

"When I was younger, my mom would do something or say something, and I would cry, and if she heard me, she would…" I trailed off, not even wanting to remember the cruel things she would say when she saw me cry. "Anyway, I tried to learn how to not cry at all, but that didn't really work, so I just started doing it quietly, or trying to at least. I wasn't always successful," I finished with a shrug.

Ash was staring at me with a look that I had never seen, and I was worried about what it meant, but it still took my breath away.

"Well," he said quietly, "I guess that more-or-less answers my next question."

"Which is…" I prompted when he didn't continue.

"Has she always been that charming, or is it a cancer thing?"

"Always. Actually, as surprising as this may seem, the cancer calmed her down some. She didn't quit drinking until she was diagnosed, and liquor made her really evil; sober, even with cancer, she's just a pretty big bitch."

"Baby," Ash said quietly, but he didn't say anything else. Instead he softly and quickly pressed his lips into mine. The kiss wasn't about sending a message or getting a reaction, it was a kiss meant to take away pain, and it worked. A tiny bit of mine faded away.

"Will you stay?" I asked him. "I mean, you don't have to, but even just for a little bit, I'd just-"

Ash was softly laughing when he interrupted. "You're not getting rid of me yet. I'm staying until I know you're sleeping, safe and sound."

My body flooded with relief and in that moment, I realized that I had fallen completely in love with him. It had probably even happened a while ago, but now that I had acknowledged it, even just in my own mind, it made it feel real and terrifying. Suddenly, my head was filled with visions of him walking away and I had to close my eyes against the pain.

"Parker?" he asked. "Baby, what's wrong? You're whole body just tensed up."

I forced myself to relax again and took three deep breaths to calm my racing heart. *One, two, three.* I shoved my face into his chest and inhaled deeply, reminding myself that he was still here and then, I lied.

"Nothing, I'm sorry. I just, I still can't believe what she said to you."

"Stop. Don't worry about me. I mean, yeah, she's your mom, so I'd kinda hoped that she'd love me and happily tell me I had her blessing, but ultimately, the only person whose approval I give a fuck about is you."

"Well, you have it," I told him. "And then some."

I heard the smile when he replied, "Good." Then he gave me a tight squeeze, dropped a kiss onto the top of my head and said, "Now, come on. Let's get you into bed."

I changed into a pair of shorts and a tank top in the bathroom and then emerged to climb under the covers. Ash had taken off his shoes and was sitting on the bed, waiting for me when I walked out. His approving look made my cheeks heat, and he laughed softly when he saw my blush.

"Come here, beautiful girl," he said softly, and I walked straight to him, stopping once I was standing between his legs. His hands rose to rest on my hips and his eyes were warm on mine as I looked down at him. I couldn't resist pushing my fingers into his hair, and it was soft against my skin as I played with the strands. Then, feeling bold, I gripped his hair gently in my fist and tilted his head back until I could press my mouth against his.

I may have started the kiss, but Ash quickly took over, sweeping his tongue into my mouth with such passion that it forced a quiet growl from my throat, and at that, Ash's control snapped. His hands suddenly pulled me into him before quickly moving to my thighs. In seconds, I was straddling him, his hard length pressing into the spot between my legs, and in response to the sensation, I felt my panties grow wet under the thin shorts I was wearing. My arms wrapped around his chest, and I ran my fingers down his back, feeling the muscles moving as he trailed his hands from my stomach, slowly traveling up until I felt him cupping my breast over the t-shirt. I didn't have a bra on, so the only thing between his skin and mine was the thin cotton, and as he rubbed his thumb across my hardened nipple lightly, I felt the action like a bolt of electricity to my core.

"Oh my God, Ash," I moaned, and suddenly his hands stilled on me.

"Shit," I heard him whisper under his breath and then he pressed his face into the crook of my neck before taking in a deep breath. "I'm sorry, baby. I got carried away."

"Please don't apologize," I told him. "I want you to keep going."

"Two reasons why I can't do that, beautiful, no matter how much I want to. One, when I finally get inside you for the first time, I don't want you thinking about anything but me. No shitty family dinners or crazy Mom drama - Just Ash and Parker, yeah?" That was sweet, and it made sense, so I nodded, even if I didn't want to. He smiled and then continued. "And two is that, as much as I want what you're trying to give me, I'm not gonna take it until I know that you're totally, completely mine. That means, you need to let me in all the way first. Tonight, we got a lot closer to that point, but we still have some work to do."

"Okay," I told him, even though I thought he was being a little silly. I wanted sex, he wanted sex. I thought we should just have sex. But, I had to admit that he *was* the expert in this situation and had two valid arguments, so I let the conversation go and crawled off his lap to climb in bed.

Ash tucked me in and then laid next to me, on top of the covers. I wanted him to get in bed with me, but this was the most I could get him to do, so I was going to take what I could get. Ash wrapped an arm around me and I laid my head on his shoulder. We didn't talk at all, he just played with my hair and I drew small circles on his chest for a little while until, before I even realized it was happening, I fell asleep in his arms.

Chapter Thirty

Ash

ALL THINGS CONSIDERED, BY THE end of the week, everything was going better than I could have hoped. Parker seemed to have finally given in to the fact that I wasn't going anywhere and every day she shared a little bit more with me about her past. She'd told me a few stories about her mom, but I got the definite feeling that she was downplaying what she'd dealt with as a child. Still, if that's what she felt she needed to do, I was going to let it go - for now.

Her mom was an abusive bitch, and I hated that Parker was stuck in that tiny apartment taking care of her almost 24/7. Part of me wanted to ask Mom and Dad to help me come up with some sort of solution, some way to get Parker out of the situation while still making sure that her mom was taken care of. That being said, as much as I was dying to do something, I knew that Parker would be pissed if I got my parents involved, so I kept my mouth shut.

The one good thing was that Katherine, Parker's mom, had decided to completely act as if I didn't exist, which suited me just fine. I was still friendly, which I knew drove her crazy and made Parker laugh, so I wasn't going to stop. I also refused to call Parker anything but Park or Baby when we were in the room with her, which happened frequently since I spent every evening there this week. We ate dinner with her mom and then did homework together at the table while Katherine watched TV and generally muttered her disapproval under her breath.

I was able to spend every night with Parker because I had called Chris and apologized about what happened Monday. He told me to take the rest of the week off. He wasn't mad, he just wanted me to take some time to relax and then come back with a clear head. I agreed, and thanked him, and that was that. I knew that I needed to call Jimmy at some point, but I was still pretty pissed at him, so I decided that that could wait.

After classes let out, I drove to Parker's, as that was quickly becoming our normal routine. I was planning on cooking dinner for her and her mom, and I was really excited about getting to make dinner for my girl.

Parker cooked every night, and I knew she felt like it was her job because we were in her place, but I wanted to make her life a little bit easier, and one way I figured I could do that was by feeding her.

When I got to the apartment, I had a bad feeling. I couldn't explain it, but waiting for Parker to answer the door, I felt on edge. When she finally opened the door and then turned around, heading straight to her room without even looking at me, I quickly shut the door and followed behind her. The second we were inside she turned back around and attached her body to mine, wrapping her arms around my chest and burrowing her face into the t-shirt I was wearing.

"Whoa, baby, talk to me," I said quietly as I felt her body start to shake with silent sobs. "Tell me what happened."

Her body continued to shudder and I led her over to the bed, sitting down and pulling her with me so she was seated in my lap. Then, I let her cry until I felt the tears start to subside. What felt like an hour later, she finally lifted her tear-stained face to meet my eyes.

"Hey, beautiful," I said quietly. "Wanna tell me what happened?"

She shrugged and looked down at my shoulder before speaking. "Oh, you know. Just my mom, reminding me every chance she gets all the ways I ruined her life."

I clenched my jaw and pressed a hard kiss into Parker's forehead. "Don't listen to a word she says, baby. None of it's true."

She was still and quiet for a moment and then she slowly nodded. "How was your day?" she asked quietly, finally bringing her eyes back up to mine.

"It was okay. I'm glad it's Friday." That finally pulled a small smile from her.

"Me, too."

"I'm gonna go start making dinner. Do you want to come sit with me?"

She nodded and wiped her face, clearing away the last remaining tears. We headed out and I got dinner ready. I was making my famous seafood risotto, something Rory used to beg me to make every week when it was my night to cook dinner. I pulled together all the ingredients while Parker watched from where she sat on the counter. Katherine didn't leave her room once until Parker went and let her know that dinner was on the table.

Parker and I were just starting to put food on our plates when Katherine finally walked out to the table.

"Well, that was just so polite of you two to wait for me," she said sarcastically, making her way to the array of medication Parker had lined up on the table for her and swallowing them all down.

"Hey, Kathy," I said with a smile. "How are you feeling today?"

She rolled her eyes but ignored me as she sat down to the table. "I can't believe this Parker. I told you that boy is disrespectful and rude, and yet you continue to parade him around here-"

"Stop, Mom. Stop now. I just want to eat dinner and then spend the evening with my boyfriend. And as I explained to you earlier, this is my apartment, and I will bring anyone here that I want."

The table fell silent and I stared at Parker. She looked up from her plate and her eyes came to mine. Then she gave me a small smile and went back to work clearing her plate.

My eyes then fell on Katherine who was staring at Parker with barely concealed rage, and I felt my body get tense. Parker ignored her mom and focused on her food as Katherine stood and looked down at her daughter.

"I should have gotten rid of you when I had the chance. Your father ruined me the day he put you inside me, and I have regretted that day ever since. And it's not enough that you got me sick, but now you're determined to make me die alone while you run around with the likes of him..." She paused to shake her head and then curled her lip before finishing with, "You disgust me."

My brain was trying to process the words that I couldn't believe were coming out of her mouth. What the fuck kind of mother could say that shit to her daughter, her only child?

Parker was frozen, fork halfway to her mouth and a look on her face that told me she was about to completely shatter. I ignored Katherine as she walked to her bedroom and moved out of my seat to Parker. Kneeling down beside her, I put my face right next to hers.

"Baby, look at me. Right now, Park, look right at me." Her eyes came to mine but they were unfocused. "Parker, don't let her get to you. You are not the reason that she is sick."

Her eyes dropped away from mine and I heard her whisper, "But I am..." Then, she was out of her chair and moving around me, heading for her bedroom. "You need to go. Now, Ash." She was looking anywhere but at me until I took a step in her direction. She matched it, moving backwards as her eyes snapped to mine and they were distant. "No, you need to leave."

"You're completely fucking crazy if you think I'm leaving you right now."

"You can't be here..." she pleaded, and the despair in her voice broke my heart.

"Why?" I asked. "Because that twisted woman has convinced you that you don't deserve love? She's wrong, and you're wrong if you believe her."

"You have no fucking clue, Ash!" she shouted. "She's not wrong. I wished *every day* for someone to take her away from me. Every single God damned day. It's all I ever wanted. The only thing I ever fucking prayed for was my mom to disappear. And now, that's happening, and it's on me."

"Are you serious?" I asked incredulously as I moved towards her, refusing to stop until I was standing directly in front of her. "Do you actually believe that bullshit?"

"It's not bullshit. It's my life!" she shouted in my face, even going so far as to place her hands on my chest, trying to shove me backwards. It didn't work, but it gave me the chance to wrap my hands around her wrists, pulling her arms around me with a quick jerk that sent her front crashing into mine.

"Parker, listen to me, baby," I told her quickly and quietly as I held her there. "Bad things happen. They happen to good people and they happen to bad people. But I promise you, you did not cause your mom's cancer. You are a good person, Eileen Parker. A beautiful, amazing, special person, and you don't deserve the life that's been given to you. I promise you, things are going to get better. One way or another, things are going to get better, and until they do, I'll be here every single day, making sure you know how fucking incredible you are."

She was quiet for a moment, and she still refused to meet my eyes.

"I don't understand..." she began, her voice breaking on a silent sob before she shook her head and stopped talking.

"You don't understand what?" I asked her quietly when she didn't speak again.

"I don't understand you," she told me, finally meeting my eyes. Hers shined brightly with unshed tears and I wanted to destroy anything and everything that had ever hurt her - starting with Katherine Parker. "I don't get why you're here right now, dealing with all of my bullshit when you could be... anywhere else. Literally, anywhere else in the world would be better than being here."

"Because you're here, Parker. There's nowhere else I want to be."

"That's crazy. *You're* crazy and I know *I'm* crazy, but I still don't freaking get why you would put up with all my-"

"I love you, Parker."

That shut her up. Well, figuratively at least, because her mouth was left hanging open as she gazed at me, in shock. I hadn't really meant for the words to come out yet, which wasn't to say that I didn't love her, because I did. More than I thought I was even capable of, which terrified me but didn't make the fact any less true. This girl had become the most important thing in my world, and I knew that as long as I lived, I'd do anything in my power to make her happy. Which, right now, meant I needed to stop her mind from traveling down the dark paths it was already starting on.

I kissed her, and I didn't hold back. I crushed my mouth to hers with a fierceness and a possessiveness that I had never felt before, and she returned the kiss like she needed it to live. We didn't do anything else, just stayed wrapped up in each other's arms as we tasted and consumed each other, and I let her feel my love through the kiss.

I knew she wasn't ready to say it back, and I was okay with that (for now, at least,) because lying with Parker in my arms and my mouth locked to hers, I felt her body tell me what her brain wasn't ready to admit out loud. With her lips pressed tightly to mine, she told me everything I needed to hear.

Chapter Thirty-One

Parker

DRIVING TOWARDS MOM'S DOCTOR'S OFFICE the Monday before Thanksgiving, I found myself thinking that, for the first time in my life, things were actually going well for me.

The past two months with Ash had been incredible. And I mean mindbogglingly crazy-in-love-and-I've-never-been-happier incredible.

After that first week of him spending almost every moment at the apartment with me and Mom, things fell into a somewhat easy pattern. We spent as much time together as we could, even if most of it was spent making out in my bed or doing homework at the table while my mom ignored us both, which was more than fine with me. I liked to think that she decided to lay off after she realized realized that Ash and I weren't just casually having sex (I mean, come on! We hadn't even progressed past heavy make-out sessions with light, over-the-clothes groping and some mostly innocent dry-humping, for crying out loud, and I'll tell you now, it was not for lack of trying on my part.) I really wanted to convince myself that she was willing to put up with Ash since he had become a constant fixture in both of our lives and didn't seem to be going anywhere, but I had a feeling that that wasn't the case.

Mom was getting weaker. She spent more time in bed than anywhere else anymore, and recently had been saying even lying in bed was too uncomfortable after long periods. After the blood tests, the doctors had determined that they needed to step up the chemo - there was really no other option at this point.

A few weeks ago, I took Mom to get scans done of her abdomen. The doctors wanted to see what was going on inside, and what they saw wasn't good. When Ash got to my place after work that night, he knew something was up with me. I finally had a breakdown and he forced me to tell him exactly what was going on.

So, I explained the entire situation. I told him how, on the day of my 18th birthday, I had moved out of the house that Mom and I shared, and how I'd cut off all contact with her. I told him how I ended up moving into an apartment near campus, and I told him how I worked my ass off to stay in the shitty place for three months until I could move into my dorm for Freshman year. I told him how I had to take out a bunch of loans to even be able to afford school, and how I then worked my ass off to keep my grades up and keep the few scholarships that I got in order to keep my spot at school. And then I explained the day that changed everything.

It had been the middle of June, just a few weeks after classes ended, and I was back to living in an apartment, but this one had been great. Small - a one-bedroom - but clean and safe with nice neighbors and a landscaping service that came once a week to maintain the hydrangeas that flourished along the brick building. I'd loved that place.

Mom called me on a Friday while I was at work. When I got off and saw the voice mail, I was a bit surprised to say the least. We hadn't spoken in over a year, and I still wanted nothing to do with her. I refused to listen to it for two days, finally giving in because, in the end, I knew it would have taken an act of God for her to pick up the phone. And an act of God was exactly what I got.

"Eileen," she answered after a single ring.

"Uh, hey, ma," I said shakily, suddenly turning back into ten-year-old-me, who was absolutely terrified of whatever she was about to hear.

"Listen," she said, dryly. "I have cancer. I need you to get over your issues and come back. You have a responsibility as my daughter, and I need you to step up to it."

"Ex- *Excuse me*?" I managed to choke out, trying to figure out what the fuck she was talking about.

"I'm sick, Eileen. I have a doctor's appointment tomorrow at ten. I need you to pick me up. We can talk then."

She hung up, and that was that.

I, of course, was there at 9:30 the next morning to take her to the doctors where they had explained to us that she was, in fact, very sick. The cancer had started growing in her pancreas, but by now was invading her liver, which was filling up with small tumors. Chemo was the only option. The cancer was too far progressed for either radiation or surgery, and even the chemo was just a life-extending solution. Mom would die, most likely in less than a year.

From there, everything had happened so fast. I gave up my apartment and found this crappy two bedroom that we could live in together. She started treatment, and my hell began again.

The problem now was that the chemo didn't seem to be doing anything. The doctors had switched some drugs around and they were hoping that it would slow down the cancer's growth, but it had become a waiting game.

So, with the exception of the cancer, everything seemed to be going well. Mom was quiet, school was good, and I was even passing Stat thanks to Ash's patient tutoring.

Despite all that, I had a bad feeling in the pit of my stomach. It was dark and noxious, and the more I tried to ignore it, the stronger it grew. Worst of all, I had no idea where it was coming from. I mean, sure, I was pretty much dreading the fact that my mom, according to the doctors, had just over six months left to live, but this didn't feel like dread. It felt like a warning... It felt like time was running out.

Because of that, I spent as much time as possible with Ash, just trying to memorize every second that we spent together. This wasn't difficult. Ash was a force of nature, and any time he was near me, I felt my body light up with the energy radiating off him. It tuned me into his frequency, so to speak, until I couldn't focus on anything but him.

I had been worried - after he told me that he loved me and I didn't say it back - that he would begin to pull away. Truthfully, I don't know why I didn't (and *still* couldn't) say the words that I knew in my heart to be true. Ash told me he loved me every day, more than once a day. If we were together, he would say it and seal it with a kiss, removing the awkwardness that would inevitably invade when I said nothing back. But he would text me when we were apart, still the same little messages as before, except now they ended with an 'I love you.' Sometimes, if I was still awake when he went home at night, I would pull out my phone in bed just to read the words over and over again. He had no idea what they meant to me.

Since my father left, the only person who had told me they loved me was Jessie. Literally no one else in my life had ever loved me. And I knew Ash loved me - it wasn't just that he told me all the time, but I saw it in the way he looked at me as if he needed me to breathe. Even if I had no idea what love was, I recognized that feeling when I saw it staring at me, because it was exactly how I felt when I looked at him.

I wanted to tell Ash that I loved him, and he more than deserved to hear it. But for some reason, I just couldn't. I couldn't admit to him how I felt. Part of me hoped that he could just tell, the way that I could when he looked at me. But I knew that was a cheap way to excuse the fact that I hadn't been able to say the words that I knew he was dying to hear.

For some reason, my heart wouldn't let me tell him I couldn't live without him. There had only been two other people that I had ever loved, and I had lost them both. For some reason, I felt like the minute I said out loud how I felt, he would be taken from me. The thought of that terrified me into silence.

So instead, I prayed that he would give me time, and I prayed that Mom would have *more* time, and I ignored the ugly feeling as I took what I could from the life that I was suddenly living. I knew if I lost this, I would need to remember every second. Ash was a once-in-a-lifetime type of love, and every day I realized more and more that if I screwed this up and lost him, I would never find anyone like Ashton Carter again.

Chapter Thirty-Two

Ash

"PARKER," I CALLED, DRAWING HER attention from her computer. I was sitting with my legs spread out, back against the wall, and feet hanging off the bed. She, on the other hand, had her back to the headboard and her feet tucked under my thighs. It was the day before Thanksgiving, and she was researching all the Black Friday sales that would be starting tomorrow night, trying to convince me that it would be fun to stand in the cold with loads of other people who wanted to race through stores to save money. I had yet to be convinced, but this wasn't what I wanted to be talking about.

I waited until her eyes were focused on mine before I continued quietly. "I want you there tomorrow."

She let out a long sigh before giving me the answer that I knew was coming. "You know I can't do that, Ash. We talked about this…"

It was my turn to sigh. I had avoided bringing this up because I hated fighting with Parker - not that it happened often, but when it did, I always felt like shit afterwards. I

221 | K . C . O ' N e i l l

knew tonight would be no different, but this was something that I was willing to fight about.

"Parker, I want you there tomorrow," I told her again, slowly this time, trying to make her understand.

She dropped her eyes before mumbling, "And, I want to be there-"

"So... Be there."

Her eyes came back to mine and they flashed with emotion. "Ash, I've explained this. I would if I could, but I *can't*. Tomorrow is Thanksgiving, I can't get someone to voluntarily give up their time with their family to come watch her, and I can't pay anyone. Which is besides the point because, *despite* our relationship, I'm not going to leave my mom alone with a stranger on what will most likely be her last Thanksgiving!"

"So bring her."

Her mouth dropped open and her beautiful face resembled a goldfish's while she gaped at me. "Are you out of your mind?" she hissed. "Absolutely not."

"Why?"

"Oh my God, you *are* out of your mind. We *both* know why."

"No," I told her, my voice rising a bit and I fought to keep it down. "I have no fucking idea why you won't get both you and your mother out of this shitty apartment for one night to come celebrate a holiday with people who love and care about you, and by extension, even if she is a raging bitch, your mother. Grandma will be there, obviously, and she can help if things get out of control, which is stupid because they wont. Everything will be fine. And Aurora is home, and I want you to meet her. I want you both there."

"Fuck *that*, Ash! I am *definitely* not meeting your sister with my mother in tow. I want this girl to *like* me, remember?"

"She already does and she hasn't even met you yet," I returned.

"And I can promise that Thanksgiving dinner with my mom will ruin all of that!" She took a deep breath. Katherine was asleep, but the walls were too thin and we definitely didn't need to wake her up.

I, on the other hand, *did* need to move. I pushed myself off the bed and paced the small room twice before turning back to face her. She had pulled her legs into her chest and wrapped her arms around them protectively, her eyes staring at the bed below her. She looked so afraid and alone, and I couldn't handle it. I didn't understand what else I could do. I told her I loved her *all the fucking time*. I wanted to bring her mom and her to celebrate the holidays with my family. I wanted her to understand that she had people who cared about her now, and she didn't need to do this alone, but she still refused to accept that, or my help. Which meant she still didn't trust me. And *that* broke my heart in half.

"Parker, you can't keep doing this. You are not alone anymore. You are not fighting this battle on your own. My family has met you four times in the past three months and they love you. You know that *I* fucking love you. Why won't you let us help you? Why can't you accept that we won't judge you for the actions of anyone but you?"

"That's not the point, Ash!" I saw the tears start to build in her eyes, and I hated it. I fucking hated that she was hurting and that I couldn't make it better right now, but I wanted... no. I needed to know if I was just wasting my time here.

"Then what is the point, Parker? Are you just not into this anymore? Are you tired of actually living, or have you decided that you need to punish yourself some more for being a 'shitty daughter,'" I shouted, using air quotes to let her know that I thought it was bullshit, "to a woman who emotionally abused you all your life?"

I saw her chest jerk as if she had taken an actual blow, and I felt like a dick, but I was way too pissed and terrified to rein it in now. This conversation was so not going how I'd planned, and I was seriously starting to freak the fuck out. "That's not fair, Ash," she whispered. "I don't know what you want from me."

I stiffened for one second, then moved towards her as I shouted, "I want you to fucking fight for this!"

Parker's eyes widened as I took three steps towards the bed and then, faster than I'd ever seen her move, she jerked her body away, cracking her head against the wall loudly as she tried to get away from my advancing figure. I froze, and then narrowed my eyes in her direction as I took in her trembling body and the small hand that was rubbing the bump on her head - she refused to meet my gaze. My heart, which had only been cracked right down the middle, shattered into a million pieces.

She had actually thought that I was going to hurt her. This beautiful, broken girl was so much more broken than I had ever imagined, and she didn't even trust me enough to know that I would never, not ever, take my hand to her in anger. That realization paralyzed me with dread until another thought invaded.

I had only ever seen one person react like that in the face of perceived possible violence, and I knew, I just knew, that Parker had been hurt by someone. Her almost frantic attempts to keep me out weren't just the result of years of feeling like she was worthless, but someone… some fucking asshole had hurt her.

And suddenly, it was all way too fucking much. I turned and backed into the wall that was two feet to my right and then sank to the floor heavily.

"I can't do this," I whispered, terrified to say the words that I knew I had to say.

"What?" she asked quietly, in a small, defeated voice.

"I can't," I repeated a bit louder, "I'm done, Parker. I have nothing left."

Her eyes came to me, and the fear in them made me want to take the words back, but it was too late for that.

"Ash, no, I-"

"No, Parker. Don't. Please, just don't. I have tried and tried and tried to get you to let me in, to get you to trust me. I have nothing else to give to you to prove that you are safe with me."

"Ash, no," she cried, sliding off the bed to land on her knees at my feet. "I do trust you, I just-"

"Don't" I interrupted hoarsely. "Don't lie to me, you still don't trust me."

"But I do…"

"Then what the fuck was that?" I asked tiredly. At this point, all I wanted to do was go home and sleep until I could forget every single thing that I knew about Eileen Parker, and everything that I didn't know, and maybe, just maybe, I could move on from this.

Parker's eyes fell, and I couldn't take anymore. It was as if something inside me snapped, and I just needed to get the fuck out. I pushed away from the wall, forcing myself to ignore when she fell back onto her ass in front of me. I refused to look at her, refused to see the pain and fear in her eyes - it would break me completely and I just couldn't do it. I ignored when she frantically called my name, getting it out twice before I was out of her room and then once more as she followed me to the front door. When I got through and slammed it shut behind me, I froze for a second as I heard the sobbing begin on the other side of the wood. I walked away from the door and left the sound of her crying behind as I ran out to my car, trying to ignore the fact that I couldn't breathe. I couldn't feel the cold air as I walked outside, and I couldn't hear anything over the sound of her crying, out loud for the first time since I'd met her, alone in her apartment with a mother who hated her.

Once I made it to my truck, without even processing the thought, I balled my fist and slammed it into the cold metal of the door. Then again. And again. Over and over until the metal was bent and distorted from my hand, and my knuckles were cut and bleeding.

With the pain in my hand to distract from the pain in my chest, I drove home. Once inside my apartment, I pulled out the unopened bottle of Evan Williams that Marco had given me as a housewarming gift and I drank until I could forget. Well, I tried at least. I guess I really only drank until I passed out, but, as I learned that night... Well, sleeping fucking sucked when all I did was dream of Parker.

Chapter Thirty-Three

Parker

I WAS LYING ON THE floor of my bedroom, crying my eyes out like one of those girls I'd sworn I'd never be. Still, I figured that could be excused because Ash was gone. I had fucking ruined everything because I don't know how to let anyone in. That's all I had to do! *Goddammit, Parker, why are you so freaking stupid?*

I let my brain berate me. It's all I had been doing myself since Ash had left the night before. The second I heard his truck pull away, I wanted to call him and tell him everything. Every little (and not-so-little) secret that I had been hiding, but I couldn't. It didn't matter anyway, now - I knew that he was done with me.

Honestly, I was amazed that it lasted as long as it did, and as my tears finally started to subside, I thanked myself for memorizing every moment I had with Ash. I mean, I wanted absolutely nothing to do with the memories right now (which was shitty because they seemed to be the only thing I could think about... that is, besides how freaking stupid I am) but I knew, once the hurt had started to heal a little bit, one day I would want to remember - remember the time that I fell in love with a beautiful boy who treated me like I was his world, and who'd made mine turn. It would be a nice thing to remember one day.

As expected, Thanksgiving had been completely horrible. I roasted a turkey and made all the fixings for Mom, who had just bitched because I made so much food for two people. Truthfully, I had bought so much food at the grocery store because Ash had told me that his favorite thing about Thanksgiving was making sandwiches with all the leftovers, and I had wanted to have enough that he could make a few at our place. But today, staring at the loaded dishes on the table and realizing that it would most likely all go in the trash, it brought tears to my eyes. It also didn't help that neither of us really touched our food. Well, we played with it a bit and pushed it around our plates, but hardly anything was actually *consumed*. Mom was sick from chemo, and I had no appetite whatsoever... but whatever.

To make things as bad as they could possibly be, Mom realized something was up when Ash never showed up. Even when I had told him that I was staying at the apartment for Thanksgiving, he said he'd spend the morning here and then pick me up to go Black Friday shopping. Obviously, none of those things happened, and Mom wasn't a complete moron unless she was drinking. She figured it out pretty quickly.

"So, that boy you've been screwing around with finally got tired of it, huh?"

"Don't talk to me about him." I refused to even look at her. That was partly because I didn't want to give her the reaction that she was looking for, and partly because I didn't want her to see the tears threatening to fall.

She laughed quietly, but there was no humor in the sound. "Don't get an attitude with me, young lady. I told you that this would happen. You should have listened to me. I *am* your mother, you know."

At that point, I stood, threw my plate into the sink, and then walked to my room where I had laid on the floor crying my eyes out - which brought us to now.

I had a splitting headache and I wanted nothing more than to just crawl into bed and sleep forever, but I knew it wouldn't be that simple. Ash was there when I slept - there was literally no way to avoid him.

So I set out towards the thankfully empty apartment - Mom laid up in bed I assumed - and headed to the fridge to grab a bottle of water. After I drank it in two long chugs, I grabbed another. I pulled out Mom's pills, not caring in the least that I was an hour early. She could figure it the fuck out. While I was in the cabinet, I also grabbed two Advil and swallowed them down before chasing them with two of the sleeping pills the doctors had prescribed Mom for when she got worked up. She had been having panic attacks when she was trying to sleep, and they had apparently been caused by not getting enough sleep. She never took them anymore - the painkillers she was on now knocked her out more than enough.

After swallowing the pills, I made my way to her room and dropped her meds on the nightstand. "If you can remember, take these in an hour. If you don't think you will, take them now. I'm going to bed." Then without another word, I left the room and walked back to mine, grabbing the water I had left on the counter along the way.

Once inside, I turned on Christina Perri, and, because I'm a masochist, listened to *The Lonely* on repeat as I cried into my pillow. It took way too long, but eventually the pills kicked in and I faded to sleep.

Chapter Thirty-Four

Ash

THANKSGIVING BREAK AND THE WEEKEND that followed it was, without a doubt, the worst few days of my life. The good news was that by Monday morning I was at least optimistic that things couldn't get any worse. And then they did, at precisely 8:05AM.

Part of me had hoped that she wouldn't show for class. I thought maybe she would be so miserable that she couldn't get out of bed, which was how I'd spent pretty much every day since Thanksgiving - the daylight hours, at least. I got wasted every night, trying to block out the memories. It had yet to work, but I was determined to see the experiment through.

I was sitting in the back of the room in my usual seat, and I had been early. I really have no idea why - probably just because I'm a glutton for punishment, but I wanted to be there if she showed up. When class started and she wasn't there, I almost felt a tiny bit of hope at the idea that she was avoiding me. Maybe that meant we could still salvage this fucked up relationship, as ridiculous as that sounds.

And then she walked in five minutes late, looking as beautiful as always in just a pair of jeans and a blue, long-sleeved t-shirt. Her hair was down around her face, so I couldn't see her eyes, but I saw the tension in her shoulders as she entered the room. She apologized quietly to the professor and then glanced up just enough to see my feet at the top of the room. Then she sat in the first available chair near the aisle.

That was when I realized that I'm just a fucking moron, and hope is a waste of fucking time. I had managed to convince myself that despite everything - the mistrust and the carefully guarded secrets - Parker had loved me. I swore that she was just too afraid to say the words out loud.

Seeing her slink into class looking perfectly fine while I felt like I was suffocating every day - that was the moment that I realized there was no way that girl had ever loved me.

I couldn't tell you the first thing about what we talked about in class. As hurt and angry as I was, I couldn't do anything but stare at the back of her head. The hour flew by and when the professor dismissed us, I watched her jump up and make a run for it. It wasn't until she had left the room that I even started putting my unopened books back into my bag before I slowly headed back out to my car.

I sat in the driver's seat with the keys in my hand for five minutes before calling Jimmy. The phone rang so long that I figured he was still sleeping, but then, right before voicemail would have picked up, I heard his voice.

"Hey, man," he said quietly.

"Hey," I replied. We were both quiet for a moment before I broke it. "Can I come over? I need to talk to you..."

I heard him let out a heavy sigh before, "Yeah. Sure."

I didn't answer, just hung up, put the car in drive and headed to my friend's house.

Jimmy lived in a studio apartment that had been built above his parents' garage. They had rented it out a few times when we were younger, but the apartment had been empty when we graduated. Jimmy moved in and had stayed put. He said he was saving money to buy a house when he and Maddie both graduated, but I knew he also stayed to help out his parents - his brother Jack was autistic, and when he started to have a freak-out, Jimmy was the best at calming him down. Jack had always liked me, and I felt the same, so we got along great.

I parked in the driveway before walking to the door that led inside. Knocking twice, I pulled it open and then walked upstairs into the loft. Jimmy was sitting eating a bowl of cereal at the small table that took up one corner of the combined dining-room-kitchen-living-room space. He jerked his head at me as he chewed in greeting and I returned the gesture as I made my way towards an empty chair.

"Hey," I said as I sat, and then I stared at the table, lost in my own thoughts, none of which were good.

Jesus. Has there ever been anyone more pathetic than me right now? Crying and bitching like a girl? Because, I totally did cry, like a bitch, drunk and in bed on Thanksgiving night... I'm a fucking-

"So, did you come here for any particular reason, or did you just want to glare at my table for a while?"

Jimmy's voice knocked me out of my downward spiral and my head jerked up to focus on him.

"Fuck," I muttered, rubbing my hands over my face, "I'm sorry, man. I just, we haven't really talked much in a while, and I wanted..." I swallowed and then just fucking said it. "I broke up with Parker."

"Shit," Jimmy replied, leaning back in his chair. "Are you... I mean, did something happen?"

"Kind of... We broke up on Wednesday. I told her that I wanted her to come to dinner with me at my parents house and she just, refused."

"Why?"

"Stupid fucking reasons. She didn't want to leave her mom, which I respect and understand, and I didn't ask her to. I told her, practically *begged* her to bring her mom, and she fucking would not do it. Basically told me to fuck myself. And then," I sighed. I still hadn't been able to forget the look on her face when she thought I was going to hit her. "I don't even fucking know what happened... But she doesn't trust me, and she's still keeping shit from me, and I can't fucking do it anymore. I just can't. Every day, every fucking day, I tell her over and over that I love her and that she's safe with me, and it's... I don't even know anymore... But I finally realized that it'll never be enough, so, I'm just... done."

"I'm sorry, man..." Jimmy said slowly. "I don't even..."

"Fuck it," I interrupted. "It's fine. How are you doing?"

"Maddie dumped me."

"What the fuck?!" I half shouted at him. "When?!"

"Well, the first time was two months ago. The day before me and you got into that fight at the rink, actually... Then, we got back together like two weeks later but she just called it off again, on Thanksgiving, actually. I'm pretty convinced that this time it'll stick."

"Holy shit, man…" I said slowly. I actually couldn't believe the words coming out of his mouth. "Why?"

He shrugged. "Stupid fucking reasons," he said with a small, unhappy smile. "I don't even know. This whole year is just… turning into everything I never expected."

I nodded because, *shit*, I could understand that. Then I murmured, "Fuck," under my breath. Jimmy loved the shit out of Maddie, and had for years. I loved Parker, but I only had her for three months; I couldn't imagine what Jimmy was feeling right now, and honestly, with as bad as my heart hurt, I was kind of glad I'd never have to know.

I hung at Jimmy's until I had to get back to school for my next class, almost saying fuck it and skipping, but then deciding against it. I spent the rest of the day in a fog, barely listening to a word that was said to me, and as soon as I could, I got the fuck home. Once in the safety of my apartment, I got wasted and blared music to block out the world. After three hours and almost an entire bottle of whiskey, I finally passed out. I dreamt of Parker again, but it was a new dream. I was standing in her apartment when Katherine walked out of her bedroom. Except it wasn't Katherine as I had ever seen her. She was healthy, and clearly drunk, weaving across the floor to get to me.

"Get out," she slurred in a cold voice. "Get out, get out, get out! You don't belong here anymore! You did this to her!" she screeched, and the sound was inhuman. "You did this!"

I tried to tell her I didn't know what she was talking about, I tried to tell her that the only thing I had ever done was love her daughter - it just wasn't enough. As I opened my mouth to speak, the room shifted. Suddenly, I was standing in a hospital room. I smelled sterile air and sickness, and I heard the steady chorus of beeps and buzzes that filled the space. I looked around the room until I found a bed, and I walked closer to get a better look.

My heart stopped when I saw Parker, except, it wasn't my Parker. She was thin, almost emaciated, and her skin looked like parchment. Her hair was missing, and her eyes were sunken and defeated.

"Why are you here?" she rasped. "I don't want you here."

I heard the beeping heart monitor speed up as she grew more agitated, and her weak body shook in the large bed as she began to shout.

"You need to leave! I don't want you here!"

I couldn't take it, I rushed to her side and grabbed her bony fingers, feeling the tears fill my eyes as I looked down at her broken body. She was dying, I knew it.

"I don't want to leave, Park," I whispered as the first tear fell. "Don't make me leave."

Her eyes turned cold and she pulled her hand from mine. "Leave," her weak voice commanded. "You need to leave. You don't belong here anymore."

Suddenly, Katherine was there again, adding her voice to Parker's.

"Leave! Get out! You did this to her! You left her, and look what happened! This is all your fault! You've killed her!"

That was when I woke up, sweat covering my body and face drenched with tears.

Chapter Thirty-Five

Parker

MONDAY MORNING POST-THANKSGIVING WENT about as bad as I had figured it would. To start, I had a breakdown in my car when I got to school and cried hysterically for fifteen minutes. This made me late for class, and also meant that I didn't get into a seat in the back. I had planned to sit in my normal spot, and if Ash came to sit with me, it meant we still had a chance. Of course, that wasn't even a possibility, because I was an emotional wreck who wasn't sleeping and cried at the drop of a hat... so that kind of sucked. But, I don't know, part of me had been expecting something... Ideally a text that said he regretted breaking up with me, or wanted to talk, but at this point I'd take anything... I didn't even care what it said about me, I was willing to do anything to get him back. But after sneaking a peek at him through my hair and seeing the glare that he was leveling at me, I knew that there was absolutely zero hope.

I forced myself to pay attention to every word that came out of my professor's mouths through each of my classes, otherwise I knew I would end up thinking about Ash, and then I would probably end up crying in class, and that just wasn't going to happen - I would make sure of it. I had cried enough for one morning.

When I got back to the apartment after school, the look that Diane gave me was part curiosity and part accusation, but then her eyes made a full scan of my face and her expression immediately transformed to total sympathy.

"Hey, sweetie," she called softly, and I couldn't take it.

"Not a word, Diane. I've had a really bad couple of days, and I don't want to talk about anything that doesn't have to do with my mom. I'm fine, everything is fine. Please," I begged, my voice breaking a bit on the word.

She nodded. "Everything's good here, sweetie. Mom's in sleeping now. She was hurting real bad earlier, so I gave her another pill, like you said to do. I think she's just gonna sleep it off. She didn't want to eat lunch. I got half a grilled cheese in her, but that was the best I could do. Just make sure that she eats dinner, she needs to put something in her stomach."

I nodded. "Thanks. I'll see you Wednesday," I told her and I followed her to the door to lock up behind her. She stopped though, and I held my breath as she hesitated.

"Parker," she began.

"Diane, please," I asked her quietly, but I saw the determination in her eyes.

"I'm just saying this and then I'll leave. That boy was a wreck when I saw him for Thanksgiving. I have no idea what happened between you two, but I've never seen him that upset, and I've seen my boy hurting like you wouldn't believe. This, this was something totally else. And now, I'm standing here and I see the exact same pain in your eyes. You two are young, and I know that you're new to this, but you need to fight for the things that matter in your life. I know you especially aren't so used to this, but when you have someone that you love like that, you hold on with everything you have."

Tears were streaking my face despite my best attempt at holding them back. "I tried, Diane," I told her quietly, "but he let me go. It wasn't my decision." It looked like that surprised her, but I was having trouble seeing through the moisture in my eyes, and I was completely over the conversation. "I have a lot of homework," I said, gesturing towards the door. She nodded slowly, and then finally turned and left without another word.

I tried for an hour to get to sleep. Then, once I realized that that wasn't going to happen, I got up and paced my room for about a half an hour. I realized I needed to do something that I'd been putting off for way too long.

I grabbed my phone and dialed the number for Jessie's cell. As the line started to ring, I felt my heart beating in my throat. I was so worked up, it was a major disappointment when the phone rang and rang before finally going through to voicemail. I heard the message and then the beep and I cleared my throat, suddenly unsure of what to say.

"Uh, hey, Jess. I just wanted to call, we haven't talked in a while and I miss you tons and tons. I was hoping that-" I was interrupted when my phone started beeping in my ear and I realized that she was calling me back.

"Oh, look," I added to the message, "you're calling me back. Cool." Then I mentally smacked myself as I switched over to the other line.

"Hello?"

"Oh my God, Parker. I can't even tell you how good it is to hear your voice! I miss you so fucking much, it's seriously not even funny. And also, while I appreciate the lame attempt to keep in touch via email, seriously, Park, fucking email? That shit is beyond stupid. I know, I know, the phone works both ways, but I'm just saying, we both suck."

Despite the fact that I was terrified to have this conversation, and I was quite possibly the unhappiest I had ever been in my life, I laughed. God, I missed this girl.

"Oh my God, Jessie, it is so good to hear your voice. And I know, the emails are freaking lame, but I'm trying. School's been crazy and… Just life."

"Fucking A," she groaned, "I know! I'm so tired of school and trying to deal with this fucking city, which is nothing like what I expected it to be… It's fucking exhausting…"

"How're things going with your dad?" I asked, knowing that even more than for NYU, she moved to New York to get to know him.

"Eh, we're still trying to figure each other out, I guess. I don't even know. It's weird, being around him with *her*… I can't stay in their house for much longer."

"What are you gonna do?" I asked, not bothering to hide the concern in my voice. "Jess, you need to be careful. New York City is dangerous, especially for a young woman living alone. You need to be careful! Do you know how many violent crimes take place in New York each year? It's insane. Do you have pepper spray? You know what? Never mind, I'll mail you-"

"Whoa, whoa," she interrupted me through her laughter. "Oh my God, I missed you!" she finally said as she got control of her giggles. "I have a nice shiny rape whistle *and* pepper spray. For real, Park," she said as her voice grew serious, "you don't need to worry. I'm well aware how dangerous this city can be. I'm always careful."

I sighed. "I know, I'm sure you are. Just, I worry about you, you know?"

I heard a quiet sniffle before, "I know. I worry about you too. But, listen, you might not have to worry so much anymore…"

"Oh yeah?" I asked when she didn't elaborate. "Why's that?"

"Well… I've been thinking, and I'm considering moving home."

"Why? What happened?" I asked suddenly.

It was her turn to let out a sigh. "Nothing, I just… I'm not so sure New York is where I belong…"

I kept my mouth shut, wanting her to make this decision on her own, but inside I was secretly praying that she came home. I wanted my best friend back.

"Ugh, anyway, I'm still considering my options, so, whatever. Now tell me, what's up with you? What have you been doing besides failing Stat for the past three months?"

"I'll have you know, I am passing Stat with a B right now." *But, shit. I probably won't keep that B for long without Ash helping me out.* I decided to worry about that later.

"Wow. How the fuck is that happening?" She asked in awe, totally understanding the plight that was my absolute suckiness at math.

"Eh, I got a tutor." I kept most of the tightness from my throat, thankfully.

"Nice. Anything else?"

"I kind of…" I let out a sigh before forcing myself to say the words. "I met a guy…"

"Oh my God, Parker! Why didn't you start with that?!" Her happy shout made me wish I had called her months ago, so we could have celebrated this together.

"Calm down, cowgirl. We broke up already."

"Wait, you said you met someone. Broke up implies relationship. Spill. Now."

I groaned. "We met at the start of the school year. We, dated, I guess, for about three months. He dumped me Wednesday."

"Damn, a day-before-a-holiday-dumper. What a dick…"

"Jessie…"

"Okay, okay, sorry. So, tell me the rest."

"That's it."

"What do you mean that's it?" she asked, as if I was a moron. Honestly, at this point, I couldn't really even argue against that.

"I mean, that's it. End of story."

"Bullshit. Why'd he dump you?"

I hesitated. "I don't know… He's a couple years older than me, and more experienced, and I guess I just… Ash is so intense, and he wanted to move faster than I guess I could… And, unsurprisingly, he got tired of it."

"What the fuck, Park? Was he trying to pressure you into having sex?!"

"No! God, no, Jessica! Not at all! I mean, he was like, *emotionally* intense, you know?"

"No," she stated shortly. "I have no idea what you're talking about."

"Yeah," I told her quietly, "I don't either…"

We were both quiet for a moment before she asked, "You okay, Park?"

"Yeah," I replied, probably a little too brightly, but I didn't want her worrying about me. She wasn't convinced.

"You sure?"

I felt the tears gathering in my eyes and I wanted to scream. I was so freaking sick of crying.

"Yeah, Jess, I'm sure."

"Alright… Well, I should run. I was in class when you called and I kind of ran out to call you back."

"Seriously? You could have just called me after!" I scolded, but I knew she heard the smile in my voice.

"Yes, seriously," she told me forcefully. "My best friend, who I hadn't spoken to in months was calling, and that took precedence over everything else. Besides, I didn't know if you would answer later. I wasn't gonna risk it."

"You're one in a million, babe." I quietly whispered the phrase that we used to tell each other all the time while we were dressing up in yet another ridiculous costume in Jessie's room. We said it so much that it became our little way of saying *I love you*.

"You too, gorgeous," she answered quietly. "Call me soon, okay?"

"I will. Stay safe."

She chuckled. "Yeah, you too."

That night, I – thankfully – didn't cry. I also didn't sleep, but, at this point, I think I'd take lying awake over the dreams any day.

Chapter Thirty-Six

Ash

BY THE TIME CHRISTMAS EVE had rolled around, I was totally over Parker.

Okay, that's complete bullshit. But I *had* convinced everyone around me that I was totally over Parker, which was good because the worried glances that my family had been shooting me for weeks after Thanksgiving had started making me feel pathetic. The nightly whiskey binges had (mostly) stopped, and I survived my finals, so I figured all was going well in my world. I also figured I was lucky as hell that Philosophy was finally over, because being stuck in a room three hours a week with the girl who still owned every piece of my mutilated heart – well... I'll just say it's a bit fucking uncomfortable.

I wasn't looking forward to the holidays, but I was glad that Rory was home and I was putting on a brave face for everyone. That being said, it was more than a little difficult. Everything around me made me think of Parker and, before I knew it, I'd be wondering how she and her mom were spending their Christmas Eve. The only thing I was sure of was that it would be nothing like ours.

My mom loved Christmas, and she always went all-out when it came to decorating the house. This year was no exception. Dad liked Christmas too; he always decorated outside (he considered stringing lights and setting up mechanical Santas to be a man's job,) but for him, it was more a matter of pride. No one's house looked better at Christmas than the Carter's - he made sure of that.

Inside the house, on the other hand - that was Mom's job, and she excelled at it. Every surface was covered with garlands and lights, figurines, candles - and of course her collection of Christmas-themed incense burners, which she displayed like showpiece items throughout the entire home.

I had loved Christmas in our house as a kid. Now, it was safe to say that the magic had worn off.

Mom had cooked a ham for dinner, and the entire family sat around the table and ate together. I spent most of my time focusing on Rory telling Grandma all about school and her life in Boston, while simultaneously picking at my food and helping myself to my dad's stash of bourbon. I knew I couldn't get drunk - there was no way I letting my mom force me into spending the night - so I was drinking slowly. Because of that, by the time dessert was being served, I was ready to go. I wanted to drive home and get blasted in an attempt to ignore the fact that, more than anything else, I wanted to go to Parker and beg her to take me back. It had been a fucking month and I still had to convince myself every day that I was doing the right thing by staying away from her.

"Ash," Grandma said suddenly, pulling me out of my head, where I was thinking about how much alcohol it was going to take to forget her tonight. Probably more than I had.

That's gonna be a problem.

"Ash," she repeated, louder that time.

"Shit… I mean… crap, yeah?"

Rory giggled quietly but Grandma ignored her. Then she said five words that I really didn't want to hear.

"Have you talked to Parker?"

I felt the breath I had been inhaling get stuck in my throat, and then I was choking. I grabbed my water and took a sip before calming down enough to feign a neutral, unaffected expression when I responded "Uh, no. I haven't."

She nodded slowly. "I figured, but I kinda hoped… I wanted to know how her mom was doing."

Fuck. I didn't want to ask. I really didn't want to ask, but… Shit. I was totally going to fucking ask.

"What happened to her mom?"

She looked at me for a long minute. "I'm not sure if-"

"Grandma," I interrupted. "What happened to Katherine?"

She sighed. "I'm not really sure, sweetie. I just know she got sick. Last I heard she was in the hospital."

"What do you mean, she 'got sick'?" I growled. "How much sicker can a person that sick get?"

And then I realized what she was saying. Katherine was immunocompromised. Even the slightest cold could be deadly if she couldn't fight it off.

"Fuck," I hissed under my breath. Suddenly, a thousand thoughts were swirling through my head, fighting for attention. I wanted to forget about Parker and her mom. I wanted to move on, I wanted to figure out where my life was headed. But at the same time, I wanted Parker. I had never stopped wanting Parker, and now, knowing that she was probably sitting by her Mom's side in the hospital, lonely and afraid, I wanted nothing more than to go to her. I wanted to feel her, wanted to hold her in my arms, and I wanted to take away her pain, at least as much as she would let me.

That fast I had made my decision. "I gotta go," I announced to the room suddenly, "I love you guys, and Mom, dinner was great. I'll see you all in the morning. Grandma," I froze in my dash for the door and met her eyes, "thank you." She smiled and nodded, but I was already on my way to the truck.

I'd made it halfway to Parker's apartment before I realized that I had no idea if she would even be home. Suddenly, I was really regretting drunkenly forcing Jimmy to delete her number from my phone. At the time, I thought it was a great idea, but being able to call her would have been fucking convenient right now.

It was pretty early, so I figured, knowing Parker, she would still be at the hospital. The problem was, I had no idea which hospital her mom would be at, so finding her there wasn't an option. I decided my best bet was to head to her apartment and wait there. I didn't care how fucking long it took, I was going to see Parker tonight whether she liked it or not.

Chapter Thirty-Seven

Parker

WALKING OUT OF THE HOSPITAL at the end of visiting hours on Christmas Eve, I'm not even gonna lie - I felt like shit. I was exhausted, both physically and mentally. I was worried about Mom. And, nearly a month later, and I was still just as miserable without Ash as I had been on Thanksgiving. Possibly more so, considering Christmas had me thinking about how great it would have been for us to spend the holiday together, and how much I wished things were different. I hijacked that train of thought when I felt the tears start to gather in my eyes - *I was not going to cry in my car. Fuck that.*

It was a depressing fact, but I had finally completed my childhood opus - controlling my tears. Mind you, it took crying about three times a day, every day, for me to finally learn to stop the show of emotion, but after repeatedly crying in public because I saw something that reminded me of Ash, it was a skill that was I was thankful to have picked up.

It had begun to snow while I was visiting with Mom, and fat flurries were swirling past the windshield while I attempted to navigate the dark, slippery roads home. My car, which was definitely standing on its last two legs (and, seriously, that was one more thing that I didn't need right now,) slid a few times across patches of ice, but luckily, between the weather and the holiday, the roads were pretty empty and I made it home safely.

I climbed out of the car into the frigid air and was halfway up the dark path to the front door before I noticed the snow covered shadow slumped on the front step. At the sight, I froze. I couldn't see more than a hunched shape shivering in the cold, and I found myself, for about the thousandth time, wishing I lived somewhere else. Right now, preferably somewhere with lights outside the front door, the better to discourage creepy people from sitting on my front step. I was debating whether or not I could make it back to my car before the creepy stranger mugged me when the shadow moved and suddenly I was staring into the same golden eyes that I had seen every night in my dreams for the past month. My breath rushed out in one steaming puff, and I felt my legs begin to shake as I told myself to get a grip because this was obviously just a hallucination.

I closed my eyes and counted to three, then opened them again. In the next second, I came to a few conclusions. First, I realized that Ash was actually sitting on my front step, and that this was not a hallucination. Next, I realized that, not only was he covered in a light layer of snow, he was visibly shivering. Finally, I realized that, as much as I had been dying to see him here, exactly like this, I was suddenly terrified of what his visit was about. And, I will restate this, because it felt important at the time, I was *exhausted*. So, I may not have reacted very well.

"What the fuck are you doing here?"

He winced and then slowly, stiffly rose to his feet.

"Can we talk?" he asked quietly. I took a minute to take in his appearance, my eyes all too eager to soak in every detail of the beautiful face that I had missed more than I would have thought possible. His gorgeous hair, longer than usual and wet with snow, hung down into his face, and the layer of scruff that I was used to was longer than I had ever seen it. Still, he looked as wonderful as ever, or, he did until I really noticed his eyes. They were sunken, haunted and dark, and ringed by ugly circles. It looked like he hadn't slept in a while. A really long while.

"I'm not really sure what there is to talk about," I answered once I had finished staring. As soon as the words were out of my mouth, my brain started screaming at me. *What the hell, Parker?! We've been waiting for this moment for a month! You're going to scare him off!*

I told my brain to go fuck itself and held my ground, trying to give Ash my most impassive stare.

"Yeah, we both know that's a fucking lie. You look like you haven't slept in a month, which is about how long it's been for me too, so…" He sighed. "Look, I've been out here for like, three hours. I'm fucking wet and cold, and it's Christmas Eve, for Christ's sake. Can I please just come up and talk to you? Five fucking minutes, Park. Please." His voice was super growly, and I had always melted like butter on hot toast when it came to Ash's super growly voice.

I groaned. "Fine! Come on," I snapped, pushing past him to head inside.

I walked straight to the stairs, not bothering to check that he was following, muttering the entire way. "I cannot even believe you were sitting outside. It's like, 30 degrees. And snowing! All those years of playing hockey have obviously damaged your brain."

Ash, on the other hand, was quiet for the walk upstairs, staying silent even after I had unlocked the front door and let us both into the quiet apartment. I ignored him while I stripped off my jacket and dropped my keys on the dining room table. When I turned back to face him, he was still standing just inside the door, staring at a spot on the carpet.

"God, Ash, at least take off your jacket. You need to get warm before you end up hypothermic. I don't want your death on my conscience."

He jumped as if he had completely forgotten I was there, and then I saw his lips tip up on one side as he moved, shrugging out of the wet jacket before draping it over a chair. I settled onto the couch and curled up in the corner, pulling my legs up and wrapping my arms around them. Ash took a seat on the opposite side and set his elbows on his knees, staring at his linked hands. It gave me the chance to stare without him noticing and I took it, taking in every detail. I was so transfixed by the sight, I almost missed it when Ash spoke.

"How have you been, Park?"

I hesitated and then decided honesty was probably the best way to get through… whatever this was.

"Pretty shitty. How about you, Ash?"

He sighed and then turned to face me. "Really fucking terrible, actually."

I nodded, trying to come up with something to say to that, but he continued. "How's your mom?"

Suddenly, it made sense. Here I was, thinking that Ash had shown up because he realized that we belonged together, and he missed me as much as I missed him. Instead, Diane had to open her big, fat mouth, and now he feels sorry for me? *Fuck. That.*

"Seriously?" I asked him, deadly quiet. His eyes narrowed on my face, which felt pale, but I ignored his glare. "It's been the worst fucking month of my life. I'm absolutely miserable without you, and you... You show up here to ask me about my mom? *That's* why you're here?"

"No, Parker-"

"No, you know what, Ash? Just save it. I can't do this. I can't have this conversation. You don't get to ask me about my mom. You don't get to show up here, and make me think..." I broke off as the tears threatened and took a moment to fight them off.

"That's not why I'm here! I mean, it is, but, I just... Grandma mentioned that she was sick, and I was worried about you!"

"Fuck that! You don't get to worry about me anymore. That's not your job!" I shouted angrily.

"Maybe so, but that doesn't change the fact that I worry about you all the goddamn time!"

I shook my head, trying to block out his words. When that didn't work, I decided that it was time to escape. In one quick move, I pushed my feet to the floor and started around the couch to head to my room.

"You need to go. I can't do this again. Just go-" The rest of my words came out as a loud squeak as he shot off the couch, moving towards me until I had no choice but to retreat, backing up until my back hit the wall. He leaned in close, and I could feel the air leaving his lips as it blew across my face. I couldn't breathe; I could barely think when he was this close to me.

"Stop running, Parker. I'm done running, and I'm telling you right now, you are too. I'm not leaving again, and you are not going to make me."

"Fuck you, Ash! We tried this. It obviously didn't work. Get out of my face!" I was using every trick in my arsenal, yet I still felt the tears start to fall across my cheeks.

"Stop lying! You still want this, I still want this. We fucking belong together, and I'm not about to let you sabotage this anymore!"

At that, I couldn't control my reaction. All I knew was that I needed him out of my face. I lifted both hands and slammed them into his chest, using every ounce of my rage and angst and loneliness to push him as hard as I could.

Ash didn't even move an inch.

"God!" I finally screamed once I realized that he wasn't going to back off. The tears were rolling down my face by now, and I just could not give a single fuck. "This is so not okay, Ashton! I have missed you every day for a goddamn month. I fucking needed you, and you left! You told me that you wouldn't leave, that you loved me and, I'll repeat, you just left! You can't do this to me again! I love you too much-"

And, that's the precise moment that Ash decided to shut me right the fuck up.

Chapter Thirty-Eight

Ash

I KISSED HER.

She was screaming at me, angrier than I had ever seen her, face red and tears streaming down her face, and I couldn't help it, couldn't have stopped myself if I had wanted to. The second I heard her say those words, those *three fucking words* that I had been *dying* to hear, I slammed my mouth down on hers.

Instantly, I remembered one of the many reasons that I fucking loved this girl. She didn't even hesitate for a second. The moment my mouth hit hers, her hands shot to my neck and she pulled my body even closer, while her tongue reached out to find mine through her already open mouth. I pressed her harder into the wall and heard a guttural moan escape her mouth. Leaning back an inch, I managed to whisper, "I love you so fucking much," before she reclaimed my mouth.

Every touch, every taste reminded me of all of the things that I had been missing for the past month, and in seconds, I was hard as a rock, pressing my hips into hers as my hands roamed her sides. My lips left her mouth and trailed along her jaw, then down to her neck, kissing and tasting her perfect fucking skin. God, this girl drove me absolutely crazy, and I loved every fucking second of it.

Suddenly, I heard her words in my head again and I had to press my face into her neck as I suppressed a smile. I took a step back, pulling her body with mine and wrapping my arms around her so that I could lift her into the air. She was lighter than she had been a month ago, and her waist felt too small, but I made a mental note to think about that later and abandoned the thought. Once I had her in the air, she wrapped her legs around me, hooking her feet behind my back. In seconds, I was moving us both into her bedroom. When I made it to the bed, I dropped us both down to the mattress, bracing my arms around her so that she wouldn't take my full weight as we fell.

Through all of this, her mouth stayed fused to mine. As soon as we were on the bed, her arms unwrapped themselves from around my neck and then I felt her warm hand on the skin of my back. I had to suppress a shudder - I had wanted to feel her hands on my skin every day since we broke up, and the sensation was completely overwhelming. The electricity was back - the feeling that I was finally, finally turned back on. My skin felt tight and hot, and the only thing I could even think about was getting inside this beautiful girl underneath me. My brain tried to argue that this was possibly a bad idea, but I was currently letting the other head on my body take the lead, and he was shouting that all systems were go.

Parker fidgeted restlessly beneath me as her hands continued to travel over every inch of my skin that she could reach, and mine repaid the favor. I let my fingers skate the skin at the edge of her waistband teasingly before switching gears and heading up to her bra-covered breast. I kneaded it through the cup gently which caused a hitch in her breath that made me smile against her lips. I rubbed my thumb over the hardened nipple I felt through the fabric and I heard the swift inhale that followed that. Every sound that this girl made was impossibly sexy - I hadn't even been inside her yet and I already knew that I'd never find anything better. Parker's fingers tentatively traced the lines and muscles of my chest and back and I felt the touch like it was a hand wrapped around my dick. God, she was amazing.

Next thing I knew, Parker had wrapped her legs around my waist and she was pressing her heat against the stiff bulge in my jeans. I heard her let out a small moan as she ground her hips into mine. That moan broke the small amount of control that I had managed to hang onto.

I moved my hand from her breast back down to the button of her jeans and flicked it open. As soon as I had pulled down her zipper, I felt her freeze and I pulled my hand away, laying it along her jaw.

"Hey, look at me," I whispered, waiting for her eyes to open before I continued.

"Ash..." she moaned, not meeting my eyes.

"Parker." Her eyes flickered open and they were hazy and unfocused. So fucking sexy... "You okay, baby?" I asked quietly, my lips so close to hers that they brushed together as I spoke.

She let out a groan. "Yes, Ash! God, keep going!" Then, her hands worked their way into my hair and she yanked my mouth against hers again. I kissed her even as I grinned and my hand moved back to the skin below her stomach.

"You're wet for me, aren't you, Park?" I asked against her lips.

"Oh my God," was her response, which prompted another grin before I took her mouth again. I kissed her hard until her body was languid below mine, and then I slowly worked my hand down, moving straight under her jeans and panties.

When my fingers finally slid against her soaked core, her mouth left mine and her head flew back.

"Holy... Ash," she panted, and I couldn't help it, I grinned a third time. I pulled my head back a few inches and watched her. Her eyes were closed and her mouth was soft, slightly open as her breath rushed in and out in short pants. Her cheeks were flushed and her lips were swollen, and I groaned watching her writhe against the bed.

"God, Park, I wish you could see yourself right now," I growled, and her eyes fluttered open and focused on me. Once I had her attention, I continued. "You are the sexiest fucking woman I've ever seen. You feel fucking incredible. So goddamn wet..."

At that, her lips tipped up and her eyes snapped shut as I suddenly but gently pushed one finger inside. She growled and then moaned, "Oh, oh, oh God, *Ash*..."

I lowered my mouth to her neck and slowly licked and kissed the skin of her throat. She smelled incredible and as I moved my finger slowly in and out, I pressed myself against her thigh. I was so hard that it ached, but this was all about Parker.

Once she was used to the sensation, I worked a second finger into her, then a third. By that time she was panting and moaning, mumbling about God and me and "How fucking amazing I felt." In that moment - watching her lose control under me, with my hand inside her wet heat - I was a smug bastard.

"Ash, I... *Fuck*, Ash, something's..." she said before trailing off, her mouth stuck in a perfect o. I decided it was time for her to come on my hand and I pressed against her clit, gently but steadily drawing small circles with my thumb. Instantly, I felt her muscles begin to clench around my hand and I worked her until I felt her tremors fade away and she had stopped screaming my name, a massive grin on my face the entire time.

See? Smug bastard.

She was completely limp beneath me as I gently removed my fingers and then pulled my hand from her jeans. I pressed a soft, closemouthed kiss to her lips and then another against her forehead. When I pulled back, I saw the small smile that curved across her lips and somehow I just knew everything was going to be okay.

"You alright, baby?" I asked quietly. Her eyes opened and met mine, and they were brighter than I had ever seen them. The smile grew and she let out a small laugh.

"Um, no, Ash. 'Alright' is not the correct word for what I am. I am amazing. I am incredible. I am-" I interrupted her with another quick kiss, but as I began to pull away her hands grabbed onto my face and she held me still.

"I love you." Her eyes stared into mine and her voice was strong as she once again spoke the words that I knew had changed my life forever.

I pressed my mouth into hers again, but this kiss wasn't quick. It was hard, long and wet - I claimed her mouth in a way that she couldn't mistake for anything but total possession. I branded her with my lips.

When I pulled away, I grasped her face between my hands and kept her close as I captured her eyes. "I love you, too."

Her lips tipped up and her eyes got bright with tears. I chuckled and then pressed one more kiss into her forehead. I couldn't keep my mouth off of her, but, the way I figured, I had a month's worth of kisses to make up, so I was getting started right away. Once I pulled away, I pushed off her and then climbed off the bed. She sat up quickly as her eyes followed my movements and her smile quickly faded.

"Please don't leave," she cried, a sudden expression of panic on her face, and I stopped and turned right back to her.

"Hey, stop. I'm not going anywhere except the bathroom to take a quick shower. Then, I promise, I'll be right back. Get ready for bed and get settled, yeah?" I took in her face, the panic fading as she nodded.

"Okay," she whispered.

I walked towards the bathroom and turned back to her where she was sitting in bed, staring at the opposite wall of her room. I stood in the doorway and took her in - her mussed blond ponytail, the slight flush that still stained her cheeks, bright green eyes, and gorgeous lips. She was the most beautiful thing I'd ever seen and I knew I would never let her go again.

"Love you, Parker," I called softly. Her face turned to mine and she gave me an amused smile, but before she could speak I moved into the bathroom and shut the door.

After a seriously quick and freezing cold shower, I had calmed myself down enough to throw my boxer briefs back on before leaving the rest of my clothes in a pile on the bathroom floor and heading back into her room.

Parker had turned off the bright overhead light and switched on her bedside lamp, so the room was lit with a soft glow. I knew she had changed, but all I could make out was a tiny tank top from where she sat in bed beneath the covers. She sat up and the blankets fell to her waist, and I could suddenly see in detail how the thin fabric stretched across her soft breasts. She had taken off her bra, and her nipples strained against the top enticingly. I was instantly hard again and my cold shower became a waste of fucking time. I grew even harder when I moved my eyes up to see hers moving over every inch of my body. Her mouth hung open and I heard her moan, "Oh, my God."

At that, I laughed and her eyes snapped up to mine, narrowing quickly. "Shut up," she snapped as her cheeks flushed and I laughed harder as I headed towards the bed. She was focusing on my groin again and her body was positioned dead center in the small bed.

"Scoot over," I told her when she continued staring, as opposed to moving so that I could climb into bed. She shook her head quickly and then moved until her body hit the wall.

I pulled back the blankets, slid into bed, and wrapped an arm around her waist and pulled her against my body. I felt her grow tight as I twisted myself until I had one arm around her neck and the other around her waist, wrapping my body around hers. I closed my eyes, but opened them immediately to reach behind me, turning off the light and plunging the room into darkness before I wrapped myself around her again.

I waited for her to relax, but it never came. Instead, I heard her squeak out, "Ash?"

"Yeah, baby?" I asked, eyes still closed.

"What, uh… What are you doing?" she asked quietly, and I grinned.

"I'm going to sleep, Park. It's late, and we have an early day tomorrow."

"We do?" she asked curiously.

"Yeah, baby, we do," I answered, opening my eyes to see hers staring down into mine. "We gotta get up early to get to my parents because I promised them I'd be there first thing. They wanna do presents all together because Rory's apparently still a child who believes in Santa, and then we gotta get to the hospital to see your Mom. From there, we'll figure it out. But to do any of that, we need to sleep."

Parker frowned. "I'm going to your parent's house tomorrow?"

I let out a small sigh because I had wanted to wait at least a day before having this conversation, but it seemed like it was going to have to happen now. I switched the light back on to find her eyes and then held them as I spoke.

"You want me here?" I asked quietly. I let out a relieved breath when she nodded, quickly and earnestly. "Alright. Then, let me catch you up.

"A month ago, I was a complete ass and I walked away from the best thing that has ever happened to me." I saw her eyes start to shine, but I kept going.

"I can't tell you how sorry I am for leaving. It was a mistake, Park. But, it was one that, I'm hoping, you can forgive because, being here with you after you opened up and told me how you feel… More than anything, I want to pick up where we left off." Her eyes still held mine, and I found her hand with my own, lacing our fingers together before I continued.

"I'm not saying that everything's going to magically get better. We still have a bunch of shit to work out and we have a lot to learn about each other, but I promise you right the fuck now Parker, I will not walk away again. And I won't let you either. This is real. This, you and me, we have something that people search their entire lives for. I fucked it up once, and I can promise that, if you give me a shot, I won't ever do it again. Do you think you can do that for me?"

I felt it in my gut when her lips turned up at the edges and she nodded. "Yeah, I can do that."

"Good," I told her with a smile of my own. "Then, tomorrow morning, you're coming to my parents' house with me and then we'll go together to see your mom in the hospital. You with me, baby?"

Her face went soft and her eyes dropped to my mouth before she nodded. "Yeah, Ash. I'm with you."

"Good," I told her with a smile. "Then lay the fuck down and let me put my arms around you. I've been dreaming about this for a month, and you're ruining it."

She snorted as I turned to flip off the light and then settled into bed beside me. "Shut up. I didn't ruin anything."

"You're right," I whispered once she was in my arms again, and then I pressed a soft kiss into her hair. "You're perfect. You couldn't have ruined this if you had tried."

"Love you, Ash," she whispered a minute later through a voice heavy with emotion, her lips moving against the skin above my collarbone.

"Love you too, Park. Merry Christmas, baby."

Then, with her smell in my nose and her weight in my arms, I fell into the first restful sleep that I had had since I walked away.

And when I slept, there wasn't a single dream. I slept like the dead.

Chapter Thirty-Nine

Parker

BY THE TIME THAT I woke up, the room was bright and my body felt strangely hot. Then, the memories of last night came rushing back. Slowly, I turned my head to the side to see Ash's sleeping face four inches from mine on the pillow. If there was ever a moment for a fangirl squee, this was it, but I contained my crazy reaction to seeing this beautiful boy sleeping next to me, and I just watched him sleep. He looked more relaxed than I had ever seen him, and I was happy to see that the dark circles were already fading from his eyes.

Suddenly, the moment was ruined by the sound of tinny hard rock echoing through my hazy brain.

"*Motorin'... What's your price for flight? In findin' Mr. Right...*"

The noise pierced the tranquility of the room, and I looked around, trying to figure out where it was coming from. I was so alarmed, I didn't notice when Ash began to stir.

"Shit," I heard, and when I looked at him, he was rubbing a hand against his hazy, hazel eyes.

Oh my God, he looks incredible in the morning.

In that moment, I decided that I wanted to wake up next to Ashton Carter every morning for the rest of my life.

Preferably, though, *without* Night Ranger preforming the wake-up call.

Ash rolled away from my side and then was moving across the room towards the open bathroom door. Grabbing his clothes from the floor, he carried the bundle into the bedroom and nabbed his phone from his front jeans pocket, at which point he moved back towards me. The phone had stopped ringing, but I saw him tap the screen a few times before groaning.

"Fuck, baby," he said, "we gotta get ready. We slept way later than we should have. I gotta call my sister real quick," he told me, already putting the phone to his ear. I glanced at the clock on the nightstand and let out a squeak. *Shit!* I hadn't slept this late in months!

Yeah Parker, my brain interjected snottily, *that's what happens when you come hard riding your ex-boyfriend's hand and then let him hold you until you fall asleep in his arms.*

He's not an ex anymore, I replied triumphantly, feeling the smile spread across my face.

Yeah, my brain agreed dreamily. *He's definitely not an ex anymore... Good job, girl.*

"Hey, Ror," I heard Ash say into his phone, and it jolted me out of my internal conversation. I shot out of bed and ran for the dresser, grabbing a pair of black pants, a gray sweater, a bra, and some panties that I took with me into the bathroom. After the world's quickest shower, I brushed my teeth, combed my hair, and got dressed, all in record time. When I ran out of the bathroom, he was seated, fully dressed, on the bed with a small smile on his face. At my entrance, he looked up.

"Ready, baby?"

I couldn't help it. I broke into a giant grin and held his eyes as I said, "Absolutely."

After stopping by Ash's apartment so that he could change his clothes, we headed straight for the hospital. Ash told me that his parents knew we wouldn't be by until later, so we could get straight over to see my mom, which I appreciated.

Mom had been pretty out of it for the past few days, and today wasn't any different, but she did look up when we entered at least for long enough to roll her eyes at Ash. But then her eyes drifted closed and she fell back into a fitful sleep.

I had bought her a few small gifts, but I forgot to bring them from the apartment, so I figured I'd just leave them at home under the Charlie Brown tree I set up, and she could open them when she went home, whenever that was. It would be something to look forward to.

Ash sat in the arm chair next to Mom's bed and pulled me down to sit in his lap. We listened to Christmas music softly play from his phone as we told each other stories about Christmases from our childhoods.

His memories were decidedly happier than mine.

At lunchtime, I was considering running down to grab sandwiches from the cafeteria downstairs when a knock came at the closed door. Ash's head swiveled towards mine before I pushed off of his lap and headed for the door just as it opened, and the air all left my lungs in one quick rush.

In walked Paul and Eliza, followed by Diane and a tall, dark-haired girl who looked about my age - Aurora, I assumed. My mouth fell open as they smiled and moved towards me as a group. Suddenly, I felt Ash at my back, his fingers threading through mine.

"Parker." Eliza greeted me with a huge smile as they got close. "It's so good to see you."

"Hey there, Parker," Paul added with a nod in my direction. Diane, however, came straight to me, ignoring Ash completely and wrapping her arms around me. "Merry Christmas, sweet girl. I've missed you."

And that was about all I could take. I pulled away from Diane's hold only to turn and plant my face directly in the center of Ash's chest. Then, I burst into tears.

"Hey," Ash cooed as he rubbed my back, "don't cry, baby. I'm sorry for not telling you that they were coming, but I knew you'd tell me no, and… Well, they're your family now, too."

That caused the tears to turn into out-and-out sobs that shook my body, and Ash's hands stopped rubbing in order to let his arms wrap around my like a vine.

"Come on, Park. It's okay, baby."

"I… I… *I know!*" I finally managed to get out through the tears as more continued to fall. "I'm just… so… *happy!*"

His body shook as he chuckled and I pulled back in his arms far enough to smack his arm. "Don't laugh at me!" I snapped, which only made his chuckles turn into straight laughter.

"You alright?" he asked softly once I had gotten my tears under control, his eyes intensely scanning my face.

"Yeah," I answered, "but I feel like I need to point out that your family keeps making me cry."

"I'll see what I can do about that. Now, do you wanna meet my sister?"

Holy shit. How did I forget about Rory? And then my face flamed as I realized that I had just made a total ass of myself.

"Oh my God, Ash. I just made a total ass of myself in front of her," I whispered angrily.

"Your point?" he whispered back.

My mouth dropped open. "My... My point?" I whispered, trying to convey the appropriate amount of disbelief at his question without being overheard.

"Yeah baby. Your point. Because, from what I can tell, my baby sister is standing about four feet behind you, smiling at every word that's coming out of your mouth. The way I see it, you should probably just accept what's already happened and start trying to salvage the situation."

Double shit. He was so right.

I wiped the tears from my face with his shirt, which pulled another laugh from his chest, and then I turned to face the rest of the room. To my utter mortification, they were all staring at Ash and I, and I could tell by the expressions on their faces that they had heard every bit of my freak out.

Alright, well. Accept what's happened. Salvage the situation.

Before I could do anything, Rory left Eliza's side and walked up to me, wrapping me up in a tight hug.

"I am so happy to finally meet you," she whispered in my ear as she squeezed me tightly. "I've heard so much about you."

When she finally began to pull away, I grabbed her arms and kept her close. "I'm glad to meet you too," I said with a smile. "This one never shuts up about you," I gestured to Ash behind me.

"It's all lies, I swear," she said, giggling, and for some completely unknown reason, I giggled with her.

Ash's parents had brought a bag full of sandwiches and chips, and once Ash walked to the vending machines down the hall to get a few sodas, we all sat around my mom's bed and ate Christmas lunch while she slept. I loved Ash's entire family, and seeing them sitting in the same room as my mom gave me a strange sense of peace. Suddenly, I felt less alone, and that feeling left me with the impression that I could get through anything as long as I had Ash and his family, standing behind me.

By the time the nurses were getting ready for their afternoon rounds, the Carters (minus Ash) all started to grab their jackets and head towards the door. I gave hugs and kisses to everyone, and told them I'd see them later tonight when we went to Eliza's and Paul's for dinner. Ash came to me and gave me a soft-but-super-sweet kiss that sent me into a total daze, and then told me he was walking his parents out and he'd be right back.

I heard the door close, and then was surprised by the sound of a throat being cleared. Glancing up, I saw Rory headed back my way.

"Can we talk for a sec?" she asked hesitantly. Her hands knitted together in front of her stomach, and she looked so uneasy that I grew wary even as I nodded.

"Of course," I replied, and I watched her let out a burst of air.

"Look, he'd probably kill me for saying any of this but... Just be careful with him. Ash is..."

"He's incredible," I finished when she trailed off, which brought her eyes to mine with a surprised jerk before they softened.

"Yeah," she said quietly, "he is. I love Ash more than anyone else in this world, and he's been absolutely miserable since Thanksgiving."

I could tell by her expression that she knew she had made me uncomfortable. "I don't really know what happened," she reassured quickly, "but, I just wanted you to know that he feels things a lot harder than most people. He's got a huge heart, but it gets him hurt sometimes. Just... Be careful with him," she shrugged.

I held her gaze as I answered the unspoken question. "I love him." I saw her eyes crinkle in the corners and a tiny smile spread on her face, but I continued. "I've loved him for a while now, and you're right, he does have a huge heart. But I promise you Rory, I'll take care of it. For as long as he'll let me."

She scoffed and waved a hand in my direction. "God, Parker, he's absolutely crazy about you, and when Ash is sure about something, he is *sure*. You tell him that, he'll have a ring on your finger in about a week."

I sucked in a startled breath, and at the same moment her expression turned to fear. "Shit, I mean, I don't know...

Crap! I always do this. Don't freak out, please! Ash'll kill me..."

She stopped rambling when she heard my laughter. I couldn't help it, between everything that had happened in the past twenty-four hours, I just snapped. Bent over, with tears rolling down my face, I laughed harder than I had in years.

And of course, Ash chose that moment to pop his head back into the room.

"Babe, have you seen..." He trailed off as he caught sight of me doubled over in laughter and Rory, who was now staring at her brother with a deer-in-the-headlights expression on her gorgeous face.

"What's going on in here?" Ash asked, suspicion dripping from his every syllable. This unfortunately only made me laugh harder.

It was official. I was definitely crazy.

But Ash loved me, so I was kind of okay with that.

Chapter Forty

Ash

IT HAD BEEN THE BEST Christmas of my life, by far. Every moment - from waking up in Parker's bed with her in my arms, to spending the day at the hospital, both our families together (and if I'm honest, it didn't really bother me that her mom spent the whole time sleeping,) as well as Christmas dinner with my family - was burned into my memory.

But when dinner was over, we went back to Parker's apartment and had the place to ourselves. I'm not even going to pretend otherwise - I was fucking thrilled.

Once we got inside and I helped her out of her coat, I headed back towards the door, telling Parker that I needed to run out to my truck for a minute.

I reached into the cab and grabbed the huge box that I had hidden behind the passenger seat. Then I grabbed the duffel bag that I had packed at my place and headed back up to my girl.

As soon as I walked in the door her eyes dropped to the gift-wrapped box in my hand and her face fell.

"What is that?" she asked warily, as if expecting my answer to be, *Why, a box of poisonous snakes to kill you with, my dear.*

I smirked and set the box next to her on the cushion, dropping the duffel at our feet before settling onto the other side of the couch.

"Open it," I told her, but she just kept staring at the box.

"I can't…" she whispered, eyes still glued to the box.

"Why not?" I asked.

Her eyes finally came to meet mine. "I didn't get you anything, Ash! That's not fair!"

I laughed, which prompted a growl to rumble from her throat. "Shut up and open the present, Parker. And, just so you know, this hardly even counts as a Christmas present, because I bought it all like two months ago and just never got around to giving it to you before."

She nodded and gingerly reached out to pull the box into her lap. I saw the surprise flash across her face when she felt how heavy it was, so I reached out to help her lift it into her lap. Her hands rested on the top of the package for about two seconds before she ripped off the bow and tore into the paper. Uncovering a plain white box, she grabbed the lid and slowly lifted it off.

I stared at her face while she stared down into the box, so I saw the first tear fall.

"Oh my God, Ash…"

"I know that you want to create again, baby. I also know you're afraid. So, I figured I'd buy this stuff for you," I gestured to the box, which was filled to the brim with art supplies - pencils, pens, paints, charcoal, watercolor sets, oil pastels, brushes, books and a few small canvases, "and maybe you could show me how to use it. Any then, maybe, if you feel like it, you could give it another shot."

My hands shook against my legs as I waited for her to respond. To say anything. She had already gotten the tears under control and she was just staring into the box with a blank expression on her face.

"Parker," I called when she still didn't react, "those pictures on your walls are incredible. They're you - brilliant and beautiful and unique. Create again. Open that part of yourself back up. You don't need to be afraid anymore."

She roughly shoved the box onto the ground and swung her body towards mine. I barely got my hands around her arms in order to stop her before she landed her mouth on mine.

"Oof. What was that for? I wanna kiss you," she pouted.

"Wait," I answered, wrapping my arms around her back and pulling her into my lap. "Do you like your present?"

"Ash, it's..." She took a deep breath, glancing down for a moment before bringing her eyes back to me. "It's incredible. I love it. I got rid of everything I had when I moved in with Mom. This is..." she trailed off and then changed gears. "You're kind of amazing, you know that?"

I smiled and pressed a quick kiss to her lips. "Yep, I know. And just you wait. I have something else for you."

"Ash!" she shouted as I smiled and grabbed the bag at my feet. I zipped it open and reached inside, quickly finding the velvet box that I had thrown in on top.

"Oh my God," she muttered as I straightened, wrapping my arms back around her before pushing the box into her hand.

"What is this?"

"Stop asking me that," I answered against the crook of her neck. "Open it." I traced my tongue along her skin until I reached her earlobe, which I sucked gently into my mouth. She let out a sexy-as-fuck moan, leaning into my body, forgotten box in hand.

"Open your present, baby," I whispered again.

I saw her hands shake as she grasped the box between her fingers, slowly prying open the lid, and I felt her body move with her gasp.

"Holy shit, Ash."

The necklace was a five-carat, princess cut emerald set in a 24-carat gold setting on a gold chain. I didn't care about any of that shit but the woman at the jewelry store had informed me, when I stopped to stare at the sizable piece of jewelry while out shopping for a gift for Rory, that it was "an exquisite piece, deserving of a woman as beautiful as the stone."

What the fuck ever. All I gave a shit about - the entire reason I had stopped in the first place - was that the deep green emerald was the exact same shade of green as Parker's eyes when she laughed.

Or cried.

I preferred to think about the laughter.

When I found out that emerald just so happened to also be Parker's birthstone, I knew I had to take it home. Stupid shit that I was, I didn't even stop to consider the fact that I shouldn't be buying expensive jewelry for a woman that I was no longer with, but it just didn't seem like an issue at the time.

I gotta say - at least this time - my subconscious really came through for me.

Parker was staring at the necklace, one hand frozen over her mouth, and I wanted to laugh, but I was actually nervous. "You like it, baby?" I asked quietly. "Cause you're kinda freakin' me out a little bit right now..."

"Ash, I can't... This is way too much. This had to have been crazy expensive," she told me, turning to look at me over her shoulder.

She was right. It was stupidly expensive.

"That's irrelevant." I reached towards her hand, quickly grabbing the box and gently pulling the necklace out. I opened the clasp and, before she could say a word about it, draped it around her neck, securing it before laying a soft kiss over the clasp at the back of her neck. "Do you like it?" I asked her again before running my nose along the skin behind her ear. I felt her shiver in my lap, and that fast, I was hard as a rock.

"I love it, Ash. It's beautiful."

"You're beautiful. Now, I believe I interrupted you right before you were about to demonstrate your appreciation of the art shit, so-"

"Ashton Carter, don't you dare reduce the best Christmas present I've ever gotten to 'art shit.'" Her eyes were flashing with anger and I wanted to laugh.

I kissed her instead.

And Parker, my *incredible* Parker, she attacked.

Chapter Forty-One

Parker

I WAS SICK OF WAITING. The second Ash touched his mouth to mine, I latched onto him and went absolutely wild. My skin felt too hot, I was restless and twitchy, and I wanted to get another look at him without any clothing.

As my mouth played with his, I quickly shifted my body around until I was straddling his lap on the couch. My hips moved against his, and I could feel his hardness pressing into the spot between my legs. I felt a growl leave my throat as his hands grabbed my hips tightly and he pressed me harder against him.

"Fuck… Ash," I spoke against his mouth, and his tongue lightly traced my bottom lip before he caught it gently between his teeth. My fingers latched on to the bottom of his shirt and I had started pulling up when his hands grabbed mine and held them still.

"Shit, Parker," he groaned as he pulled his lips away and rested his forehead against mine. "I didn't-"

"Shut up," I interrupted. "Just, shut up and *please* take me to bed."

My eyes had been closed, but I felt his hesitation and I opened them to see him watching me.

"You sure?"

I let out a snort of laughter that jostled me in his lap. As I shifted against his length, the laughter sharply became a groan of pleasure.

"Yes, Ash. I'm sure," I told him.

He didn't make me say it twice.

That fast, I was in the air. I hooked my legs around his back as his fingers dug into my ass, and then we were headed towards my bedroom. Ash didn't bother closing the door or turning on a light as he took us straight to the bed. This time, instead of collapsing on top of me, he sat on the edge of the bed with me in his lap again. I pushed him straight to his back, hands roaming his chest as I chased him with my mouth, tasting and kissing every inch of his lips, so I felt it when he grinned.

"Fuck, baby," he groaned. "You are so fucking sexy when you can't keep your hands off me."

I smiled but otherwise ignored him as I moved my hands back to the bottom of his shirt, leaning back so that I could pull it off. I was impatient, and the impatience was making the process even harder until I was ready to just rip the thing apart.

Thankfully, he assisted my efforts by leaning up to grab the shirt behind his head before yanking it off. I felt a rush of wetness between my thighs as I took in his chest, and I couldn't control the moan that slipped from my mouth. He was almost too incredibly perfect - the smooth, tanned skin, the lickable eight-pack that molded his tapered waist, and the dark line of hair that started below his navel and ran straight down between the perfect v formed by his hips and into his jeans.

Oh my God, he can't be real. The thought floated through my head uncontrolled as I took in his form with unconcealed longing. Except, he grinned, as if he completely knew what I was thinking at that precise moment. Either he could read my mind or... *shit.*

"I totally said that out loud, didn't I?" I asked, and he nodded. I answered with a nod of my own, and his words from the hospital floated through my head. *Accept what's happened. Salvage the situation.*

So, I grabbed his neck and pulled his mouth back to mine.

As his tongue teased, his hands worked their way under my sweater, and I groaned as he started kneading my breasts. "God, that feels good," I moaned. I dragged my hands from his chest just long enough to grab my shirt and pull it over my head.

Even though I had always expected to be nervous when this moment finally came, being with Ash felt completely natural - as if he had always been a part of me. I already ached to have him filling me, as if my body knew exactly where he belonged. I knew he was nervous about moving faster than I was ready to, but I wanted to show him how much I wanted this. How much I wanted *him.*

When my sweater hit the floor, Ash leaned back an inch to sweep his eyes down my flushed skin. I felt his stare burning into my chest and the slightest hint of embarrassment over my plain, peach-colored cotton bra, but Ash's heated gaze warmed me until it felt like my insides were burning. Slowly, his eyes came back to mine and at the look in them, my already wet panties were absolutely drenched.

From there, it became an exploration. We slowly undressed each other, inspecting every inch of skin that we uncovered with both fingers and mouths. We worshiped each other with quiet, reverent kisses as we learned the curves and lines of each other's body.

Next thing I knew, we were lying on top of the covers with our heads at the bottom of the bed. Ash had settled on top of me, and he shifted his weight back onto his knees as his hands came to my hips, gently grabbing my panties to pull them down my legs. I was completely naked with another person for the first time, but I realized I didn't feel embarrassed by his molten stare. I didn't want to shy away from his eyes - eyes that were filled with need. The sensation was heady - overwhelming yet comforting. Reckless and yet completely safe. It was a mixture of contradictions, and I loved it.

"You're so beautiful, Parker."

His voice had gone super-growly, and I shifted on the bed, unable to wait anymore . He was sitting back on his heels, wearing nothing but pair of black boxer briefs that hugged his thighs, and his eyes moved over my body for a few long moments before he brought his mouth to the inside of my knee. He pressed his lips against my skin as he kissed and licked his way up my thigh and I squirmed beneath him. Just as he started to reach where I wanted him, his mouth left my skin and I felt it press against my other leg, starting the slow, torturous process over.

I groaned and shifted again. "Ash..."

I felt him chuckle against me, the small exhales of breath tickling my skin as he whispered, "Patience, baby. We have all night, and I need to make sure that you're ready for me."

I lifted my head to glare at him between my legs. "Trust me, I'm ready."

His mouth moved higher as he shook his head. "I'll be the judge of that."

Suddenly, my head dropped to the mattress as he pressed two fingers into me, and I sucked in air.

"Fuck," he rasped against my thigh, "fucking drenched."

His fingers moved slowly in and out, and his mouth moved closer until in one swift movement, he placed his mouth right there.

"Oh God, Ash, oh my God…"

I moaned unintelligibly as his fingers pumped faster and his mouth sucked and licked my sensitive skin. Mere minutes later, I felt my body start to tighten.

"Fuck, Ash, I'm…" I groaned, and my hips started to lift from the bed until Ash wrapped his free arm around one of my thighs and anchored me against his face.

"Come on, baby," he growled against my skin, "Come for me."

My body shattered.

I vaguely remember screaming his name and shouting about God as he continued to work me, dragging out the orgasm until I was completely boneless and sinking into the bed. I barely noticed it when he finally pulled away, leaning back to rub an arm across his mouth before his heat disappeared from between my legs. I moved to find him but he was already back, crawling up my body to lay a long, wet kiss against my lips. His hands moved to his hips, and I broke the kiss to watch as he removed his last piece of clothing.

Oh my God…

Okay, so, now I was *definitely* nervous. He was huge! I mean, it's not like I had ever seen an actual penis before to compare it too, but he seemed way bigger than I had ever imagined, both in length and girth. There was no way that thing was going to fit inside me!

"That's not going to fit…" I told him, staring at the massive (but still strangely beautiful) appendage between his legs .

"It'll be fine, baby. I promise," he answered with a small smile, stretching out over top of me and breaking my stare. My eyes darted to his and I felt them bug out a little.

"Are you crazy?" I asked, wrapping my hands around his arms. "Ash, you're like, huge! I'm telling you…" I trailed off when I realized that he was laughing. "Are you laughing at me?" He *clearly* was. "Go ahead, laugh, but we'll see who's laughing when you try to put that thing in me!"

His laughter cut off abruptly when his mouth crashed into mine once again. As usual, I couldn't control my response. I was licking my tongue across his lips when I felt him glide against me, and a shaky moan burst from my mouth.

"Fuck, Parker, I need to be inside of you," he whispered softly, his lips fluttering against mine as he spoke. "I'll go slow, I promise, okay?"

I was still a little hesitant, but his eyes looked almost pained. I wanted tonight to be good for him, too. So I nodded. I watched as he grabbed a condom from the bed and ripped it open, rolling it on with one hand as he kissed me, slow and sweet. As I felt him position himself, I braced.

"Breathe, baby," he urged, holding his hips still and laying soft kisses against my neck until I dragged in a ragged lungful of air. Once I had relaxed again, I felt him start to press into me.

The sensation was strange - it didn't feel great, it didn't really hurt, it just felt... different. Then, he pushed a little further and I felt the first real twinge of pain. My breath hitched and he stopped, pulling back a bit to let me adjust before pushing in a little bit more. I was drenched and he slid against me easily, but, as I established, he was huge. My body was fighting to keep him out.

He started a leisurely rhythm of in a little, then out again, then in a bit more and the slow friction caused a burn to start growing in my stomach. *That felt good...*

"Fuck, Parker. You're so fucking tight..." he groaned, his voice tense. The muscles in his arms all stood out as he held the rest of his body completely still, only moving his hips a few inches at a time.

In a flash, I was filled with a sort of desperation for him. I started meeting his small thrusts, helping him to open me up, until I was dying to feel him inside me, as deep as he could go.

"Ash..."

He ignored me and kept moving slowly, steadily, driving me even crazier.

"Ash," I repeated... "Fuck, Ash, I need you. I need all of you..."

His voice was choppy and his breathing heavy when he answered. "Don't wanna hurt you..."

"Fuck it, Ash, I need you," I urged, and he moved to put his hands on my knees. Using slight pressure, he opened me up wider and then, in one smooth thrust, his hips were pressed against mine and he was fully inside.

I let out a serrated scream at the sudden slash of burning pain. *Fuck, fuck, fuck that hurt!* Ash stayed completely still and a strangled sound made its way from his throat as I tried to will away the tears that had filled my eyes.

"Fuck," Ash groaned, pulling his head out of my neck, "you okay, baby?"

I couldn't speak, nodding fast and hard with my eyes squeezed shut.

"Parker," he called, and once the pain had started to fade, I opened my eyes to meet his gaze. "Love you," he whispered. "I love you so fucking much."

I took a deep breath as the pain receded, leaving only an intense fullness that left me wanting more.

"I love you too. Now move." He smiled from above me, and it was so stunning that it took my breath away. I'd never seen him look happier. Figures, he'd feel that way after he took my virginity. *Men…*

"Bossy little thing, aren't you?" He smirked, and I moved to smack his arm lightly, but my hips twisted and my arms dropped to the bed. At the feeling of him sliding inside me, my hands balled into fists in the sheets.

"Holy shit…" I breathed as he let out a groan, and the moment was broken. Ash started moving for real - long, steady strokes that left me breathless - and all logical thought left my head. Every brain cell I had was completely focused on the things going on inside my body, the sensations that Ash was making me feel, and the fact that I knew I'd never feel anything quite so amazing again. Or, at least not until the next time he was inside me.

I had been wrong, earlier. Ash fit like he was made for me. Like he was the other half of my puzzle, and we had just put the pieces together. It… was… *phenomenal…*

"Fuck, Parker," Ash groaned. "So tight, so wet… So fucking perfect."

I smiled as he spoke, then let out a gasp when his thumb moved between our hips and pressed against me.

"Fuck baby, you feel too good. I'm not gonna last… Need you to come with me." His words were forced, urgent, and they sped up my impending orgasm. Then his thumb pressed and rolled and I fell apart.

I barely heard his muttered "Fuck" as I started to shake and shout his name, and then he was pounding into me, dragging out my climax and turning my shout into a scream.

When I finally came back down, Ash was lying with his full weight on top of me and we were both breathing heavily. He finally recovered enough to gently pull out of me, and then he moved quickly to the bathroom. He was back in a flash, wrapping an arm around me and pulling me into his body. I was completely shattered, exhausted, and sated in a way that I had never been before. I felt a lazy smile spread across my face.

"That was…" I trailed off.

"Fucking everything, baby. That was everything." His words were quiet and heavy, and I felt them rock through me, warming me to the core. I snuggled deeper into his arms, not caring in the least that I was still naked, and before I could say anything in return, I fell asleep.

Chapter Forty-Two

Ash

THE NEXT MORNING, I WOKE up before Parker. It gave me a chance to watch her sleep, which was one of the things that I had missed the most about her while we were apart.

Before, when I spent every night in this apartment, I would almost always stay until Parker had fallen asleep next to me. We would talk about anything and everything - favorite movies and books, places we wanted to visit, things we wanted to do before we died - but she'd eventually fall asleep in my arms, and I would stay, just watching her breathe. It soothed me somehow, knowing that she was safe and sleeping, and I loved that I had the chance to do it again.

After what happened last night, I knew now, more than ever, that there was no way I was ever letting go of this girl. Truthfully, if what happened last night had happened sooner, I doubt that I would have even been able to walk away from her in the first place. Parker was pure perfection and I knew that, if I even tried, I'd never find anyone better.

When she turned over in her sleep and the sheet that was covering her fell to her waist, I couldn't control the need to put my mouth on her. I pressed soft kisses against the skin across her chest, down to her breasts, and then back up to her neck. I was pressing my lips to her jaw when I felt her move, and I looked up to meet her eyes.

"Hey," she said quietly, a small smile playing its way on to her lips.

"Morning, baby," I whispered. "Hospital today?"

Her smile faded and then she pulled out of my arms, sitting up in bed while shooting me a nervous glance.

"Yeah, I mean… I was gonna spend the day there, but you don't have come…"

"Park, if you think I'm letting you out of my sight, you're crazy."

"I just mean, I understand if you don't want to sit there all day, and I'm just-"

"Stop," I interrupted. "I'd follow you anywhere, Parker. Wherever you are, that's where I want to be."

She smiled then, a smile so bright that it overpowered the early morning sunlight streaking through the window. I knew she was probably sore from last night, but if she kept looking at me like that, I was going to just say fuck it and sink inside her anyway.

To avoid that, I rolled away from her and slid out of bed. "Come on," I told her. "Get dressed."

She shot me a confused look. "Visiting hours don't start until nine. We have two hours."

"We're going to go get breakfast."

Now she looked like she thought I was crazy. "Wait a second. You're telling me that we woke up in bed together this morning, both completely naked, and your first thought was *breakfast*?"

I grinned. "Far from it, beautiful. My first thought was to fuck you until you couldn't walk. But, since I know you want to make it to the hospital sometime today, and I know that you're probably gonna feel pretty sore once you start moving around, my *second* thought was breakfast."

By the time I was finished, her eyes were hooded and her face soft with desire. "I mean, we don't have to go to the hospital today..."

"Up," I commanded, and I watched her frown and then roll her eyes before I walked to the bathroom, laughing the entire way.

We climbed into my truck and drove until we found somewhere to eat. We were seated quickly - the place was nearly empty - and I ordered coffee while Parker asked for chocolate milk, which made me laugh.

"What?" she asked once the waitress had walked away to get our drinks.

"This is only the second time I've seen you order a drink, and both times it's been liquid chocolate," I said with a smile, and she fired one back in return.

"So?" she asked. "I like chocolate. Got a problem with that?"

"Not at all, baby. In fact, I'll make a note of that for the next time you get pissed at me. You like regular chocolate too, or just chocolate in drink form?"

"Regular chocolate works too."

The waitress returned to drop the drinks and I ordered pancakes and eggs. Parker went for the Belgian waffle with strawberries on top, and then we were alone again. I had fixed my coffee and was taking the first sip when Parker spoke again.

"How many women have you slept with?"

I choked and set the mug down with a thunk. "Seriously?" I asked once I had finished coughing.

"Yeah… I wanna know."

I took a deep breath. "Honestly? I don't know… I, uh, I mean, I guess I got around in high school and some when I was a freshman and sophomore, but…"

"Wait, you really don't know how many people you've slept with?"

"I guess when you think about it, it sounds terrible, but no. I really don't."

"Well, are we talking like tens, hundreds, thousands…?"

"Fuck, Park of course not. Tens, I guess. I just… I didn't really care about much back then. I got fucked up a lot, I was pissed at the world half the time, pissed at my dad the rest of the time… I just, I looked for ways to escape. Sex was a good way to do that."

Parker nodded, but her expression had grown distant and I knew she was disappointed.

"Don't look at me like that, baby. It's not-" I groaned. "It was always just sex. Nothing more - no connection, no relationships. You're the only person who's ever made me want more."

She nodded slowly, stirring her milk with the straw. "So, it's *not* just sex with us?"

"Are you fucking kidding?" I asked incredulously. "I almost don't even want to answer that. Do you really think that that's why I'm here?"

She shook her head almost frantically. "No! No, it's not that… You just, you make me nervous. I mean, I'm sorry,

I'm not trying to throw this in your face, but you left and, seriously Ash, it kind of devastated me. Being with you... It's the first time I've ever felt happy to be living my life... I'm afraid to lose that again."

Fuck. I hated that I had done that. I hated that I had walked away and given up on her. But I would spend every minute of every day for the rest of my life trying to make it up to her.

"Don't apologize. You're right, and I understand if you don't trust me, but-"

"Actually," she interrupted. "The weird thing is, I really do. I've never trusted anyone more. I think I just... I don't really trust myself."

"Trust yourself with what?"

"I'm afraid that I'm going to do something - find some way to fuck this up. Self-sabotage is kind of my thing..."

I chuckled softly. "Well, no worries then. Try as hard as you want. There's not a chance in hell that I'm going anywhere."

She looked unconvinced but then shook her head. "I'm sorry. This is, I'm just stupid. I, you don't have to promise me anything. We just-"

"Stop, Park. I get it. I really do, and..." I took a deep breath before giving her the honest to God truth. "Look, I know that we're young, and we have a lot to learn about each other. I also know that we haven't really been working at this for long, and I really know that I didn't help the situation by walking away from you. But, please hear me when I tell you this - I will do whatever it takes to make this work. You... You make me feel alive, you make me feel like things can only get better. Even if I'm having the worst fucking day of my life, just being around you makes everything okay. Trust me, Parker. It's not just you. I need you, too."

She was quiet, staring at me in a way that I knew meant she was about to tell me that she loved me. It hadn't even been two days, and yet she had said those words to me so many times that I was beginning to recognize when it was coming.

"I love you."

I couldn't help it. I cracked a huge grin. Her face fell and then her eyes narrowed in my direction. "What?" she snapped.

I laughed. "Nothing. It's just, I haven't really forgotten. You tell me about every half an hour."

Her cheeks filled with color and she looked down to the table, worrying her napkin between her fingers. I caught, "Yeah, well..." before she started mumbling so badly that I couldn't hear a word she said.

"What was that?" I asked.

"I said, I have a lot of 'I love yous' to make up for." I shot her a confused look, and she rolled her eyes before she continued. "You used to tell me that, all the time. I loved it."

I smiled but she wasn't done.

"I loved you then, you know. I loved you the night of the party. Probably even before that... I was just so, afraid I guess. I don't know how to love someone, or what to do when someone loves me... I've never had that, and with you... Well, it scared the crap out of me. I was afraid of what would happen when I admitted it." She flashed me a sexy smile then. "Although, I have to say, if I had known how you would react, I would have told you a long, long time ago..."

I groaned. "Do me a favor. Don't remind me of all the time we wasted. It's in the past. Just focus on all of the things we have to look forward to," I told her, my voice dropping as I spoke. I watched her breathing pick up a bit. She loved it when my voice got low. She reacted every time.

"Oh yeah?" she asked quietly. "What kind of things?"

I leaned forward across the table and crooked a finger in her direction. I moved until my lips were an inch from hers, and her eyes fluttered shut.

"Well, for starters…" I whispered, and her face drifted closer to mine, "there's your waffle and my pancakes." Her eyes snapped open and landed on my grin and I leaned back as I saw our waitress approaching.

"Ash…" she groaned while I laughed softly. "That's not even funny! You should know that you're playing with fire. After last night, you can't expect to get me all excited like that and then-" she squeaked as her plate was set in front of her and then glanced up at the waitress. The middle-aged redhead was trying to hide her smile; I was out-and-out laughing, and Parker just gazed at her breakfast like it was the most interesting thing that she'd ever seen.

God, I fucking *loved* this girl.

It was after we had finished eating, while we were waiting for the check that I realized something that made me laugh out loud. Parker shot me a questioning glance as I was shaking my head.

"I just realized," I told her, "this is our first date."

Her eyes narrowed. "I think we're kind of past the first date stage, Ash."

"Yeah, but this is the first time I've actually taken you somewhere."

She shrugged. "You took me to the coffeehouse."

"Didn't count."

"Why didn't it count?"

"Dates end with a kiss," I informed her.

She thought about that for a moment. "We kissed after the party."

"That party sure as fuck did not count as a date."

"Why not?"

"Well, for one thing, you didn't come to that party for me. You came to get fucked up. And because, if I'm gonna take you out - no, scratch that - *when* I take you out, it won't be to go to a fucking party at Marco's."

She smiled and then shrugged. "Okay."

"Okay?" I asked, thrown by her sudden agreement.

"Okay," she repeated and then rolled her eyes at me. "I'm not going to argue over the fact that you want to take me somewhere nicer than Marco's house for our next date. Seems counterproductive to my interests."

I laughed. "Well then. Okay."

Once we had paid and walked outside, I pulled Parker into my body and kissed her - hard, wet, and long. It was the morning after Christmas - freezing cold and bright with the sunlight reflecting off the snow on the ground - and we stood on the sidewalk wrapped in each other. My arms wound around her neck as she leaned into the kiss, and it was like nothing else existed but us.

Yeah... I made that first date official as *fuck*.

Chapter Forty-Three

Parker

ONCE MOM WAS RELEASED FROM the hospital, time flew by. The weeks blended into a kaleidoscope of mornings at school, afternoons with Mom and long, seriously awesome nights with Ash. I couldn't even begin to describe how much I appreciated having him around. Mom had been in and out of the hospital a few more times, and she'd been getting sick so often that they had stopped treatment altogether for the time being. The doctors told us that they'd start it up again when she was stronger, but I knew that, at this point, her getting any stronger was a long shot.

She was smaller, frailer every day. Her arms had become nothing but gnarled, wrinkled twigs, and her legs looked barely thick enough to support her weight. I was watching her literally waste away - she hardly ate anything but cheerios anymore - and Ash had become the perfect distraction.

By the time February had rolled around though, we were both starting to go a little stir-crazy. Ash understood that I couldn't leave my mom, but neither of us liked the fact that, when we weren't at school or work, we spent all of our time in my tiny apartment. The most exciting decision we made was what to make for dinner, and I had started to feel guilty, and a little concerned that Ash would get tired of our boring life.

Every time we talked about it though, he assured me that wasn't the case. He repeated that he didn't care where we were or what we were doing, so long as we were together. But I still worried.

Despite all of that though, those weeks were still some of the happiest of my life. I learned to live in a state of semi-ignorance - happy to pretend that things would stay this way forever. Mom and Ash settled into an easy detente, and she even left me alone most of the time - which I refused to acknowledge as a sign of dark things to come. Instead, I pretended to be oblivious and focused on classes, work, and getting closer to Ash.

It was a Monday afternoon, and I was listening to music and writing a paper when I heard the knock at the door. I was a bit surprised - no one ever came to our place but Ash, but he was working, so I had no clue who it would be. Before I could climb off the bed to see who was there, my phone rang from the mattress besides me and I saw Ash's name light up the display.

I flipped it open as I headed towards the door.

"Hey, baby. Aren't you supposed to be at work?"

"Did someone just knock on your door?"

I narrowed my eyes suspiciously and stopped walking through the apartment.

"Uh, yeah-"

"Okay," he interrupted. "Just listen to what she says, and hurry. I'll see you soon, beautiful."

I started to ask what the heck he was talking about, but he had already hung up.

Okay, new tactic.

I opened to the door to see Diane, holding a large white box and staring at me with a wide smile.

"Uh, hey," I waved and stepped back to let her in. She walked through the door and then thrust the box at me.

"Here, sweetie. Everything you need is in there. I brought stuff to make dinner for your Momma, so you don't need to worry about us."

"What's going on, Diane?"

"Just take that," she nodded to the box in my arms, "and head to your room. Go on, I was told that if you weren't ready in an hour, he'd drag you out of here, ready or not."

I had no idea what to say, so I did as I was told and turned to head to my room.

Setting the box on the bed, I gently pulled off the lid. The first thing I noticed was the note.

My beautiful Parker,

I know that you probably haven't even realized it, but today is Valentine's Day, and I have a very important question to ask you.

Will you be my Valentine?

I'm hoping that your answer is yes, because otherwise all my planning will go to waste.

Everything in this box is yours. It's now four o'clock. I'll be at your front door at five to pick you up.

Love you.

Ash

I read the note twice, my smile growing the entire time. Then, I unpacked the black, strapless, knee-length dress and a pair of black, sequined ballet flats, with which I instantly fell in love. Last but definitely not least was a strapless, black lacy bra that looked so insanely sexy that I was almost afraid to put it on. To match that was a pair of black lace panties, which were so soft I wanted to live in them. I experienced a moment of embarrassment when I realized that Diane had just given me a box containing sexy lingerie, but I shrugged it off and replaced the embarrassment with excitement.

For about ten seconds I freaked out like a total girl. But, come on, this stuff only happened in books!

Then, I ran straight to the bathroom and got ready for our date.

Ash was there at exactly at five, as promised, and he took us to eat at the Ivy Inn. The place had been built on an estate that dated back to the 1700's, and the food was absolutely amazing. Dinner was perfect - conversation flowed easily (as it always did between Ash and I) and I found myself strangely disappointed when the night ended. Ash led me back out to his truck, and I was so busy trying to immortalize every moment of the perfect evening, I didn't even notice when his truck turned out of the parking lot and away from my apartment.

"I didn't say it earlier, baby, but you look amazing."

His quiet words caught my attention, and I turned to face him in the fading twilight. "Thanks," I returned with a small smile, "but I should be thanking you. You picked everything out."

"Trust me, no I did not," he laughed. "I went to the store, and told the woman your size and what you'd like. She picked a bunch of stuff and then I decided on that. Don't get me wrong, I made a good decision, but I didn't work that hard."

I shrugged. "Doesn't matter. Still the most romantic thing anyone's ever done for me…"

"No offense baby, but you don't have a whole lot of experience with romance."

It was my turn to laugh. "And you do?"

Ash lifted a shoulder and took his eyes from the road to glance at me. "No, I don't. I guess it just comes naturally with you… You make me want to give you the world."

I felt the heat flow into my cheeks before I looked away from his face. He turned off the road and when I looked out the window, I felt my mouth pop open.

"We're going ice skating?" I asked, completely bursting with excitement, and he grinned at my expression.

"I can see that you're happy about that. Good. I was actually kind of worried."

"Why wouldn't I be excited to go ice skating?"

He shrugged. "I don't know. Doesn't matter. I'm just glad you're happy."

I was bouncing in my seat as he parked the truck. "I've never been ice skating before!"

"Good. That means you'll need to hold on tight to me to stay standing." He leveled me a sexy wink as he turned off the car. "Here," he said, handing me a sweatshirt from the backseat. "Bring this in, I don't want you to be cold in just that dress."

Ash climbed down from the truck and walked around to help me out, and then he held my hand as we walked towards and through the front doors.

It was almost seven, and yet the building was completely empty. I took a look around, trying to take in the details. I had never been to Ash' workplace before, but I could picture him here. He seemed to relax the second we walked in the door, the same second that we were hit with the smell that I could only identify as cold.

"Where is everyone?" I asked as Ash led me towards the back of the giant building. He rubbed the back of his neck and gave me a sheepish grin.

"I kind of asked Chris to shut the place down. We have it all to ourselves. Well, we will, once we get rid of Jimmy. He should be in the office."

"Wait," I asked as he continued to lead me across the space, "you just asked your boss to shut down his entire business for a night? And he agreed?"

Ash laughed softly. "Chris is more than just a boss. He's Jimmy's dad, for starters, and he was my hockey coach for 12 years. Honestly, he'd do just about anything to get me on ice - including closing down the rink." We were walking into a small staff room when I heard a voice from the even smaller office inside.

"Yeah, yeah, yeah, we all know that he likes you the most. You can shut the fuck up about it any time..."

Ash laughed. "Parker, do you remember Jimmy?"

I nodded. I hadn't really spent any time with the guy, but Ash talked about him enough that I knew the basics. As he walked out of the office towards us, I took in his shaggy dark blond hair and almost strangely light brown eyes, and it hit me how different the two men were. Jimmy was bigger, brawnier - he looked more like what you'd expect from a hockey player. He wasn't really my type, but Jimmy was attractive - despite, or maybe because of, the slightly crooked nose that had clearly been broken a few too many times.

"Hey," I told him. Even though I knew they were close friends, I wasn't sure what to make of Jimmy. The only other time I'd met him, he'd pretty much just ignored me completely. He was totally different from Marco, Ash's other friend, and I had wondered more than once what had brought those three people together.

"Hey, Parker," Jimmy answered, and his smile seemed genuine which helped me relax a bit. "Do you guys need anything before I head out?" he asked Ash as he headed for the door.

"Nah, man, were good." Jimmy nodded but Ash spoke again before he could get out the door. "You talked to Maddie?"

Jimmy shook his head. "Not for a few weeks." He shrugged and then headed back towards the door. "I'm out of here. Have fun, guys. And don't forget to lock up, Ash."

One Jimmy was gone, Ash walked me over to where they kept the skates and pulled a thick pair of socks from his pocket, handing me those and a heavy pair of ice skates that he pulled from a cubby inside the skate shack.

I smiled at how much he had planned to make tonight happen and started to get ready. Ash pressed a kiss into my head and then walked out of the room, promising to be right back. I had just finished lacing up one skate when I heard music start to play over the speaker system. I smiled as the sound of Rilo Kiley filled my ears. I had introduced Ash to the music of Jenny Lewis a few weeks ago, and he'd been obsessed ever since. We both liked the same types of music, and I loved playing him something new that I'd heard, and listening to the songs that he'd play for me.

When he came back, I was ready to go. He threw on skates a lot faster than I did, and he held my hand as we hobbled our way over to the ice.

I learned very quickly that I was a horrible ice skater. One could probably even say that I was worse at skating than I was at math, although that was still up for debate. I fell on my ass (and took Ash down with me) more times than I could count. But, as much as it hurt, I don't think I've ever laughed harder. Ash on the other hand, was obviously at home on the ice. He tried to help me keep my feet by skating backwards in front of me while holding my hands - a failed endeavor - but I appreciated the effort nonetheless. I also came to really appreciate the fact that we had the building to ourselves, especially every time that I ended up flopping around on the ice like a fish in a dress.

My mother would have been disgusted. Ladies *definitely* didn't roll around on the ground – let alone ice - wearing dresses.

After I'd fallen half-a-hundred times, I finally shook off Ash's hands and told him I was going to do this on my own. I took tiny steps while he skated in circles around me, helping me up each time I fell. Usually he would grab my hands and pull me up before pressing a soft kiss to my lips and then skating back away, and every time I'd smile like an idiot as I once again started to stumble across the ice.

Two hours later, I finally had enough of falling down. My body was sore and all I wanted was to go home and take a hot bath. Ash led me back off the ice and helped me pull of my skates. Once I had put my shoes back on, Ash told me to sit while he went to shut everything down. I watched the lights fade from super bright to a dimmer overnight setting, and then he was back, pulling me up from the bench I where I sat. I stood with a groan, which made Ash smile. He put our skates back on the shelves and then walked to me, bending down to swing me up into his arms.

"Ash!" I squeaked, wrapping my arms around his shoulders as he walked towards the door. "What are you doing?"

"Carrying you."

"Well, obviously! Why?"

"You're in pain, *obviously*. Stop complaining - we both know you like it," he said, giving me a cocky grin as he took us both through the door.

I thought about that and decided to keep quiet as he locked the door behind us - while still holding me, might I add. He correctly read my silence as my agreement and chuckled about it the entire way to the truck. I decided at that point to not speak to the cocky bastard at all, which he also seemed to find amusing.

When we got back to the apartment, I continued not speaking to Ash as I thanked Diane and asked about the night. Ash continued to chuckle as I gave him the cold shoulder, so as Diane said goodnight and headed for the door, I held it open for him as well.

The jerk laughed. "Shut the door, baby."

"No. Why should you stay? I'm not speaking to you."

He prowled towards me, smile still on his face, but his eyes had gone dark.

"That's fine. You don't need to talk for what's about to happen." He leaned in close to me and reached over my shoulder to grab the door and push it from my hand until I heard it click shut. I automatically stepped back into it.

"Ash..." I warned, but my voice was already going breathy. *Damn this man and his ridiculous effect on me!* He was getting closer, pressing me into the wall with his hips. I could feel him hard and heavy against my stomach.

"I've been thinking about getting inside you all... fucking... night, baby." He punctuated each word with a kiss and my legs started to shake.

"Don't you dare. I'm mad at you."

"Why you mad at me, baby?"

Goddammit. His voice had gone super growly. He knew what that did to me!

"Because you're a cocky son of a bitch."

"Yeah," he whispered, kissing the corner of my mouth. "You love me anyway though..."

He had a point.

Ash chucked at my faltering resistance and then his mouth was on mine and I was in the air, moving towards my room. He got us inside and shut the door, and approximately eight seconds later my panties were gone, his pants were unzipped, my skirt was up around my waist, and he had me pinned to the wall with my legs around his hips as he slowly sank into me.

He groaned, low and loud, once he was fully inside. I had started taking the pill this month, and there was nothing I loved more than feeling him inside me with nothing between us. I still hadn't gotten used to the subtle change that somehow felt huge. I loved knowing that we were linked in that way - no separation, no barriers.

Ash started to move, slow and steady at first but the pace picked up to punishing as we both got closer.

"Fuck, Parker. You are so fucking perfect. There is nothing better than being inside you."

I agreed with that, but I couldn't speak. I felt my body start to tighten as Ash began to pound into me, his mouth coming back to mine. His kiss was wild, full of passion and emotion, and it pushed me over the edge until I was shouting into his mouth and clawing at his back. Ash followed me over the edge a few seconds later with a muffled grunt and a whispered "Fuck." He held me for a few moments as we both recovered and then he gently pulled out and set me on the floor, holding on for a few seconds as I attempted to stand on legs made of Jell-O.

He pressed a soft kiss into my mouth and then helped me take off my dress. When he got a look at me standing in nothing but the lace bra, I saw him clench his jaw. I moved to take it off but he stopped me before pushing me towards the bed. He quickly stripped and followed me under the covers, rolling on top of me and pressing me to the mattress as he kissed me reverently, but still heatedly.

Not long after that, I felt his hot, hard length press against me, and we both groaned when he slowly pushed his way inside.

Ash slowly, sweetly, made love to me. It wasn't wild, it wasn't rough, but it was passionate, and when we came together, quietly whispering each other's names and staccato 'I love yous,' I realized something profound with a resolute certainty.

Lying in Ash's arms, his body still joined with mine as we both reveled in the aftermath of our lovemaking, I had finally found *exactly* where I was supposed to be.

Chapter Forty-Four

Ash

ABOUT TWO WEEKS AFTER VALENTINE'S Day, I started to feel a heavy sense of foreboding. Katherine looked a little bit worse every day, and it was clear she didn't have much time. I had thought that Parker would be at least a little affected, but for the most part, she seemed to act as if time was frozen. I worried that life was going to knock her on her ass when it all caught up to her, but at least I knew that I'd be there to help her pick herself up when it happened.

Parker and I were lying in bed listening to Death Cab for Cutie. "What Sarah Said" had just started playing when I turned to my side and looked down at her.

"Have you made any plans yet?" I asked hesitantly. I didn't want to upset her, but she needed to at least consider what she was going to do when the time came to make the choices that were headed her way.

She squinted up at me. "What kind of plans?"

"I mean, once... She doesn't have a lot of time left, Park. You need to start thinking about what you're going to do once it's just you."

She shrugged and dropped her eyes from mine. "I know, I just... It's hard to explain."

Since we'd gotten back together, Parker had shared more about her childhood with me. I still didn't know everything, but as much as I didn't like it, I wasn't going to push her. She knew that she could tell me anything, and I knew that she trusted me. Still, I knew that a lot of what she still had to tell was stuff that she had never told anyone, and I knew that it was hard for her. Parker had never let anyone in before - never trusted anyone to give them all of her - and I knew that she was trying, despite how hard it was for her.

Regardless, I wanted to understand what was keeping her from admitting, even to herself, the fact that her mom would be gone soon.

"Try for me?" I asked quietly.

She was lying only two inches from me, but she scooted her body over until we were pressed tightly together. I wrapped my arms around her and laid back down, holding her tight as she gave me another piece of the puzzle.

"My mom... I've hated her since I was little. It wasn't so bad, back when my dad was around. At least, from what I remember, but I don't remember a lot. I know they fought, but she pretty much ignored me. Once he was gone, when it was just me and her... It was bad, Ash. Really bad. I hated her so much. She used to get so drunk..." She let out a shudder and I squeezed her tighter, pulling her out of the memory.

"It's okay, baby," I whispered. "You're okay."

She nodded before continuing. "I guess I just always wished she had left and my dad had stayed. Or even that he had taken me with him? I don't know, I just didn't want her around, I didn't want her to be my mom. As I got older... I don't know. I guess that now, it's hard for me to accept that she'll really be gone when the deepest, darkest parts of me have been asking, begging for this for years and years."

I felt her body start to shake with sobs and I gently rubbed her back as she silently cried. "It's just..." she said in a watery voice, "You know how people say be careful what you wish for? I guess that's kind of the story of my life. But, I swear, Ash. I swear I didn't wish for this. I never wanted this."

"Shit, Parker, of course you didn't. This is not your fault."

"She thinks that it is," she whispered as she finally stopped the tears. "Sometimes, I really think that it is my fault."

I looked down at her and she met my eyes, correctly reading my indignant disagreement. She shook her head and then said, "There are people who believe that every thought we have carries mass. It's basically, the power of positive thinking. If enough people think good, happy thoughts, the world will be a good, happy place. But, the converse applies as well." She shrugged. "Maybe I just had so many bad thoughts-"

"Stop," I said abruptly. "Baby, you are not the reason that your mom got cancer. I swear to you. That's just not the way the world works."

She sighed. "Then maybe there's a God and He just really hates me..."

I was so not the person to get into a religious debate with. I had my own issues with the idea of an all-powerful heavenly being, mostly stemming from the fact that I knew for a fact that bad things happened to good people.

"I'm still undecided on the entire idea of God, but I can tell you this. Over the past few years, I've wondered a lot about why the shittiest things seem to happen to the best people, and I didn't start to understand it until a few months ago."

She waited for me to continue and when I didn't she asked, "And what happened a few months ago?"

"I met a girl. A girl who I wouldn't have met otherwise. A girl who completely changed my life and who made me want to be a better person. A girl who made me believe in myself for the first time in years. I may not understand why I had to go through some of the shit that I went through, but it all led me to you. And I'd do it again. I'd revisit the worst days of my life, and I'd live them all over again if I knew that, at the end of it, I would walk away with you holding my hand."

She opened her mouth to speak, but I kissed her, quickly sliding my tongue between her parted lips. She made a noise of surprise that morphed into a low moan, and I felt myself start to get hard. Before I lost all self-control, I pulled back and met her darkened eyes.

"I want you to know, no matter what happens, you will walk away holding my hand. I know you're afraid. I know you probably just want to run and hide. If that's the case, I'll run with you. I'd follow you anywhere, and I'd take you anywhere you wanted to go, so long as I'm there with you. I love you, and I won't *ever* let go of your hand."

She kissed me, pushing me to my back as she climbed on top of my body. Her legs straddled mine as her mouth worked against my lips and her hands moved under my shirt. *Fuck*. It was absolutely insane how much I loved this girl. She embodied everything I had never known I wanted, but now that I'd had her, I knew I'd never want anyone else. If she ever left me, she'd take everything.

"God, Parker," I groaned as she moved her hands to her shirt and yanked it off. Next went her bra, and then my hands were on her breasts as she moved her mouth back to mine. It wasn't long before my shirt was gone, and the rest of our clothing quickly followed.

She wrapped her hands around me and positioned me where she wanted me, rubbing the tip of my dick across her drenched core twice.

"Oh God." I barely got the words out before she impaled herself in one quick movement, causing my breath to freeze in my lungs.

I heard her guttural moan and then she started to move, gliding up and down slowly, fucking tortuously. I wanted to grab her hips, speed her up, but I restrained myself, letting her have her moment of control.

She felt absolutely incredibly, and the sight of her moving up and down on top of me, breasts bouncing with every slide, was the sexiest thing I had ever seen.

She rode me slowly, steadily driving us both closer to the edge until her movements turned frantic, almost desperate. That's when I wrapped my hands around her hips and thrust up into her. I heard the strangled growl as I pounded into her from below. In minutes, I felt her muscles contracting around me and I almost lost it. Instead, I pulled her body down to mine and then flipped us so that she was underneath me as I slammed my hips into hers. Within minutes I felt her start to come again and it forced me over the edge with her, taking me under - to the place where nothing mattered but her.

Lying on top of her, still buried in her wet heat, I realized that, for the first time in years, I didn't feel broken. I didn't feel like I was missing parts of myself. For so long, I'd felt like someone had smashed me apart and then tried to glue the pieces back together, but they'd missed a few necessary parts.

It was like Parker filled the holes. I was complete again, and I only had her to thank for it.

And I planned to thank her. Every single day, for the rest of my life.

Chapter Forty-Five

Parker

ON MARCH 5TH, I TOOK Mom to the doctors. It was a Monday afternoon, and Ash was at work. He offered to go with us, but I told him not to worry, that we would be fine on our own.

While we sat in the exam room, waiting for the doctor, I thought back to the day in November when we had come to the office. I remembered the woman who I had seen sitting in the waiting room, the woman who had looked so close to death, and I realized that she was probably gone now. For some reason, even though I had never even spoken to her, the thought made me indescribably sad.

After the physical exam, the nurse left and Dr. Bradley took a seat on the swivel stool in the room. He leveled his eyes on Mom, and just looking at his face, I knew.

"I'm sorry, Katherine, but I don't think that you have any more than another three months."

I felt the breath rush out of me as if his words had landed a physical blow. I mean, sure, I knew that she wasn't getting better, but *three months*? That was hardly any time at all.

I saw Mom shrug. "Figured as much."

"How are your pain levels?" the doctor asked. "Getting worse?"

She nodded as an ugly laugh burst from her mouth. The laugh soon turned into a cough. Once she had smothered it, she looked back up to him.

"It hurts every second of every day."

He nodded. "I'm going to up your dosage of the methadone. It'll make you even more out of it, but I'm guessing you're okay with that."

She nodded again, and he gave her a sad look as he stood to leave. Then his gaze came to me, and I froze.

"I'm truly very sorry."

It was my turn to nod. I had nothing to say. I was numb. Ice spread outward from my heart, moving through my arms and legs, and into my head. It blocked out everything - the pain, the fear, the guilt. It all faded away as I wrapped myself in the cold. Wrapped myself up until there was nothing else left.

By the time Ash got home, the ice had formed a shield so thick that I felt completely removed. Mom was already asleep and I was lying in bed staring at the ceiling when I felt the bed depress next to me, so I assumed he'd used the key I'd given him after Valentine's Day to let himself in.

"Hey." The word was careful, hesitant.

"Hi," I answered quietly, keeping my eyes on the ceiling. I didn't want him to see, and his eyes saw everything.

"Everything okay? I texted a few times, and I called. Where's your phone?"

I shrugged. "I'm not sure. Sorry. I didn't hear it…"

I felt his eyes narrow on my face at my dismissive tone. "What's going on, Parker? What happened at the doctors?"

"Nothing, Ash." I sat up and tried to move around him to climb off the bed, but his body blocked mine. "I need to pee," I told him, trying to get away.

"No, you need to tell me what happened at the doctor's."

I sighed. He always saw through my bullshit.

Seriously. Freaking. Annoying.

"He didn't say anything that we didn't already know. Three months. That's our new timeline."

"Okay," he said slowly. "Okay, three months. Well, at least we know now, right?"

"Yeah," I agreed, "at least we know. Now, please let me up."

"I'm confused, Park. What exactly is happening here? Why do I feel like you're pissed at me?"

"I'm not." The sharpness in those two words shocked even me.

"Yeah, that fucking convinced me," he groaned. "What the fuck is wrong, Park?"

"I don't know!" I shouted, unable to keep it in anymore. "I don't fucking know. I'm fucking numb! I don't know what to think, or how to feel. I don't know if I should be happy or sad or angry! I don't know how to handle any of this!"

Before I could move away again, Ash pulled me against his body, wrapping his arms tightly around my shoulders. The instant I hit his warmth, I burst into tears.

"You shouldn't want me," I cried into his chest. "You shouldn't have to deal with this. I'm fucking crazy," I shouted, pulling away to stare up at him, ignoring the tears flowing down my cheeks.

Ash didn't look at me like I was crazy. He looked at me like I was something precious, but I knew otherwise.

"You don't understand," I continued. I needed to make him see the truth, "you don't know what I'm really like. I'm nothing. I'm *no one*. You deserve special and I'm not special. I will never *be* special!"

"Tell me, Parker. Tell me what she did to you to make you think that."

I cried in his arms as I realized that I had no other choice. He'd never understand why he should walk away from this until I told him everything.

So, I did.

I told him about the alcohol. I told him about the men. I told him about being locked in the closet at the top of the stairs. I told him about the times I hid under my bed, listening to the shouts and screams coming from downstairs. I told him about the (rare, but always memorable) beatings, and I told him about the words. The bitter, nasty, hateful words. *I was worthless. I was less than worthless. I was the biggest mistake my mother had ever made, and no one would ever love me because I was a selfish bitch who only cared about herself. I'd never amount to anything, and everyone I loved would leave me behind because I was absolutely nothing.*

Ash didn't speak as I talked, just held me as I unloaded everything I could - the thousands of reasons why he would eventually want to walk away. Through it all, he just let me get it out until there was nothing left.

When I finally fell quiet and wiped the tears from my face, I chanced a glance up at him. His face was a mask of fury, and his jaw ticked.

"She hit you?"

I nodded.

"How bad?"

I shrugged, but he wasn't letting it go.

"How bad, Parker?"

I sighed before I answered. "I guess pretty bad. She used a belt - hurt like a bitch for days. But, she wasn't the worst."

His arms went super tight and I couldn't breathe for a second. I tried to figure out what I had said that he had reacted to, but I honestly had no idea.

"What do you mean she wasn't the worst?"

Oh. *That.*

"There were, uh," I swallowed, trying to choose my words carefully. "Two... boyfriends. She left me with them, and I guess they didn't like that."

"What does that mean?"

"Well, the one beat the shit out of me because I was listening to music in my bedroom. The other tried to get me to suck his dick when I snuck down to the kitchen for food. When I said no, he slapped me around a bit before I could make it back to my room and lock the door."

"I know I'm gonna regret asking this, but what the fuck did Katherine do?"

"Well, she actually kicked out the one that tried to fuck me. She said, and I'm loosely quoting here, that she wouldn't fuck anyone who tried to fuck her piece-of-shit daughter. The other one she kept around for a while. Then he left. They always left."

"Fuck." The expletive was ragged, and sounded like it had been ripped straight from his chest. "I want to rip apart every person who ever hurt you, starting with that woman. I know it's a fucked up thing to say, but she is getting everything that she ever deserved. The only one who doesn't deserve anymore of this shit is you."

"No, Ash, you still don't get it. She was right-"

"Don't you dare," he snapped. "Don't you dare tell me that she was right about anything. She was a shit mom, and you deserved so much more than her. She's just a miserable woman who hated her life and took it out on the only good thing in it."

"You don't know that," I tried to explain.

"But I do, baby. I know you. I know that you are a good, kind, loving person who I am honored to know. You're beautiful inside and out, Eileen Parker, and I swear, I'll work every day to make sure that, one day, you see that."

I shook my head as tears filled my eyes. "You can't want-"

"Don't tell me what I want. I know what I want. And I want you. I want you on the bad days and the good, whether you're happy or pissed the fuck off. I want to wake up next to you every morning. I want to sleep next to you at night. I want to marry you, and make babies with you, and fucking grow old with you. I know exactly what I want, so don't tell me that I don't want you."

Well, *shit*.

I really hadn't been expecting that.

"Ash, I-" But he kissed me.

I really wished it wouldn't be a giant lie to say that I hated when he kissed me to shut me up. But, it meant that his lips were on mine, and under any circumstances, that was a good thing. When he pulled away, he rested his forehead against mine and whispered, "Don't. You'll ruin it. Just nod, smile, and say 'Okay, Ash.'"

His voice was super growly and he'd just completely kissed the wits out of me.

So, I nodded, smiled, and whispered, "Okay, Ash."

Chapter Forty-Six

Ash

IT WAS LIKE THINGS WENT from 'kind-of okay' to 'completely and totally fucked' overnight.

Katherine was deteriorating so fast, it had become uncomfortable to even be in the same room with her. She looked like a walking corpse, and she barely spoke at all. The doctors had upped her painkillers and she moved around the apartment like a zombie. Her skin was pale, her eyes were sunken – even I was having a hard time looking at her.

I knew it was really sinking in for Parker. Her eyes were always haunted, and every time she looked at her mom, I saw a slight flinch, as if the sight physically hurt her. We both walked on eggshells in the apartment, trying to stay out of Katherine's way even as we tried to keep her as comfortable as possible.

The truth was, Katherine was dying. There was no way she would last another three months.

I had started staying at Parker's every night, too afraid to leave her alone with her mom… just in case. Early Friday morning, I woke up to the sound of shuffling in the living room. Leaving Parker asleep in bed, I threw on a t-shirt and boxers and walked out to find Katherine going to the bathroom on the living room floor. When she saw me, she cried out and looked around, suddenly realizing where she was. Then, she was sobbing in a heap on the soiled carpet.

I picked her up and took her into the bathroom. I helped her clean herself up and then left her sitting on the toilet seat lid while I went and cleaned up the carpet. When I walked back into the bathroom, Katherine's eyes were once again vacant. She didn't say a word, and I silently led her to her room and got her back into bed.

I couldn't imagine how Parker was feeling. I struggled every day with the fact that, as much as I hated this woman, I still felt like she deserved some compassion as she died.

I'd always heard people say, when talking about someone with cancer or some other debilitating or life-threatening disease, 'It always happens to the best people.' Except this time it hadn't, and as wrong as it felt to say that, it was the truth.

It helped a little that my mind imagined two different people in my head. There was the sick, broken woman we were living with now, and there was the cold, bitter woman who I had met almost half a year ago. The two caricatures were so different that my mind tried to isolate one from the other. I told myself that I was allowed feel sorry for this woman whose body was almost completely destroyed.

Every sliver of sympathy still felt like a betrayal to Parker.

Thursday night at work, I told Jimmy everything. All about Parker's mom and what we were dealing with. I knew he was right when he told me to just let myself feel however I was going to feel, but it wasn't that easy.

I was cycling through anger, sadness, rage and guilt faster than my brain could keep up. One minute, I felt sorry for Katherine, the next I was once again filled with fury over what she had done to her daughter. Then the guilt slid in… On and on and on.

The worst part was that I didn't know how to help Park. All I wanted to do was take away the pain and I couldn't. It made me feel absolutely helpless, and that wasn't a feeling that I had ever enjoyed.

To make up for it, every night we laid in bed and talked about the distant future. Where we would be in five years, ten, twenty. I wanted to fill her mind with thoughts of a happy future. I knew that right now it seemed impossible, but one day this would all be behind us, and her eyes would be bright again. I needed to make sure she didn't forget that.

Because I knew how hard it was to remember once you forgot.

Chapter Forty-Seven

Parker

THAT SUNDAY WAS THE DAY that everything changed again.

The hospital had given us a card a while back with a number to call if we needed a nurse at the house, and so far I had managed to avoid using it. But I was worried about Mom, so I made the call.

She had been refusing food all weekend. I couldn't even get cereal into her anymore. She slept almost all the time. It was a fight to wake her for her meds, and she didn't leave her bed unless it was to go to the bathroom, but she had even stopped doing that. I had to change the sheets and give her a bath three times in two days.

She was giving up.

My suspicions were confirmed the second the nurse arrived.

He reminded me of Charles, just a bit younger. A heavyset, redheaded man with a British accent, he walked in the door and saw Mom on the couch and I watched his face fall.

"She needs hospice, sweetheart."

Fuck. Fuck. Fuck.

I am not ready for this.

Not at fucking all.

I felt Ash move in behind me as I looked desperately at the nurse. "What? No, she still has…"

He shook his head as he walked to the couch where Mom was sleeping and knelt down at her side. "She's jaundiced. Her liver's starting to shut down. I'd say she's got less than a week."

I felt my knees go out the same second Ash's arms shot out to hook beneath my arms.

"I got you, baby," he whispered as he turned me in his arms and then wrapped them around me. I went completely limp, and my breathing turned heavy as I tried to process his words.

Less than a week…

This time next week, she'd be gone.

I banished the thought from my mind.

Get your shit together, Park. You need to figure this out.

I pulled away from Ash to stand on my own before turning back to face the nurse again. "Okay. What should I do?"

"Pack a bag for her, sweetheart. Some nightgowns, comfortable clothes, whatever she likes to wear. If she has anything you think she'd want - a blanket or sweater, books or anything like that - you can bring that too. Enough for a week and then you can go from there."

Yeah, if by "go from there" you mean, "she'll be dead so it won't matter."

"Alright. I'll get it now. Do I need to call for an ambulance, should I drive her, or…?"

"Just pack, darling. I'll make the calls."

I nodded and gave Ash's hand, which was wrapped around mine, a squeeze before I dropped it and walked away. I listened from the other room as the nurse called the hospice unit at the hospital and asked them to ready a bed. Then, I heard as he called for an ambulance to come for Mom. I grabbed her clothes and things and threw them into a bag. I knew it was a long shot, but I grabbed a few of her old magazines that sat on her nightstand on the off chance that she was lucid enough to read them.

Once I had her bag ready, I walked back out to the living room. Ash's eyes locked to me immediately, and I felt them search my face. I knew he was waiting for the breakdown that we both knew was coming, but I was holding it together. For the moment, at least.

Fifteen uncomfortably quiet minutes later, the knock came at the door. The nurse let in the EMT who looked at Ash and I sympathetically.

"We just need to get her downstairs. I was going to bring up the stretcher, but…"

Yeah. The elevator.

"I'll carry her," Ash volunteered immediately, which didn't surprise me at all. Over the past week, he'd been amazing with Mom.

I knew it was hard for him. I was fully aware that he hated her. He had told me, flat-out, that he hated her, but I knew he was trying to make things easier for me. He was a really good man, and he felt like it was his responsibility no matter how much I had tried to convince him otherwise.

The EMT and nurse stood back as Ash bent down to lift Mom's tiny frame into his arms. She let out a quiet groan as he settled her weight in his arms, and then seemed to drift right back to sleep, her head resting against his shoulder.

I almost lost it at the sight.

The five of us moved downstairs together, where a second EMT was standing with a stretcher. He nodded as we approached and then helped Ash settle Mom on the cushion. Once she was situated, they strapped her down and then started to wheel her out of the lobby.

While outside, I watched in an almost catatonic state of disconnected shock as they loaded her into the ambulance. *She was leaving*. She was leaving this place, and she'd never be coming back. Ash's held me tightly in his arms, giving me a squeeze as if she knew exactly what I was thinking, and we watched in silence as the ambulance pulled away and the nurse walked back to us.

"They'll take her over and get her settled. Head over whenever you're ready, and bring her bag, alright?"

I nodded and he reached out a hand which I awkwardly shook. He nodded his head at Ash and then he was gone.

We walked back upstairs and Ash led me into the apartment with an arm around my shoulders. He hadn't let go of me since he had put down Mom, but at that point I wasn't sure if it was more for my benefit or his. I had caught his eyes once on the way upstairs, and I could see something working behind them, but I couldn't even handle trying to deal with that right now.

"Parker," Ash began, and something in me snapped. I had been standing in the center of the room, but suddenly I was on the floor and I was crying harder than I ever had before. In the next second, Ash was wrapped around me and he held me as I cried.

This was not a silent cry.

I wailed.

I screamed.

I *completely* fell apart.

It felt like hours had passed by the time the tears started to slow. As the fog began to clear, I took stock of the situation - my head was pounding, my eyelids were sandpaper, my ass hurt from sitting on the floor, and all I wanted to do was sleep.

It was time to go to the hospital.

Ash pressed a kiss into my hair and then gave me a hand to hoist myself up. He grabbed the bag from where I had left it by the couch as I grabbed my phone and then we were out the door. I didn't say a word as he led me to his truck and helped me up into the passenger seat.

Ash kept the radio off as we drove to the hospital and neither of us spoke. I still felt raw, and even though I had cried more than enough tears for a lifetime, I could feel them gathering again, pooling in the corners of my eyes as we got closer and closer to our destination.

Once there, we parked and walked half a block to get inside and then Ash navigated the way to the hospice unit. When we walked through the door into the wing, my first irrational thought was that it was much prettier than I had expected.

It didn't look like a hospital. The walls were a warm brown, and glass sconces hung between the doors to the individual rooms, most of which had been left open.

Making our way towards the nurses' station, we were intercepted by a nurse leaving a room on our right.

"Hey there," she called, stopping us as we passed. "Are you guys here for Katherine?"

Ash told her that we were, and then she was leading us further down the hall.

"Here she is. If you guys need anything at all, please just give a shout. My name's Alice." I nodded as Ash thanked her, but my eyes were already on Mom.

I let a few tears streak down my face before I wiped them away and went to sit on the couch. Mom was asleep, and I found myself wondering if she even knew where she was... or that we were here. I wondered if she was really ready to die. I wondered if she had any regrets.

I wondered if she really hated me.

Around dinner time, Ash offered to go get food but I told him I wasn't hungry, so he stayed with me. We didn't talk at all, just sat together on the couch until about ten o'clock. By then my body was stiff and I just wanted to go to sleep. Ash pulled me from the couch and led me back out the doors to the truck. Even as he drove, he held my hand until we were back at home.

That night, neither of us really spoke. Ash seemed to know that I was working through things in my head, and he gave me the mental space that I needed. Physical space, on the other hand, I neither needed nor wanted, so I was glad that he stuck to me like glue. He was so hesitant to have me out of his sight that I half expected him to follow me into the bathroom.

Other people may have been frustrated at his borderline-overbearingness. Not me. I was frayed – I felt like someone was pulling on my edges and I was unraveling. Ash's presence was like a balm that sealed the fibers and helped to keep me together.

We didn't speak - we barely even kissed. We just lay in bed, side by side, lost in our own thoughts. I rested my head on his chest, and his hand tangled in my hair, playing with the strands in a way that normally would have soothed me right to sleep.

Not tonight. Not with the thousands of thoughts that were fighting for supremacy in my mind.

Hours later, long after Ash had fallen asleep, his chest smoothly rising and falling under my cheek, one thought grew to dominate the others, and it was that thought that finally calmed me enough to put me to sleep.

I knew, without a doubt in my mind, I would fight to the death to keep Ash with me for the rest of my life. I had been running for so long - running from my fear... my loneliness. Running from my life.

I had tried to run from my mom's sickness too. I had actually tried to *outrun* cancer. And, like it had been bound to do, it caught up with me, knocking me flat on my ass in the process.

The one lesson I would walk away with - the one message that I would carry with me for the rest of my life - was that running never got you anywhere. You can run and run, as fast and as far as your feet (or your mind) will carry you, and after it's all said and done, you'll look up and realize that you're in the exact same place where you started.

I was done running.

Finally facing the fact that in less than seven days my mom would be gone for good, I knew I would hold onto Ash in a way I would have never dared before.

Now that I was learning what it meant to really lose someone, I would be dead or damned before I let anyone take Ash from me ever again.

Chapter Forty-Eight

Ash

MONDAY MORNING, PARKER AND I both spent the first twenty minutes of our day emailing our professors and letting them know that we'd be out for, most likely, the entire week. Park was reluctant - I think she wanted to take the situation day-by-day, which I could understand, but I wanted her fully free to face whatever was coming our way. I didn't want her worrying about school or me or anything that wasn't related to taking care of things with her mom. It took some pleading on my part, but finally she agreed.

We made the trek to the hospital and spent another long day sitting on the tiny loveseat. For better or worse, Katherine slept the entire time. At this point, I was torn between wanting her to just fade away quietly, and begging for her to wake up just one last time... for her daughter's sake.

I sensed that Parker was holding out hope for a grand gesture - a deathbed apology from Katherine that would never come. Even if she woke and was lucid enough to speak, I knew she wasn't lying in bed dreaming about all the things she had done in her life and looking for absolution. As much as I hated it, Parker would never get the closure she needed - I knew that. Still, I wanted my girl to at least get a chance to say goodbye - a real goodbye that Katherine would hear, for whatever that was worth.

Parker had been quiet upon leaving the hospital again, but I wasn't going to suffer through another night like the last. I had practically been able to hear Parker's mind racing all night, and I knew that she had gotten almost zero sleep. She'd been a zombie all day, and she actually fell asleep for two hours in the afternoon, her small body curled into my chest on the tiny couch. I had to pee five minutes after she fell asleep, but I sat there, my arm wrapped around her shoulders and her head on my chest, until the nurses on their rounds woke her up.

When we went back to her apartment, I went straight to the kitchen and grabbed everything I needed to make grilled cheese. Parker didn't want to eat at the hospital, so neither of us had eaten since breakfast, and I was starving.

"I'm making grilled cheese, baby. You want one or two?"

She glanced my way briefly and continued to head towards her bedroom. "Don't worry about me. I'm not hungry." Then she was gone.

I let her go, focused completely on making four sandwiches as quickly as possible. When they were done, I piled them all on a plate, then grabbed two bottles of water and followed her into her room.

She had already changed into a pair of yoga pants and an old t-shirt, and she lay on her side in bed, staring blankly at the wall.

I set the plate next to her, toed off my shoes, and got comfortable in bed, leaning back against the pillows before pulling the plate on my stomach and dropping a bottle of water against the curve of her stomach.

"Eat, Park," I said, taking a bite of the warm sandwich. I may have been no master chef, but I sure could whip up some comfort food.

"I'm not hungry," she flatly responded. I gently grabbed her shoulders, hoisting her up to a sitting position, and placed a sandwich in her hand. "Eat."

She rolled her eyes but took a bite.

"Roll those eyes all you want, baby, but you lost too much weight when we broke up. That was two months ago, and you're still too small. You need to eat."

She didn't say a word, which I assumed meant she was annoyed with me, but I didn't complain as she finished the sandwich in small bites that she chewed with painstaking care. Once she had finished one sandwich, turning down a second, and I had swallowed two, I carried the plate and the leftover back out to the kitchen, leaving it on the counter to get back to her. She had curled back onto her side, her empty gaze directed back towards the far wall.

I stripped down to my boxers, dropped my clothes on the floor, and climbed onto the bed. Once there, I pulled Parker to my side, wrapping my arms tightly around her as I pressed a kiss into her hair.

"We need to talk, baby," I whispered, instantly regretting my word choice when her body froze solid. "Hey, no," I said, reaching down to pull her face up to mine, which she reluctantly allowed. "Not that kind of talk. *Never* that. Get the thought out of your head."

She pulled her lower lip into her mouth, but then nodded, holding my eyes for what felt like the first time in days. "What's up?"

I hadn't planned on telling her like this. I knew she had tons of shit going on, and she probably didn't need to add my fucked up past to that mix, but, for a few reasons, I wanted to do this now.

Things were about to change for us in a huge way. Once Parkers mom was gone, she would be free - able to leave behind the fucked up past that had brought us both here, to this moment in time. When that day came, I didn't want anything holding us in the past, and right now my secrets were doing that.

I also kind of hoped that telling her my story would distract her from the thoughts that had been dominating her mind for the past two days.

So I told her everything.

"When I was younger, I wasn't a fan of my home. It seems so fucking stupid now, honestly, especially knowing what you went through, but... You know my dad and I fought, but it was over the absolute stupidest stuff. My mom used to try and talk to me all the time, try and get me to see things from his perspective, which would just get me pissed at her too. But Rory... Rory *always* took my side. She would come to my room after we'd finished screaming at each other and she'd sit down on my bed and just... God, it sounds stupid, but she would tell me knock-knock jokes. I'd be pissed as shit, and she'd just walk in and start telling the most stupid fucking jokes you've ever heard. But, they would always make me laugh. She was seven when she started doing that, so you can imagine how bad the jokes were, but it didn't matter. She made it bearable to be in that house…

"As I got older, everything changed. I started high school, became 'cool,' or what the fuck ever. I played hockey, so I knew a lot of older guys on the team, and I started going to a lot of parties. I snuck out of the house all the time, especially after a fight, just to get fucked up. I drank a ton, smoked way too much weed, even did the occasional line of coke. Anything to find a temporary escape.

"Rory and I drifted apart. She knew, like my family knew, the shit I was getting into. She knew even more than they did how often I would sneak out, only to crawl back through my bedroom window at 3AM, fucked up so bad I could barely walk let alone scale the tree outside my room.

"I went to college. Doing the same shit, all the time. It's actually ridiculous to think about what I could have accomplished if I wasn't getting wasted every night. Because, through it all, I kept a 3.8 GPA. I worked towards med school, spending fifty percent of my time on graduating, and the rest on just blocking out the world. I started to avoid my parents, and then Rory, until I hadn't spoken to any of them in weeks, months even."

I took a deep breath, trying to steel myself for the next part. The part that I avoided remembering. The part that made the guilt surface, threatening to tear me apart. I laced my fingers through Parkers, laying her hand on my chest and letting her warmth fill me with the strength to revisit the night that I fucked everything up.

"It happened April 23rd, my sophomore year. I went to a party at some guy's house off-campus. Normal night for me, which means that I got absolutely blasted. Marco was there, and some of his friends who I didn't really like, but they always scored good shit, so whatever, right? When they started laying out lines, I didn't even think.

"It was so…" I shoved my free hand through my hair, trying to make sense of a senseless night. "It was just so fucking stupid. I didn't even like coke, it wasn't my thing. But, that night, I didn't care. *Most* nights, I didn't care.

"I guess it was cut with something, or it wasn't coke, I'm not really sure. But, it fucked me up. I mean, I had never even experienced that level of 'fucked up' before. I don't even remember the rest of the night. We had started partying early, like 7:30. The next thing I knew, it was 3AM. I had come down enough to actually think a little, and I remember checking my phone. There was, uh…" I cleared my throat, wondering why I didn't leave this part out, "a girl. We had hooked up a few times, and… Whatever. Anyway, I checked my phone, and I had a voicemail and a missed call. From Rory. At 9, six hours earlier."

I froze, my throat starting to close up as my heart pounded. Parker must have realized that I was losing it because she rolled up onto her knees, pressed close to look down at me as she wrapped her hand around the side of my neck. The touch was grounding, as was her voice as she whispered, "It's okay, baby. It's in the past. I'm here."

I gave her a quick nod, feeling myself start to calm with her hand on my skin. "I knew something was wrong right away. Rory hadn't called me for months. I had blown her off so many times that she had just given up. So, I checked the voicemail."

Suddenly, my sister's quiet, terrified voice filled my head. *Ash, I need you, please.* She had been crying, quiet sobs that punctuated her words and gave her voice a strange staccato rhythm. *I'm sorry to call, but... It's my boyfriend. I just, I'm really scared, Ash. Please, please can you come here? I just want to go home...*

I shook my head, clearing the sound that still woke me some nights, creeping in while I slept.

"I listened to that voicemail three times, Parker. Three times. I couldn't focus, I was still too messed up. And then, the words made sense. I didn't even know she had had a boyfriend, but she had given me his address and asked me to come pick her up. God, Parker, she was fucking terrified when she left that message. Jimmy tried to stop me, but I was gone. It had been six hours since she called, and I had to get to her.

"It took me twenty minutes to get to the house. I was so bombed, I'm still amazed I made it there alive. When I pulled up and saw her car parked out front, I didn't even knock. Just walked inside the house, right through the unlocked front door.

"I found her right away. She was lying on the floor in the living room, surrounded by broken furniture. The place looked like a fucking bomb had gone off, and... Rory, she..."

I couldn't block it out. Couldn't stop the vision from bursting to life, and then I was standing amongst splintered wood and shattered glass, staring at my baby sister. The same sister who had always defended me from invisible monsters. The sister who told the world's worst knock-knock jokes in an attempt to make her asshole brother smile.

There had been so much blood, *God*, I'd thought she was dead. It wasn't until she pushed up on a shaky arm and cried out my name in a pained whisper that I even knew she was still breathing. When I got close, I saw the bleeding cut on her temple, the already darkened bruises lining her arms and legs. Her clothes had been hanging off her battered and bent form, torn so badly they looked like nothing but rags.

Suddenly, I felt my body being pulled up, and then I was sitting, with Parker on her knees between my outstretched legs.

"Hey," she said quietly, placing her hands on my jaw and forcing my eyes to hers. "You disappeared on me. It's okay, you don't have to do this…"

I shook my head between her hands. I needed to get this out.

"Sorry. I'm okay, I promise." She nodded, clearly unconvinced, but shifted forward until her legs pressed against mine, tangling us together. She kept me in the moment by grabbing both of my hands and gripping them tightly as she let me get it all out.

"Jimmy had followed me from the party. Suddenly he was there, walking in the open door a minute after me. I'd been frozen, staring at my sister as she cried, but completely unable to do anything. And then, he was picking her up and carrying her to me. He tried to pass her to me, but I wouldn't take her. I told him to go, take her to the hospital. I said that I would be right there. He just nodded and left.

"Once they were gone, I walked through the house until I found him. The motherfucker was asleep in bed. Do you believe that? He was fucking sleeping after *beating and raping my sister*, and leaving her bleeding on his goddamn floor." I heard Parker's swift intake of air as I finally said the words, but I couldn't stop. I needed to get it all *out*.

"I didn't even see him. I dragged him out of his bed, dropped his ass on the fucking floor, and started beating the shit out of the guy, and not once did I even see his face. All I saw was Rory on the floor. Clothes ripped, blood everywhere. It's all I could think about. The rest was just fucking... autopilot."

"I would have killed him, Parker. I'm not exaggerating, I'm not just saying that. I would have killed him if Jimmy hadn't called Marco. Thankfully, or not, depending on how you look at it, he'd been up getting laid instead of sleeping, or else I probably wouldn't be here right now. He showed up and, it took some effort on his part, but he stopped me.

"Marco called an ambulance, and then told me to leave. I went straight to the hospital, to Rory. She had to have surgery, and then I remember the cops coming, and leaving, but coming back. And that's when I got arrested. Standing in a fucking waiting room with my entire family, begging any fucking God that was listening to make my baby sister okay."

Chapter Forty-Nine

Parker

I COULDN'T BREATHE. I couldn't think. I wanted to tell him to stop, that I couldn't listen to this anymore, but I was frozen solid the entire time Ash spoke.

My mind was racing as I pictured the beautiful girl I had met at Christmas, who I had talked to on the phone countless times since then. In a way, Rory had become the sister I never had, and hearing about what had happened to this girl I loved felt like taking razorblades to the skin, using them to pull back the fat and muscle to get at the bone underneath.

Ash told me that his dad got him out after four days spent in jail waiting for a judge to grant bail, which at the time had seemed like a long shot.

"His name was Will," he says, and I can hear the disdain when he says his name, like it's a dirty word that he can't stand to have on his tongue. "And he almost died. He was in a medically-induced coma for two weeks before the swelling in his brain went down enough to try and wake him. He woke up, but it was bad, Park. I mean, bad. He was in the hospital for a month and a half. Lost the sight in his right eye. It was really close."

His voice came out broken when he said those words, and I heard his aching within them.

"And then… When Rory came home from the hospital, she was… To this day, I still wish I'd killed him for what he did to her. He broke her. In some ways, she never came back…"

His voice broke off, and I knew he'd been sucked back into the moment. This time, though, I didn't let it hold him. "So, what happened?"

"What happened is that I ruined everything. If I hadn't lost my shit and almost ended his life, Rory would have had everything she needed to put him behind bars. But, then… We both ended up getting a fucking slap on the wrist. Will's dad had money, not as much as mine, but still. They worked out a deal with the judge. It was the only way to avoid dealing with fucking attempted murder charges, which was something that, sure, would have sucked. But, it meant that fucker got off, which I was not okay with. I was beyond pissed at Dad for making the deal. Not that I wanted to fucking go to prison, but I would have if it meant that asshole got locked up too. Instead, he's living free and easy because I fucked up twice."

Ash fell silent, and I wanted to say something but my mind was moving too fast, sifting through thoughts too quickly for me to grab onto one with both hands. Finally, I found words.

"So, house arrest?"

He nodded. "Yeah, fifteen months. It was total lock down. I didn't work, didn't go to school. Just sat in that house and went crazy..." One of his shoulders rose in a halfhearted shrug that I answered with a nod.

"So what happened to him?"

"From what I understand, pretty much the same thing as me. My dad wouldn't tell me too much, but I heard from friends of his that he transferred to Virginia Tech, so at least he's not here anymore."

"And Rory?"

"I don't know if she'll ever be okay. We've only ever talked about that night once, but I know she's still healing. I think Boston will be good for her, but I worry about her being so far away. Still, I'd do that anyway, so..."

Suddenly, thinking about the girl who had been through something so traumatic, I felt a shudder chase down my spine. I had my own scars, but they were relatively small, nothing more than puffy tissue that had healed wrong and caused the occasional itch. Her scars though - I couldn't imagine living with those memories, those wounds. In one night, someone had stolen her innocence, her happiness, essentially her entire life with an act of violence so horrifying, it made my heart hurt.

I felt the tears well in my eyes, and I tried to brush them away, but Ash's hands held tight to mine.

"So, what about you?"

He shrugged. "What about me?"

"Have you dealt with everything?"

He made a sound that I thought was supposed to be a laugh, but it was too hard, too cold and too forced. "You sound like my mom. I'm fine. I'm not the one who got raped."

"You were still a part of something traumatic. There are bound to be effects. And I can't say that I've ever been in that position, but I'd imagine almost killing a guy would fuck with your head. Anger, frustration, guilt would all be normal."

"Fuck *that*. I don't feel a goddamn *shred* of guilt over what I did to that dick head. He deserved so much worse than what happened. He should be dead, and if not that, at least locked away for a long time. The only thing I feel guilty about at all is the fact that my sister laid on that floor covered in blood for hours waiting for me to show up."

I was surprised by his answer, but only a little. I'd never had a sibling, but I'd probably be pissed enough to seriously harm anyone who ever hurt Jessie with very little guilt afterwards.

We were both quiet for a bit, lost in our own thoughts. Mine centered on the fact that this beautiful man had been willing to throw away his entire life for his baby sister. His, apparently, were much darker. He broke the silence with quiet, almost remorseful words.

"I don't deserve you."

"That's stupid. Don't you dare try to give me some bullshit speech about how you lost it on some dude and now we can't be together, or whatever asinine thing is about to come out of your mouth."

His eyes narrowed, and then he responded sharply. "Let's get something straight before I tell you what I was actually trying to say. First, I didn't lie when I said that I have absolutely no remorse for what I did to that motherfucker. None. At all. If Marco hadn't shown up, I would have finished the job and wouldn't have lost a second of sleep over the fact that that son of a bitch wasn't breathing anymore.

"Second, I said I don't deserve you, and I don't. Not for the reason that you're obviously thinking, but it's irrelevant - my point stands. I did not say that we couldn't be together. I've told you repeatedly I'm not letting you the fuck go. That doesn't mean that I'll ever be fucking good enough, but it does mean that I'll fucking work every day to make you so happy that the rest doesn't matter."

I took that in and then glared at him. "Okay. Want to tell me why you don't deserve me then?"

"Were you even listening? Fuck, Parker, she called me six hours before I got there! I was too fucked up to know that my goddamn sister was being beaten and fucking raped by her fucking boyfriend. If I hadn't been out doing stupid shit, I would have gotten there before he fucking hurt her! I asked her, the one time we fucking talked! I asked her when she called me. She said that she had gone over to watch a movie, and Will was acting weird. She got nervous, and then he started to get rough... wanted to have sex and she was saying no but he was forcing the issue. She went to the bathroom and called me, then tried to hide. He forced his way in! He fucking broke his way into the room and I... I fucking..."

His body tensed as his voice broke on those words, and I just knew he was going to try and move, but I couldn't let him. I needed him to stay here, with me, and I needed to make him understand that he couldn't keep blaming himself for what had happened to Rory. Sure, if he'd have been at home studying, he probably would have gotten her call and stopped Will before... But it was in the past. It had happened, and he needed to move on.

We both needed to *move on*.

I moved, one second facing him on my knees and the next I was straddling him, wrapping my legs around his back to anchor my weight to his.

"No, stop," I said as I felt his hands move to my hips. "Please, I need you right here."

"Parker," he warned, voice low and I felt his hands shaking as he gripped the skin above my ass.

"Listen to me, Ashton." I grabbed his face, holding his eyes to mine and forcing him to see the way I saw him. "I'm not going to tell you that you're wrong. You probably could have been there sooner if you were doing anything else. You could spend the rest of your life thinking of all the ways you could have stopped it, but none of it matters. It happened. You got her out of there, and in your own way, you took back a little of what he stole from you. I'm not saying that you made the right decisions, but ultimately it was not your fault."

"You don't-"

"Would you tell Rory that it was her fault for dating him in the first place?"

"No! I wouldn't fucking blame her for something that he did!"

"That's my point," I shouted back. "It was something that he did! And, regardless of all the ways that things could have happened differently, if you blame yourself for this for the rest of your life, it will destroy you."

His eyes dropped from mine and he stared at my throat in silence for thirty very long seconds.

"How do I do that?" he finally asked, his voice betraying just how broken he was. "How do I just let go of that guilt, Park?"

I wished I could give him an insightful answer - some perfect set of steps that would heal his heart and help him find himself after losing so much - but I had nothing that wise. It had taken Ash for me to move past my guilt, so I told him what I knew.

I shrugged, and then whispered, "Let me have it. You took my guilt, so let me have yours."

I heard another one of his forced laughs, but this one contained at least a trace of humor buried beneath the anguish. "Is that how this works?" he asked, his eyes finally coming back to rest on mine.

I nodded and gave him a small smile. "Yeah, from what I can tell."

I saw the corner of his mouth tilt up, and at the sight, I pressed my lips to his. I meant for it to be a short kiss, a quick reaffirmation of my love for him, but the second our mouths connected, Ash grabbed the moment and held on tight. One hand dove into my hair to keep me in place and within minutes he had me gasping into his mouth as his tongue massaged mine and his other hand lavished a searing torture on my breasts.

In minutes he had me naked on the bed. He knelt between my legs, my back to the mattress and his head between my thighs. When his mouth touched me, it sent a spark through my body that electrified my nerve endings. The sensations were almost too much as his mouth roved over the sensitive skin, his fingers working their way into my drenched opening. I felt his breath, hot against my flesh as he whispered, "God, I fucking love how you taste."

That sent another rush of wetness that he must have felt, because I heard a hungry groan. Then his teeth gently scraped across my clit as his fingers curled inside me and I was falling, falling, falling. I waited to land, waited for the end to the shaking and the tremors, but every time they started to fade Ash pulled or pushed or licked or sucked or swirled and I was coming again. I lost count of how many times the waves receded and then crashed over me again as Ash tortured me. There was no other word.

Fucking.

Exquisite.

Torture.

Finally, he pulled away, once I was boneless and my voice was hoarse from screaming his name. He moved to lay beside me, probably ready to let me sleep after the ordeal he'd just put me through, but I needed him. I had just come and come and come, and yet, I was achy. I wanted him filling me, needed the connection of our bodies joining together. I craved the sensation of feeling him lose control as he moved inside me.

I didn't bother to undress him, instead just opened his jeans and wrapped my hand around him.

"Baby, you don't…" he started in a low voice that soon turned into a groan.

"I want you, Ash," I told him, and even I could hear the blatant need in my voice.

"Fuck," he whispered, sitting up quickly to pull off his shirt before pulling himself out of my softly stroking hand to shed the rest of his clothes. Then he was falling between my legs and giving me exactly what I needed.

After his intense oral assault, I had expected him to take me hard. I had expected him to fuck me - no restraint, no apology. Instead, he slowly and sweetly made love to me, and the power in our connection stole my breath more than once as I felt him deep inside me, in a place that would only ever belong to him. His motions picked up speed, and we both grew urgent, desperate. Breath mingling with our foreheads pressed together, Ash laid a possessive kiss on my lips before he growled, "I love you so fucking much."

Then, we were both coming together, and the beauty of the moment washed over me, warm and arresting. It had me holding him close even as he tried to pull away.

"I love you, Ash."

His eyes stared into mine, and they were lighter than I'd seen them look in weeks. It brought a smile to my face, and when his eyes fell to my lips as they curved upwards, he rewarded me with a smile of his own. It was still small, and it was definitely amused, but it was a smile so I was going to take it.

"I love you too, baby."

Then, without once thinking of horrible things happening to people I loved, or the fact that I had no fucking clue what tomorrow would bring, I laid surrounded by the warmth of the man I loved, and I fell into a deep, dreamless sleep.

Chapter Fifty

Ash

I WOKE TO THE SOUND of Regina Spektor ringing through Parker's dark room. The second after my eyes opened, I was wide awake and filled with dread. I knew Parker was awake when I felt her weight press across my chest as she reached towards the nightstand where her phone sat. I heard her answer, and I found myself praying that it was anyone, anything else, but at the sound of her voice I sat up and wrapped an arm around her shoulder, burying my nose in her hair and taking a fortifying breath.

"Okay," I heard her whisper. "We'll be right there." Then she flipped her phone closed. I didn't speak, instead just turned my face to press my lips to her throat and stood to pull on my clothes from the day before. She followed me out of bed and we both got dressed in complete silence. My mind was strangely blank, but I knew Parker's was probably racing, thinking about what she was going to have to do.

It was time to say goodbye.

We pulled up at the hospital before six. Parker hadn't said a word since we got the call, and I was letting her have her space for now. When we got to the hospice unit, I stopped her with a hand on her arm.

"Go ahead in, baby. I'll be right there, I just need to call my parents." She gave me a blank nod that left me wondering if she had even heard my words but I let her go so I could do what I needed to do and get back to her and Katherine.

Dad answered on the first ring. "Ash." I heard the sympathy in his voice and I knew that somehow he already knew.

"Hey, Dad. We're at hospice. She doesn't have much longer."

"Alright, son. You just tell us what you need us to do."

"I want to bring Parker there later. I want her around family. Is that okay?"

"Of course," he said immediately. "You guys are both welcome to stay for as long as you need."

"Thanks," I said quietly, trying to convey just how much I meant that one word. A word that I didn't say to my father nearly as often as I should have. "I need one other favor." I asked him to do something that should have been done ages ago, and I wasn't surprised when he instantly agreed to that as well, even though it would take some string-pulling and check writing early in the morning. I thanked him again before hanging up and then moved straight through the double doors towards Parker.

She was standing by the bed when I walked in. Her hand rested on the mattress, but she didn't try to reach out. She didn't touch her mom at all. Just stood close, her eyes trained on the slow rise and fall of Katherine's chest as if she could control her breathing and keep her alive through sheer will. I stood behind her, letting my chest press into her back before twining my fingers through hers. I didn't speak, just gave her my support as she stood still and stared at a woman who would soon be gone.

We stood there, perfectly still and silent, for 89 minutes.

And then, in one quiet moment, suddenly she was gone. The room felt somehow emptier, and the sound of her rattling breath ceased as her soul left to go... wherever it was that she would end up.

Katherine Rose Parker died at 7:34 on a Tuesday morning in March, with no one in attendance but her daughter and her (though she didn't know it) future son-in-law.

I had expected to feel relief. I had expected to feel some guilt at that relief. I had expected to be content in the knowledge that the woman who had made Parker's life a living hell was no longer in the world. I had expected to be glad that it was all over. But, none of those emotions were present at 7:34 that morning, or 7:35, or anytime thereafter.

All I thought was that I had just witnessed a very sad end to a very sad life.

All I felt was determination. Determination to live a life that I could be proud of, that Parker would be proud of. A life that brought more people to my deathbed than two kids whose feelings were such complicated tangles of emotion that it would take years to sort through them.

Staring at death that morning, I knew that I would work every day for the rest of my life to make sure that when I died, it would be *nothing* like this.

Once Parker had said goodbye, I pulled her from the hospital. We had made it to my truck before her tears started to flow, and I slid across the bench seat to lift her into my arms as we sat in the parking lot. She tried to stop the tears, or at least slow their descent, apologizing for the show of emotion.

"Baby," was my response.

"Don't 'baby' me," she snapped through sobs that just kept coming. "This is just... so... stupid! I... didn't even... like her!"

I rubbed her back lightly as I answered, "Yeah, but she was still your mom. Let yourself be sad. It's okay. I'm sad. Stop thinking that you're not allowed to feel whatever it is you feel."

After that she quieted and soon she was taking deep breaths as the last of the tears fell and she wiped the wetness from her eyes. Once I had her settled back into her seat, we headed straight to my parents' house. I knew I needed to stop by both of our apartments for clothes and stuff, but I wanted to get her around people who cared about her. I needed to make her feel secure, because I knew she probably felt like she was waving in the wind right now. I was going to tether her back to the ground.

Once we got to my parents, Mom sat us down at the dining room table and started piling plates of pancakes, eggs, bacon and sausage around us. I ate while I watched Parker pick at her food, but I didn't push her this time. Once we had finished eating, we talked about the service. Parker tried to protest when my parents said that they were going to handle everything, but eventually she gave in. Parker told them that she had just been planning on a quick, graveside service, and once the plans were laid out, my mom headed out to door to visit the funeral home, and I led Park up to my old bedroom.

Once inside, she took a quick look around the room before she walked straight to the bed and flopped down, face first. I followed her and sat beside her hip, letting my hand skate up and down her back slowly.

"Mmm, that feels good," I heard her mumble into the pillow, and it pulled a small smile from me.

"You wanna take a nap, baby?"

She nodded. "If that's okay. I just need to sleep for a few hours so that I can think again. Right now…" she gestured with her hand something that I guessed meant her mind was chaos, and I nodded. I could totally understand that.

"Alright. I've got to run out for a bit, but I'll bring some clothes for you when I come back. Is there anything else you want from your apartment?"

She finally turned her head to face me, face unreadable as she considered the question. "Can you just grab my phone charger?"

"Sure, baby. I'll be back soon, okay?"

She nodded and I dropped to press my lips into her temple before I stood and left her lying in my bed. I moved back downstairs to where my dad was sitting in the living room, staring at the dark TV.

"I'll be back in a little bit, Dad."

"Hold up a second, Ash," he said as I moved towards the door, rising from the armchair that he had been sitting in. "How's she doing?" he asked once he was finally a foot from me.

"She's okay. Trying to sleep now," I told him with a shrug.

He nodded. "I just wanted you to know that I did what you asked. She'll be here tomorrow at 8 and I'll head over and pick her up at the airport when her flight gets in."

"Thanks, I appreciate it."

He nodded again and then his eyes drifted away from mine. "I know that this is rough for both of you, but I'm glad that she has you by her side for it." His eyes came back to mine and they were apologetic. "I know we don't always get along, and I may not say this enough, but I'm proud of you Ash. You're a good man."

I took a deep breath as the words penetrated the exhausted haze that was starting to invade my brain. The only time my dad had ever said those words growing up was in regard to hockey. To hear him tell me that he was proud of me because of who I am... Well, it meant more than I had thought it would.

"Thanks, Dad," I answered, and we both ignored the hitch in my voice. "I'm gonna run, I wanna get back before she wakes up." He nodded and then I was out the door.

Chapter Fifty-One

Parker

WHEN ASH LEFT ME LYING in his childhood bedroom, I spent ten minutes trying to hold back the tears I knew were inevitable. Then I just said fuck it.

I cried for thirty minutes before I passed out. And once I was asleep, I slept longer and deeper than I ever had before. So deep, in fact, that all three times Ash tried to wake me later that day, I slept right through it. I slept through the afternoon and then into the evening, finally waking once Ash was lying in bed next to me. When my eyes flickered open, the first thing I saw was his golden gaze watching me, and as soon as our eyes met he smiled.

"She lives," he joked quietly.

I rubbed the heel of my hand into my eyes and sat up, glancing around to take in the dark room. "Wow. What time is it?"

"Nine thirty. You slept all day."

"God, I'm so sorry-"

"Park, baby, stop. You're fine. You obviously needed the sleep. Don't worry about it."

"Okay," I whispered, still unable to believe that I had slept for so long.

"You hungry?" he asked, sliding to sit on the edge of the bed.

I considered the question and then nodded.

"There's pizza downstairs. Do you want some? I can heat it up for you."

"No need. Cold pizza sounds perfect." I started to move off the bed to follow him, but he stopped me with a gentle grip on my waist.

"Stay here. I'll bring it up for you." He gave me another smile and then pressed a kiss to my forehead before pushing away from the bed to leave the room. I took the opportunity to make my way to the bathroom, getting resettled on the bed by the time he made it back upstairs, a few slices of pizza loaded onto a plate in his hand. We ate quietly. I wasn't sure what thoughts were running through his mind, but for the first time in days, mine was blissfully empty. When we had finished, Ash gave me the bag of stuff he had packed at my place. Opening it, I grabbed out some shorts and a t-shirt, and then paused.

"Is it okay if I take a shower?"

"Of course. Whatever you need."

I grabbed my toiletries from the bag and then walked to give him a quick kiss before I headed out the door. I meant to take a quick shower, but once I was under the hot water my mind switched back on and wandered to the morning. I let the water beat against my back until the memory of the way her breathy rattle had just stopped flowed down the drain with the runoff. Once I was done, I toweled off quickly and then threw on my clothes before leaving the steam filled room and walking back across the hall.

Ash was asleep when I entered, lying on his back with one hand under his head and the other resting on his chest. He was wearing a pair of plaid flannel pants and nothing else and I let my eyes travel over the exposed skin as I threw my stuff towards my bag on the floor and crawled into bed next to him. I managed to get the covers out from under his body without waking him up and then I slid in next to him. I propped my head up on my hand and then just watched him sleep.

Ash had a raw energy that filled the air when he was awake - it was something that drew your eye to him and kept it there. When he slept, the energy was still there, but it wasn't as intense, not nearly so all-consuming.

Still, my eyes didn't leave him once as I watched him take slow, soft breaths. His lips were just slightly parted and I had to resist the urge to touch them with mine - an urge that was pretty much always present, which luckily meant that I had had a lot of practice.

I planned on watching him sleep all night. I didn't expect to sleep at all after my long nap, so I settled in to wait with him until morning. Instead, after a half an hour of uninterrupted and peaceful staring, somehow I ended up with my eyes closed, my head resting on his chest, dreams of Ash in my head.

I knew the moment I woke that I was alone in bed. It took me another second to realize that Ash was speaking.

"Baby, wake up."

I felt his lips against my head and I smiled at the sensation, turning to try and find his warmth, and then pouting when I finally opened my eyes to see him smirking as he leaned over me.

"Why aren't you in bed?"

"Because. You need to get up."

I groaned. Even after sleeping all day and night, all I wanted to do was lay in bed with his body next to mine.

"I think you should just come back to bed..." I tried, letting my voice get low. He knew what I was up to and I heard a small chuckle.

"Come on, baby. We have company."

That got my attention. "We do?" I asked, instantly awake. I moved to sit up as he backed away from the bed nodding.

"Yeah, well, you do."

I narrowed my eyes. "Who's here?"

He smirked again and kept moving towards the door. "Get dressed baby, and then come downstairs."

I called his name but he was already heading down the stairs. I flew out of bed, mind racing as I tried to figure out who would have possibly come to see me at Ash's parents' house, coming up with absolutely zero answers. I had no other family, and no friends but Jessie. At a loss, I finished throwing on a pair of jeans and a t-shirt from the bag Ash had packed for me and then headed towards the stairs. It wasn't until I was nearing the kitchen when I heard the familiar voice that convinced me I *had* to be dreaming.

I moved faster, breaking into a run as I rounded the corner to see her. Jessie. Sitting at the dining room table and staring at Ash like she had died and gone to heaven. She was so distracted she didn't notice me enter the room, but Ash, who was leaning against the far wall, looked to me right away. I completely ignored him as my feet came to a total stop.

Jessie followed his gaze until her brown eyes stopped on me. Then, faster than I could blink she was barreling out of her chair towards me, red hair streaming behind her as she flung herself against my body and wrapped her arms so tightly around me that I couldn't breathe.

"Oh my God," I breathed, "you're really here."

A second later she was pulling away to smack my arm. "Of course I'm here! I should have been here weeks ago! What is wrong with you, Parker?! Why wouldn't you tell me that..." Then she was sobbing and wrapping her arms around me again. Of course I started crying too, and we stood in the kitchen with only Ash in attendance (thankfully) while we both worked out our tears. Once we had calmed down a bit, I wiped my eyes and looked at Ash.

"You did this?" I asked quietly, biting back a new wave of tears when he gave me a small nod. I mouthed the words *Thank you* which earned me a small smile before he walked towards the door.

"I'm gonna take a shower. Why don't you guys go to the den? Mom and Dad'll leave you alone in there." Then he pressed a kiss into the top of my head before leaving the room. Jessie had gone quiet and her body had stopped shaking but her arms still held me as if she was never going to let go.

"I'm sorry, Jess."

I felt her take a deep breath before she pulled away. She wiped the tears from her eyes before bringing her bright eyes to mine. "You need to tell me. Everything."

She was right, and there was a hell of a lot to tell, so I led her to the den and started to talk.

It took three hours. Three *painful* hours to fill in all the missing pieces from my childhood and the last year. Three hours where Jessie asked loads of question, and repeatedly told me that she couldn't believe I didn't tell her any of this. I tried to explain as best as I could, but now, even I had a hard time understanding it. Until Ash, Jessie was the only person that I was close to. I had trusted her more than anyone else in my life, and I still hadn't been able to let her all the way in.

But, as we talked I realized that everything was different now. Mom was gone. I had Ash. And, I knew that there were people in my life who cared about me, even loved me.

My entire life had changed over the past few weeks, and with it, my outlook. I could leave everything else behind and just focus on where to go from here. I didn't need to hide from anything or anyone, and I didn't need to hide myself.

I could just *be*.

And on that thought, it was like a weight had been lifted from my chest. I determined my life now - I was in charge of where it would go. It was a heady realization.

Once I had told Jessie all about Mom, the conversation naturally flowed to Ash, and I caught her up on what had happened since the last time we talked, which had been right before Christmas.

"Seriously, Park, he's a keeper," she said, a small smile on her face.

"I know," I sighed. "How did he even find you?"

"I have no clue," she answered, turning to me. "It was actually Paul who called. I was super freaked out at first, truthfully, but he explained who he was and told me about your mom. Then he said that he would arrange a plane for me as soon as I could make it." She lifted a shoulder. "What does he even do for a living?"

"I have no clue. He explained it once, but it was a little... shady." She widened her eyes at me and I couldn't help it, I giggled.

It felt great.

A second later Jess joined in and our giggles turned to pure laughter.

And that felt even better.

Chapter Fifty-Two

Ash

OVER THE NEXT TWO DAYS, Parker and I spent almost every second together. Jessie was usually there too, but she was at least staying at her mom's house nearby, so I had my girl to myself at night. That being said, I didn't mind Jess's presence at all.

She was outrageously funny. She was also at least half-certifiable, I was sure of that, but at least her antics seemed mostly harmless. Parker and Jessie told story after story about growing up together, and I realized I was seeing an entirely new side to Parker - a side that somehow managed to surprise me. They talked about sneaking out to parties and skipping school to go to the beach. They talked about summers and holidays spent together, and as I got to know Parker's only real friend besides me, I was glad that she had had someone when she was younger, someone to make her shitty situation a little bit better.

I kept a close eye on Park, but she seemed to be holding up pretty well. She had cried twice, apologizing both times which I told her again was crazy. Her mom died, and even if that mom was a shitty person, death screwed with everyone. I knew that, even after everything that she had been through, Parker regretted never getting to have a positive relationship with her mother. I hated knowing that she had to live with that forever, but I knew that the feelings would fade. I also knew that I would work my ass off every day for the rest of my life to make her happy, so I wasn't too worried.

We had spent Tuesday night at my parents, but Wednesday we went to my apartment. It was the first time Parker slept in my bed, and I found myself stupidly excited about that simple fact. I had spent weeks sleeping next to her at her place, and even a night with her in my childhood bedroom, but we had never slept in my bed before. I tried to keep my hands to myself and let Parker take the lead. As much as I wanted to christen the bed, I wanted it to be her decision.

Apparently we were on the same page, 'cause we christened the fuck out of that bed.

Twice.

She was awake when I opened my eyes the next morning, lying in bed and staring at the ceiling. I checked the clock on the nightstand and was surprised by how late we had slept. It was already ten, which meant we had two hours before we needed to be at the cemetery. I pressed a quick kiss to Parker's cheek and then pulled her with me into the shower. I expected her to complain, but she stayed quiet as I removed her clothes and tugged her under the hot water. I washed myself quickly but spent more time massaging shampoo into her hair and soap into her skin. I was painfully hard, but I ignored it.

Once we were both clean, I hopped from the shower, drying myself quickly before wrapping her up in a towel, and then we headed into the bedroom to get ready.

Parker wore a plain, black dress that hit her mid-thigh and hugged her curves. She looked stunning, even on her way to her mom's burial. I had thrown on a pair of black pants and a black, button-down shirt and once we were set, we headed out to the truck.

It took twenty minutes to get to the cemetery, and we were both quiet for the drive. The day was chilly and overcast, and I expected rain drops to start falling any minute.

When we made it to the burial site, I noticed a handful of people already there. I saw Mom and Dad, with Rory behind them. Grandma was there as well, as I knew she would be. She loved Parker as much as she loved Rory and I, and I took a moment to reflect on how glad I was that Parker was finally getting a family, complete with a grandma who was more than willing to make her favorite pie.

I also noticed Jessie with two older people, a woman and a man. Based on the little that I knew about her, I assumed it was her mom and step-dad. I brought my attention back to Parker as we both climbed down from the truck, and I moved to her and grabbed her hand before leading her towards the small crowd. There was one other man, who I guessed by his pastoral outfit was there to perform the service.

If I had to pick one word to describe the burial, it would be short. The pastor said a few words, general notes on life and death and God, and I blocked most of it out. He offered to let Parker speak, but she just shook her head and stayed quiet. Then, Katherine was lowered into the ground.

And that was the end.

We all hugged and talked for a few minutes once it was all said and done. Everyone there was invited back to Mom and Dad's house for lunch afterwards, and we all headed out pretty quickly to re-congregate there.

Mom had apparently gone all out. As soon as we walked in the door, her and Grandma were busy setting trays of lunchmeat, rolls, cheese, salads, fruit. Way more food than we needed for the nine people in attendance, but I knew it made her feel useful so I didn't say a word.

There was also lots of alcohol, and despite the fact that it was only 1:30 and a Thursday, everyone partook.

With the day's dark business over, the tension had left the air and now, everyone was focused on celebrating. Not the fact that Katherine had died, but rather that we were all still alive, still living and loving and breathing. We celebrated our lives as we reflected on loss. I, for one, knew I'd never had more to celebrate.

I was in love with a girl who had taken away my pain, my loneliness, and who, every day, took away a piece of the suffocating guilt that I had been living with for two years. I had my family around me, and Parker had a room full of people dedicated to showing her that we cared for her, and, perhaps best of all, I knew that her dark days were at an end.

From this day forward, I was determined to help us both live in the light.

That night, surrounded by the people who had made and shaped me, and the people who were a vital part of my life, it was like the last pieces of me found their way back and I was finally whole again.

Completely unbroken, and finally ready to live the rest of my life with the woman that I loved.

Chapter Fifty-Three

Parker

WHEN I WOKE UP, I was instantly aware of three things.

Despite the fact that I completely blacked out the night before - remembering nothing past the point where Jessie and I decided that it'd be a good idea to play a version of Scattergories that required you to drink for every missed answer - I was not nearly as hungover as I should have been. I had no clue what that meant, but I was thankful. Besides a slight headache, I felt fine.

Secondly - I was in Ash's bed again. I didn't remember deciding to sleep here, but I was glad that we had. Now that the entire ordeal was over, part of me never wanted to step foot in that apartment again. I knew I was stuck there at least until my lease ran out and I could find something new, but I planned to mooch off Ash with as many nights spent at his place as I could get away with.

I was also aware that someone - whom I could only assume was Ash - was pressing warm, wet kisses into my shoulder.

It felt *awesome*.

I felt my lips tip up as I took my eyes from the wall and turned to find Ash's face moving towards mine. A soft kiss later (one that I tried, unsuccessfully, to prolong) and he was pulling away to smile warmly at me.

"Morning, baby."

"Good morning," I muttered, staring at his mouth attempting to will it back to mine. He chuckled, but my attempt at mind control had no effect. He stayed put.

"Do you know what today is?"

I forced my eyes to him and took in his playful expression before shaking my head slowly. He smiled widely and the look of pure happiness in his eyes took my breath away.

"Today is the first day of the rest of our lives together."

God, I loved this man.

So, I decided to tell him that.

"I love you."

He chuckled. "Love you too, baby. Now sit up. I want to talk to you, and I want you focused."

I pushed myself up on my elbows and then he pulled me into his lap, wrapping his arms around me tightly.

"I just need you to listen to me, okay?"

I felt a tiny slice of unease pierce my calm, but I ignored it and nodded my head.

"I know that the past few months... Well, we kind of went about this whole thing in a pretty unconventional way. I get that. And I know that it really hasn't been that long. We've known each other less than a year, so I can understand if you're worried, or you have any reservations. But, I love you. I will always love you, and only you, Eileen Elizabeth Parker. You are absolutely everything to me. So, I want to ask you a question."

I froze and then my mouth blurted something that somehow passed straight through my filter without even slowing down.

"Are you about to propose?!"

"I'm going to ignore the sheer panic I just heard in your voice and just say no. We can deal with that later."

He was right, my voice was panicked. But, strangely, once I heard him say no, I felt disappointment flood my veins.

What the heck was wrong with me? Was I really disappointed that he wasn't going to ask me to marry him?

Yes, yes I was.

Because I would have said yes.

For some reason, I started talking.

"No! I mean, yeah, I kind of panicked for a second, and maybe it's totally crazy, but... I would have said yes... Not that, you know, you actually asked, but-"

Clearly my filter was broken.

"Did you just say that you wanna marry me?" His voice was quiet and his body was still as he spoke.

"Well, I mean, yeah..."

Suddenly, I was flying through the air, landing on my back with Ash on top of me. His mouth was pressed to mine and my tongue was reaching out to his as I let the kiss I had been desperate for block everything out.

We pulled at each other's clothes with frenzied grasps, desperate to remove the barriers until there was nothing left between us. As soon as the last pieces of clothing were gone, Ash was sinking inside me.

He groaned, stopping for a moment once he had completely filled me.

"Ash," I moaned, trying to move under his weight, which was pressing me into the mattress. "Ash," I said again, and he must have heard because then he was moving. In and out in smooth strokes that obliterated every thought from my brain besides the ones that were trying to process the way I felt.

With each powerful thrust, I felt myself start to tense, climbing higher and higher as my hands started to claw at his back and grab onto his hair. Through it all, he just kept building, kept stoking the flames that were working their way through my body, rendering me completely mindless as I focused on nothing but him.

"*God*, baby," I heard him choke out, "fuck, I can't..." Then, the thin thread of control snapped and he was pounding against me. My hips rose to meet each thrust and less than a minute later, I was screaming and crying his name, coming harder than I ever had before. He followed me a second later, coming through four almost painfully hard thrusts before coming to a stop, still buried inside me.

Ash rested his forehead against mine, keeping enough of his weight off me so that I could breathe. We both fought to regain control of our breathing, and as my thoughts slowly started to repopulate my mind, I let out a sudden giggle. However, with Ash still in me, the movement and the sensations that it caused turned the giggle into a groan.

"Fuck," Ash sighed, slowly pulling out and sitting up slowly. I followed him up, giggling again.

"I'm afraid to ask, but do you wanna tell me why you're laughing?"

"I just..." another laugh cut off the words. "What was that?"

He shot me his cocky grin and then shook his head. "My girl just told me that when I propose to her, her answer will be yes. I wanted to mark that occasion."

My laughter was cut off and I felt the happy tears start to pool in my eyes. "Oh."

It was Ash's turn to laugh. "Yeah. Oh."

We were quiet for a moment, still recovering, until I remembered that he had been trying to ask me a question.

"So, what we're you going to ask me?"

"Well, I was going to ask you to move in with me, but based on what just happened, I'm thinking I might already have my answer."

I frowned. "What about my place?"

He shrugged as he spoke. "I doubt your landlord will care if you break your lease, but if he won't let you out, I'll pay it until it's up."

"You're not paying my lease, Ash," was my automatic answer.

"If it means you living here, waking up in my arms every day, going to sleep next to me at night, I sure as fuck am."

"Ash…"

"No, Park. I'm serious. We're moving forward, and that means you living here. Or we can find a new place, I don't really care, but I want you with me. First day of the rest of our lives, remember?"

I wanted to argue - it was crazy for him to pay my rent so that I could live here - but at the same time, I had never wanted anything more than I currently wanted to live with Ash in this apartment. I felt the smile start to spread across my face, which he noticed.

"I take it that's a yes?" he asked with his usual cocky grin.

I loved that grin. I loved his entire gorgeous face. I loved the way he treated me. I loved the way he made me feel special. I loved the way he kissed me in the morning when we woke up together. I loved the way that he held me at night before we fell asleep. I loved that he didn't put up with my bullshit, and that he always knew how to say the right thing.

I just loved *him*.

"Yeah," I said quietly, "that's a yes."

The smile he gave me then wasn't cocky. It was full of nothing but love and happiness.

"Love you, Park," he whispered then, touching his lips to mine gently.

"Love you too, Ash."

He was right. It was the first day of the rest of our lives, lives that we would spend together, and lying underneath him, feeling nothing but my love for him and the peace that came with knowing that my entire ordeal was over and behind us both, I felt completely relaxed for the first time in years, and totally whole.

Suddenly, I thought of that stupid nickname that still made me smile, Just Parker. And, I realized that, for the first time in my life, that's all I was. *Just* Parker - without the guilt, and the loneliness, and the anger. All that was left was me. Nothing but pure Parker.

And Ash.

In the early morning light of Ash's bedroom, I let that thought fill me with warmth, and a content smile settled onto my face.

The first day of the rest of our lives together…

My smile shifted from content to blissful.

It was going to be a fucking beautiful life.

Author's Note

So much work has gone into this story, and it's surreal to be writing this, here at the end. First, I just want to say a major thank you to my best friend/husband, Jude. Not only are you the best editor I've ever had (wink, wink) but you were the biggest and best support system I ever could have asked for. For that, I'll always love you. Even when you grow old and wrinkly.

Next a great big thank you to anyone who looked at this in it's opening stages (and a HUGE thank you to Jennifer here) when it was downright painful to read. My friends are the best friends, simply for reading what I wrote and NOT telling me to just give up.

Next is the hard part. When I decided to embark on this project, it was a sort of therapy for me. My Dad was a lot like Parker's Mom in a lot of ways, and because of that there were a lot of demons to exorcise. Despite his problems (and really, who doesn't have problems,) I loved him until the end and watching cancer tear him apart was the hardest thing I've ever done. It's hard to lose a loved one - any loved one. It's arguably harder to stand by them, despite all the things they've done over the years to hurt you, and focus on the positives. Still, wherever you are Dad, and whatever you're doing, I miss you and love you every day. And that will never change.

Cancer is ugly. You don't need me to tell you that. But people can be uglier. So, if you know anyone (repeat:

ANYONE) dealing with abuse - be it physical, verbal, or sexual - please help them. The internet is many things, but it's an especially great resource for information and assistance. If you need it, I urge, beg, plead with you to seek those resources out and use them. You could be the one to save someone when they need it most. And everyone needs saving sooner or later.

Lastly, thanks to the readers because without you guys, this would never have been possible. If you enjoyed the book, please let me know either via social media or by leaving a review. It's more help than you could possibly know. Thanks again, and don't ever stop being awesome.

K C O'Neill is a full-time Mom, a part-time editor, and a writer down to her soul. After spending too many years in a job that wasn't nearly creative enough for her liking, she left to spend the days writing about the people living in her head and chasing the two demon-toddlers who've invaded her home. It's hectic, it's loud, and it's messy, but it's life, and it's beautiful, and she wouldn't have it any other way.

Connect with K C O'Neill

Online @ katrinaoneill.com

On Goodreads @ K.C. O'Neill

On Facebook @ KCOneillWrites

On Twitter @TrinaMarieOh